# LAND OF NO PITY

*Toni T-Shakir*

Cover by Leva Ross, TruElementz Unlimited

Published by Shakir Publishing LLC
www.shakirpublishing.com


ISBN: 099860920X
ISBN 13: 9780998609201
Library of Congress Control Number: 2017904550
Shakir Publishing, Los Angeles, California

# DEDICATION

*"Continue to build yourself, don't stop and settle for mediocrity. You are not limited. Use your mind to think outside the box, be courageous, and start making things move for yourself."*

*Your words of inspiration that fuel and guide me every step of this turbulent journey. Thank you for showing me the true meaning of unconditional love and undying loyalty. My love for you spans the universe and goes beyond eternity.*

# AUTHOR'S NOTE

I grew up as a part of America's lower class. The characters I've created in this story are the people I can write about with the most honesty and knowledge. The profanity, the terminology, and modes of expression contained in this novel are purely for the realism of this world.

For the gang members who may happen upon this book: if a disrespectful term is used about your hood, please do not take it personally. It's not intended as an attack on you or your tribe. It is only a testament to the book's authenticity.

All events and characters in this book are fictional. Any resemblance to persons living or dead is purely coincidental.

on the journey of life, a warrior walks alone,
though surrounded by many.

dialogue within far supersedes the chatter
of the many.

the warrior's actions must be justifiable only
to himself in order that he may be content in
times of ease and moments of adversity.

the righteous heart endures while the weak
falters.

the warrior's war has no ending, and the
beginning may start at any time.

the struggle is to stop from falling for
anything. we are the trailblazers to pave the
way for those that follow.

we come from the bottom of nature's
coldest sea, rising to spit righteous venom.

a silver fox by day, the shining serpent by
night . . . woe to the enemies of patient rage.

to fight the struggle is to go the distance,
to win is not caring how far to go . . . forever
we march forward!

O.G. Hitter
1999

# PROLOGUE

**1986**

Eight-year-old Elijah Hassahn brushed his teeth vigorously as the shower ran loudly behind him. Using his free hand, he wiped the steam from the mirror and stared at his brown oval face and hazel-brown eyes. *I haven't read my Bible verse for today,* he thought, as he spat toothpaste into the sink. *I hope Momma won't be mad at me for not keeping up with reading. Maybe I should read it real fast so I can tell her what I read today when I see her.*

"Hurry up, boy. We gonna be late!" Big 9-Lives shouted. His nephew was always making him wait.

Elijah's eyes grew wide. He'd almost forgotten about the appointment. He quickly rinsed out his mouth, then rinsed out the toothbrush and placed it in the little blue cup, which had been there since before he was born, on the sink. To him, everything in the house seemed to have been there before he was born. The tidy but old one-story, three-bedroom house had been passed on to his mother, Fatima, and uncles, Big 9-Lives and Cannon, by his grandmother who had recently died.

Elijah walked across the cold green linoleum floor and pulled back the plastic flower-decorated shower curtain. He hurried under the hot water. *I won't have time to read,* his thoughts raced as he scrubbed his body with the big block of generic soap. He was worried. He couldn't tell Uncle Big 9-Lives that he needed a little extra time to do Momma's daily reading. His uncle hated when his mother made Elijah read the Bible. "Religious spookism shit," he always yelled at her. *What he mean by spookism?*

Heavy pounding on the bathroom door caused him to jump and drop the soap.

"I said bring your ass on. I ain't gonna keep telling you!", Big 9-Lives hollered from the other side of the door, his voice high-pitched and intense as usual.

"All right, I'm coming!" Elijah shouted. He rinsed off the soap and turned off the water. From his uncle's tone, he knew he needed to speed dress and be ready to in the next ten minutes. Big 9-Lives wasn't mean or physically abusive, but when he gave an order he expected it to be followed. Occasionally, both of his uncles Big 9-Lives and Cannon roughed him up and taught him how to throw gang signs, but that was just to "Teach you how to be a man," as he was told.

With a towel wrapped around his waist, Elijah exited the bathroom onto the worn brown carpet in the hallway and walked to the bedroom that he shared with his mother when she was home. The family photos that decorated hallway walls caught his attention before he made it to the door. He paused for a minute to gaze at his mother's graduation picture, which was surrounded by smaller pictures of her and his uncles when they were young.

Fatima's beautiful brown almond-shaped eyes seemed to stare at him accusingly. With her high cheekbones, full lips, flawless caramel-brown complexion, and long straight black hair that highlighted her Native American mix, she was the essence of beauty. Tears welled up in his eyes. He regained his composure and slipped into his room when he heard his uncle's footsteps coming from the dining room. The last thing he wanted was for his uncle to see him crying. His mother's presence lingered with him in his room. The big picture of Jesus Christ that she had him kneel before and say prayers before bedtime; the chair where she sat and talked to him about right and wrong, God and the devil; her peach terrycloth robe hanging from a hook on the back of the closet door . . . it all made him miss her more.

Elijah slipped on his gray hooded sweatshirt and matching pants, put on black-and-gray Pumas, and headed down the hallway. "I'm ready, Unc." He poked his head into his uncle's bedroom. Big 9-Lives, phoned pressed to his ear, gave him the one-minute hand signal and went back to handling his business on the phone. Elijah stood there for a minute watching his uncle with open admiration.

Big 9-Lives was a dynamic figure in the neighborhood. Even though he was not a big man in stature, his presence still demanded attention. His slight built but hard body, intense dark eyes, along with features that showcased his black and Native American heritage, gave him a natural air of danger. He had become part of the Crip movement at its beginning in the seventies, and when the Westside Crips began breaking up into subsets, he and a small circle of his childhood homies formed their own gang, and his claim-to-fame was being the leader of the gang. He was the only father figure Elijah knew, and Big 9-Lives took pride in teaching all that he knew.

Elijah gave his uncle a smirk, nodded slightly, turned and walked away from the bedroom doorway. When he made it to the porch, his uncle Cannon was finishing a set of bench presses on an old worn bench that sat in the middle of the yard. He placed the massive wheels of pig-iron weights back onto the rack before sitting upright. A curl bar and a few sets of dumbbells were scattered around the bench, along with a forty-ounce bottle of Old English 800. The early morning sun beat down on the sweat dripping from Cannon's brow and chest, making him look bigger than he already was.

"What's up, Neph?" Cannon flashed Elijah a smile as he bobbed his head to Tom Tom Club coming from the speakers in his '62 Chevy Impala squatted low in the driveway.

"Nothing, 'bout to go see Momma." Elijah smiled and bounced off the porch to get his customary playful headlock from his uncle.

Cannon, Big 9-Lives younger brother, was a huge man, tall and broad faced with a wide nose. He reminded Elijah of the picture of George Foreman that hung on the wall of their makeshift gym in the garage. His biceps covered Elijah's entire head as he wrapped his arm around it. "How you gonna get outta this, li'l nigga?" he chided Elijah.

"Let me go, sucka," Elijah said with a laugh.

Cannon let him go and threw a combination punch that lightly tapped the side of his head and chest simultaneously. "Get on the balls of your feet, turkey," Cannon teased as he bounced around lightly with his arms up in a boxer pose. Elijah mimicked him, dancing on his feet with his dukes up.

"Let me see a right-left-hook combination," Cannon instructed. Elijah did as he was told. "Uppercut, right-straight-left," his uncle said. "Duck and counter." Cannon swung a slow left hook intended to give Elijah enough time to duck it. Elijah didn't miss a beat. "Good, good." Cannon smiled.

Elijah knew Cannon loved these moments, so he never missed an opportunity to let his uncle know that he was paying attention to his boxing lessons. At one time, Cannon was considered a rising star in the professional boxing world, but with the introduction of crippin' in South Central Los Angeles, he gave up his aspirations and took to the streets like a fish to water. He didn't lose his passion for the sport, so he kept his mini garage gym in pristine condition. To Cannon, Elijah was the heartbeat of the gym. Every chance he got, he gathered the local kids together, promising them candy and soda, to stage boxing matches with Elijah being the number-one contender.

Suddenly, a deep hoarse voice interrupted them. "You working?" A man dressed in filthy clothes pushing a basket filled with what looked like pieces of garbage stopped in front of the house.

Cannon, shirt off with blue khakis sagging off his boxers and white-on-blue Chuck Taylors, walked calmly to the fence and whispered in a hushed tone to the man. Elijah strained to hear but couldn't catch much of what was being said. A quick hand-to-hand exchange took place and the man continued his slow trek up the street with his basket. Elijah watched the man as he walked up Ninety-First Street towards Budlong Avenue, wondering what he and Cannon had talked about.

"Let's go," Big 9-Lives said as he stepped outside and walked toward the Cadillac that was parked behind Cannon's '62 Chevy.

"All right, Neph, give my li'l sis a hug and kiss for me," Cannon said as he sat on the bench in preparation for another set of presses.

"Come with us," Elijah said innocently as he walked to the passenger side of the Cadillac.

"Nah, young gun, I'd rather see her when she gets home." A hint of sadness flashed across Cannon's face.

"All right, see you when I get back." Elijah jumped into the passenger seat as Big 9-Lives turned the ignition.

---

As Big 9-Lives pulled into the parking lot of Patton Hospital's Mental Health Facility, Elijah felt that feeling again—a nervous pit in his stomach. During the ride, he'd snuck glances at his uncle from time to time, hoping he would say something, but Big 9-Lives remained silent for the entire trip.

They entered the waiting room and Elijah felt a wave of fear clawed at his spine. The air was much too cold and he shivered involuntarily as he looked around. Vending machines with food and drinks lined the wall. A few people were in line to buy items. A woman removed a hot tray from a microwave as the old white man in hospital patient attire stood next to her with empty eyes. An elderly black man sitting at a table with a middle-aged woman and two children stared at Elijah. The man's stare caused Elijah's entire upper body to shake continuously.

Elijah quickly followed his uncle to a table across the room. He was always afraid to touch anything, so he sat stiff and uncomfortable with his hands in his lap, trying not to make eye contact with anyone. They waited for nearly forty-five minutes before his mom entered the visiting room.

Fatima was wearing a light blue-and-white hospital-issued pant-shirt set with white slippers. She shuffled her feet forward methodically, eyes focused on the floor in front of her. A male orderly in white scrubs held her arm and spoke softly in her ear in an African accent as he ushered her toward Elijah and Big 9-Lives.

Big 9-Lives sighed. *Ah, Fatima,* he thought, as he saw his sister head toward them. This was not the sister he knew.

Elijah ran to hug her, wrapping his arms around her waist, and burying his face into her midsection. His mother, her eyes empty, her arms at her sides, mumbled incoherently in a barely audible tone. She didn't seem to notice him holding her. Elijah looked up in confusion. *Why isn't she hugging me?* Her lips were crusty white and she smelled of something sweet but also sour. Tears ran down his face.

"Momma?" he asked as if he was unsure it was really her. She looked down and stared at the floor like a zombie, mumbling her bizarre dialogue with the angels and demons occupying her head.

Elijah was frightened. He pulled and tugged on her. "Momma, what's wrong?" he pleaded as he fell into an open bawl. There was no response.

This had gone on too long for Big 9-Lives. He knew enough to know that his sister was pumped full of enough drugs to tranquilize a horse. With anger and hurt etched across his face, he grabbed Elijah. "Let's go," he demanded.

Elijah pulled back and wrapped his arms around his mother in a struggle to hold on for dear life. He yelled uncontrollably.

Big 9-Lives dug his fingers in-between Elijah's death grip. "I said, it's . . . time . . . to . . . go!"

The male orderly stepped in to assist Big 9-Lives in separating Elijah from Fatima, fearing that she would tip over at any moment from the violent tug-o-war between the boy and his uncle. Finally, Big 9-Lives pried him away and forcefully carried him out the door as Elijah cried and yelled, his arms stretched out in direction of his mother.

Once they reached the car, Big 9-Lives held Elijah in place with one arm as he opened the door with the other. Then he jammed Elijah into the passenger seat and slammed the door. Elijah sat with his eyes downcast in his lap as he cried the entire ride home. Even after the wailing stopped, the tears continued to flow along with the light sniffle that came after a hard cry.

Big 9-Lives never looked at Elijah or said a word as he drove home. He was a tough man and had seen a lot in his thirty years, but seeing his nephew upset over Fatima was almost too much to handle. Pulling into the driveway, he shut off the car and turned to face Elijah. His little body grew tense, and Big 9-Lives felt bad. The kid had been through enough. He didn't need to be scared. But he also needed to toughen up if he was ever to survive. Fatima was gone—at least the way she used to be—and the kid had to learn at some point that she wasn't coming back.

Big 9-Lives stared at him, trying to think of how to best word his nephew's first real lesson. He cleared his throat and looked away before turning back to him again. "Elijah," he began, "today is the last day I'll forgive you for acting the way you did, so I hope you got it out your system." He paused and took a deep breath. "You'll no longer be treated as a boy. Today you became a man, and men don't show uncontrolled emotions—that's a weakness. Even if you hurtin', the next man ain't never supposed to know it. If it's a situation where you feel you must cry, do it when you by yourself. And once it's done, put your game face back on."

Elijah nodded his head and sniffled.

"Life for us is like being in war," Big 9-Lives continued, "and war is hell. In war, soldiers are lost, and just because that happens, we can't stop fighting and strategizing. The war continues. You gotta understand that your mom's one of our soldiers lost to the struggle. You can still love and honor her, but you gotta press on. She gave you love and morals that are vital to being a balanced man. Her job is done." He paused to let Elijah absorb what he said.

Big 9-Lives thought of his own mother and felt an emptiness pass through him. "I won't love you like your mother did," he stated calmly. "My job is to put iron under the silk gloves that she formed. I'll provide you with the necessities, but you'll work for your own wants. It's time for you to learn to be your own individual self. Don't try to be me, or anyone else for that matter, and last but not least, you'll swim or sink. Should you sink, I won't shed one tear, because this is survival of the fittest, and Budlong Avenue niggas is built from the best of material! So, get in the house and wipe all that soft shit off your face. Duty calls!"

With that, his uncle exited the car and left Elijah sitting with his thoughts, his chest tight from crying.

Elijah skipped up Budlong looking forward to getting home. Having his mother back at the house after six months apart was a relief. At the corner of Ninety-Second Street, a little ugly gray poodle ran to the gate, barking and growling at him like it did every day on his way to and from his school, Ninety-Fifth Elementary. Elijah stopped and kicked the gate, and the poodle ducked and ran. Once it realized Elijah was no real threat, it ran back to the gate, barking and carrying on its antics. Elijah laughed and ran off.

A block away from the house, a queasy feeling erupted in his stomach. He had been getting this feeling for the last couple of months every time he got ready to go inside. Though he was happy his mother was home, there was something different about her, something that he couldn't quite wrap his mind around. There were times when she sat and stared out the window for hours. When he tried to read to her or have conversations about his events at school, she'd randomly giggle, mumble, or make an absurd statement like, "One of Snow White's dwarves is poisoning my food." Although these one-sided interactions persisted, he never stopped trying to reach her, and he never left home without his customary hug and kiss.

Elijah noticed a large pale owl sitting in the tree across the street from his house before he turned inside his gate. He paused to look at it. "Momma told mc owls can't see in the daytime," he mumbled. The owl seemed to stare directly at him and goose bumps rose on his arms. In one swift motion, the owl flew toward the sky, spreading its large wings, flapping away as leaves from the tree floated to the ground. Elijah watched the owl until it disappeared. Then he stomped up the porch steps and headed inside.

He dropped his backpack by the door and began removing his jacket as he walked through the semi-dark hallway. He hesitated as he stepped into the living and saw his mother sitting in the old brown Lay-Z-Boy recliner in front of the picture window that gave a view of most of the block. Elijah thought it was odd that she was facing the doorway instead of staring out of the window as she usually did. Her eyes were lucid and inquiring.

"Sit down, son." She waved to a cheap kitchen chair that she had placed in front of the Lay-Z-Boy.

Elijah hesitantly approached, not knowing if he was in trouble for some reason. He finished taking off his jacket and threw it on the sofa before easing into the chair in front of his mother. She appeared radiant beyond words. He had never seen her dressed this way. She wore an all-white dress that came all the way to her ankles, white clogs, and a white scarf covered her head that lay across her neck and shoulder. She reminded him of a nun or one of the black women who attended the Nation of Islam mosque down the street.

"Did I do something wrong?" he asked.

"No, baby." She sat up straight and proud as she studied him for a moment with affection. A warm smile spread across her face. "Baby . . ." She leaned forward slightly to look him in the eyes, as if she was trying to reel him into fully understanding what she had to say. "I did the best I could for you. I love you more than life itself. What I do, I do for you. I know that you won't understand for a long while and it's going to be difficult for you." She smoothed her dress and looked out the window briefly.

Elijah squirmed in his chair. He looked at the seashell sitting on the coffee table then down to the plastic runner beneath his feet. He rubbed his feet back and forth over the runner as he uncomfortably sat there. He forced himself to look at his mother to let her know that he was paying attention. Intuitively, he knew he shouldn't interrupt because what she was saying at that moment was very important for both of them. She hadn't had a clear, sensible conversation with him since returning from the hospital.

"When you become a man," said still looking out the window before turning back to face him, "you'll be more than just a common man. You're a strong warrior, a king of kings, and it'll be you who'll bring our family name the recognition it deserves."

She lowered her eyes to her lap and took a deep breath. "Elijah . . ." she said in a sad tone, "my demons have become too strong, and God has told me what I must do to defeat them. He also told me that you must be a witness to it all so that you'll know I'm brave in my duty and not in despair or fear, and from this you'll grow strong in being a witness so that nothing in this world that attacks you will be able to break you."

A tear slid down her cheek. Elijah trembled as tears burned his eyes. He didn't understand what she was saying, but it seemed important. He tried to get up from the chair to approach her, but she stopped him with a wave of her hand.

She wiped her tears and looked at him with deep regret. "Make sure you don't become the evil that we fight against, Elijah." Her bottom lip trembled. "The angels are always near to keep account of your deeds, so be righteous even in war." She looked up to him again and sat up extra straight, as if resolving herself to what she had been struggling with. "I love you, my king . . . I'll always be with you."

With those final words, her right hand rose in one fluid motion from where it had been resting between her thigh and the armrest. Elijah's eyes widened as a small .38-caliber revolver appeared in her hand. His heart dropped to his stomach as the barrel of the gun touched her right temple and the hammer reared back with the clicking of the spinning cylinder. He jumped toward her in horror.

"Momma . . . no!" he shouted as the pistol jerked with a large explosion. A tongue of fire reached out and licked her head, wiping what appeared to be a smirk from her face.

Time slowed to a dreamlike state. As Elijah rushed to grab her, a spray of blood splashed his face and clothes, and the smell of gunpowder and burnt flesh filled his nostrils. In slow motion the slug exited the left side of her face, leaving a messy hole. Before he could catch her, she tilted left and slumped forward, inert and lifeless. The hot pistol hit the floor with a thud.

Elijah cradled her body, screaming hard enough to almost burst open his chest. As one breath ran out, he gulped more air and screamed again. His heart raced as sweat fell from his forehead mingling with the blood splatter and tears resulting in the resemblance of a scene out of a horror movie.

His uncles charged into the living room in a panic. Cannon made no attempt to mask his emotions when he saw the horrific mess in front of him. He unconsciously knocked Elijah out of the way and cradled Fatima in his arms. Elijah reached out to her, wailing in sorrow.

Tears streamed down Cannon's face as he stroked his sister's hair and rocked her back and forth. "No, no, no," he repeated. "Hold on, baby sis."

Big 9-Lives, eyes wide and panicked, tried to remain calm and think at the same time. He snatched down the nearest thing he could get his hands on, a flimsy curtain. "Move! I gotta wrap the wound!" he yelled. His brother and nephew continued to cry and didn't move. "I said move!" he screamed, and physically pushed them out the way. "Go get the car keys!" he ordered Cannon, who reluctantly hurried to do what he was told.

Big 9-Lives's hands trembled as he wrapped the material around Fatima's head to stop the bleeding. His breath came in short spurts as he tried to process what was going on. He knew from prior experience that calling 911 from this part of town would be useless. Help wouldn't arrive for at least forty-five minutes, and that would be on a good day. Lifting her lifeless body, he rushed her to the car and laid her in the backseat. Elijah was right on his heels, traumatized and frantic.

Cannon burst out the front door and handed the dangling keys to his brother. "Wait here with Elijah," Big 9-Lives said, and hurried to the driver's door.

"Nah! I'm going!" Cannon protested as he ran for the passenger door.

"No!" Big 9-Lives snapped, eyes wide, veins bulging from his neck. He was on the verge of choking Cannon in the stress of the moment. "Pull your mutha-fuckin' self together!" He clenched his fist, closed his eyes, and shook his head to calm down. "Elijah seen too much. He don't need to see anymore . . . We can't leave him here by himself, so you gotta stay," he said in a lower tone.

Cannon knew by the tone of Big 9-Lives's voice that he was at his breaking point and he needed to pull it together. Although he was more physically imposing than his older brother, he respected him and knew that his word was law. So, Cannon took a step back and grabbed Elijah's hand. Elijah was still hysterical, not knowing whether to try and force himself into the car or run to the house, but Cannon's grip took away both options.

Elijah watched in a daze as Big 9-Lives got into the Caddie and shot out of the driveway like a madman heading to Martin Luther King Jr. Hospital on 120th Street and Wilmington Avenue.

Cannon and Elijah moved to the porch. His uncle wept uncontrollably as a shell-shocked Elijah looked at him. His emotions were out of control, ranging from fear to despair to rage, and finally false hope. *Momma said that God listens to prayer,* he thought. He got on his knees and prayed fervently. "God, please save my momma . . . please don't let her leave me. I promise I'll be good from here on out. In Jesus' name, Amen!" He stood up and looked at Cannon. "It's okay, Unc," he said innocently. "God's gonna save Momma." Cannon looked up briefly, shook his head, and buried his face back in his hands. Elijah reached over and hugged him.

Two hours passed before Big 9-Lives pulled into the driveway. Elijah and Cannon stood in anticipation. Big 9-Lives sat in the car for a moment, gripping the steering wheel. He slowly exited the car, averted his eyes, and delivered the news. "Sis didn't make it. She's gone," he whispered.

Elijah's entire world rocked and swayed, and he stumbled as if he had been hit by a powerful blow. Cannon fell to his knees, pounding the pavement with his fist, and bawled in agony. Elijah caught his balance and looked from Big 9-Lives to Cannon, confused. Then he turned, ran inside the house, and locked himself in his room.

After police investigators and visitors came and went, Big 9-Lives went about the business of arranging a proper burial for Fatima. A week later, her funeral took place at Angeles Funeral

Home on Crenshaw Boulevard and the hood came together to pay homage to Big 9-Lives and family.

Elijah remained silent throughout the service. He had cried alone in his room, fluctuating through all the emotions of trauma until the day of his mother's funeral. His tears had dried up and he couldn't cry anymore. He was numb. He looked at those attending the funeral, feeling virtually invisible. Others mourned but he just stared, eyes dried, in his bubble. Big 9-Lives never tried to force him to speak. He just gave Elijah mental space and respected his grief.

For months after the funeral, Elijah continued in silence and self-imposed isolation. Then one afternoon he came out of his room with a little pep in his step. "I'm going outside to kick it for a bit with my friend."

Big 9-Lives looked at him in surprise. He had told all of Elijah's little buddies to stay away for a while until he had healed some. Elijah didn't seem to notice they weren't coming over. "Alright" he said, confused, trying to process how Elijah went from being silent and morose one day to upbeat and communicative the next. "Just be careful," was all that he could think to say.

Elijah sprinted out the door and straight to Akili and Musad's, two brothers he had known his entire young life who lived five houses down. They were excited to see him. They laughed, talked, and roughhoused like any other boys their age. The brothers knew not to bring up his mother and the three carried on as if it never happened.

To those around him, Elijah had returned to being the intelligent, charismatic boy they all knew, but unknown to them a part of him had died along with his mother. At times when he was alone, he could feel something empty and dark floating just below the surface of his being, and in those moments he gritted his teeth in anticipation, knowing in his soul that both the good and wicked would one day be witness to that darkness.

# CHAPTER ONE

## 1988

Palms tree swayed under the soft blue sky and bright California sun as Elijah and three friends—Musad, Akili, and Julius—waited on Vermont Avenue for traffic to clear to cross the street. The last car in the massive wave of fast-moving vehicles passed and the four youths darted for the other side of the street like a small band of hyenas searching for food. On the other side, a stray dog, all skin and bones, was pulling scraps from a garbage can. When the boys approached, it looked up with desperation and danger written all over its face. The boys heeded the dog's warning immediately.

"Come on, cuzz, this way," Musad, known to his circle as "Li'l Teflon-Black" or "Li'l Teflon," directed the others up a garbage-cluttered alleyway. The small band moved with silent purpose through the concrete jungle of South Central Los Angeles. They hurried past the stretch of boarded-up buildings and storefronts that resembled the remnants of a Middle Eastern warzone. Unkempt toddlers in soiled diapers, oblivious to the hell around them, played in some of the front yards of the inhabited places. A gray hooptie sped past with three black male occupants throwing up gang signs at the foursome. Akili, known as "Big Teflon-Black" or "Big Teflon," the older brother of Musad, immediately responded by throwing up the gang signs of his own.

"We ain't got time for that shit!" Li'l Teflon snapped at his brother. "We got business to handle."

At twelve years old, Li'l Teflon was clearly the brains to his brother's brawn. The two looked almost identical: broad lips, prominent African bone structure, and skin the darkest shade of black. But where Big Teflon, age fourteen, was tall and wiry with natural cuts, and had hazel-brown eyes that contrasted his dark skin, Li'l Teflon appeared severely undernourished with pitch-black emotionless eyes. He looked about nine years old instead of twelve, but his eyes revealed the old corrupted soul that occupied the tiny person.

*Why Big Teflon always do what that li'l nigga tell him to do?* Elijah thought as they headed down the alleyway. Big Teflon was the most physically dominant out of the bunch; he'd gotten his reputation from knocking out men twice his age and size, so it puzzled Elijah that Big Teflon never resisted his younger brother's orders.

Elijah unconsciously tugged at his long ponytail before slinging it over his shoulder where it hung down his back. He quickened his steps to keep up with the others. Two years had passed since the death of his mother and he had refused to cut his hair. No one knew why he chose not to cut it, including him. Though it had been a struggle, Elijah was learning to survive and thrive in a world without his mother. At ten years old, he resembled a male version of her, the same strong black and Native American features under soft caramel-brown skin. The central quality in his face was pain, and his smile was a witness to it—pain so old, deep and dark, that it became personal and particular only when he smiled.

"That's it right there, cuzz." Li'l Teflon pointed to a peach-colored stucco house with a large front window. The darkened window obscured any attempt to see inside. A wooden four-foot fence surrounded the property, but it seemed more for appearance than it offered protection. Li'l Teflon peered around suspiciously. "Li'l Nine, you goin' in with me."

Elijah nodded in agreement. He now went by the nickname "Little 9-Lives" or "Li'l Nine," but most often he went by "Nine" when he was with his friends. He inherited the name from his uncle, Big 9-Lives, the co-founder, and leader of the Nine Os Budlong Avenue Crips. Being raised under the powerful influence of a gang leader, Elijah's indoctrination into the gang lifestyle was complete. His uncles were his heroes, so he naturally adopted the moniker. That was how names were carried on in LA gang culture. Just as a father named his son "Junior," and Junior then named his son "the Third," it was the same concept with gang names. There was "O.G." (or Big), then there is "Little" (Li'l), "Baby," "Tiny," and "Infant," in that order. Adoption of Big 9-Lives's name was a natural consequence of Elijah now being raised by his uncle.

Li'l Teflon led them through the gate and to the side of the house. Out of the view of passersby, he reached into his oversized khakis into a stash he had sewn to the inside pant leg and pulled out an L-shaped crowbar. "Ju-Ju, you gonna be the lookout. Stay on this side of the house. You see anything suspicious, whistle the bird chirp, and keep your ass outta plain sight."

Julius Grant, who went by "Ju-Ju," was the misfit of the bunch. His over-weight chubby frame, low-cut afro, light-brown round face, big marble eyes, made him look like a thirteen-year-old stuffed teddy bear. He tried to respond to Li'l Teflon, but the words got caught in his throat. Dark sweat marks appeared on the armpits of his fake Izod shirt as he started sweating bullets as if he'd just ran a marathon in the desert.

Li'l Teflon turned to his brother. "Bro, you gotta lift me up to the window so I can pry it open." He motioned to a small square window toward the backside of the house. "Once I get in, put Nine through. We'll make sure everything is clear, then we'll let you in through the back door."

"Come on then." Big Teflon moved toward the window. Li'l Teflon and Elijah followed suit.

After a few steps, Li'l Teflon realized Ju-Ju was still standing in the same place and hadn't moved to his position. "What the fuck you standing there looking stupid for?" he said through gritted teeth.

"Why . . . why we . . . doing this in broad daylight?" Ju-Ju stammered. "We need to come back when it gets dark." Eyes shifting around, he looked like he was on the verge of bursting into tears.

In unison, the three friends turned and glared at him. "Because, you stupid fuck, nobody's home right now," Li'l Teflon said, irritated. "Would you rather come back when someone's here and ask them if it's alright to burg they house? Shut the fuck up and do what I told you."

Ju-Ju still wasn't quick to move. He was about to protest again when Big Teflon took an aggressive step toward him. "You fat, soft bitch, what did he say?" He clenched his fist, rearing up to slap the shit outta Ju-Ju.

"It's cool," Elijah said, grabbing Ju-Ju by the elbow, edging him forward. "Just go lookout for us," he instructed as Big Teflon shot daggers at Ju-Ju. "Everything is straight. We'll be in and out in no time."

They all knew how much Big Teflon hated Ju-Ju. He had an uncontrollable resentment for him and only tolerated him because he was his brother's "do-boy." Li'l Teflon used him continuously. Ju-Ju stole food out of his house and money out of his mother's purse to give to him. Any dirty work that needed to be done or was a little too risky, Ju-Ju was the candidate to get it done. Li'l Teflon knew that Ju-Ju just wanted to be a part of the "in-crowd," and needed his protection from his brother, so he manipulated Ju-Ju into doing his dirty work as a sort of payment for keeping Big Teflon off his ass.

Ju-Ju nodded to Elijah. *Nine's always looking out for me,* he thought. But he needed to focus. His last hesitation had almost cost him an ass whipping. Elijah stepped in at just the right time, and he wasn't going to waste the opportunity to get somewhere. His fat, wobbly frame moved with deceptive quickness to his position.

Elijah stepped past Big Teflon, who looked ready for violence. *Why did I help Ju-Ju's fat ass anyway?* he thought, as he and Big Teflon engaged in a momentary silent standoff.

Elijah didn't fear Big Teflon like so many others did. Yes, Big Teflon was older and much stronger, but his uncles had taught him to fear no man. Big 9-Lives always told him, "If you can't win with fists, then win with guns and sticks," Elijah hoped it never came to that with the Teflon brothers. They were his friends, and their strength was to be used against outsiders, not each other. *But isn't Ju-Ju one of us too?* he wondered. He had mixed emotions about Ju-Ju. He didn't dislike nor like Ju-Ju; he saw him as sort of like a movie extra—at times he served a purpose, and at other times he was unnecessary and in the way. He didn't really have an opinion as to whether Big Teflon should be cruel or kind to Ju-Ju, but his uncle Cannon always told him that there should always be a real purpose for any act of violence.

"We ready now?" Li'l Teflon asked, breaking up the stare-down between Elijah and Big Teflon. He stood there smiling as if he was about to get on a ride at an amusement park. His two-sizes-too-big Dickie suit and dirty Chucks were almost comical.

Elijah suddenly had an urge to laugh. *Li'l Teflon really loves this shit,* he thought. "Come on, homies, let's rock 'n' roll."

Before the words were out of Li'l Nine's mouth, Li'l Teflon had one foot in his brother's hand for a boost up. Crowbar in one hand, he used the other hand to catch the windowsill as Big Teflon thrusted him up and held him there. At level with the window's lock, he jammed the crowbar into a barely visible crack, grunting as he strained and wiggled. Changing hands to get more strength, he went straight back to work on the window.

Elijah began to get a little nervous because Li'l Teflon was taking too long and making too much noise. Big Teflon's legs and arms were visibly shaking under the strain. Just as Elijah was about to tell them to just let it go, the wood groaned with a loud cracking sound and the window flew open. Li'l Teflon looked down at them and smiled before scrambling through the opened window into the house.

Elijah got his boost up and went in behind him. Li'l Teflon waited for him to land in what appeared to be the bedroom, then led the way out to the hallway. The house was dark except for the light rays penetrating the cracks in the curtains. Elijah followed behind closely, eyes scanning as they walked quietly. The wooden floor creaked as they made their way through the well-furnished old house. It was obvious that whoever lived here kept it nice and clean. The smell of Pine-Sol and polish was very apparent.

Li'l Teflon stopped at the next room they came to. "You check under the bed and in the closet," he whispered. Then he went straight to a large oak dresser with a mirror sitting on top of it and rummaged through the items on the dresser and through the drawers. Whatever he found interesting or believed was valuable, he swiftly stuffed into his pants, hoping Elijah couldn't identify exactly what he was taking, so he could steal it for himself.

"What you doing?" Elijah asked, looking over Li'l Teflon's shoulder. Li'l Teflon glanced up briefly, obviously irritated, then continued rummaging through the drawers. "We're supposed to be checking to make sure no one is home and then let your brother in," he added.

Li'l Teflon ignored him, as his hands and eyes moved in a synchronized controlled rush. "I'm going to finish checking out the rest of the house. You go to the back and let Bro in," he said in a hurried, hushed tone.

Frustrated, Elijah headed to the back door. "That nigga always doing some sheisty shit. He think mutha-fuckas stupid and don't be knowing what he up to. He only look out for himself. He don't give a fuck about nobody else," he mumbled. As he walked the hall alone, he began to get the feeling he was being watched. He heard his heart beating through his chest. He picked up the pace, suddenly not wanting to be alone.

When the door opened, Big Teflon stepped in, eyes roving all around at once. *He looks like one of them old runaway slaves in the movies,* Elijah thought. Big Teflon followed him as he retraced his steps back to the room where Li'l Teflon was, but he was nowhere in sight. Elijah looked around puzzled. "He was just here," he mumbled.

They set out to search the rest of the house and found Li'l Teflon in a back room that served as an office of some sort. A large leather chair sat behind a polished oak desk and cabinets surrounded all four walls. Two of the cabinets had been pried open and two black gym bags sat in front to be filled. Elijah and Big Teflon walked over and peeked into the cabinets. They were thrilled to see the array of weapons: old swords, knives, hatchets, pistols, and a few rifles that looked to be more collectables than weapons of war.

Elijah knew what Li'l Teflon was up to but asked anyways. "Why are we splitting the guns into separate bags?"

Li'l Teflon looked up at him. "I'm separating them so Bro don't have to carry it all. It may be too heavy."

Elijah wasn't convinced. He knew Li'l Teflon was up to no good. "The big homie, 1-Punch, said only one of us should carry the bag to the homegirl waiting in the G-ride. The rest of us are supposed to go in a separate direction back to the house."

Li'l Teflon tried to think of something to say to hide his intentions, but the look on Elijah's face told him that he was already hip to exactly what he was trying to do. He decided to forego the lie and come clean. "Alright, this is my plan . . . we gonna keep half the pistols. Me and you are gonna hide them before we go back to the meeting spot. No one will ever know we got them. It'll be between the three of us. Ju-Ju don't even need to know."

"Cuzz, the 1-Punch ain't goin' for that shit," Elijah protested. "He's the one who put us up on this lick. Don't you think he already knows what's in here?"

"Fuck 1-Punch!" Li'l Teflon's old, corrupted soul emerged in full force. "If that nigga wanted everything, he shoulda brought his ass up in here instead of sending us to do his dirty work! Shit, if he notices some of the pistols missing, we'll tell him we were rushing and musta overlooked them." For emphasis, he yanked the bag toward him and began filling it. He paused again and looked up at Elijah. "Matter of fact, that nigga ain't my big homie, no way," Li'l Teflon said. "He's from the Orchard side . . . fuck him!"

Elijah understood the finality of those words and figured it worthless to try to change his mind. For this mission, Li'l Teflon was the de facto leader, so when it was all said and done the call was his to make. But if they got put into the "circle" for this, Li'l Teflon would be responsible.

Elijah grabbed a sword and a hatchet out of the cabinet and stuffed it in the second bag. "Since we're making the rules up as we go along, these are mine to keep!"

Li'l Teflon thought about protesting, but he only wanted to have to carry the guns. *What the hell he gonna do with a damn sword and hatchet?* But they didn't have time to waste over dumb shit. He zipped the bag closed while mumbling under his breath, "Huh! The circle, fuck the circle, and the niggas in it. I'm the muthafuckin' circle, nigga!"

Big Teflon never spoke a word. He stood in the shadows and only did what his little brother decreed was to be done. He exited the back door and moved swiftly to the G-ride with the guns that were to be given to 1-Punch. The other bag was strapped to Li'l Teflon's back like a hiking sack. Ju-Ju was told to go a separate way by himself and wait for the crew at home. Li'l Teflon and Elijah went back to the house to hide the guns in Elijah's room since his uncles never snooped through his stuff. With their spoils safely tucked away, they headed to 1-Punch's house to see what he would add to their pockets.

Li'l Teflon smiled and exclaimed with arrogance, "Mission accomplished! Do or die, crip or cry, till the casket drops!"

# CHAPTER TWO

Fifteen miles away on the far west side of Los Angeles, a struggle of different proportions was taking place. Fourteen-year-old Elise Cortez sat on her bed and stared out the window as she stroked her straight black hair with a flat pink brush. The beaming sun and chirping birds meant nothing to her, as her stomach churned with anticipation and dread. It was almost four p.m. and she was silently wishing her aunt Maria would make it home early from her Saturday yoga class.

The small voice that haunted her mind daily for the past few years was at it again. "You're better off dead," it whispered. "You'll never be happy on this earth. Take a handful of pills or use your belt to hang yourself. It could all easily be over. You're worthless anyway, so what does it matter?" She looked at the thick brown belt hanging from her closet door. Putting down the brush, she grabbed her Winnie the Pooh stuffed animal and clutched it to her chest. She caught a glimpse of herself in the mirror on the dresser and noticed how much she was beginning to look like her mother.

"Momma, why did you leave me?" she whispered.

When Elise was three years old, she and her mother, Teresa, migrated from Belize to the United States. Four years later, her mother was diagnosed with uterine cancer that spread rapidly. After the dreaded process of chemotherapy and all the other treatments, Elise watched her mother wither away and die. She barely knew her father—the only relationship she had with her father consisted of the occasional letter and an old, worn photo her mother had kept. After her mother's death, all communications with him ended.

Her mother's sister, Maria, took custody of Elise and got her US citizenship. Unlike the financial hardships Elise and her mother had to endure, Maria and her husband, Thomas, were well off. They ran a private dental practice in the Wilshire District, Thomas the dentist and Maria the dental hygienist. They owned a large two-story, four-bedroom house off Olympic and Pointview and both drove $80,000 cars. Judging from the outside, they were the perfect couple with an almost perfect life. But like any other family, there were flaws and secrets. Due to a botched medical procedure when she was in her twenties, Maria was unable to have children of her own. This condition left her with occasional bouts of bitterness and feelings of inadequacy as a woman. During these bouts, Maria directed her negativity toward her husband and Elise.

Elise tossed the bear aside and buried her face into the pink comforter on the bed. Hopelessness came over her. *Aunt Maria doesn't even love me. I'm a stranger here,* she thought. The sound of keys and footsteps coming up the stairs startled her. She bolted up as her heart raced and her hand trembled slightly, her eyes searching the room for some sort of sanctuary.

The bedroom door slowly creaked opened, admitting Thomas into her world. He poked his head in, peeping around the room until his eyes came to rest on her sitting on the bed with her arms clutching her knees against her chest. He looked her up and down.

In the six years since she had been living there, she had transformed from a pretty, little girl into a beautiful work of art. Her body had fully developed into that of a grown woman, and her Belizean mixture of African and Hispanic roots were in perfect proportion—her skin tone the lightest shade of brown and tan, her eyes an exotic mix of green and blue, her hair naturally long and flowing to the middle of her back, and her body petite but curvy in all the right places. But despite her outward appearance, her innocent face and mind were still that of a child. This was one of the traits Thomas loved most about her.

It was time for his usual Saturday afternoon visit to Elise's room. It would be a while before her aunt returned from her yoga class and she already knew he would be there. He took a full step into the room. His short well-tapered afro and closely cropped mustache and beard were already gleaming with perspiration. He nervously pushed his square-framed bifocals up the bridge of his wide nose as he edged his six-three, two-hundred-pound frame over to the bed, towering over her. Elise tensed up as he extended his hand toward her. She took her eyes from his face and moved them to the small blue box in his open palm. He nodded for her to take it; she slowly removed it from his hand and lifted the top halfway. Inside, there was a small silver pendant of a bear with crushed diamond pieces a thin silver necklace. Over the past couple of years, he'd given her these sorts of gift that he called "treats."

"Do you like it?" he asked.

She felt the urge to throw it in his face. Instead, she nodded her head. As if her answer gave him the green light, he put away all pretense and became a man possessed, grabbing her face with warm, sweaty hands that repulsed her. She felt helpless. He had warned her before not to tell anyone about their "secret" because no one would believe her, she would be kicked out into the streets, and her aunt would hate her forever. Whenever she resisted or tried to put up a fight, he simply overpowered her. He kissed her neck, cheek, and mouth hungrily, panting and sweating as he climbed on top of her. She struggled under his weight, but he gripped her arms. The smell of sweat, after-shave and desperation overwhelmed her. Silent tears fell from Elise's eyes as he removed her clothes, pulled his pants to his ankles and manipulated her body. In her head, she went to another place . . .

She was a little girl again, playing with her mom in the tiny living room of their house in Watts. They squealed and laughed . . . Her mother tickled her sides, and they rolled around on the carpeted floor. The smell of vanilla bean filled her nostrils—her mother's scent. Sometimes, she would hug her mother from behind just so she could smell her.

"I'm here, Elise . . ." Her mother's voice echoed in her ears.

The moment his movement stopped, Elise returned from her mental escape. Exhausted, he rolled off her. Feeling contaminated, she ran to the bathroom adjacent to her room and showered under scalding water, scrubbing so hard that her skin began to bruise.

Tears and emotions mounted until she collapsed to her knees and wept uncontrollably. At the height of emotional pain, something in her head suddenly snapped. Elise felt numb all over, hatred and desperation boiling in her veins. Her brain stopped consciously functioning and her body began working on its own. Rising, she stepped out of the shower and paddled dripping wet downstairs to the kitchen. Water dripped from her body as she mechanically climbed the stairs. When she reached the top, she detoured to the master bedroom instead of her own. She pushed the bedroom door open and heard the shower running in the adjoining bathroom. She steadied herself, holding on to the post of the king-sized bed. She could hear Thomas humming a tune as she watched the steam and bright light from the bathroom seep out into the bedroom.

She was a woman possessed. He would never touch her again. She glided over to the bathroom and quietly opened the door. His silhouette moved behind the steamy glass door. "Please, God . . ." she whispered, and without hesitation, she flung open the shower door. Thomas startled and squinted his eyes as shampoo ran down his face.

Elise pulled out an eight-inch butcher's knife and thrusted it at his chest with all the strength her small body could muster.

"No!" he screamed frantically. He arched backward, which was his saving grace. It prevented the full force of the thrust, only allowing a few inches of the blade to penetrate his chest before he slipped and fell backward, slamming his head.

Elise charged into the shower and was on top of him. She pulled the knife from his chest, raised it above her head, and stabbed him again, this time striking into the soft tissue of his shoulder. Deep red blood gushed from the wound as she took to the air with the blade again.

"No, please!" he yelled, as he grabbed her wrist to restrict any further knife action. With his free hand, he slapped the side of her face so hard that her head crashed into the shower door, causing glass to rain down on them both. Blood, steam, and hot water mingled together.

"You'll never touch me again! I hate you!" she seethed.

Elise was running on pure adrenaline; she didn't feel the slap nor the open wounds from the glass. Tears and blood ran down her face as she strained to break his grip from her wrist. His strength and desperation for survival was unyielding and her hand went numb.

"Elise, stop! Please . . . I'm sorry . . ." he pleaded.

The very sound of his voice gave her a new boost of strength and determination. Elise quickly grabbed a large jagged piece of glass from the floor. Before he had time to react to the new threat, she buried the glass into neck at full force. His hand gave way of her wrist and fell helplessly to his side. As tears streamed down her face, she stabbed his torso over and over until the muscles in her arms burned.

As if awakening from a dream, she became conscious of his lifeless body and his glossy eyes staring up at her.

"Oh my God! What've I done?" she whispered.

Suddenly, all the cuts and bruises she received began to throb in pain. Her hands were on fire. The shower rained down on her as she realized she was drenched from head to toe in blood. She jumped in horror. Had her hands been the creator of such destruction? She retreated from the shower and backed out of the bathroom on rubbery legs. In a panic, she didn't know what to do. What'll I tell Aunt Maria? What's she g do to me? She'll hate me!" Realizing the seriousness of what she'd done, she picked up the phone and dialed 911.

"You have reached 911, what is your emergency?"

Elise looked around the room in panic. "I killed him . . ." she blurted without thinking.

"You killed who ma'am . . . ma'am?"

"Oh my God . . . I killed him." Elise broke down in sobs.

"What is your name?"

"Elise . . . I–I just killed my uncle," she stammered.

"Why did you kill your uncle?"

Elise suddenly felt trapped, as if the walls were closing in on her. She hung up the phone and paced the room like a caged animal. The phone rang, startling her. Her body shook in fear. She backed away from it and ran to her room. Naked, wet, and covered in blood, she hid inside the closet, curled up into a ball, crying hysterically.

Short thereafter, emergency personnel arrived and searched the house. Two police officers found Elise curled up in a corner of the closet. She screamed as they lifted her out to be attended to by the medics. She was so hysterical that they had to strap her to a gurney before taking her out of the house.

Once she was placed in the ambulance, still handcuffed to the gurney, she struggled and screamed until her lungs gave out.

⟡

The police discovered Thomas lying on his back in the shower, water still running and ricocheting off his pale flesh. When the medical examiner concluded his evaluation of the body, Thomas was documented as having eighty-six puncture wounds to his torso and one fatal blow to the neck.

Elise was arrested and taken into custody. She was held in Los Padrinos Juvenile Hall until investigators received the results of the rape kit that had been administered because of the statement she'd given the police. It was confirmed that sexual intercourse took place, but the question now was whether it was consensual or not.

After countless hours of interrogation and investigation, it was determined by investigators and the California District Attorney's Office that it was a classic case of sexual and emotional abuse that resulted in a crime of passion.

Elise entered the small visiting room wearing an orange county-issued jumpsuit and oversized shower shoes over thick orange socks. Her cuts and bruises were still fresh, and the more serious ones had dressings on them. Dried blood was visible through the dressing on her hand and arm. The clothing hung off her, as if she had lost twenty pounds. Her hair was matted to her scalp, and her face sagged under the heavy weight of the large bags under her eyes.

Maria sat at the small circular table in one of the beige plastic chairs. Her usual flawless hair and makeup was in total disarray. Her outfit—a buttoned-down shirt, blue jeans, and white tennis shoes—were wrinkled and stained as if she hadn't changed for weeks. Her puffy red eyes stared at her niece with hate as she made her way to the table with her head down. Maria didn't rise; she didn't trust herself to not reach out and choke Elise. When she'd received a phone call from the police, she was sitting in her car in the parking at work, getting ready to make it home for the day. She'd sat in the car for a half-hour, without blinking, as the shock of what she had been told seeped into her conscious. Later, when she learned the details of what had happened, her body seized up with rage and anger at the thought that her niece would lie so horrifically, that she would viciously murder her husband.

Elise lowered herself into the chair across from her aunt. Tears rolled down Aunt Maria's face, and Elise tried to stop her legs from shaking. She wanted to reach out and touch her aunt, say something to her, but she was paralyzed by fear and shame.

Gritting her teeth and stilling her face into a mask of determination, Maria leaned forward and spoke as if she wished the words themselves would kill Elise. "Out of the kindness of my heart and for the love of my sister, I took you into my home," she hissed. Her pale face became redder with each syllable.

"What appreciation did you show me? You came in and destroyed my life and slandered my husband's name with your lies. You seduced Thomas in a moment of his weakness. Then when you couldn't have him for yourself, you murdered him out of jealousy." She had formulated all of this in her mind to cover her shame and pain for being married to a child molesting rapist, not wanting to accept that she somehow ignored all the signs: his sidelong glances, the way his eyes would linger just a second longer on her niece when she left a room; his nervousness and look of guilt when she returned home from yoga on Saturdays. It was too much to bear. "You are the devil! I hate you and never want to see you again. Burn in hell!"

Elise couldn't believe what she was hearing. Her shoulders slumped even further and she bawled. "Aunt Maria, it's not what you think . . . I would never hurt you like this on purpose," she said in-between sobs. "Uncle Thomas raped me, and I couldn't take it anymore. He'd been doing it for years. I wanted to tell you, but he told me that you or no one else would believe me, and that I'd be kicked out of the house. I was so afraid that you'd hate me. You're all I have. I should've told you. I'm so sorry that I hurt you. Please, Aunty, forgive me." She reached her hand out, hoping Maria would believe her and accept her embrace.

"You little lying bitch!" Maria yelled as she rose from her chair, causing it to tumble backward. She grabbed her purse, turned around, and walked out of Elise's life forever.

After the case was processed, Elise was released from juvenile hall, placed into the custody of Child Protective Services, and taken to a group home. A few months after entering the group home, Elise began having bouts of nausea resulting in vomiting and lightheadedness. She had missed several menstrual periods and notices changes in her body, most notably an expanding waistline. With a lump in her throat, she put the pieces together and figured out that she was pregnant. She hated herself and what she felt was a monster growing inside her.

Out of desperation, Elise began starving herself, barely eating enough to stay breathing, and stayed away from everyone as much as possible. She wore loose-fitting clothes to hide her growing belly. The rest of the ten or so girls in the home stayed away from her, assuming she was off in the head. That was fine with her, because it kept them away and out of her business.

After months of hiding an unwanted pregnancy, she was awoken late one night by a sharp pain in the abdomen and liquid running down her leg. She got up and made it to the bathroom where she locked herself inside and labored there on the cold bathroom floor until she gave birth to a baby girl. She had already prepared for this moment by reading books on giving birth, so she knew the umbilical cord had to be cut. Using an old pair of scissors, she gave it a quick snip. With the little strength she had left, she wrapped the newborn in bath towels without even looking at her baby's face, and cleaned up as best she could.

Surprised that no one was woken up by the baby's cries, she crept back into the sleeping area, retrieved a blanket and plastic bags, and went back to the bathroom. She wrapped the baby in the blanket and placed it in the plastic bag. Making sure no one was watching, she held the bundle to her chest, feeling it move as she snuck outside into the darkness and down the alley. Her feet padded down the dark walkway littered with glass and trash as she approached the big blue garbage bin. Using her right hand, she opened the lid while clutching the bundled baby in her left arm. Without hesitation, she threw the bundle inside and slammed the lid shut, muffling its cries.

She felt no emotional attachment to the baby, no remorse or natural motherly instincts. Absolutely nothing. The bundle was thrown away like old food. She then walked back to the group home, got into bed, and went to sleep as if it never happened.

# CHAPTER THREE

## 1990

The night's darkness was just giving way to the first rays of light. The purple hue of the sky, along with the bird's first songs of the day, bestowed a sense of oneness with all things. Elijah wouldn't be able to explain if asked, but the break of dawn always made him feel a deep calmness and clarity.

He stood in the cut at the Twin Apartments on Ninetieth Street, two three-story apartments complexes that sat directly opposite of each other in the middle of the block between Vermont and Budlong, eating a bag of Ruffles potato chips, his six-a.m. "grinder's" breakfast. During these hours, Elijah usually had the block to himself. He took a sip from his orange juice and peered toward Budlong. When grinding through the wee hours, quick, unhealthy snacks from the all-night liquor store was the usual meal. He'd been popping NoDoz tablets like candy all night to stay alert for police, enemies, and customers alike. The salty chips helped to settle his stomach, as the pills made him a little jittery. But it was better than the alternative of drinking coffee, which was no surprise coming from a thirteen-year-old. A "curb server's" best time for business was from midnight until seven a.m. All the vampires came out at night, and if he wanted to sell his product, he had to be there when they fiend the most.

For the past six months, all-nighters had been a way of life for Elijah. His normal routine was to hit the block around six p.m. and not see the house again until seven-thirty or eight the next morning. Once home, he usually slept until one in the afternoon, ate, worked out, read a little, showered, then back to the block to do it all over again. Periodically the routine got broken up a bit when his uncles were around and decided to check and see if he was going to school. If he got caught, Big 9-Lives would come down on his head and he would have to go to school regularly for a week or two just to appease him. Once Big 9-Lives got preoccupied again with business or some fling across town, it was back to the block as usual.

Tired of the phone calls from the school, Elijah devised a plan to keep them at bay. He'd paid an old neighborhood crackhead to go to the school and play the part of his uncle. Arriving at the school with Elijah, escorted by the secretary to the principal's office after a short wait, the crackhead had given the principal the spiel in his most sorrow-filled voice. "My wife, Elijah's aunt, is in the last stages of a terminal illness, and I have to work two jobs just to make ends meet because we don't have any insurance to cover the medical expenses. As much as it pains me, I need Elijah home as much as possible to help out with his aunt." Pausing, as if he was trying to hold back tears, the crackhead sighed and continued. "If possible, can you allow Elijah to receive a month's worth of schoolwork at a time and attend classes periodically? Just until my wife go home to be with the Lord."

The principal had eaten up the fake story. "Of course, we'll work something out to make this a little easier for your family. I'll meet with Elijah's teachers and work out a home study lesson plan for him. He's a smart student, so I'm sure he'll be able to handle the workload," he'd said with sympathy.

"Thank you so much for your help, sir. This will take a big load off our family," the crackhead concluded. He stood up, shook the principal's hand, and exited the office with Elijah trailing closely behind him.

"You did that shit." Elijah complemented the smoker, excited that he got exactly what he wanted. They exited the school and parted ways.

This new freedom virtually gave Elijah a license to come and go as he pleased as long as he turned in his lessons. He'd have the work completed and sitting in his sock drawer within a few days. Academic curriculum came easy to him; the problem was sitting still in a classroom for seven to eight hours a day. He couldn't adapt well in a school setting. He had simply concluded that school was a waste of time. It made you no money, and much of the shit he learned wouldn't benefit him in the real world. He could use those seven or eight hours to get money!

And that was exactly what Elijah was doing as he wrapped up another long night doing what he did best—hustle. The house lights were turning on as the sun peeked up in the horizon. The neighborhood was waking up to face the day's struggles. Kids being bussed from South Central out to the Valley schools were the first ones out the door into the morning dew. Many of them were older, but he viewed them as children. He felt like a seasoned adult compared to them, a grown man trapped in a little boy's body.

He saw Ju-Ju exiting his apartment. Even with the semi-darkness, he could recognize Ju-Ju's fat-rolling walk from anywhere.

Ju-Ju spotted him and made a beeline toward him. "What up, Crip?" Ju-Ju greeted him with fake toughness.

"Ah, you know . . . just Budlong Ave'n!" Elijah responded, peering around Ju-Ju to examine the approaching man who seemed to have appeared out of thin air.

"Damn, cuzz, you out early this morning. How long you been out here?"

Just then, the man approached. "Y'all working?" he asked.

"Yeah! What's up . . . what you need?" Elijah asked.

"Let me get a dub."

"Hold up," Elijah said, and jogged out of sight to the back of the apartments. He slipped his hand in a crack between a brick wall and the apartment building and retrieved his stash. Removing a twenty-dollar piece of crack, he resealed the Ziploc baggie, placed it back in the stash, and ran back to the front. He looked both ways before he dropped the rock into the man's hand.

The man rolled the rock around in the palm of his filthy hand as he examined the product. "Damn, you can't do no better than that?" He tried to work his con game to get more, a tactic crack-heads used regularly.

"I don't do no damn bargaining! This shit ain't legal, and this ain't the fucking swap meet. Now gimme my money before One Time roll up," Elijah said firmly. The man hesitated, still wanting to press his luck. Finally, he handed over a dirty crumpled twenty-dollar bill.

"You gonna have to hook me up better next time," the man said, then turned and left.

Elijah stuffed the bill into his pocket, scanned the block, then turned back to Ju-Ju. "I've been out here all night," he said.

Ju-Ju stood dumbfounded. He'd been so caught up in watching the small transaction that he had forgotten the question he asked. He'd never seen his friend handling a drug transaction before. Yes he knew Elijah hustled, but seeing him in action was a different story.

"Oh, oh . . . damn, you haven't been home?" Ju-Ju said, amazed. "You ditchin' school again?"

"Fuck school!"

"Your uncle is going to trip. You know how he is about you going to school."

"Unc's outta town right now wit' Big Wiz, doing the same thing I'm doing right here. He can't be mad at me for getting mine. I don't see his ass in college nowhere. Shit! Just like school don't put money in his pocket, it don't put none in mine either. He told me I had to supply my own wants, so that's what I'm doing."

Another crackhead walked up, a woman this time. Elijah went through the same routine with her as the last customer. Ju-Ju watched him in his element. In truth, he was fascinated by the sight. Ever since they did the house burglary for 1-Punch a few years ago and only got eighty dollars to split between the four of them, Elijah had refused to go on any more licks with them. He said he wouldn't work for bread crumbs. Where the Teflon brothers were satisfied with twenty bucks each and the extras they got from the stolen guns and jewelry Li'l Teflon had pocketed and kept secret, Elijah wasn't. His uncles had taught him enough to know twenty dollars wasn't shit for a job like that. They all still hung out together, but whenever Li'l Teflon came up with plans and schemes, Elijah wished them well and headed in the opposite direction.

It blew Ju-Ju's mind how Elijah, at thirteen years old, had the heart, smarts, and freedom to be out on the block all night by himself selling dope, watching for the enemies, and dodging police at the same time. He had no knowledge of how buying and selling drugs worked, and he knew that his mom for damn sure wouldn't allow him to stay out all night. Shit, even if she would allow it he didn't think he had the balls to do it.

"You better get on to school. You're gonna miss the bus." Elijah jolted him out his thoughts.

"Oh, I can ditch and hang out with you. I know you heard the homie Hitter dumped up Baby Sidewinder from Tramp yesterday."

"Yeah, I heard."

"That nigga Hitter's a madman! I heard he served cuzz outta that big-ass U-Haul moving truck he's been riding around in.

They say Baby Sidewinder and Tiny Duck supposed to try and put something together for some get back. I can stay here and watch your back in case they come through," Ju-Ju rambled with excitement.

Elijah studied him as if he was trying to figure something out. His long penetrating stare always made Ju-Ju uncomfortable. Slowly, Elijah peered up the block before speaking. "Nah, you go on to school. I'll be goin' home in a li'l bit to get some sleep." He turned back to face him. "I don't need nobody to watch my back . . . I stay strapped!" He reached in his pocket and produced a small .380.

Ju-Ju stared in adoration. *Damn! This li'l nigga really is a beast,* he thought. Elijah turned to go retrieve his stash before walking home.

---

After school Ju-Ju headed over to the Teflon brothers' house. Naqael, their younger sister, opened the front door for him and immediately turned around to walk back to her bedroom. Ju-Ju was in and out of their house so much that she didn't bother to acknowledge him or alert her brothers of his presence.

Ju-Ju stepped inside and watched her ass as she disappeared into her bedroom. "Ol' dusty bitch, act like she can't speak," he mumbled.

Virginia, their mother, walked from the kitchen with a Newport dangling from her lips. "Hey, baby, you want some food?" she asked, grabbing an open can of Colt .45 from the busted speaker that sat in the corner of the room and took a long swallow.

"No, ma'am, I just ate," he lied. His eyes unconsciously went to her deformed, corn-riddled filthy bare feet. He resisted the urge to shudder in disgust. Against the stained brown carpet, he couldn't decide which were nastier, his mother's feet or the floor.

"Hey, babe, bring my plate," a deep voice shouted from the back room. Ju-Ju couldn't tell which boyfriend it was this time. She had a new man in the house damn near every month.

"Coming, babe. They in the bedroom," she told Ju-Ju, and hurried to the kitchen.

Ju-Ju trailed her to the kitchen on his way to the Teflon brothers' bedroom. He made sure he didn't touch anything in the living room as he passed through. Everything in there was dirty. The mismatched sofas were sagged and stained, and the coffee table was littered with cigarette butts, and empty beer cans and wine bottles. A big roach crawled across the picture of white Jesus that seemed completely out of place in the house. The odor of old lard and stinky seafood grew stronger as he entered the kitchen.

The kitchen was ten times worse than the living room. Blackened stains covered the walls and ceiling, and roaches had their own freeway running back and forth. Ju-Ju glanced at the big tub marked "Lard" sitting on top of the filthy stove. *Why they always have the same food: lard, Kool-Aid, eggs, lunchmeat, and sack of potatoes?* he wondered. He could never survive without his mother's country fried chicken. She made it for him at least twice a week.

The Teflon brothers were in their junky bedroom talking when Ju-Ju walked in. Big Teflon sat with his shirt off, lips and fingers greasy from eating the canned corn, over-cooked green peas, and canned salmon that had been transformed into a hard-greasy train wreck that Virginia claimed to be salmon croquettes. Ju-Ju could tell by the look of the meal that Virginia must have just gotten her county check, because that was considered a special family meal, according to her standards. They barely acknowledged his presence as he sat at the foot of Li'l Teflon's bed and removed his jacket. A head nod from Li'l Teflon and a cold stare from Big Teflon was all he received as a greeting.

Big Teflon still didn't like Ju-Ju. One day, after trying to work out a solution to the problem, Li'l Teflon had taken him over to

Ju-Ju's house in the hopes that it would lighten him up a little if he became more familiar with Ju-Ju. But seeing Ju-Ju's nice things and the good food he ate only infuriated Big Teflon more. Everything concerning Ju-Ju fed his rage toward him. He hated Ju-Ju's clean house, his clean clothes and shoes; he hated that Ju-Ju's mother, Brenda, was sober and cared for her son; he hated Ju-Ju's voice, his fatness, his cowardice . . . everything.

Ju-Ju sat and listened as Li'l Teflon ran down his latest idea. Li'l Teflon was convinced that he'd discovered the big move that would put them over the top for good. "I went over to the west side to buy some weed from the homie Cujo. He took me into the back room to weigh it up—that's where they keep the weed, work, and the safe full a money. If we could get our hands on the safe, we'd be set."

Big Teflon listened attentively, thinking of all the ramifications of what was involved. *This is risky*, he thought. He decided to voice his concerns. "So much could go wrong. The first problem is somebody always in Cujo's spot, so it's impossible to get in and steal the safe without a shootout. Secondly, if we somehow made it in successfully, how in the hell we gonna get the safe opened without knowing the combination? Lastly, Cujo and his crew are our homies—Nine Os, regardless of the fact they from the Western side. If word somehow got out that we hit Cujo's house, the big homies gonna come down on our heads." Big Teflon speaking up was an uncharacteristic move for him. Usually his younger brother would lay out the plans and he'd simply play his part.

Li'l Teflon instantly sprang to his feet and paced back and forth in the tiny cluttered room. He rubbed his chin and stared at the floor, formulating his words. "The Western side ain't our homeboys," he said, still pacing and gazing at the floor. "They a bunch a rich pretty-boy cowards who rode the back of the real Nine Os head-busters to get rich. They claim to be 90s, but they busted asses don't never put in no work on the enemies." His face became a mask of disgust as his voice grew louder and he pounded his fist into his hand for emphasis, driving home his point. The word spreading through the hood was that the big homies from the Budlong side, Big Wizard and Hitter, were about to smash on the Western side anyways, so why wouldn't he use this to his advantage?

"If it do come out that we got 'em," he ranted, "Big Nine is gonna have our backs. His nephew Li'l Nine is our road dog and will ride with us regardless. He won't have a choice . . . he ain't gonna go against his nephew for them bustas. Once Big Nine steps in, they can't do nothing but accept their loss or get smashed."

Li'l Teflon explained how they were going to get the safe open and get in the house when no one was there. "The safe isn't nailed to the floor, and it's little enough for us to carry. We'll simply carry it away and worry about opening it later." He paused for a minute to let his words sink in, then continued. "Gettin' in the house when no one home ain't a problem. Us and 60s playing the Rollin' 100s in football next Sunday at Southwest College and all the homies gonna be there. Cujo and his squad ain't gonna miss this to sit in no dope spot all day. We hit the spot while they at the game, then go to the game afterwards as if we had nothing to do with it. Who'll know exactly when we arrived at the game? No one! That'll be our alibi if we ever needed one: 'We was at the football game the whole time'!"

Li'l Teflon didn't plan on being refused; taking from others was his game and he loved it. Ju-Ju noticed the twinkle in his eyes as he spelled things out. From as far back as Ju-Ju could remember, things like this was Li'l Teflon's only passion. He didn't even concern himself with the girls in the hood as the rest of them did. His focus was stealing, smoking weed, and trying to come up on something to eat. The highest priority on Li'l Teflon's short list was stealing, and nothing or no one was exempt from his sticky fingers: mom, grandma, friend, or foe; if you slipped, Li'l Teflon was gonna get you.

Li'l Teflon finished laying out his master plan with dramatic flair. Big Teflon admired his little brother with a mischievous smile. Li'l Teflon returned an evil grin of his own. Both knew without having to say it that the plan was a go!

# CHAPTER FOUR

Li'l Teflon could barely see over the steering wheel as he swung the dark blue beat-up 1976 Monte Carlo onto Ninety-Fourth and Manhattan and pulled over to the curb. Kids rode their bikes up and down Ninety-Fourth while a few elderly women sat gossiping on their front porches. Li'l Teflon positioned the smoker rental on the west side of Manhattan. The three underage boys dressed in all black couldn't have looked more suspicious if they tried.

"Them niggas need to get the fuck on. We can't be sittin' out here like this too much longer. Them nosey-ass ol' ladies probably call the police on us," Li'l Teflon said. As soon as he finished speaking, Cujo, Squeaky, Big Iceman, and G-Down exited the house down the block, jumped in a gray BMW, and presumably headed to the football game.

Li'l Teflon waited five minutes, then turn to Ju-Ju, who was sitting in the back seat, and said, "Go knock on the door to make sure nobody still in there."

Like an obedient child, Ju-Ju wobbled out of the car, went up to the door, knocked, came back, and gave them thumbs-up. "All clear!"

"That's what's up. Get in," Li'l Teflon ordered. Once Ju-Ju was in the car, Li'l Teflon pulled away slowly. Turning off Ninety-Fourth, he again parked on Manhattan Place, out of the sight of the women on the porch.

"Get in the driver's seat and wait until you see us come out," he told Ju-Ju. "When you see us, pull in front and pop the trunk."

Suddenly, reality set in. Paranoid and shaking like a leaf, Ju-Ju desperately wanted to find a way out. "Don't you think we should get Nine in on this one? He'll come for this amount of stuff," he said.

"Nine doing his own thing," Li'l Teflon said, pulling his black hooded sweatshirt over his head and drawing the string. "That nigga just wanna sell dope all day and night. I told him, 'Why stand out there day and night for money we can get in minutes.' He don't want to listen to me, so we're leaving his ass out."

"Stop asking so many mutha-fuckin' questions," Big Teflon interjected. "We already got everything in motion, just do your part!" Ju-Ju just stared blankly at him.

"What the fuck you starin' at, nigga?" Big Teflon asked with aggression.

"Man, we ain't got time for that shit. We got work to do," Li'l Teflon scolded his brother.

Ju-Ju and Big Teflon continued staring each other down. With a face filled with animosity, Ju-Ju slowly diverted his eyes back to Li'l Teflon. Over the years, he had grown tired of being the punching bag. He knew Big Teflon could kick his ass, but what was once fear had grown into resentment bordering on hatred. Still, he had yet to gather enough courage to openly challenge Big Teflon.

"You ready, Bro?" Li'l Teflon broke the tension, pulling his brown gardener gloves on tight. "Let's get it!"

They got out the car with their tools, hugged, looked both ways, and darted through the alley. It led to Cujo's backyard cordoned off by a low-rise brick wall. An effortless jump landed them in the spacious yard.

The yard was littered with old beer cans and bottles. What used to be grass was now a lawn of dirt and debris. A few tattered lawn chairs sat around a small leaning table under an orange tree. A homemade chicken-wire pigeon coop stood midway up one side of the brick wall. Li'l Teflon looked at the birds inside the coop and had a fleeting thought: *I should take a few of these mutha-fuckas for souvenirs on my way out . . .* But he quickly shook the notion; a much more important mission was at hand.

Li'l Teflon wasted no time when he got to the window. He took out the crowbar and began wrestling with the lock on the window's safety bars. In under a minute, the bars groaned and parted with a loud clank. He sat the crowbar aside, slid the windowpane up, and hoisted himself halfway through. Just then, he heard the growl of what sounded like a wild wolf. Thrusting himself backward out the window with no regards of how he landed, he could smell hot dog breath as the teeth from the face of an all-black pit bull lunged for him. Mere inches away, he could hear the rapid snapping of the dog's fangs as its saliva spittle dripped onto his face. A few more seconds and his face would have been ripped to shreds.

Big Teflon instinctively lurched back, eyes wide, confused. He shifted from one foot to the other as the dog's face reappeared in the window. Its legs were too short to jump all the way out of the window, but that didn't stop the effort. The dog howled and scratched the wall, whimpering, dying to get to the intruders.

Li'l Teflon landed on his ass, scooted backward, and bounced to his feet with all intentions of getting up outta there, but once he realized the dog couldn't make it out of the window, he settled down. He brushed off his ass so his brother wouldn't see his trembling hands. "Shit! Why didn't Ju-Ju's stupid ass say something about a goddamn dog in there!" he shouted, still trying to gather his composure.

"What we gonna do now? Let's get out of here," Big Teflon said, looking around as if he expected someone to come out and grab them at any moment.

Li'l Teflon shook his head and pounded it with the side of his fist as if he was trying to get his brain to work. "No, no, no . . . hold up!" He closed his eyes. "Let me think for a minute."

"We gotta hurry up!" Big Teflon said, ready to abort the mission.

"Not yet. There's gotta be a way . . . fuck!" Li'l Teflon kicked up a chunk of dirt in frustration. "Ain't no fuckin' dog about to stop me from gettin' rich," he growled.

After a bit of contemplating, he believed he had a plan. He turned to his brother, suddenly in a rush, and said, "Go 'round to the front door, and knock and make noise like you trying to get in. While you keep the dog occupied, I'll creep through the window. Once inside, I'll hide in another room. Wait a few minutes, then come back to this window and make more noise. Once he runs back to the window, I'll slam the door and lock his ass inside. I'll let you in through the back door and we get the safe . . . got it?" Big Teflon nodded. "Go then!"

Big Teflon turned hesitantly and headed toward the front of the house. As soon as Li'l Teflon heard the dog's faint barking, he went into action. The plan worked to perfection. Within no time, they were loading the safe into the trunk of the car. Their adrenaline-spiked hearts pumped wildly as they drove back to the Budlong side of the hood. The Teflon brothers struck again!

The garage (if it could be called that) in the back of Virginia's house was made of old wooden planks and leaned as if it was propped on a kickstand. There was a wide-open space where the door was supposed to be. The garage was filled with old miscellaneous items that would never be used. One match thrown the wrong way would ignite the shed like a summer brush fire. Li'l Teflon sat on the hood of the car parked at the garage's front entrance as he punched numbers on the enormous gray block cell phone he'd stolen out of the house. Ju-Ju and Big Teflon stood just inside the garage staring perplexed at the small metallic safe tucked in the corner.

"Li'l Nine? Nine? . . . Check it out, cuzz, we got a problem," he said into the phone. He filled Elijah in on all the details of the lick before ending with the final dilemma. "We've tried everything and can't get this fuckin' safe open for nothing in the world."

Elijah remained silent on the other end of the phone while his brain scrambled for a solution. Finally, he said, "I'll come up with something, but I want a cut out of whatever's in the safe if I get it open for y'all."

Li'l Teflon smacked his teeth in frustration. He was expecting help, not ultimatums. "Look, if you get it open I'll give you something, but it won't be an equal cut because you wasn't there when we had to take all the risks."

Elijah agreed to check it out. He would negotiate later once he got the safe open.

Li'l Teflon hung up and alerted the others that Elijah was on his way. A half-hour later, Elijah showed up. The three of them were waiting with extreme anticipation to hear his plan.

"Get it in a box and put it in the car. We have to get it down the street to the big homegirl Lady Rawdog's house," Elijah instructed. They all looked disappointed, as if they thought he would show up with a blowtorch, or some shit, like in the movies.

Li'l Teflon wasn't quick to move. "What do we need to take it to her house?" he asked suspiciously.

Elijah already knew that Li'l Teflon just wanted to know the method he planned to use to open the safe so he could steal the idea and cut him out of the deal. He smiled to let it be known that he was up on the game. "Cuzz, just roll with the flow. I'm going to get it open for you," Elijah said like an old slickster.

Li'l Teflon reluctantly gave in. He hated caving to Elijah, but the safe had to be opened. Slowly, he nodded to his brother and Ju-Ju, gesturing for them to load it in the trunk for the ride to Lady Rawdog's place. "Let's get this shit over with," Li'l Teflon said. He got behind the wheel, slammed the door, and pulled out into traffic.

# CHAPTER FIVE

Lady Rawdog's shabby one-bedroom apartment sat at the end of Ninetieth and Vermont. For the most part, a black security gate at the front kept out the riff raff. The barred gate couldn't be opened without a tenant buzzing you in, so Elijah had already called ahead to let her know they were on their way. As soon as they pulled up to the building, Lady Rawdog's round face and shot-out perm could be seen leaning out the second-floor window. She had to move the makeshift sheet curtain to hand them the remote that opened the driveway gate.

By the time they made it upstairs to her apartment, she had already sent her daughter, LeLe, to the back room and was waiting for them with the door opened. They sat the safe in a corner of the living room and took seats on her worn sofa and loveseat that used to be beige but was now a coffee brown from all the dirt on it. Li'l Teflon and the others waited expectantly while Elijah laughed and joked with her.

Not long after, a Mexican wearing greasy jeans and a tool belt knocked on the door. Lady Rawdog let him in and showed him the safe. He dropped his tool bag next to it and went to work. Within three minutes, the safe door lay open. She pressed two-hundred dollars into his hand and warned him, "Forget that you ever came here and did a job." He nodded, counted the money, and smiled all the way out the door.

As soon as the door closed, Li'l Teflon greedily reached into the safe. He smiled as he pulled out the stacks of cash wrapped in rubber bands, fluttering each stack near his face to feel the breeze from it and smell the scent. Next came twenty-seven individually wrapped plastic sandwich baggies with knots at the top, each containing an ounce of crack. Stacking the baggies neatly next to his feet, he then pulled out two Glock .40 pistols and admired them affectionately. The last of the safe's content was five pounds of high-grade Indo bud and two scales—a triple beam and an electric. After counting the cash, the total amounted to $6,800.

"Damn, li'l niggas!" Lady Rawdog said with hungry eyes. "Who y'all sting for all that?"

"You asking too much. Remember, you never seen this," Elijah said. Without asking the others he took a pound of weed off the table and handed it to her. "That's for your silence."

She raised her eyebrows at him, feeling insulted. "Li'l nigga, if I didn't love you and your uncles, I'd fuck you up. You could never give me anything for my silence because mine is automatic and goes without saying. I've been doing this shit before you li'l niggas could balance your heads good! I'm a real O.G. that's true to this. Don't you ever get at me like that again!"

Elijah put on his most charismatic smile that he knew she loved. "My bad, Aunty." He hugged her and kissed her hard on the cheek. "I didn't mean it like that. I just don't want my uncles or the other homies knowing about this."

Lady Rawdog smiled even though she didn't want to. "Li'l nigga, don't be trying to charm me. You worse than your uncle, Big Nine, thinking you can manipulate me! Y'all do what you got to do, then get that shit and your asses out of my house." She clutched the pound of weed to her chest and went into her bedroom.

Li'l Teflon started putting all the spoils from the safe into a gym bag until Elijah held up his hand for him to slow his roll. "Hold up, cuzz, let me get my issue."

Li'l Teflon paused, then continued packing the goods. "We'll meet up at the house later and break it . . ."

"Nah, my nigga." Elijah shook his head. "I got shit to do later. Let me get mine now."

Li'l Teflon furrowed his brow. "What you feel you should get for calling a fuckin' locksmith?"

Elijah huffed. "Yeah, it sounds so simple now, but you couldn't think of it!" He glared at Li'l Teflon. "Just give me a thousand dollars, a pound of weed, and tramp ounces uh the work."

Li'l Teflon did the math in his head and scowled. "Eight-hundred dollars, a pound a weed, and two ounces a work is all you gonna get. Take it or leave it!"

"Fuck it, give it here," Elijah said, taking his cut. Li'l Teflon went back to packing the rest.

"What about me? I want mine too," Ju-Ju said.

"You'll get yours later." Li'l Teflon quickly packed up.

"Nah, every time you tell me that, I end up not getting shit. I want my cut this time," Ju-Ju said, suddenly feeling defiant and tired of being stepped on.

Big Teflon stood swiftly, his nose flared in anger. "Who the fuck you talking to like that, busted-ass nigga? You fuck around and get nothin'!"

Ju-Ju glared at him, only slightly trembling. "Shit, I never get nothing anyways, but this time I want mine and I'm going to get—"

In one fluid motion, Big Teflon balled his hand into a fist and swung his arm, his knuckles connecting to Ju-Ju's jaw like Barry Bond's bat on a one-hundred-mile-per-hour fastball. The cracking sound echoed throughout the apartment and Ju-Ju hit the floor.

Hot pain scorched Ju-Ju's face and dots danced in front of his eyes. The walls shook.

Then everything went silent. Ju-Ju sat there for a moment, stunned, and then he felt a rage course through him that he'd never felt before. To everyone's surprise, Ju-Ju sprang back up with the look of a madman in his eyes.

"Ahhhh!" he yelled while charging Big Teflon. With all his might, he threw a wild, slow George Foreman haymaker that caught Big Teflon square on the side of the head.

The sudden burst of violence caught Big Teflon completely by surprise. The blow stumbled him, but he was able to catch his balance and take a few steps back, retreating as Ju-Ju continued his charge. Once he got over his initial shock, he anticipated and ducked the second uncoordinated punch. Rolling left, he countered with a fierce left-hook-straight-right combination that sat Ju-Ju on his pockets again.

Like an enraged infant, Ju-Ju waddled back to his feet and attacked, nose and mouth bloody, tears running down his face he yelled at the top of his lungs and swung with all his might. Big Teflon hit him with a beautiful flurry of devastating blows that cut his face up like a razor blade.

"Y'all li'l niggas stop this shit in my house!" Lady Rawdog shouted as she ran from the back room. Veins popped out of her neck and eyes bulged in fury. She kicked off her tan house slippers and quickly pinned up her hair in a rushed ponytail, ready for a fight. Her young daughter peeked out of the bedroom door with frightened eyes.

Elijah grabbed Big Teflon. "It's over." Big Teflon shook free from his grasp and looked as if he was ready to attack him as well. Elijah swelled up in attack-mode ready. "I said the shit is over," he said through gritted teeth. "Y'all niggas disrespecting the big homegirl's house. You been using this nigga for free for years. Now you up. Give him his due and stop being greedy!"

Big Teflon seemed to finally come to his senses, as if he snapped out of some trance. The tension in his posture eased up.

Elijah turned to Li'l Teflon once the threat of his brother was no more an issue. "Give Fat Boy his shit!" he demanded, pointing to Ju-Ju.

Li'l Teflon paused a minute to weigh his options. He looked at Ju-Ju in disgust as he lay on the floor with his shirt pressed against his face, bleeding like a stuck hog. The risk of confrontation with Elijah wasn't worth the problems it could possibly cause. "Alright. We'll give him his shit, but after this, he won't go on a lick with us ever again."

Li'l Teflon reached into the bag and dug out $500, a pound of weed, and five ounces of work and slammed it on the dining room table. "That's all he getting. If he wants more, he can get it in blood." He glared back and forth between Elijah and Ju-Ju.

Elijah coming to Ju-Ju's defense left a bad taste in Li'l Teflon's mouth. Strapping the gym bag over his shoulder, he headed for the door.

"Come on, Bro, let's rock-and-roll!" Li'l Teflon said. Big Teflon fell in behind his little brother as they left Lady Rawdog's with the bag of goodies that would play a major role in changing all their lives forever.

# CHAPTER SIX

"Elise . . . Elise . . . Ms. Cortez, wake your ass up."

Elise thought she dreaming until she felt the tug on her wool blanket and friction of the creaking metal of her small cot. She rolled over and was startled to see Superintendent Ms. Givens's ugly face hovering over her.

"What?" Elise breathed sleepily.

"Don't 'what' me. Get your ass up and start my coffee."

Elise glared at Ms. Givens with deep hatred. She could barely contain herself from grabbing her neck and trying to break it.

Ms. Givens turned and stalked back towards her own room once she saw that Elise was awake. Elise angrily tossed the blanket back. The cold chill whipped through her shirt. She had to pause when her bare feet touched the cold floor.

*I gotta get outta here before I kill this bitch,* she thought as she looked around the dark room at the other sleeping girls. *Why does she always pick on me?*

This was Elise's fifth group home in three years, and the courts had already labeled her a troubled child. She never seemed to fit in. She earned the reputation as the quiet girl who should be left alone because of all the fights she had been in with the staff and the other girls. The bumps and bruises she'd received from the older and bigger girls in all the other homes had turned her into a seasoned brawler, but Ms. Givens hadn't taken heed. She and Ms. Givens argued and even tussled a few times when Elise first arrived at the facility, but Ms. Givens was relentless. She reported Elise to Children Services, who in turn threatened to place Elise in juvenile hall if she continued her rebellious and violent behavior.

Elise had a little over a year before her eighteenth birthday when she would be able to leave for good, so she sucked it up and tried to deal with what Ms. Givens was dishing out. She agonized every day from Ms. Givens's continuous scheme to make her life miserable and get her thrown into juvenile hall.

Elise stood up, stretched, and dragged herself to the kitchen to put on the coffee pot. As she waited for the water to boil, tears formed in her eyes as she thought of that fateful day. *All I did was defend myself,* she thought. *Why am I being punished for killing a man who was raping me? Why won't Aunt Maria forgive me and come get me outta here. This is not a home; this is jail.*

The red light on the coffee pot flashed and the beeping snapped her out of her agony. She poured the coffee in a small white mug and spit in it, then stirred it nonchalantly with a spoon. She carefully eased her way to Ms. Givens's room with the hot beverage and placed it on the nightstand. The bathroom door was close but the light was on. Just then the toilet flushed. Elise turned quietly, hoping to get out before Ms. Givens finished in the bathroom.

"Elise . . ." Ms. Givens called from the bathroom. "I left a load of clothes by the washing machine. Put them in before you go back to sleep."

Elise looked at the clock: 4:25. *How dare this bitch,* she thought as she scowled at the bathroom door. "Okay," she mumbled, then she left.

Instead of going to the laundry room, she detoured to another room filled with sleeping girls and walked over to the corner cot near the window. "Diabla." she called softly.

Diabla rolled over and looked at Elise through sleep-filled eyes. The light from the streetlamp coming through the window made her squint as she tried to focus and get her bearings. The light revealed her thick lips, high cheekbones, and prominent Hispanic features. Diabla, real name Sophia, was a member of the Eighteen Streets, a ruthless Hispanic gang. She and Elise had started off as bitter adversaries, and they had come to blows a few times when Elise first got to the home, but they eventually came to respect each other as two riders in the struggle. That respect grew into a fast bond and Diabla was the closest thing that Elise had to a family.

"What time is it, *mia*?" Diabla asked groggily.

"I'm leaving," Elise said.

Diabla rubbed her eyes and sat up slowly. "What are you talking about? Where're you going?"

Elise shrugged. "I don't know. I just gotta get outta here, and another group home is not an option. This musical-chair ride has gone on long enough. I don't belong in one of these places no more. I didn't do anything wrong, but I'm forced to be trapped here with no one in this world to love me.

"You can't just leave without having a plan." Diabla grabbed Elise's hand. "First you have to have somewhere to go."

Elise didn't respond. She stared blankly as her mind raced.

"I know you're a soldier," Diabla moved closer to her, "but making it on the streets of LA is not an easy task for a girl with no support." She looked out the window. "Maybe I can talk to Shy-Girl," she said more to herself than to Elise.

Being from the Eighteen Streets, Diabla had many contacts. Their gang was comprised of many different cliques and sub-sets throughout southern California down into Mexico. She was from the Smiley Drive clique in west Los Angeles.

"Alright, I won't tell you not to go, but at least go and stay with my homegirl until I get out. I only have six months left to complete my court order, so it don't make no sense for me to leave when I'm at the finish line. You're almost at the finish line too, and I'd rather you stay, but I understand your situation is different from mine, so all I can do is support your decision."

Elise was adamant about leaving. No amount of rationale was going to change her mind. She had had enough.

---

The next morning, Diabla contacted Shy-Girl and arranged for Elise to stay with her. Diabla's word was enough for Shy-Girl to welcome Elise as an unofficial member of their Eighteen Streets family.

After being out of the group home for a few weeks, it didn't take long for Elise to figure out that she had a serious dilemma with providing for herself. She was under-age and she encountered every obstacle a juvenile runaway could face.

"I need to get some money to take care of myself. I can't stay broke like this," she voiced to Shy-Girl one day.

"Don't trip. As long as I have, you have," Shy-Girl reassured her.

Elise wasn't satisfied with this. She didn't want sympathy or charity; she wanted a solution. "I need to be of some use," she said desperately. "You already feeding me and giving me a place to stay. I appreciate it, but I gotta find a way to feed myself and buy my own things."

Shy-Girl nodded and probed Elise with her eyes. "I respect your independence," she said with a sense of satisfaction. "Let me talk to the homeboy, Pelon. I'm sure he can find you something to do to earn some money. I got you, *mami.*" She patted Elise's knee.

---

"*Que pasa,* homegirl!" Pelon greeted Shy-Girl. Unlike the stereotypical view of Mexican gang members, Pelon didn't wear the oversized Dickies hiked up to chest level, and every other word he spoke wasn't *homes.* Aside from the occasional mix of broken Spanish and English, his slang talk and swagger was that of the urban black gangster. His clean-shaven head, Jordan tennis shoes, and matching Tommy Hilfiger outfit passed him off as a player-hustler type, but Elise knew that he'd kill in a California second.

Pelon eyed Elise up and down suspiciously. His suspicion quickly turned to sexual attraction. She was gorgeous, with long straight hair and a curvaceous body.

Elise caught a quick glimpse of Pelon's look and instantly knew what it was—lust. She stared at him with disgust. She hated him, because he represented the wrong she suffered. She was staring at her uncle all over again and wanted to bury the butcher knife in his face, but she kept her face smooth and revealed no emotion.

Not appreciating Elise's silence, Pelon decided to have a private talk with Shy-Girl. "Shy-Girl, let me holla at you for a minute." He tilted his head, gesturing her to the bedroom. "How you know this chick?" he whispered once the door closed.

"She was in a group home with Diabla. She ran away from there and has no family, so I did Diabla a favor and took her in for a while. She's good people though. I wouldn't have asked you to help her out if I didn't think she was," Shy-Girl explained.

"But she's a *morena*! Even though she looks good . . . just because she's good enough for Diabla to lick her pussy doesn't mean she's good enough to be involved in *barrio* business," Pelon snickered.

Shy-Girl muffled her laugh with her hand. "Fuck you, *vato*!" she said between giggles. "Don't be putting that lesbian jacket on my homegirl Diabla. It's not like that; they're just *amigas* and Elise isn't a regular *pena*—she's Belizean, asshole."

"I'm just bullshitting," he laughed. "But you know how Diabla's crazy ass is, and I wouldn't put anything past her. I'm gonna talk to homegirl to see where her head is."

Elise stared Pelon up and down as he came out of the room. He sat across from her on the cream-colored ottoman. She looked him directly in the eyes without any sense of intimidation.

"So, *mia,*" he said, his eyes deeply probing Elise, "Shy-Girl told me that you and Diabla are *amigas.*"

Elise nodded in response. She didn't have too much to say and wanted him to get on with it so she could get out of his presence.

"She tells me you need work," he added as he checked his pager. "So, what are you at?" He looked at her with a devilish grin.

"What do I need to be at?" Elise asked unflinchingly.

"Ah, you know . . . a little bit of this, a little bit of that."

"I don't know what 'a little bit of this, a little bit of that' is, but whatever'll get me some money without me having to belittle myself I'm with it."

Pelon nodded. "You know how to be an actress and how to use a gun?" he asked with amusement on his face.

"I've never done either one, but I'm a fast learner."

Pelon rubbed his chin and examined her closely. "I got a few things in the mix right now. I think you just may be the person for the job. I'm sure you've figured out by now that I don't sell suits for a living, so what I'll need you to do will involve risk. Are you ready for risk?"

Elise stared at him with an unreadable expression. "Is risk ready for me?" she said without humor.

Pelon returned her stare for a few seconds, then he stood up and extended his hand to Elise. She stood and shook his hand in agreement.

"Let the games begin," Pelon declared. "Be on standby for my call." With that said, he saluted Shy-Girl and headed out the door.

Elise stood there for a minute, watching him as he exited. *Yeah, let the games begin,* she thought, as the door shut behind him.

Climbing the outside stairwell of the Super 8 motel, the severely obese Mexican Border Brother was so drunk he could barely walk. He used Elise more for balance than succeeding in his attempt to feel her up. He had been drinking tequila and Coronas like water for most of the night at the local bar. She strained to keep him and herself from falling over. In his attempt to whisper sweet nothings in her ear, he overwhelmed her sense of smell with a combination of tequila, tamales, shit, and hot breath. She was on the verge of puking.

After what felt like a triathlon, they finally made it inside a room that smelled of cigarettes where she dropped him like a sack of potatoes onto the cheap boxed mattress, then got to work struggling to take off his tight-fitting cowboy boots. She never understood why the drug lords from Mexico always dressed like imitation cowboys.

"Hurry up, *mia* . . . suck my deek." He slurred and swayed as he tried to sit upright.

With his boots off, Elise moved to take off his pants and shirt. Lying there in tight, dingy, white crime-fighter drawers with black nylon dress socks, he was a fat human pig. She turned her face up in disgust.

Abruptly, he reached out and grabbed the back of her head with unexpected speed and strength, and pulled her toward his crotch.

"Come on, *mia*, put et in ju mout."

She began to panic. "Relax! You're hurting me!" She struggled to resist his force while trying to act calm at the same time. She might as well had been talking to the wall because he didn't understand anything she said. He pressed harder on her head and neck.

"Stop it!" she yelled, jerking her head and neck from his grasp.

"Ju bitch!" he growled, slapping her face with enough force to send her flying across the bed.

Before she could regain her wits, he was straddling her, ripping at her clothes. Her heart rate shot through the roof and she had to think fast. She viciously dug her fingernails into his eyeballs and face with the ferocity of a tigress. He recoiled from the sudden attack, easing the amount of weight necessary to keep her pinned down. Her free arm snatched the porcelain lamp off the nightstand next to the bed, and in one fluid motion, it exploded against the side of his head and face.

Just then the door crashed open with Pelon and two other masked men entering with guns drawn. The Border Brother crawled on all fours, dazed from the lamp blow. Blood gushed from the cuts on his face and head as the three men began duct taping his mouth, hands, and feet.

As one of the men was preoccupied with the duct taping, Elise grabbed his gun that was lying on the nightstand. She pressed the barrel into the incapacitated man's forehead and squeezed the trigger. The gun failed to discharge; she hadn't removed the safety. Frantically, she slid the top shaft back and forth to make it fire. Initially, Pelon and his crew were startled by her erratic behavior, but he recovered quickly and snatched the gun from her grasp, using his forearm to shove her off balance and landing on her ass.

"What the fuck wrong with you?" he barked. "We haven't got the shit yet and you're gonna kill 'em? You trying to get us busted, bitch?"

Elise was seeing red. She couldn't believe she had put herself in this position. The man's foul breath clung to her nostrils, and she still felt his fingers fondling her skin. *No!* Her uncle's face floated in her mind and she pushed it away. She looked at the fat man tied up on the floor to Pelon with equal hatred and disdain. Never again would she let a man hurt her . . . *never again.*

# CHAPTER SEVEN

The plump Mexican waitress delivered a fresh hot batch of homemade tortilla chips with chunky salsa. Her traditional garb matched the many flags decorating the walls of Margarita's Mexican Restaurant. "Thank you," Elise said with a smile as the waitress refilled their drinks.

Diabla was anxious to get caught up on the hood news and gossip. Her freedom from the group home gave her a renewed energy and zest for life. Her eyes roved everywhere at once, taking in the sights and sounds. The quaint, little restaurant was abuzz with activity.

Rancheras played in the background as families with their children chattered in rapid Spanish. The dark Gothic eyeliner, shadow, and long eyelashes, along with the bright red lipstick on her thick lips made Diabla look like a pretty clown with evil intentions. Her long ponytail curled around her neck and lay casually on her right breast.

"I'm glad you made it home. Now we can do everything we talked about," Elise said.

Diabla, out of habit, rubbed the upside-down cross that was tattooed on her wrist. "I know, *mia.* Shy-Girl has been telling me what you've been doing with the homeboys. Are they treating you right?"

"Fuck no! Every time I do something with them, they give me a few hundred dollars. At first I was cool with it because I've never had money of my own. I thought the few hundred was a lot. But Pelon's homeboy Pee Wee was trying to hook up with me and felt he could earn some brownie points by telling me that Pelon was taking advantage of me." She paused for a moment and sucked her drink through the straw.

"The guys I've been setting up are big-time drug dealers connected to Pelon's uncle," Elise continued. "He knows when they are coming to LA and what they're bringing. He puts me in the right place at the right time to meet them. I make them think they're gonna get some, then once I find out where they're staying, I call to let Pelon know. He comes and robs them. If the dope or *fadia* is not on them at the time, they torture the connect until he tells them where it is. Pelon is getting hundreds of thousands of dollars and throwing me bird crumbs." The bitterness was evident in Elise's voice.

Diabla popped a tortilla chip loaded with salsa into her mouth. "That's how the homeboys are, especially that *vato* Pelon," she mumbled around the food in her mouth. "I don't know why Shy-Girl didn't warn you. She's probably getting a cut of the money, so she's keeping her mouth shut," she speculated.

Elise stared out the large window at the traffic bustling through the streets. Her thoughts had her momentarily entranced. "I'm not mad at them for using me." She turned and looked Diabla in the eye. "Being mad doesn't get me my fair share—only getting even does that."

"What are you talking about 'getting even'?" Diabla wasn't feeling the implied threat. "Check it out, I'm with you on whatever, but no matter how scandalous Pelon is, he's a homeboy and I can't let nobody hurt him."

"I'm not talking about physically hurting him. I'm talking about getting what's rightfully mine. Ever since Pee Wee told me that shit about Pelon, I've been thinking about how to get what they owe me and I came up with an idea."

Diabla studied her over the rim of the heavy glass mug as she drained the remainder of the Coke. "Fill me in on this idea." She set the glass down.

Elise felt giddy with excitement. "On the next job Pelon calls me for, I'll perform all the normal duties, but when I'm supposed to call him to let him know where the robbery is gonna take place, I'll contact you instead. I'll spike the mark's drink sometime during the night with a roofie. This will make tying him up easier since we won't have the homeboys' muscles to do it. If he resists giving up the info to where the goods are," she looked at Diabla deadpan, "I know how to make him talk."

The implied prospect of torture gave Diabla goosebumps. She thought hard on the pros and cons of the plan. She took a bite of the enchilada to buy some time with her thoughts. "It sounds good, but what about Pelon? What will he think when you don't call him or if he finds out from his uncle that the guy's been robbed?"

Elise played with the food on her plate as she said nonchalantly, "I'll call him and say the mark already had a woman with him and a circle of friends so I couldn't get to him. It wouldn't sound out of the ordinary because we've encountered similar predicaments on a couple of jobs in the past. Pelon finding out from his uncle that his boy got robbed—shit, anybody could have done it in his line of work."

Gradually, optimism filled Diabla's eyes. "Damn, I think this can really work. The actual robbery will be easy. I've been doing that since I was twelve. We just have to make sure Pelon doesn't figure out what we've done when it's over." With a hint of reluctance, she made her decision. "Fuck it, I'm in!"

⁂

Rancheras blared from the old-school jukebox in the smoke-filled pool hall. The wrap-around bar was occupied with overly made-up Mexican women and Mexican men dressed in tight jeans, cowboy boots, and hats. Coronas and tequila flowed constantly throughout the hall.

Elise leaned over the table with the pool stick aimed at the stripped ball she was trying to knock into the corner left pocket. Her tight maroon miniskirt was hiked so far up that a hint of her butt cheeks peeked out. Her blouse, tied in a knot at the front, exposed her toned brown stomach. Her matching stilettos accentuated her calves and made her legs appear longer than they really were. Her hair flowed with red highlights and her lips were covered in rose-red lipstick. Her pool stick slammed into the ball. It ricocheted off the eight ball and missed the mark.

"Hey!" the man called out, and raised his tequila shot in the air before draining the glass. "No good for you," he said with a heavy accent before bursting into drunken laughter. "My turn." He picked up his cue stick and moved around the table.

Elise smiled. The man—her mark—was drunker than a skunk. *This is going to be easier than I thought.*

As he took aim, Diabla walked swiftly from the bar area and passed Elise a shot glass of tequila. The exchange was made without even a glance between them. Diabla walked toward the restroom and Elise moved to the other end of the table with the drink. She watched as her date banked a shot into the side pocket and yelled in exhilaration.

The man wrapped Elise in a sexual embrace in celebration. His hand went under her miniskirt and fondled her ass. She placed one hand on his chest, slightly pushing back from him, and offered the drink just in time to deflect the kiss he was aiming her way. She had been pretending to drink all night, pouring her drinks into his glass when he wasn't looking.

He laughed, took the drink, and downed it.

"It's time to go." She pulled him close, whispering in his ear as she grinded her crotch against his.

"Yeah . . . it time to go, *mami.*" He swayed as he kissed her exposed cleavage.

Diabla watched with malice over the rim of her mug as Elise walked out of the pool hall with the man hanging on to her for balance. As soon as they were out of sight, she drained her mug and headed out behind them.

A wave of fresh air washed over Elise as she ushered the man to the rental car waiting at the far end of the parking lot. She felt his weight getting heavier and knew she had to hurry. She got him to the car and dug into his pocket for the keys as she strained to keep him upright. He reeked of alcohol, and she had to turn her head away. She got him into the car and nodded to Diabla who was already waiting in her car to trail them.

The man drifted into sleep as Elise sped out of the parking lot. Within minutes both cars were turning into a darkened alley off Venice and Clyde. They killed the lights on both cars and turned into an empty lot that led to an abandoned factory.

Diabla was instantly at the passenger door with her .380 pistol in hand. They dragged him out and carried him into the factory. The duct-taped his wrist and ankles to a chair that they had placed there earlier.

Elise swiped smelling salt under his nose and jolted him awake. His head swayed back and forth as his eyes strained to focus. He looked at Elise and Diabla in confusion. Diabla dashed him with a pot of cold water to further wake him up.

*"Espabilate . . . ¿Donde esta la mota?"* Diabla said in Spanish.

"He speaks English," Elise said.

"I know. I just want to make sure he fully understands." She smirked.

Elise shouted in his face, "Listen, I'm giving you only one chance to tell me where it is."

"I don't know . . . I don't know what ju talkin'," the man slurred.

"Oh, you don't, huh?" Elise walked to the corner of the room and returned with a hammer. Without hesitation, she raised hammer and slammed it into his kneecap.

His knee made a crunching sound and he screamed. Diabla braced herself behind him and muffled his scream with a rag. Before he could recover, Elise smashed the other knee.

It didn't take long before he was begging to tell them where the goods were. Elise continued the torture a little longer, loving the power it gave her. It filled a void within her, that huge hole left by the torture she'd endured by her uncle's hands, and being left to fester in the system. She was done being a victim.

The information he gave them led to a hidden compartment in the trunk of the rental car. They took their time unloading the pounds of weed from the trunk over to their car.

"Wait in the car," Diabla instructed Elise.

Diabla went back into the building where the man was still tied up. She took out a small pouch containing a syringe loaded with raw heroin and a rubber strap. She tied the rubber strap around his bicep and tapped on his forearm until she saw a vein. She inserted the needle and released the drug into his vein.

The man mumbled and grunted under the duct-tape covering his mouth.

"Calm down, *papi*. This is the easy part." She looked him in the eyes as she stood there with a smirk spread across her lips.

His pupils dilated, his body went limp, and his head tilted back. The job was done.

She headed back to the car, jumped in the passenger seat, and glanced at Elise. No words were necessary. Elise backed out of the parking lot, into the alley, and headed into the night.

It took a week for Diabla to find a buyer for the low-grade weed. They were some Crips from Venice Shoreline that she went to junior high school with. They gave her an under-value price of $200 per pound. Sixty thousand dollars for one night's work wasn't nothing to complain about.

For Elise it was about more than the money, it gave her a sense of power. Before long, she was doing robberies by herself just for the adrenaline rush. Still, she couldn't shake the depression and sadness that consumed her. No matter how much money and material things she acquired, happiness continued to elude her. *I'm a stick of dynamite,* she thought grimly, *just waiting for the right time and circumstance to explode.* The thought caused her hands to tremble in anticipation.

# CHAPTER EIGHT

Elijah walked down Ninety-First Street, went through the cuts, and was on Ninetieth at Ju-Ju's two-bedroom apartment, ringing the doorbell in under five minutes. Brenda, Ju-Ju's mother, opened the door dressed in a big pink terrycloth robe, fuzzy slippers, and a much-too-happy smile on her face. Brenda always looked like she was wearing makeup, but half the time she wasn't. Her permed, short, straight black hair made her look stylish and modern, like she kept up with the times with next to no effort.

Brenda was like many black women who came from the South in hopes of better days on the West Coast. Instead of reaching the glitz and glamour of Hollywood, she landed in the concrete jungles of South Central LA. She had Ju-Ju at sixteen years old, struggled through high school, took whatever job came her way, and had been around the block a time or two because of Ju-Ju's father, who was hardly around anymore, but unlike many others in the neighborhood, he paid child support for Ju-Ju's care. Unlike the vast majority of the county-check moms in the complex, Brenda actually spent the money on Ju-Ju instead of on hair, nails, and swap-meet clothes. Through trial and error, she learned how to survive and make it day by day as a single black mother with a child to raise without the help of welfare.

"How you doing, Ms. Brenda?" Elijah greeted politely.

"Oh, hey, Elijah. I'm alright," she replied, walking away from the door.

"Ju-Ju here?" he asked, stepping inside the apartment.

"He's in his room."

He softly closed the door behind him. "Sure smells good in here, Ms. Brenda. You cooked something?"

"Uh-huh, you eaten yet?" she asked him.

"Yeah, I ate. I'm a just holla at Ju-Ju a minute if that's cool." Staring at Brenda, he saw where Ju-Ju got a lot of his features: the round face, full lips, and brown curious eyes. *Damn, Ju-Ju is really the ultimate momma's boy*, he thought.

"Elijah, sweetie," Brenda purred as she stepped over her lazy white cat, Powder, "I want to talk to you for a few minutes, then you can go on back to the room and see Julius." She scratched her head, swayed back over to the sofa, and sank down on it. She sat with her legs crossed in a no-nonsense way, her eyes solely focused on him. "I wanna know who messed my son's face up like that."

Immediately, Elijah felt like he was in trouble and being interrogated. He didn't like the feeling at all. "With all due respect," he started, measuring his words closely, "that's a question you have to ask your son. I'm not gonna stand here and lie to your face and tell you that I don't know what happened to him because that would be disrespectful to you. But at the same time, it would be disrespectful to Ju-Ju on my part if I told you something he don't want you to know, ma'am."

His direct assault on her prying caught her off guard. Brenda was at a momentary loss for words, then decided to try a different approach. "You two stick together like peanut butter and jelly, don't you?"

He peeped toward Ju-Ju's bedroom and saw the door was closed. "Yeah. Sorta."

"You know, Elijah," she scratched her nose, then smoothed her robe, "because you didn't lie to me like I'd expected you to, I'm going to respect your position, *li'l man*." She smiled sweetly. "But I'm going to ask something of you."

"Yeah. Anything."

"Look after my son. Julius hasn't had a man, a male figure in his life, much to teach him. . . what's the word I'm looking for, chile? *Strength*. The strength of a real man."

"And you think I can teach him that? Strength?" he asked, puzzled.

"Of course you can. Listen, I'm a woman and can only do so much and teach him so much. But your uncles taught you so much. Your uncles taught you strength . . . strength that Julius don't have. Not much anyway. And I knew your mother well. I know that she taught you morals. You're not like those little black-ass boys with them African-sounding names who Julius be trying to run with. I know that I'm losing my grip on him and won't be able to shelter him much longer. I'm no fool. I know he's getting into things he shouldn't be, but he's getting to an age where I can't stop him."

"Yeah. I hear that a lot from grownups 'round here," he readily admitted.

"So I'm charging you with looking out for him as best you can. Your friends don't know it yet, but you're the leader and that's why I'm asking you. Do I have your word that you will do your best?" She waited for his answer.

"I'm no leader. I'm a loner!" he answered with a hint of defiance. "But to the extent that I can look out for him, I will. You have my word on it."

She studied him closely. "Gosh. You remind me so much of your mother. God rest her soul."

"What's up, Nine?" Ju-Ju interrupted from the hallway. "I didn't even know you was here. Come on, we better go to my room before she talks you to death."

Brenda rolled her eyes at him. "Shut up, boy. And who the hell is 'Li'l Nine'?"

The boys looked at each other with mischievous looks in their eyes.

"His momma didn't name him no damn 'Li'l Nine," she said. "His name is Elijah!"

They burst out laughing and turned down the hallway toward the bedroom.

"All these crazy-ass names," she mumbled behind them.

Elijah entered the small but comfortable bedroom. N.W.A. and Public Enemy posters covered the walls, a beach cruiser laid propped against door entering the closet, and everything was neat, a testament to the habits Brenda instilled in Ju-Ju. Elijah sat at the foot of the bed and turned on the thirteen-inch TV and Nintendo.

"What's up? You want some Super Tecmo Bowl, homie?" Elijah asked.

Ju-Ju sat next to him and picked up the other game control. "Why not? Nothing else to do but whoop your ass today."

"So what did you wanna holla at me about?" Elijah asked.

Ju-Ju put his eyes on the screen, trying to figure out the best way to ask Elijah for help slinging dope. "I've been holding on to what I got from that house lick just like you told me. But I want to sell it, or at least some of it, to get some money," he nervously managed to get out.

"Oh, you wanna sell dope now?" Elijah said, half-condescending, half-amused at his friend.

"Well, yeah, you know, sorta like, but not all New Jack City, just make a li'l money. I need you to show me the ropes."

Elijah shook his head in disappointment, knowing he had to keep it real with his partner. "Ju-Ju, you ain't no hustler. Not even a little bit. Shit ain't easy as you think it is. I can't be trying to hold your hand like we in a potato-sack race. It's every man for himself, and I've got enough on my plate trying to keep myself from falling off and losing money. Hell, I gotta keep myself from losing my freedom and my life. Feel me?"

"You won't have to hold my hand. Just show me what to do."

Elijah paused the game and turned to look at him. "Look, homie, I ain't gonna sugarcoat it. Other homies lie to you and keep you around so they can use you for whatever they trying to get done. That's it. I ain't got no reason to lie to you. I don't need you to do my dirty work. I do my own. So I'm a keep it all the way real with you when I tell you this."

"Tell me what?" Ju-Ju asked eagerly, as if he was wishing to hear something that would change his life.

"I'm not gonna show you how to sell dope because you're not built like that, homie."

Ju-Ju looked sick, like he'd lost his puppy. Was he hearing correctly? "Is that why everybody treats me like . . . like . . . I'm different when we hang out?" he asked. "Because I'm not built like that? Wow." He shook his head in anger.

Elijah looked at him, the silence thick between them. His shoulders slacked and he exhaled. "Look—"

"Nah, what makes me so different from y'all? I grew up on this block like everybody else. We went to the same schools. What's the difference between me and you?" Ju-Ju kept at it, refusing to just back down.

"A lot."

Ju-Ju wasn't trying to hear that. He put up with his friends' bullying for too long. He was tired of being their do-boy. "I can be a rider. I'm ready to do whatever, whenever. I just need you to show me a thing or two is all. I don't have uncles or nobody who taught me everything like you, but I'm tired of everybody treating me like I'm weak 'cause I'm not. I'm not. On my mama, I'm not weak." He lashed back with even more determination.

"Man, you're just talking. All emotions right now." Elijah began to grow agitated.

Ju-Ju smacked his lips. "Think so? Sure about that, Nine?"

"Check this out, homie." Elijah stared at him as he would a brother. "I'm not who I am or do what I do just because of my uncles. My uncles can't feel for me what I feel for myself, only I can feel that! And only I can deal with it every day."

"Everybody is going through something, feeling something, man."

"Alright, you really wanna know the difference between me and you?"

"Yeah. I wanna know."

"You got love in your life. You got family that loves you and you love them, right? You're not ready to die and leave them. You fear death. You fear pain. You fear jail. But me, I don't have nobody that loves me in that way, so I fear none of it. My uncles, they got hood love for me."

"What you talking about, Nine? Hood love?"

"Like two male lions try'na raise a cub to be a lion. That kinda love. That's what it is. They don't love me in the regular sense."

Ju-Ju furrowed his brow in confusion, trying to understand.

"And not only do I not fear death, but I run toward it. I wake up every day with suicidal thoughts."

"You wanna kill yourself, Nine?"

"I don't know . . . sometimes." Elijah was conflicted in his feelings about living and dying. Sometimes he just wanted all the pain to end. He missed his mother and often wondered what it would be like to be with her again. "But I'm too strong, or maybe not strong enough, to take my own life. So, I live my life in a way that gives my enemies the opportunity to do it for me."

"Kill you?"

"Yeah. They can try, but I'm a competitor. So I'm not gonna make it easy for anyone to kill me. And if they don't come correct, come right with guns blazing at me, I'm gonna kill them first."

"You sound crazy when you talk like that, Nine." Ju-Ju was getting nervous. He'd never heard anyone talk this way. He knew that Elijah's mother's death changed him. It was subtle, but he noticed a difference in Elijah's eyes, as if he were always a little bit distant. But he was shocked to hear him say that he wanted to die.

"Yeah. It is what it is," Elijah answered, "but I'm never happy. Even when I smile or laugh, it's not from the heart. I don't give a fuck about dying. I don't give a fuck about going to jail. So miss me with that 'I'm ready' shit! You not ready for any of this!"

"But I am. On everything I love, I'm ready." Ju-Ju insisted.

"How can you be ready for something you don't know shit about?" Elijah had to rein in his speech to keep the spittle in his mouth. He stood up. "How? You ready to die? You ready for misery? You ready to ride the beef for the rest of your life in prison? Or will you be the pussy mutha-fucka helping homicide detectives hunt niggas like me?"

Ju-Ju stood up. "I ain't no snitch! I might be a lot a things, but a snitch ain't one."

"Better not be! Snitches wind up in ditches with ninety stitches, Ju."

"Huh?" Ju-Ju was now overwhelmed and confused.

"Anyway, nigga, you ain't ready so shut the fuck up with that lame shit. Just be yourself. And play some Tecmo Bowl, cuzz."

With that, Elijah unfroze the game and started to play. His body temperature had risen and beads of sweat formed on his forehead. His body trembled. Adrenaline. *How dare this soft-as-cotton-ass-nigga sit here and say that shit?! He ready? Humph*, he thought.

They sat in a thick silence, minds preoccupied with thoughts of the exchange as they played the video game. Elijah knew he had to calm down to present his solution to Ju-Ju's problem. Helping

Ju-Ju get rid of the drugs would ultimately serve his purpose even more than it would Ju-Ju's. He had already greatly benefitted from Big and Li'l Teflon's portion of the drugs.

After their blowout at Lady Rawdog's apartment, it took Li'l Teflon a little over a week to get over his ill feelings about what he felt was betrayal by Elijah for taking Ju-Ju's side. At the end of the day, Li'l Teflon was about money, and he knew that he could get it quicker if Elijah dealt with the drugs because he'd already had clientele. Selling drugs wasn't Li'l Teflon's thing, so they both put their pride aside and came to a business arrangement: all the cocaine would be turned over to Elijah and he would pay the Teflon brothers $375 off each ounce.

Elijah thought about telling Ju-Ju that he would give him $300 off each ounce, but he'd give him the same deal he gave the Teflon brothers. "I ain't gonna have you tagging along trying to learn how to sell dope," Elijah suddenly spoke, breaking the silence, "but I'll get rid of it for you and give you $375 off each one."

Ju-Ju was startled. "That would be—"

"Eighteen-seventy-five," Elijah rattled off the figure. "It'll take me a couple weeks to get rid of yours because I gotta get mine off too. So, don't be sweating me about the money. When it's gone, you'll get what you got coming."

Ju-Ju couldn't believe his ears. He had never dreamed of possessing nearly $2,000 of his own money. His mind raced with what all he could do with it.

Elijah nearly elbowed him off the bed. "Snap out of it, Fat Boy. I ain't got all day. Go grab that shit out the closet so I can go."

Ju-Ju jumped to his feet, nearly tripping as he hurried to the closet. "How you know I had it in the closet?" he asked, looking back over his shoulder. "I never told nobody where I stashed it."

"You didn't have to. I just know these things. And you can bet Brenda and the cops do too. So, find another stash if you wanna outsmart they asses."

"Here, cuzz." He handed Elijah the five ounces of hard white cocaine that had been carefully wrapped in sandwich bags. "I 'preciate you doing this for me. If you ever want me to do something, anything at all, just let me know."

"Whatever, man," Elijah responded and he put on his jacket. "Alright, cuzz. I'm 'bout to roll. Duty calls." He stuffed the work into the deep pocket of his leather bomber jacket, then tugged his gloves on tight.

Ju-Ju stopped him as he reached the bedroom door. "Nine?"

Elijah turned to face him.

"This might sound crazy, but don't ever feel like nobody loves you. Your uncles do love you like you're their own son. I see it in the way they talk to you and how they treat you. And even if they didn't, I have homie love for you like a brother."

Elijah half-smiled, half-scowled. "Homie love, huh?"

"Yeah."

"See you, Ju-Ju."

Elijah made it back to his house, went to his room, and grabbed his pen and paper. As he calculated the twenty-seven ounces of cocaine from the house burglary, he factored in that two ounces were his. The other twenty-five he would sell piece by piece, making $1,000 off each ounce, then he minus $375 on each ounce to both Teflon brothers and Ju-Ju. He smiled and leaned back with his hands behind his head—$17,625. *That's lovely for a lick I didn't have to risk my neck in,* he thought as a warm feeling bubbled up inside of him.

Elijah was well on his way down the Road to Perdition. A path that he'd unwittingly chosen for himself. The Teflon- brothers and Ju-Ju were not far behind him . . . four blind mice on a dark road.

# CHAPTER NINE

**1992**

It was a beautiful spring day in South Central LA and the Budlong-Aves were out on full display, enjoying the camaraderie of one another. The aroma of grilled meats and weed filled the air throughout the block. There was no beef (except on the backyard grill) or drama among the circle—only jokes and laughter were in abundance. Dice rattled in the background as Ghetto Boys' "Scarface" blared from the house speaker propped on the front porch of the duplex unit in the middle of the block.

"Dub! You don't five or nine." One of the dice players placed a bet with his homeboy.

"Bet!" Li'l Teflon responded. "I'm from Budlong Avenue, and if I don't hit a nine for the hood my name ain't Teflon." He shook the hell out of the dice in his right hand and turned them loose. Two blue dice with white spots slowly tumbled out. "D-i-i-ice!" he chimed.

The dice rolled across a clear patch of space as everyone in the circle followed them with greedy eyes. "C'mon . . . nine . . . dice."

One of the blue dice stopped rolling near the pile of small bills in the cash pot curtained off by Converse and Nike sneakers. Five spotted to the sky. Its twin spinning on its corner slowed like a break-dancer doing a backspin. Four spotted to the game gods.

"Yeah! Pay me, mister," Li'l Teflon said with wild eyes. "I told you I was gonna hit the hood!"

All the space was taken and people were shoulder to shoulder in the circle except for a couple of females around Ju-Ju on the porch. Dice were shaking, rattling, rolling back and forth—fives, tens, and twenties were heading for the cash pot nonstop.

The Budlong clique cars lined Ninetieth Street like a showroom floor of a classic car dealership: the Teflon brothers' twin gunmetal black 1977 Cutlass Supremes sitting on mustard- and mayonnaise-striped Vogue tires with fourteen-inch Dayton rims; Ju-Ju's nut-brown Cutlass on Deez and Vogues; Elijah's 1979 Crip Blue Cadillac Coupe de Ville also on Daytons and Vogues; and Big 9-Lives' gray Mercedes 190E. It was a good day. Everyone was living and enjoying the moment.

"Fuck Nachos!"

All heads swiveled on cue to the direction where the ultimate disrespectful word for Nine O was shouted—"nacho." Then, in a blur, gunshots sprayed the dice game and everything in the vicinity. People scrambled for cover from the rolling drumbeat of the Tec-9 aimed out the window of the passing car. Bullets crashed against metal, glass, and wood.

Though no one could see the ski-masked shooter, it was clear that he operated the Tec-9 with pure hatred. The eyes behind the mask told it all. A dark, evil, blind hatred filled those wicked eyes.

The old beat-up blue LTD, continuing its assault, made its way down Ninetieth Street past the crowd. Before the car could make it off the block, Ju-Ju sprung from behind a parked car firing his semiautomatic .38 Supra. Ten shots from the extended clip knocked the side and back windows out, while three more hit the trunk, causing it to fly open. The LTD took a few more shots, swerved violently, and crashed into a parked car. The occupants—driver, shooter, and backseat driver—scattered out of the car like cockroaches.

Ju-Ju continued to let the pistol rip after them as he charged up the middle of the street. His bullets missed their mark, allowing all three of the intruders to get away on foot. He presumed they were Eight-Tray Gangstas.

"Aw shit, cuzz! The homie's down!" someone yelled.

Elijah got to his feet to see who'd been hit. To his horror, he saw his uncle Cannon lying face-down on the ground, no movement, no signs of life. Time slowed down again to that same dream like state he knew all too well. He rushed to Cannon's side and slowly turned him over. Two neat holes with minimal blood decorated his chest. Cannon's head tilted slightly to the left in a slow death roll, and a pool of blood spilled from his mouth. Elijah didn't need to be a doctor to know that his uncle was gone. As much as he wanted to turn his eyes away from the nightmare, he couldn't. He stared into his uncle's face as if he could will him back to life.

"Ah nah, nah, please no . . ." Big 9-Lives pleaded. "Come on, Elijah, we gotta get him to the hospital."

Elijah was shaken out of his daze when he heard "hospital." Tears blurred his vision.

Big 9-Lives placed his arms beneath Cannon's armpit and lifted his torso. The stream of blood from his mouth thickened and flowed heavier, painting his shirt and the front of his pants red. Elijah grabbed both ankles and together they lifted and loaded him into the back of Elijah's Cadillac. Big 9-Lives snatched the keys from his him, got behind the steering wheel, and sped off. He was visibly shaking with tears in his eyes as he darted the Cadillac in and out of traffic. This was the most emotion Elijah had ever witnessed from his hard-as-steel uncle. He hadn't acted this way when his sister died. He was always the picture of calm.

"It's gonna be alright bro . . . hang on," Big 9-Lives repeated over and over.

Elijah knew this was a lie that Big 9-Lives was telling himself and not Cannon, because it wasn't going to be alright by any stretch of the imagination. Cannon was dead.

Silent tears rolled down Elijah's face. No wailing, no questions, no pleading, nothing. Tears just flowed.

Upon entering the hospital's emergency room with Cannon, the diagnosis was "dead on arrival." Elijah continued in his silent dream—another teacher, another protector, another loved one, another soldier . . . gone.

A few weeks later, Elijah parked in front of the Nine Os stucco apartment building behind Li'l Teflon's Cutlass. His impulse had taken over before he could get comfortable at home. Cannon was on his mind. He had told Li'l Teflon on the phone that he had to even the score, then drove over to the other side of Budlong and parked on the block. He opened the trunk and took out the AR-15 assault rifle that was wrapped in a coat. He stood in the back of the dimly lit apartment building under the cover of darkness with the assault rifle clenched in his hands. He couldn't stop thinking about the times he had shared with Cannon, wishing he could erase the memory of seeing him gunned down. The guilt, anger, and animosity had taken over him. This rage that caused his stomach to burn and head to spasm with a nonstop ache needed to be released. He sat in the back of the apartment building complex, dressed in an all-black ninja suit. Toying with his AR-15, his thumb picking at the selector switch. *Semi-auto? Fully-auto? Fully automatic tonight,* he decided.

"Fuck that, cuzz! I'm going! Them tramp bitches gotta pay!" Ju-Ju's protested. He was insistent on trying to force his way inside the stolen car with the others.

"I said you ain't goin'." Li'l Teflon physically barred his way. "I know you'll bust your gun in the heat of the moment, but you ain't ready for what we on tonight."

Until this point preparing for the mission, Elijah had remained silent. He wasn't feeling the vibes of his companions. When he called Li'l Teflon earlier to get a G-ride for the mission, he wasn't expecting him to show up with his brother. They'd arrived with an eight-shot riot-pump-action twelve-gauge shotgun, a ten-shot Colt .45 pistol, and their brown work gloves and ski masks. Now Ju-Ju had shown up, .38 automatic in hand, while they were preparing to move against the Eight-Trays. *Hell, I only wanted that nigga Li'l Teflon to bring me a stolen car. I want to do this shit solo,* he thought as he watched the confusion.

"Check it out, homie," Elijah said. "I don't need all this bitchin tonight. That's why I wanted to go by myself." He looked toward his companion. "Ju-Ju, it's his," he pointed with his head toward Li'l Teflon, "G-ride, so if he don't want you to go, just fall back this time."

"Whatever, cuzz!" Ju-Ju stormed off to his car, pissed off at them all. He sped off in his Cutlass in frustration.

The remaining three piled into the primer-gray Chevy Nova. Li'l Teflon was an excellent car thief. He'd used a spark plug to crack the car window; just a dime-sized piece of the heavy carbon casing on any spark plug would did the trick. *Ready, aim, fire* into the window and watched the resulting spider web of glass replace the car window. Elbowed it a couple times, entry gained. Steering wheel lock, no problem. With all his might, he'd gripped the wheel and turned it to the left far as it would go, then to the right, each time the steering wheel's internal lock mechanism cracking a little more until it was finally broken and the wheel freed. Flathead screwdriver, the big one with the one-eighth head, slid into the lip under the wheel on the left side of the steering column. He'd peeled away the metal. Mini flashlight gripped in his teeth, he saw the wires and levers. "Ah, there it is." Jamming the flathead into the exposed mess, he turned over the ignition. The first go and the compartment lights came on. Second go and the motor choked. Third try was always the charm and the motor turned on. No one hotwired a car with two sparky wires except in the movies.

Li'l Teflon was behind the wheel, Elijah was giving directions from the passenger's seat, and Big Teflon sat the backseat gripping the pump shotgun. The murder crew was rollin'.

"Ride through Ninetieth place between Budlong and Normandie first. If they not hanging out there, drive over to Ninety-Sixth and Normandie to see if they out," Elijah said.

"Them bitches on Ninetieth is hiding out. Time to hit Normandie," Li'l Teflon whispered. They took a left on Normandie, driving slowly as they hunted for victims. Just past Ninety-Fourth, a crowd of stray Gangstas—male and female—were drinking, smoking, and selling dope.

"Oh, there they go right there," Big Teflon said with excitement. All three kept their eyes straight ahead, trying not to arouse suspicion as they passed the crowd.

Coming to Ninety-Sixth Street, Li'l Teflon tapped the right turn signal. "I'm gonna circle the block. When I hit the corner off Ninety-Fourth, y'all hang out the window and serve 'em." Li'l Teflon anxiously looked in the rearview mirror.

"Nah," Elijah said, looking straight ahead, "This is personal. I'm gonna get out and get up close to these Tramps. Hit Ninety-Fourth and pull inside the alley where you can wait."

Without further comment, Li'l Teflon pulled the car to a stop inside the alley behind Normandie. Elijah racked one of the .223 rounds into the chamber of the AR-15 and hopped out. Big Teflon jumped out of the backseat with the shotgun. Both dressed in all black, the darkness of the alley covered up their presence when Li'l Teflon killed the car lights.

"Y'all niggas hurry up," Li'l Teflon said, gripping the .45 and checking his surroundings. The alley was clean by any standard indicating that the crackheads and bums hadn't been through there in a while. *Good, won't have to shoot no one for being in the wrong place at the wrong time,* he thought.

Big Teflon caught up to Elijah around the corner of Ninety-Fourth Street. Elijah stooped to peek around the corner of the apartment building onto Normandie. Cars drove north and south in an ongoing pace.

"Lennox sheriffs is always on Normandie, cuzz," Big Teflon said, knowing they were taking a significant risk.

"Yeah, so?"

"What the fuck are we doing then? You want us to get caught out here holding our dicks and guns? Let's get 'em loco." Big Teflon sounded and looked anxious to find cover in the shadows from the oncoming headlights.

But Elijah didn't care about the police. All that mattered was getting the enemy and sawing their heads off with a burst of hot lead from the AR-15 in his grip, and if the police showed up, they could get some too!

He peeked out just enough for one eye to get a quick glimpse on Normandie. "Shhh," he warned. "Halfway up the block, two of 'em coming our way." He braced himself anxiously.

They saw two men cripped down: blue shirts, pants and shoes, limping arrogantly as they walked directly toward their death.

"Stay the hell out of my way. Wouldn't wanna shoot you before I cut these niggas down," Elijah cautioned Big Teflon.

"I hear ya, I hear ya, cuzz."

"I'm gonna get 'em. Once I hit these two, I'm running into the crowd up the block." Elijah licked his lips. "I'm counting on you to wait here. Not up the block, not around the corner in the car, right here, homie, 'case I need cover fire on the way back this way."

Big Teflon's wide nose flared up in anticipation. He nodded his understanding. "You hear that, Nine?" he asked suddenly as if he was startled by something strange.

"What?"

"Sounds like . . ." Big Teflon bopped his head to the beat. "The Payback!"

Elijah took the pause as an encouragement to record James Brown to memory. In that moment, he suddenly understood the meaning of song.

"What the fuck?" he mumbled to himself.

Out of nowhere, the brown '77 Cutlass Supreme whizzed past them southbound on Normandie, James Brown's voice howling on the wind, rumbling bassline about three seconds behind.

"Who dat, cuzz?" one of the Eight Trays said, now close to the corner.

Elijah and Big Teflon stepped from behind the building the two Eight Trays were caught looking in the opposite direction, eyes following the brown Cutlass. The car stopped in front of their homies. They weren't aware that two of hell's angels with tools of death stood at their backs.

"Cuzz got a heat!" someone warned, as the Cutlass pulled to the curb and the driver's side door flung open. The driver bounced out of the car on the crowded street corner, gun in hand.

"It's just them Bang-side 90s" Elijah growled at their backs. The two men turned around, startled at the masked gunman. Their eyes grew huge when they saw the AR-15 leveled at their chests.

Elijah got comfortable with the assault rifle. It must've weighed about six pounds, thirty rounds in the magazine, locked and loaded. He considered these two fools for a second. They looked to be in their late teens, dark faces now ghostly pale, and their mouths in the shape of an O. Their faces painted in tattoos that made Elijah certain of their gang affiliation—Tramps!

Elijah didn't flinch, didn't blink an eye. With his blood boiling, nose flaring like an angry bull, sweat collecting in the black cotton gloves, he felt like a man on fire in the ninja suit, with the sudden urge to rip his clothes off and feel the cool air. His body temperature spiked and then dived south. The cold blood iced his veins, giving him the cool he needed to do the deed. Before the enemies could spin in their Converse . . .

*Bloooom*!

The shotgun blast went off beside Elijah, so close that black powder and fire off the barrel licked his elbow. "Sonofabitch!"

Big Teflon and his sawed-off shotgun had roared to life, hitting one of the men up close and personal at point-blank range in the chest. He'd shredded his blue top with double odd buckshot and racked another shell into the shotgun before his vic landed about seven feet away from them in the street—roadkill.

Simultaneously the AR-15 began its deadly tap dance with a distant chopping sound, like helicopter propellers, unique to military-grade assault rifles.

*Chop! Chhhhoop! Ccchooppp!*

The second man's face melted into his skull as his head suddenly evaporated, crumping like wheat under a reaper's sickle.

Elijah ran up the block hugging the AR-15 before the last body settled on the ground. Headlights momentarily blinded him but then passed by at a good rate of speed. A stream of bullets from the Cutlass driver hosed down the crowded corner. People were running, dropping, and cowering on the ground from the mad gunner.

*What the fuck is he doing here*? Elijah thought as he recognized Ju-Ju as the driver of the Cutlass. *His ass should be somewhere in bed right now.* He charged on with a full head of steam.

Ju-Ju, still letting off shots into the crowd, faded back to the driver's door. Out of bullets, he jumped in the Cutlass and smashed from the scene. James Brown screamed from the trunk.

On the corner, heads began to raise, believing the massacre was over, only to have Elijah start in with a storm of bullets on them. Big Teflon and the shotgun joined in the deadly symphony.

Elijah was frustrated, wishing Big Teflon had for once just listened to him and waited back on the corner. Now who was going to provide cover if the enemies collected themselves and surged forward on them? But that was an argument for another time.

They fired on anything moving and left everything smoking, chipping paint, stucco, and drywall from the scene. Hell hath no fury like two Nine Os.

"Let's go, cuzz!" Big Teflon shouted.

Elijah couldn't hear a thing. His ears rang with the sound of gunfire.

"That's enough! Let's go!" Big Teflon yanked his arm.

Elijah looked toward Big Teflon, a thousand-yard stare in his eyes. *Did we come together? What the fuck am I doing here?*

Big Teflon turned and headed back the way they came, nearly slipping and breaking his neck on the shell casings rolling under his shoes. The copper was spread evenly on the corner . . . shells for days.

Elijah surveyed the death and destruction they'd brought down on Normandie. *Damage: maximum. It'll take all the king's army and all the king's men to put these chumps back together again. Why am I always thinking these sick nursery rhymes? Must be that evil inner child at it again,* he mused to himself.

An injured man mourned as he crawled to nowhere in particular. Elijah squeezed the trigger, popping him in the back. The sewer flowed with blood.

Elijah took off back down the way he came to the getaway car waiting for him in the alley.

Mission accomplished.

# CHAPTER TEN

Los Angeles sparkled after the unseasonably early spring showers. The morning air was crisp, the sidewalks washed clean and clear of leaves and debris, and the snowcapped San Gabriel Mountains peaks were visible for a change. It reminded Elijah of his early childhood when he was simply "Elijah" and all the girls in the neighborhood sang it so beautifully to him. The music of ice cream trucks sounding in his little ears; sweet Red Vines, Lemonheads, and Jolly Ranchers tickling his tongue; a wishbone-shaped slingshot and marbles in his pocket; a time when LA was as close to paradise as his young mind could imagine it to be.

Despite today's beauty, a gray depression gnawed at his soul. Was it reaction to the Normandie murders? A veteran of the killing fields of South Central, only murder seemed to stir the deep settlings within him. It was an unemotional urge to kill with no strings attached, but what about Big Teflon? Was his comrade as unattached and emotionally immune to death? Something had to be going through his mind, if not occupying it completely. Something like when would it be their turn to die in a hail of bullets? *Isn't that how we all go out? With a bang.*

As a kid, Elijah attended those same Sunday church services like everybody else in the neighborhood with his mother Fatima. She offered her tithes, took part in Communion, sang in the choir, and did all the church folks stuff. What effect had those Sunday church attendances and Bible study classes have on him? *Humph!* How could you take serious the word of those who were whores, drug-heads, and pimps Monday through Saturday but were the holiest people on Earth on Sunday? To him, the blessing was that he was free of the church bonds that regularly held the people in church pews around him. He'd convinced himself that the penalty of fire and brimstone for many was a burden that he did not carry because there was no church in the wild. For him, God was sort of nonexistent, and a great mystery God, if anything. What bothered him was that his life seemed to be a constant cycle of death, hospitals, and cemeteries. Wouldn't it be wonderful to wake in the morning to an entirely different life? Yes, it would. *Fuck a wish,* he thought, *this is reality.*

Elijah opened the door to the garage. Inside, the home-style boxing gym and his uncle awaited his arrival. He let his eyes roamed over the gym equipment, guessing that they'd sunk at least five grand into it. A beat-up gray mat spread from wall to wall. A heavy punching bag hung from the ceiling in the corner. An accuracy bag was suspended between two straps made for jabs and footwork, speed bag, jump ropes, free weights, along with whatever the latest infomercials had sold them, and posters and autographed memorabilia of Tyson, Holyfield, Sugar Ray Leonard, and Muhammad Ali completed the decor. The gym was a mixture of all the family's likes. Cannon had hung an enlarged photo of the two of them in sparring gear. He almost broke down seeing it, so he directed his eyes toward Big 9-Lives.

Although not physically imposing, Big 9-Lives was exceptionally fit. His high-pitched almost squeaky voice spoke at a breathtaking clip and stopped only to look at his pager, which beeped constantly. "Sup?" he mumbled, working his fingers into leather gloves with thumbtack holes in them. The little gloves somehow fit his big hands.

"Aw, you know," Elijah responded, sounding somewhat deflated. "Another day like the last."

"What's the matter? You sound fucked up like a busted six-by-nine."

Elijah ignored his last comment and went to the corner where the sand-loaded heavy bag awaited his punishment. He slowly wrapped his hands in flesh-toned Ace bandages and slipped into the Spartan-padded mixed martial arts gloves.

"Hey, man, you gonna fuck your hands up on that bag in those gloves."

"Yeah, so?" Elijah came back at him smugly. "Why you worried about it?"

Big 9-Lives shook his head. "Hard head make a soft ass."

Elijah opened up a can of whoop ass on the heavy bag, throwing combination punches that Cannon had taught him.

Big 9-Lives bench-pressed his weight and more under the heavy pig-iron plates. The bar could almost be seen bending with his strength. He was the powerhouse lifter of the quiet sorts.

The tapping of leather on leather, and the clinking of the weights behind heavy breathing went on for a forty-five stretch. They didn't converse much outside the gym, and even less inside the Nine Os man cave. Big 9-Lives told him what was necessary and saved the small talk for lawyers, bail bondsmen, and women. Family ties and money, guns and courage, death before dishonor, was what they talked about mostly. It was all toward the strength of their relationship, and they could enjoy each other's company for hours on end in a comfortable but nonrestrictive silence.

At fifteen, Elijah was unquestionably loyal to Big 9-Lives. With the loss of Cannon, they'd become more like brothers than uncle and nephew. The tragedy and everyday struggle had brought them closer together. Big 9-Lives had even stopped sweating him about attending school, looking ahead to college, and career moves. He'd been in the trenches long enough fighting these street wars to know that Elijah was a young soldier making soldier moves. Elijah had chosen his path in life, and limited as it was, it was still his choice. Big 9-Lives would never bring himself to castrate his nephew by taking away his choice. Besides, who was he to preach being a "good-boy"? All he could do was try to teach him how to live off the fat of the land, how to be the best and bravest warrior imaginable, and how to survive in South Central LA.

After finishing a set of ten reps of 250 pounds, Big 9-Lives sat upright and carefully flexed his tight muscles. His dark eyes transitioned to coffee brown in the deep afternoon light falling through the window. He took in Elijah banging away at the punching bag. Caressing his goatee, he studied him for a moment. "Elijah," he blurted.

Elijah halted and turned to him.

"I see you've been preoccupied in your thoughts lately," Big 9-Lives said. "What's on your mind?"

The question caught Elijah off guard. His uncle never tried to pry into his thoughts. "Shit," he started, "so much goes through my head, I wouldn't know where to begin."

Elijah turned back to the punching bag, his sweat-wrinkled rags hanging on his body like a gym rat. *Why he wanna know so much all of a sudden?* he thought. He hoped this wasn't the start of a new trend.

"Well, begin with what's pressing you the most, Neph."

Elijah rested his gloved hands on the bag, eyes pinned on the mat under his Reebok running shoes. Trying to gather his thoughts could be like trying to collect scraps of paper in a cyclone at times. "I know this might sound like a crazy question, but do you believe there is a God?" he asked.

Big 9-Lives tsked and wiped the sweat from his upper lip. "Nobody can say if there's a god or not! You have a bunch of self-important mutha-fuckas who say they know the answer. But truth is, the religious types and scientists are all guessing and trying to manipulate the next man with they mixed-up theories about God." He paused to allow what he'd just said sink in.

"Mom's told me before she . . . died that God told her to make the sacrifice. She always spoke of God and the Bible. I–I just wonder that if there's a God, why is our life so hard and so much hell going on in the world?"

Big 9-Lives squirmed in agitation. "Look, man, don't start clouding ya head up with all these irrelevant-ass philosophical questions. I don't say much about your mom, but since you brought her up, I'm going to give it to you raw. Your mom had a mental disease. Fatima lost her mind. The voices she heard wasn't no god. They were at best her imagination, and at worst, if they came from a spiritual source, they were demons in my book! If, for the sake of argument there is a god, he sure as hell don't give a fuck about us. I'd been going through hell for as long as I can remember. Shit, if God do exist, he'd be our enemy and I'd hate him!" Big 9-Lives drank from his water bottle, twisted the cap back on, then tossed it to Elijah. "You know what gets us through?" he continued, not waiting for an answer. "Our own inner strength, our own will, our determination, our faith in self."

"I know but—"

"Can you believe in a god that tells your mom to kill herself in front of you, her own child?" Big 9-Lives interrupted. "The closest you will ever get to knowing God is turning to look within yourself. We're the gods who are at war with other gods and demons in the shape of men. As far as looking toward a make-believe god in the sky that rules everything, that loves one race and hates another, fuck him! The key to life is to keep living. Keep winning, nigga!" he said in his usual fast clip. "Anything else we need to know, we'll find out when it's meant for us. Till then, fuck remorse, fuck guilt, fuck shame, fuck heaven and hell, and fuck fear! Remember what I told you, either you conquer or ya ass get conquered . . . period."

Elijah stood silent processing what his uncle had said. He stared at the wall, seeing what only he could in the stucco. He spoke in a low tone. "I have dreams . . . nightmares every night."

"Nightmares?"

"Yeah, sometimes I see Momma and Cannon."

"You don't see me in any of those dreams, do ya?"

"Nah, but sometimes I see other homies we've lost" Elijah craned his head to see the hard expression on his uncle's face. "Majority of the time it's the enemies and evils hunting me, killing me. I hate even going to sleep at night."

"Damn, nephew, why you didn't come talk to me about this shit sooner?"

"I don't know." He shrugged his shoulders. "But do you think it's all because of the way I live?"

"No!" Big 9-Lives said emphatically. "It's because you weighing your conscience down with all these weak-ass questions you keep asking yourself. Once you get all that emotional shit out your head, the dreams will go out with 'em, and if they didn't go away, fuck it . . . live with 'em. It comes with the territory." He paused for a moment, then said, "You know what? Maybe this shit ain't for you. If you weak in the knees, get out the streets. I got a bitch in Hollywood you can stay with. Or better yet, you can use some of the money you got saved to get your own place on the other side a town. Go back to school or something, start a new life."

"What about you?"

"What you mean, 'What about me'?"

"Why don't you move and start a new life?" Elijah asked.

Big 9-Lives thought for a moment. There was a time when he almost left . . . "I tried the square life—"

Elijah burst out laughing as if he'd heard the funniest joke.

"What the hell you laughin' at, nigga? I did and it doesn't work for me. Surviving in the jungle is what makes me feel alive. Everybody got to know they place in life. Being a king in the land of no pity is my position, my place in the grand scheme of things."

"I feel ya, Unc." For a moment Elijah thought about what it would be like to live a 'normal' life, but he could never imagine a different lifestyle. This was who he is. Hate it or love it, this was his home.

"Don't get me wrong. I got some moves in the works that's gonna help me scale, you know, expand game right along with my mind, but this ain't about me. This is about you, nephew. And it seems to me like you at a crossroad."

"I have to decide which way I want to go?"

"Yup."

Elijah gave him one of his rare smiles. "There's no decision to be made because if it ain't about crippin or Nine Os, it's about me and you rollin' till the wheels fall off."

"You accept whatever comes with that, Elijah?"

"Yeah, whatever's clever."

"Alright, now. Remember you made the decision," Big 9-Lives said with grim finality.

With no further words, they resumed their workout. Their dynasty would survive after all, because they'd certainly kill for their hood and die for their family.

# CHAPTER ELEVEN

Elijah's dope house was a major step up from having to hustle out on the streets all night long. The money from the twenty-seven ounces afforded him the safety of being inside while doing his work. The spot moved about a half-kilo a week. Big 9-Lives was his supplier and cooker, and by the time his uncle cooked the cocaine from soft to hard, the ounces swelled up to twenty-two with just baking soda and water. Unlike most youngsters who gambled their money off or spent it on cars, clothes, and jewelry, Elijah's money went into the safe at his uncle's stash house in the Underground Crip neighborhood. Weed was his only habit, getting money his number-one priority. Elijah used females for sex and company from time to time, then sent them back to wherever they came from. The dope spot was his girlfriend.

Blunt smoke filled the air in the shabby two-bedroom duplex inside the "neighborvilles," a stretch of identical duplex units spanning from Ninety-Second to Ninety-Sixth Street on Western Avenue. Guns and crack decorated the living room end table as if they were legal. 2-Pac's "I Get Around" played on the cheap stereo system. The spot also served as the official hangout for the usual suspects. Big Teflon was there most of the time. Occasionally he brought his own dope sack to sell, but he was mostly there just to kick it with his boy.

Ju-Ju and Li'l Teflon never came to sell dope, as it wasn't their thing. They were still robbing and stealing, only now they did it for bigger stakes. Ever since Ju-Ju went on the suicidal solo mission on Normandie, the other three finally accepted him as their equal and not just a "do-boy." Li'l Teflon and Ju-Ju were now everyday hang-and-bang road dogs.

All four were gathered in the spot, and as always, Li'l Teflon had the floor telling war stories. His appearance alone was comical, so he kept them laughing. He was seventeen years old and still hadn't grown much. Most times Elijah wasn't laughing at what he was saying, but he couldn't help it at the thought of this little ugly mutha-fucka who had the swagger of a giant. Couldn't nobody tell Li'l Teflon he wasn't the shit!

Elijah lounged on the beanbag in a wife beater, blue Dickie shorts, and blue-and-white Pumas with his hands interlocked behind his head as he listened to Li'l Teflon's tale. As he'd grown older, he'd come to terms with the fact that Li'l Teflon was a cutthroat, but he was *their* cut-throat. Before he didn't understand, but now he did—Li'l Teflon was a survivor, a scavenger who enjoyed the game of survival. He rejoiced in his conquest and even found humor in the instances where he got caught. To Li'l Teflon, winning and losing came with the territory, and he embraced both with a smile. Elijah figured that jail had help to make Li'l Teflon the way he was. He'd been in and out of juvenile hall and group homes since the age of eight. Once he learned there was better food, clothing, and living conditions in jail than there was at home, jail no longer frightened him and believed it wasn't so bad at all. As Elijah saw it, how could someone live the life Li'l Teflon did and not be a cutthroat?

Li'l Nine was already chuckling before Li'l Teflon could get to the heart of his story. Ju-Ju slouched in the beat-up recliner chair half listening and half watching the basketball game on TV. He'd heard these stories before and was there for most of them. Big Teflon sat back on the couch with his Nike Cortez resting on the table, twisting more blunts.

Li'l Teflon was in full "show mode," and his oversized blue khaki suit and low afro made it more comical. "Nah, cuzz, for real." He tried to convince them of the truth in his story during the loud laughter. "I got the bitch on the bed, I stick my hand between her legs, and I could've sworn I seen a puff of white smoke."

"Man, knock it off!" Elijah interjected.

"Real talk." Li'l Teflon raised his right hand as if giving an oath. "I thought I was trippin' for a minute. So, I'm tryin' to stay sexy with her but investigate what I just saw at the same time. You know, I'm kissing on the bitch neck and shit, but my eyes is looking down in the pussy area while I'm taking off her pants." He was physically acting out the scene as he spoke.

"Once I get her pants down, I see this bitch's panties is packed with a ton a baby powder. I ain't talking 'bout a li'l dash; I'm talking the whole damn bottle." Laughter erupted. "But I ain't 'bout to let no extra powder stop me from hittin' the pussy, so I start fingering her. All of a sudden, she talking 'bout 'No! Stop!' Bitch, my dick is hard as this iron lamppost. You 'bout to give me some pussy. I keep rubbing it, she still trying to play the 'no-can't' role. Man, I flipped that hoe over on her stomach and pinned her down with the old arm bar to the back of the neck move," Li'l Teflon chuckles at the memory. "So, I slid the dick up in her. She like, 'Oh, shit, Li'l Teflon!' The dick took all the fight outta her. She started throwing that pussy back at me. I was so busy trying to get up in her that I hadn't paid any attention to the hand I was fingering her with. I finally realized that my hand felt extra creamy. This wasn't just pussy juice. I looked at the hand—that mutha-fucka was covered with white pasty cream like cottage cheese or some shit. Seemed like as soon as I saw it, the funk from her pussy shot from between her legs like a spray gun. Nigga! That shit hit my nose and knocked me out the pussy. I said, 'Goddamn bitch! What kind of evil you got in that mutha-fucka?"

Everybody burst into laughter. Big Teflon rolled off the couch onto the floor holding his stomach. Elijah stayed on the beanbag but covered his eyes with his forearm and kicked his legs wildly in laughter. Ju-Ju just shook his head.

"I started screaming, 'Ju-Ju'!" he continued. "We at the Embassy Suites, so you know they have them double rooms. Ju-Ju ran out the back room with the strap, thinking it's going down. I said, 'Cuzz, smell this bitch's pussy.'"

"This nigga crazy," Ju-Ju chimed in. "He really wanted me to bend down and smell her pussy. I said 'Nigga, I can smell it from here!' He called her all kinds of funky pussy bitches and hoes and kicked her outta the room. Shit, he fucked my pussy off 'cause my broad had to go catch up to her homegirl."

Their laugh session was interrupted by pounding on the front door.

"Sheriff's Department—search warrant!" someone shouted.

The back windows came crashing in from being hit with baseball bats. Without hesitation, Big Teflon got to his feet and dived through the side window, glass and all. Elijah was a step behind him. As he cleared the window, eight white men, who looked like they should be playing football for the Nebraska Cornhuskers, crashed through the front door, screaming with guns drawn, "Get down! Get down motherfuckers!"

The one-second hesitation by Ju-Ju and Li'l Teflon cost them. Both were pounced on and cuffed. One policeman screamed frantically through his handheld radio, "We have runners who've fled the east side of the location."

Big Teflon crashed landed on his shoulder, rolled with the momentum, instantly jumped to his feet, and was in an all-out sprint. Elijah came out of the window more controlled, landing on one knee and one hand. In one fluid motion, he was up and running right behind Big Teflon. Crackling from the police radios and frantic voices could be heard behind them as they hurdled over the chain-link fence into a backyard that led them to the next block. As they sprinted up the drive, through another backyard and crossed the street, an ugly black poodle-shepherd mutt jumped on their trail, barking and snapping until they leaped the next fence and left it barking in their footsteps.

The faint chopping sound of the Ghetto Bird helicopter could be heard approaching in the distance. They looked at each other in a silent acknowledgement that they had to end this footrace and find cover because there is no out running the Ghetto Bird once it makes it to the scene.

Big Teflon took a chance and doubled back toward Western Avenue through one of the passageways off the alley and Elijah decided to follow suit. When they made it the busy street, they looked both ways and dashed across into another passageway that led them to their homegirl Big 12's backdoor. They frantically banged on the door until she opened it.

Seeing the blood dripping from Big Teflon's right arm and their disheveled appearance, Big 12 already knew what was up. She quickly ushered them into the house. She took Big Teflon into the bathroom, plucked out some of the glass from his arm, and wrapped a homemade bandage around it. She then ran to grab her car keys and headed for the front door.

The Ghetto Bird was now flying low, circling the area of the drug spot. Big 12 went out the front, then pulled the car from the street-side parking into the driveway and up to the side entrance of the house. Big Teflon and Elijah scurried to the back of the car, opened the back door, and lay on the floor. Casually, Big 12 drove them back to the Budlong side and dropped them off at Big

9-Lives spot. They both silently thanked whatever higher power there was for sparing them from going to jail.

⟡

The lead police officer sat on a kitchen chair turned backward with his forearms resting atop the backrest. "You know you guys are going down for a long time for these guns and dope on you." He eyed Ju-Ju and Li'l Teflon. "Tell us who your friends were that got away and we'll take it easy on you."

"I ain't see nobody get away. Did you see somebody get away?" Li'l Teflon asked Ju-Ju sarcastically, sitting with hands cuffed behind his back. *This pink pig ain't got nothin' on us.*

"Nah, I ain't see nobody get away. Did you see somebody get away?" Ju-Ju responded.

They kept this exchange up until the officer couldn't take it anymore. The officer abruptly jumped from the chair, causing it to crash to the floor on its side. "Alright motherfuckers. You want to be smart asses? We'll see who'll be laughing when you're getting sent up the river!"

Li'l Teflon laughed. "Damn, boss, you need to calm down before you have a stroke. You take your job too serious." Ju-Ju joined in the laughter.

The lead officer nodded to his partners. One stepped forward and gut-checked Li'l Teflon so hard that it knocked the wind out of him. Li'l Teflon folded like a chair and gasped for air. Ju-Ju tried to stand and protest but he was kneed and body slammed to the floor by another cop.

The lead cop grinned. "How about now? Do you remember who your friends are that ran?"

Li'l Teflon, finally able to breathe, raised his head to look the cop in the eye. "Suck . . . my dick, bitch," he barely managed to get out.

The aggressive rookie raised his leg to kick Li'l Teflon but was pulled back by the lead cop. "Just get 'em outta here," he ordered.

"We'll see how tough you are when you're looking at all that time in prison."

The two cops roughly grabbed Li'l Teflon and Ju-Ju by the cuffs and dragged them to their feet. As they were exiting the door, the lead officer stepped in front of them and drew his face close to Ju-Ju's. "If you change your mind and want to save yourself, all you have to do is reach out to me."

Ju-Ju stared at him with pure hatred. "If you change your mind and want to have your momma give us some head, reach out to us. Man, get the fuck out my face, stanky-ass breath."

The officer smiled deviously and stepped aside and nodded his head. The others escorted Li'l Teflon and Ju-Ju to an unmarked police car and forced them head-first inside. They were transported to Lennox Sheriff's Department where they were booked, photographed, and slammed into a filthy holding cell.

Because Li'l Teflon was seventeen and Ju-Ju was two weeks away from turning eighteen, both were hauled off to Los Padrinos Juvenile Hall. For Li'l Teflon it was simply a minor adjustment to go from freedom to captivity. He was at his second home.

For Ju-Ju, however, this was a milestone in his underworld career. He was determined that he would use the jail time to complete himself as a real street warrior. He would make his name ring throughout the system.

# CHAPTER TWELVE

**1994**

Big 9-Lives took out a short lease on a modest one-bedroom apartment in a large cobalt stucco complex in Westchester, a neighborhood by the LAX Airport. Like most of the area, the buildings and boulevard were lined with California palm, evergreens, and well-manicured shrubbery. As he drove home he practically spazzed out behind the wheel of his Mercedes Benz 190E, a car that every day felt less like luxury in the ranks of Porsches, Ferraris, Lamborghinis, and Bentleys. The crazy high-end autos made his blood pressure spike. For some reason the fear of "life without the possibility of parole" didn't make him change his mind. The thought of his final resting place with no tombstone didn't bother him. Something inside of him was coming to life or something inside of him was dying, but either way, he knew it was time to scale up and bring his operations to a bigger market. Time to assemble all the pieces and turn the machine on.

The corner of his mouth creased upward at the thought of "machining," building a great enduring, moneymaking criminal enterprise—a mob. The key was to have a clear vision of what was to be accomplished, then work out the airtight blueprint to make it happen. The rest was hard work and dedication and not losing the faith in the vision when things didn't go exactly as planned. Nobody said it was going to be easy. It was climb or die in a cold crevice in the streets alone. No two ways about it: the plan was to climb, and the higher he got, the further up he could take his family.

Since he was in the area, he breezed by the snazzy 3-1-0 Motors, just a cruise-by for a quick look-in. Yeah, his blue Ferrari was still on display. He would be dropping thirty grand for a down payment someday soon. It didn't matter that he didn't have the legal means to show where the money was coming from; he'd just walk in and drop the grocery bag of cash on the car dealer's desk and tell him to figure it out. He'd walk out with those keys if it was the last thing he did.

Big 9-Lives stepped into his apartment around one. He had very little furniture. A solitary painting of *Black Scarface* graced the living room wall, with nothing else in the living room or kitchen. A few dishes in the sink and a couple of Chinese takeout boxes were in the dining area. When he walked into the bedroom, his large television was situated on top of the black- and gold-trimmed bedroom set. He picked up the remote control, aimed it at the television, but changed his mind. He felt more like hearing some music. The remote swung to the mini stereo and the CD player clicked on. A hypnotic, bouncy Snoop Dogg anthem began to play. He dug into his pocket for cellphone, flipped it open, and hit his nephew.

"Elijah, where are you?"

"Over here in Six O's hood." Elijah then he paused for a moment and Big 9-Lives overheard him say, "Damn, girl, hold up."

Big 9-Lives could hear a female's high-pitched voice laughing and talking on the other end. "You over there fuckin' with Li'l F-Bone's niece again?"

"Don't trip. I just stopped through for a quick minute. What's up?"

"I told you not to be over there too much. The 60s are the homies only to a certain extent. They get shifty over in they hood. You really startin' to like that li'l hoodrat or something?"

This time Elijah dropped his voice. There was a garbled exchange between him and girl. He laughed and she talked shit. "Nigga, who the fuck he callin' a hoodrat? I heard his ass."

Elijah said, "Kick back, girl, this my uncle." He fended her off. "Hello?"

"Speak."

"Yeah, back to what I was saying. I ain't worried about these cats over here, they bleed just like us!"

"That ain't the point. Don't put yourself in dangerous situations when it ain't necessary. Oh, and tell your li'l bitch she better watch her mouth. I don't give a fuck where she from or who niece she is."

"That makes two of us," Elijah stated with cockiness.

"Look, get over to the spot in the U.G. I'll meet you there."

"I'm on my way. Give me about twenty minutes."

"Twenty minutes? It only takes about five to fly from the 60s to the 100s."

"Yeah, I know, but I'm 'bout to get my dick sucked first."

"Nigga, don't be telling him I'm about to suck yo dick!" the girl screamed in the background, pretending to be mad but laughing at the same time.

Big 9-Lives smacked his teeth. "You could've kept that info to yourself. I don't wanna hear about you getting your little dick sucked." He hung up and stuffed the cellphone in his pocket. He sat on the side of the bed for a minute, his eyes lost in the carpet. His nephew was a hot mess these days. He had to bring his plan together and get them out the city before week's end.

Elijah stepped inside the apartment and faced the solitary portrait on the living room wall. An oil painting of a man cladded in nothing but a loin-cloth, muscles ripped across his bronzed skin from head to toe, strain chiseled into his face as his hand gripped the chain and lock that held him captive. He stared at it for a minute. *Why does Unc always have symbolic picture in all his spots?* he thought.

The curtain was drawn tight enough to block out most of the sunlight and only slivers came inside. The white plug-in fan was rotating, cooling the room. Elijah carefully closed the door and secured the deadbolt. The unpleasant smell of work backed up his nose for a few seconds: a mixture of sweat, musk, and cocaine. His uncle was in the lab.

Two boxes of baking soda were on the kitchen counter, one already opened and showing the baking soda crusted around the rim of the box. Cooking up coke was enjoyable except when the powder was of a low grade and gave problems gelling together. What Big 9-Lives had started a half-hour ago had evolved into a controlled experiment, like pharmaceutical engineering.

Big 9-Lives braced himself on his knuckles, staring down into the gumbo pot on the stove, looking at what would be the finished product. “This shit ain’t coming out right. I can’t quite put my finger on the problem and it’s frustrating the fuck outta me,” he said, visually agitated. “That was the longest twenty minutes I’ve ever heard of,” he added without looking up.

Elijah’s lips curled into a sly smile. “Aw, you know how these broads be with that I-don’t-want-you-to-go type shit.” He studied the contorted expression on Big 9-Lives’ face.

“I need to bring this work together. I wanna be done with this last nine-piece today.”

“What’s wrong with it?” Elijah stepped closer to peek in the pot.

“I’m not sure.” He looked up. “Come look at it.” He grabbed a worn oven mitt and carefully took the jumbo-sized beaker out the boiling water, examined it, then set the glass cookware onto the tile counter that wrapped the kitchen.

"You want me to whip it up for you?" Elijah asked.

"You think you can do better then be my guest!"

A smile creased Elijah's face as he put the oven mitt on his right hand. He looked over the cooking utensils that were laid out on the counter. "Is this the only baking soda you got?"

"Yeah. Just bought it today."

"I see." He turned the fire up on the stove and opened the fresh box of soda, hit the cocaine once, then three more times. He dropped the beaker back into the pot, shook it up in small circles then pulled it out, turned the beaker on its side and rolled it until the gel wrapped around the mold of the beaker.

Big 9-Lives looked into the glass at his nephew's work. "It's better than what I could do with it, but—"

"Something still wrong, huh?" Elijah began pouring hot water from the pot directly into the beaker, dropped it back in the pot, then shake, rattle, and roll.

"Okay, how about now?" They looked it over again.

"If this can stretch just a little bit more . . ." Big 9-Lives mused.

"Uh-huh, I see. It comes together evenly. Let it cool."

They spent the next fifteen minutes tinkering with their experiment before it had the stamp of approval. Big 9-Lives tried not to comment on his nephew's whip but he had to nod his head at the youngster's improvement in that department. He'd taught him everything that he knew about work . . . well, not everything. Cannon had the best whip hand in the family, but Big 9-Lives was no slouch either. Now Elijah was on his way to out whipping them both.

Big 9-Lives ran cold sink water around the outside of the beaker before immersing it in a crock-pot half filled with ice water. This shocked the dope into hard white. Leaving the work to cool, he dried his hands. He pulled a blunt from his shirt pocket, lit it, hit it, and blew a Chronic cloud over the kitchen. "I called you over because we need to rap on a serious note."

Elijah pulled up a seat on the barstool. "Shoot!"

"What we 'bout to move on soon is gonna to take focus. All these li'l bitches and dumb shit you been having goin' on is gonna have to stop."

"I'm focused."

"You think you are, but be careful of distractions because they'll throw you off course. Whatever takes you away from your goals or don't help you reach them is to be given less time and energy as possible."

"Unc, you already know when it's time for biz, I'm on deck. But shit, I ain't no robot! Today my goal and priority was getting some head and pussy. So, I gave it the needed time and energy to achieve that goal." Both got a chuckle out of his slick comment.

Big 9-Lives passed him the blunt. "Anyways, a lot of shit is changing. It's too much killing going on out here in LA for no more than a street number. It's necessary to bust heads at time, but when we first started this Crip shit we wasn't about just running out and shooting anybody who wasn't from our turf. We used our fists and hands to show who we were. Now there's too many cowards running around with guns killing for nothing, and the crazy thing is only a handful of real soldiers eating and progressing from all this mayhem. A lot a the real ones dying and going to prison for no gain, leaving our next generation to go through the same cycle of cursed poverty." He pointed and said, "Pass the Chronic, nigga."

His machine-gun talk paused long enough for him to suck down the blunt. A cloud developed over his blue wave cap. "We changing directions—King-Kong scale change!" He looked at the blunt.

"Unc, what the fuck're you talking about, Donkey Kong or the streets?"

"Well, if you shut up and listen you'll learn something. What I'm saying is that we gonna make the necessary sacrifices to get rich so those who come behind us can inherit a better life. They won't have to sacrifice or scrape and struggle just to make it. They'll go to the best schools and have the best life connections—the shit that was damn near impossible for us to do. In other words, we'll make the sacrifice and die if necessary so they can live and succeed." He looked around at nothing in particular as he braced himself to give his nephew the blueprint.

"Recently I got an offer from Big Cadillac from the Western side who wants to give us access to they outta-town spot in Oklahoma. In return, Big Cadillac wants my assurance that I'd get the li'l homies, Big Wizard and his brother Hitter, to understand that all 90s are one. The bottom line is they got the Western homies shook and Big Cadillac need a way to neutralize them without bloodshed. I'm the solution to their problem, or so they think."

Elijah took the roach from his fingertips as his uncle shared the new info with him. "Why they want you to take responsibility for what they got going on down there? Not only that, but why they let Wiz get down there in the first place if they feel that way?" He sucked down the roach before leaving it in the ashtray on the countertop.

"They don't want me to take responsibility. It's a business move on their part. They know that me and Wiz got a good relationship, so if I'm their business partner, they figure Wiz will give them more consideration, and if that happens then they feel it will be a little extra from the real threat: Hitter."

Big 9-Lives grabbed a roll of paper towels, ripped off two, and laid them out on the counter. He removed the chilled beaker from the crockpot, grabbed a nine-inch butcher knife, and began to work the cocaine patty free from the glass. Once he got it out, he laid it on the paper towels to air-dry. The experiment was successful.

"I'm gonna jump in the shower and put on some fresh gear," he said, "Why don't you wrap that work up so we can get it in traffic?"

"Got it."

Big 9-Lives headed for the bathroom while Elijah went to the kitchen. He pulled a box of sandwich bags off the shelf over the stove. Shower water could be heard coming from deep inside the apartment. He snatched a couple bags out of the box and packaged the cocaine into one, then doubled it before tying it off in a knot. The only thing left to do now was wait on his uncle in the shower. He was hungry as a mutha-fucka.

⟜⟝

Big 9-Lives and Elijah walked into Lucy's, a classic Mexican-American restaurant in the hood. There were only four customers, all eating separately at the counter. The fellows didn't wait to be shown a table; they grabbed a booth in the back of the restaurant. Big 9-Lives had changed into a casual Fubu jeans and gray embroidered denim jacket ensemble. Elijah didn't stray too far from khakis and Chucks, and today was no exception. Big 9-Lives put his cellphone between them and settled at the table.

A short, slim, raven-haired Hispanic waitress carried away old plates of food scraps, one hand balancing a weighty tray and a couple drink glasses in the other as she made her way to the kitchen before returning with pen and pad in hand. Big 9-Lives ordered and chilled out with a smirk on his face, liking the quiet coziness of the place, the soft music coming from the ceiling, and the woman serving them.

"Earlier, back at the spot," Elijah started, "you mentioned that those cats were trying to compromise with Wiz and Hitter."

"Oh yeah, they been did that. That's how the homies Wiz and them got down there in the first place. But now they want me to come on board 'cause now they realize the position they in. At any minute, or for any reason, Wiz and Hitter can push them out the way and they wouldn't be able to stop it." He dipped a chip into the little cup of red sauce and smashed it between his teeth. They took turns crushing the basket of chips and sauce.

"We gonna take full advantage of this riff they got going. I got something going in the works right now in Atlanta, so I'll be heading that way. I want you to go down to Oklahoma and work that end. You'll take Big Teflon with you."

Elijah smiled. He liked the idea of having his road dog with him out of town. Who knows what was waiting in Oklahoma.

"How much money do you have saved?"

Elijah did some quick calculations in his head. "Once I get rid of my last li'l bit of work, I should have anywhere from thirty-five to forty stacks."

"Alright. They want us to buy our dope from them instead of my regular connect. If we do, they'll match whatever we buy on consignment, and they'll transport our work with theirs so we won't have to take the risk."

"What's the price?"

"Fourteen thousand a key. You'd put up twenty-one thousand for a kilo-and-a-half and I'd put in for three-and-a-half for a total of five kilos. The Western homies will front us five more. The five we pay for will go with you to Oklahoma City; the five they front will go with me to Atlanta."

Big 9-Lives wiped his fingers off on a napkin, and grabbed a pen from his jacket pocket. He used a napkin to scribble down some figures. Ounces went for $1,000 each, wholesale to the curb servers. A kilo had thirty-six ounces in it, but after he cooked it up, it would swell to forty-five. Forty-five ounces at $1,000 each would mean a profit of $45,000 off each key, and five kilos multiplied by $45,000 equaled $225,000. He shoved the napkin over to Elijah. "Off that," he said, "you keep seventy thousand for yourself and shoot the other hundred and fifty-five to me."

"What about Tef?"

"You pay him whatever you think is fair out of your own pocket."

"What do you think is fair?"

"I'm gonna leave that up to you. I can't speak on your money but I'm gonna give Wiz fifteen stacks outta mine just to keep things running smooth."

"Fifteen thousand dollars? For what? They don't have nothing to do with this transaction!"

They paused their conversation as the waitress arrived with the large tray carrying their order. She placed their plates in front of each of them. "Can I get you anything else?" she asked with a cordial smile.

"No thanks," they both responded as she removed the empty containers from the chips and salsa. She gave Big 9-Lives a flirtatious side glance before she walked off.

Big 9-Lives immediately dug in, polishing off the food in greedy mouthfuls. "Out of respect," he said between bites, picking up where the conversation left off, "we gotta keep a strong bridge between our two families. Keeping my influence with them is important. That's why when you get to Oklahoma you gotta make time to spend with Wiz. When it comes to crucial hood matter while you are there, follow his lead. If you cross paths with Hitter, always be respectful."

Elijah wasn't feeling this part. He felt like his uncle was the founder and big homie for their side of the hood. Why should he have to pay these niggas to keep the peace? That was what they made guns for.

Big 9-Lives saw the rebelliousness in his nephew's eyes, knowing what he was thinking. Sternly, he said, "There ain't gonna be no beef or disrespect from you to the homies—period!"

Elijah smacked his lips. "Whatever you say and put in motion should be respected without question is all I'm saying. I know they brother Big K-Mike, Rest in Peace, was your road dog and had just as much status as you, but Wiz and Hitter demanding from the hood more than I believe they older brother would've. I ain't from the Western side, I'm from Budlong Ave. just like them. I shouldn't have to worry about them when I get there. Just put your foot down, and that's that!"

"You right as far as me being the big homie, but it's more to being a leader than you understand."

"Like what?"

"Like, it's not always about individual force or charisma. Intelligence and wisdom is first and foremost, and how you manage yourself and relationships with others is next. You must find the proper balance of fear and respect from those you lead, and from your enemies and potential enemies too. As a leader, you have to recognize those who solidify the base of your force and fear."

"You kinda losing me." Elijah wasn't getting it.

"See, Wiz and Hitter are both leaders in their own right. They command just as much fear and respect from the outsiders as I do. In some cases more because they young and uncompromising. At least with me a person will feel like diplomacy might work. So, by me being able to claim them as my li'l homies from my clique it adds to my power, my leverage with outsiders. Each individual must be led differently. You can't push a hard line on homies like Wiz and Hitter 'cause they're leaders, too, and they'll rebel if they feel threatened or disrespected. If they become enemies, they can cause a possible downfall. Crash the whole house. So don't forget, they're our allies. If something was to happen to us, they'd be the ones to hold the streets responsible. They respect me and I respect them—that's what our relationship is built on, not me telling them what to do or how to do it."

Elijah tried to process it all. He would follow his uncle's lead; however, he wanted him to handle things. "When do we leave?"

Big 9-Lives leaned forward. "There's one more piece of business we need to handle before we leave. It's for the hood's benefit as a whole, and Wiz and Hitter have a special interest in it. The move'll be a plus for you when you get to Oklahoma. That nigga, Dirt-Mike, from Back Westside Eight-Tray Gangstas moved over from Normandie to our 10-10 Apartments on Ninetieth and Vermont with his sister. He even had the nerve to come up in the apartments and pull a strap on one of the Tiny-Loc's, Li'l Kaos, and the young homie, Li'l Snoop from 11-8 East Coast."

"I heard about that shit, but I thought it was just a bogus rumor," Elijah said. "What person in they right mind would move into their enemy's main stomping ground, and on top of that, he one of the main characters Hitter and Wizard's family was warring with."

"Wiz called me this morning to let me know he heard about the incident," Big 9-Lives said. "Hitter was on his way back to personally take care of it."

"What did you say?"

"I told him it wasn't necessary, we got it."

Elijah leaned forward with murder in his eyes. "That's what I wanted to hear. And you know what? Fuck the plans with the homies and what the move does for the hood. I ride on the Tramps for my uncle Cannon! Draw up the plan. I'm ready to rock rock-and-roll!"

Before they realized, five o'clock flew in quickly. It wasn't nothing new that they were out kicking it together this long. The waitress picked up their empty plates with a smile. "The dessert is so fresh today. Some churros?"

"Yeah, why not," Big 9-Lives said with suggestive eyes. "Two to go."

Elijah stopped to take care of the check while Big 9-Lives went outside to his Benz to meet a client—a quick hand-to-hand transaction in the parking lot. He gave the man a small paper bag and received one in return.

Elijah got in the Benz with his uncle, handing him a churro stick. "You should a gotten the waitress's phone number. I think she wanna give you some pussy," he teased.

"You late, li'l nigga, I already got it."

# CHAPTER THIRTEEN

Dirt Mike crouched on the side of the apartment building clutching a .45 Colt. His dusty black skin and dark clothes blended with the darkness of night. He waited patiently for the Nine Os to show up so he could give them the surprise of a lifetime.

Unbeknown to him, he was being watched by two sets of eyes from the window of a house sitting directly across from his position. Two killers were resting right on top of him. So preoccupied with carrying out his ambush, he never stopped to consider why the neighboring complex was so uncharacteristically dark. All porch lights and indoor lights were off as if this small section of LA was experiencing a blackout. Dirt Mike was a shadow against the building. It might have seemed like a benefit to his plan.

Inside the house, guns were cocking and the venetian blinds were being disturbed. "Let me show you how it's done, youngsta."

"Nah, let me get this one," the youngsta protested.

The men went back and forth in whispery tones, shuffling their pistols from one hand to another in anticipation of what was to take place next.

"This one takes a more *experienced* method. Wait here until you hear the music. Once it gets started, head out the front door and cover me, just in case," the older man said. He eased out the back door clutching a nickel-finished .357 Magnum, six hollow points to do the job. Even though he was moving with the quietness of a stalking house cat, he felt too much noise was being made.

Creeping from behind the house, he could see Dirt Mike's shadow still crouched facing the front entrance and street. He was clueless to the dark figure inching closer to his rear on the other side of the flimsy chain-linked fence.

The .357 hammer cocked with a deadly crack. *Boooom*!

The blast went off like a lethal hand cannon on the unsuspecting man. The first blast caught him in the left shoulder, blowing him from his crouched stance into the side of the building face-first. He bounced off the wall like a cartoon character. Suddenly, Dirt Mike sprang to his feet and bolted for the street, leaving his pistol on the ground.

Two more blasts quickly followed, one hitting him in the leg, the other crashing into the apartment building, sending concrete and paint chips flying in all directions. With two .357 slugs lodged in him, he shouldn't have been able to run, but his fear and adrenaline allowed him to defy the natural laws of science and medicine. The last three blasts—one after another—caught him in full stride, destroying his back. He folded like a cheap sweater, the thrust sending him spiraling to the asphalt.

With a dying man's will to survive, Dirt Mike somehow clumsily climbed back to his feet and stumbled forward, trying to reach the front door of his sister who foolishly moved into one of the Nine Os hangouts.

"Help me . . . please, somebody . . . help!" he screamed from the depths of his soul before falling to the ground. He clawed forward to reach his sister's door, losing blood and strength with each inch gained.

When he finally reached the door, he stretched out his arm and banged weakly against the lower section of the metal screen. “Help me,” he whispered. “Oh, God . . . help me.”

Suddenly, two masked gunmen hovered over him. “Sup, nigga?” the older one said.

“Oh, God, please, I don’t wanna die . . . please God.” He had turned sinner to saint in a matter of seconds.

“Too late for all that. Lucifer already has his arms around you to bring you home!” the youngsta said, raising his 9mm Beretta to Dirt Mike’s face.

“No!” Dirt Mike managed to let out, but a single shot from the gun silenced him.

In a moment of sick humor, the youngsta looked to his older companion after the fatal shot was dealt, and in a demonic voice echoed, “Flawless victor!” as an ode to the video game Mortal Combat.

Big 9-Lives and Elijah turned and disappeared into the night.

---

No matter how fast she ran, the footfalls continued to dog her trail as she made it down the long dark corridor. She expected to be tackled at any moment. The prospect of being caught terrified her. The corridor gave way to a two-way passage. She chose to go left.

Up ahead in what appeared to be an exit surrounded by a bright light, a male figure stood blocking the way. She couldn’t figure out who he was but decided she’d rather take her chances with him than with her pursuers, so she continued forward. Coming upon the figure in the light she noticed his soft but pain-filled eyes and smooth brown face. He held a Native American-styled hatchet. Specks of blood sprinkled his face. His clothes were blood soaked, and the hatchet dripped blood into a puddle surrounding him. She tried to stop, but her momentum carried her within inches of his face. As she looked into his eyes, she became paralyzed. He made no attempt at stepping aside to let her pass, nor did he attempt to attack her. He only stared with the hint of a sinister smirk that touched the corners of his mouth, but not his eyes. She only had a split-second to react when she heard the beastly voice behind her.

"You bitch!"

Before she could turn to face her attacker, she was tackled. She squirmed and fought for dear life, enabling her to position herself on her back to better use her hands. Hovering inches above her was the face of a fat Mexican man who smelled of shit, sweat, and hot peppers. He had been wounded and blood oozed from a large gaping hole in his forehead. Her terror intensified as he gripped his sausage fingers around her neck and began choking the life out of her.

Suddenly, the face transformed into a boar with two six-inch fangs. It roared a guttural laugh. An instant later the boar-face changed into a grotesque demonic figure with horns and fangs. On the brink of passing out, she used the last reserve of strength and screamed a high-pitched shrill.

"Enough!" came the command. Just like that, the grip on her neck released and her attacker was gone. Holding her neck and gasping for air, she looked around and realized that the command had come from the mysterious man with the hatchet. He stood in the same position, the same smirk frozen on his face.

Getting to her feet, she charged him in a rage. With all her momentum, she lunged for his face. At the point of impact, he turned into mist and she fell uncontrollably into the light. The scene became a breathtaking view of lush green mountains and rolling meadows. She took it all in before taking a sudden drop into the abyss, falling rapidly into the jagged rocks below . . .

Elise shot upright in the bed with a screech. Her breath came in snatches. Sweat beads covered her forehead and down her chest, rolling under her breasts.

"You alright?" Diabla asked, pressing their nakedness together.

"Yeah! Just . . . just a bad dream." Deep inside Elise knew this was no ordinary dream. It was a cryptic vision that contained a message. Until she could understand these messages and gain some knowledge of the unseen tides that were influencing her life, the visions only served as nightmares. Nightmares that continued to feed her rage.

"Let's get up," she said. "We have work to do today."

# CHAPTER FOURTEEN

The early morning sky in Oklahoma City was overcast with the potential of bad weather as the Greyhound bus pulled into the station. Elijah popped a cassette in his Walkman. He and Big Teflon shuffled off the bus into the crisp bone-chilling air and quickly into the bus terminal. He bobbed his head to "Shed So Many Tears"; something about 2Pac's words had become his strength. In his heart, he knew that even if Cannon wasn't there physically, he was still with him. Not like a ghostly sidekick following him around, but more like a strong presence guiding his steps, his guardian angel. He didn't know why, but thinking that way sort of put him at ease.

"I'm gonna call this nigga Wiz and tell him we here," Elijah said. "Why don't you grab our luggage off the bus while I do that." They went in opposite directions: Elijah walked to the bank of telephones and Big Teflon back to the bus.

As Elijah dropped the quarter into the coin slot, he recalled most of what was told to him about this dangerous young boss, Big Wizard (or Wizard), and his bloodthirsty brother, Hitter. They were the younger brothers of O.G. Big Killa Mike, K-Mike for short, who had been Big 9-Lives's best friend and road dog. The two co-founded the Nine Os on Budlong Aves together.

Their father, the reputable Clarence X, had been the treasurer and first lieutenant for the Fruit of Islam (FOI) in the Nation of Islam's (NOI) Temple 27 in South Central Los Angeles for over two decades, his FOI being some of the most disciplined radical black men in the city due to his training. He drilled the Nation of Islam's ideology into his sons, starting with Big K-Mike, his oldest. They were taught a mixture of community activism, self-defense, and financial independence. K-Mike later joined the Crip movement and shared much of those FOI/NOI teachings with his new comrades and built a formidable gang in the Budlong Aves. He trained his little brothers, Wizard and Hitter, as if they were mini soldiers in boot camp. The result was two severe militant Muslim Crips.

Big K-Mike was killed in the mid-eighties, gunned down in front of his two younger brothers, Wizard and Hitter, by a rival gang member associated with the Back Westside Eight-Tray Gangstas. That incident led to the brothers declaring their own personal war against those they held responsible, the Eight-Trays. The five-year war caused all sorts mayhem—shootings, fire bombings, violent retaliation—that built Wizard and Hitter's reputations as the best of the best of South Central's soldiers. The streets soon learned that both Wizard and Hitter (now called "the Brothers" by their enemies) were built for war and hard to kill. A deadly one-two punch that never seemed to let up on their enemies.

After witnessing the slaying of Big K-Mike, Hitter went through a transformation that caused those close to him to often question his sanity, and he became a loose cannon. He went from being a good-natured considerate kid to being a black-hearted man of zero tolerance for whatever he believed went against the code of the street warrior. He lived in an existence of controlled madness.

Wizard was troubled by his brother's condition but never attempted to tell him what to do. He compromised with Hitter, learned to teach him without preaching, guide him without force, and love him without condition or strings attached. Hitter accepted his brother and allowed himself to find balance in his security.

In the aftermath of the LA uprising after the Rodney King verdict in April 1992, a peace treaty of sorts developed between the Crips and Crips, the Crips and Bloods, and LA black men as a whole. On all sides of the conflict, the possibility of peace talks had suddenly gained inspiration. The idea of a ceasefire with the other side, once dismissed outright, became the subject of serious debate. Before long, under the direction of the Black Muslims, blue, red, orange, and purple rags were tied together and raised over the city. Ceasefire!

With the street war on pause, the Brothers turned their attention to an old unfriendly enemy: poverty! Their new priority was getting money. They had continued to hustle during the wars, but it wasn't their top priority due to the bullets and bombs being hurled their way. The struggle they'd gone through for the set and the turf gave rise to a deep sense of entitlement, and it was time for the turf to break bread or else. To them, the "haves" had an obligation to spread the wealth with the "have nots," and it was time to take a piece of that wealth from the tight-fisted Western side Nine Os.

With that grimy attitude, the Brothers turned their hungry eyes and force on them. The Western homies had many out-of-town dope spots sewed up, Wiz and Hitter demanded in. The Western O.G.s sent their calls to voicemail, avoided them at functions, and spun them from one O.G. to another. They didn't take the threat serious; after all, they were all Nine Os.

The board was set and the game of chess was ready to begin. Wiz elected to open. His first move was to move in and set up a base of operations in the heart of their turf. He chose Ninety-Fourth and Western in one of the row houses that stretched from Ninety-Second to Ninety-Sixth Street. The Brothers officially christened the houses "neighborvilles." With Moet and Black Talon bullets, they declared the neighborvilles on Budlong Avenue territory. From there, they took Jesse Owens Park, then on into the back-streets. Their moves were aggressive, like pitching a tent on your enemy's back porch.

The Western side Nine Os armed themselves, moved operations to a new spot in the U.G.s, and resisted the Brothers' extortion demands. They tried to find a way to save their turf, but the Brothers rained bullets wherever they tried to regroup. Wizard and Hitter looked at things like this: they'd just come out of a five-year war with some of the best killers in LA, and this little scrimmage was nothing more than a walk in the park.

Before long, O.G.s from all sides were petitioning Big 9-Lives to reign in his homies. Big 9-Lives made a visit to them at their headquarters in the neighborvilles. He found them settled in like they were born and raised on Western, laughing and talking as if they didn't have a care in the world. After some diplomacy and a whole lot of haggling with both sides, Big 9-Lives convinced the Western O.G.s that it was in their best interest to give up some of their opportunities to the Brothers. They caved and offered to open Oklahoma City to Wizard if he called off the war. That was Wizard's objective all along. Checkmate!

Hitter wasn't satisfied. He never really had a goal or purpose, real or imagined. He wanted to continue to go at them, but Wizard calmed him down long enough to get their foot in Oklahoma. Once in, Hitter began another campaign that was part force, part finesse. He managed to work his way into every state that the Western homies were flooding with drugs. Slowly but surely, the Brothers filtered in their own handpicked soldiers to go into these states and traffic drugs on their behalf. It was a hood-style takeover.

All these events led up to Elijah being able to come in behind their bulldozing and heavy lifting to eat from the table with them. Everybody who was somebody in the underworld, enemies and allies alike, had no choice but to tip their caps to the ever-growing legend of the Nine Os Brothers. Wizard and Hitter deserved bronze statues in front of Jesse Owens Park.

---

Elijah and Big Teflon pulled out of the bus station in the rented Chrysler Wizard sent to pick them up. Cool rains drizzled from the cold gray skies, and ten minutes later it started to hail. As one of Wizard's workers drove, Elijah was thinking about his uncle, wondering how he was doing in Atlanta.

The Chrysler pulled into an apartment complex a few blocks from the projects and the three got out and grabbed their things from the trunk. The wrought-iron front door to Unit C opened. A short guy dressed in baggy jeans, a sweatshirt, and winter boots walked out holding a forty-ounce bottle of Old English 800. He cupped his hands around his mouth and called out to Elijah. "What's up, cuzz?"

Elijah raised his chin in response, straightened out his pants, and put his bag over his shoulder. hugged and dapped each other's fist before the guy stepped aside and let Elijah and Big Teflon enter the apartment.

Unzipping their jackets, they exchanged greetings with the men present and took a seat on the coffee-colored sofa. Wizard was in the middle of an exercise routine. He sat facing them on the old faded carpet.

"Make yourselves at home," he said, starting a set of sit-ups.

"'Preciate you scooping us up," Elijah said.

"Don't trip. Big Nine put me up on what y'all got goin'. You welcome to grind in one of my spots if you want."

Elijah politely declined. "Thanks, but Big Cadillac already set up a spot for us to start off in."

"Suit yourself," Wizard said between reps. "But be careful with them cats. They soft as baby shit, so watch your own back. My advice to you is to get rid a your first couple sacks with them, then shake 'em and get your own spot, or fuck with me. I'll be throwing some business your way regardless. Your uncle got at me 'bout my cut, so I'm gonna make sure you have free access to get your bread up. But when I give a call on hood business, you'll roll with me, no ifs, ands, or buts."

Wizard finished another set of sit-ups and stood, sipping from a bottle of Evian water. No matter how many times Elijah had seen him over the last few years, he always appeared different, as if he modified his looks to remain discreet. Today it was short wavy hair with a light chinstrap lining his jaw, which gave him a boyish look to his face. He was the clean-cut fly guy, around thirty or so, around five-nine, with chocolate-colored skin and an agile middleweight boxer build. He always dressed in college-stamped jogging suits with a tank top underneath to floss his link chain. An average person meeting him in passing would never suspect that this unassuming man commanded a small army. After being in his presence for a while, it became evident that there was an aura of "bigness" about him.

Elijah surveyed the room with slight confusion. "No disrespect to you or anybody in here, but I'm confused by all these dudes from different hoods in here. I mean, I'm with you and Hitter without question, but I don't know these other cats." He was dumbfounded when the seven individuals introduced themselves. At first he thought they were all O.K.C. Nine Os until he learned they were a mix of 90s, 60s, Mansfield's Gangsters, Crenshaw Mafia Bloods, and 4-Trays. How could Bloods and Crips, Rollins and Gangsters, all work the same spot together?

"These are my people." Wizard waved around the room. "Some are my cousins and some considered cousins. I was raised in the

Nation of Islam, and all of us who were part of that movement are family. We might have strayed from the Muslim way of life, and bang from different hoods, but our Muslim ties override our geographical affiliations. When I say 'go,' we all go. As long as you keep it solid, this circle you see right here will be with you before majority of the homies who claim our hood. These are the soldiers who been riding with me through all the wars over the years. This my secret sauce, the key to my success, to have ties and affiliation throughout LA and other states."

"I respect that, homie." Elijah leaned back and fired up the blunt. "You've been doing this long enough, longer than me anyway, so I'm rollin' with your flow." He offered the blunt to Wizard.

"I don't smoke, homie." Wizard waved him off and started a set of push-ups.

"Damn, I thought everybody smoked weed," Elijah said in disbelief. He put the blunt in rotation to the right, beginning with Big Teflon.

Wizard laughed. "Not me. I don't smoke, don't drink. My drug is pussy and money," he said in-between reps. "And I get a lot of both."

Before he could start another set, the cellphone on the coffee table rang. Wizard picked it up and said, "Hello." He paused and then responded, *"Wa alaikum assalaam."* Wiz listened patiently. The blunt circled the room. "Alright . . . alright, calm down. I'll call him now. Don't trip. I'll get it all straightened out. Later." He ended the call, then called someone else, waiting for someone to pick up.

"Man, what's going on?" Wizard sounded agitated. "Look, man, just leave dude alone. I'll give you what he owe outta my own pocket. What you mean you only want it from him?! It shouldn't matter, as long as you get it. Man, you full a shit! You just looking for a reason to fuck with him. Leave the shit alone. He'll have it in a couple days alright later." He hung up the phone and set it on the table. With a sigh, he opened a window to air out the place.

"Man, my li'l brother. That nigga stress me out with all the wild cowboy shit he be on." He focused his attention on Elijah again. "Check it out. You playing in a different league now. You have to learn to broaden your horizon. Get to know different people outside the hood. We ain't gang-banging just for the fuck of it no more. We smash our enemies when it's necessary, but that's not the priority any more. It's a dead cause to kill for a color or street number now. We've put in work for the hood, more than most will do in a lifetime. After all the wars, all the pitfalls, we still here, still standing. Niggas like us don't have shit to prove anymore; we've established who we are. So stay focused, stay balanced, and don't let the money corrupt you."

"I hear you, homie, that's real talk." Elijah nodded. "But in our lifestyle, how do we stay focused in a world of craziness? My uncle tells me to stay focused all the time, but really, what's focus?"

Wizard cocked his head sideways at him, "That's a good question. Most young cats would've simply nodded in agreement with what I was saying as if they understood while the information went in one ear and out the other, but I see you're actually listening.", he stared at Elijah intently. "When I was a kid, one of my teachers in the NOI used to always drill into our heads that mastering ourselves should be our life's work. I discarded most of my teachings somewhere along the way, but that's one of the lessons I always try to remind myself of. That's one of the reasons I don't use drugs or drink. I want to be clear-headed and in control in whatever I do so I can keep my eyes on the prize through all the traps and bullshit that comes my way on a daily basis. That's focus. Right now your focus should be on getting rich—everything else is secondary."

"Yeah, for real. That's what I want to do, get rich," Elijah agreed, soaking up all the game Wizard was running down to him.

"Hitter over in the projects and I want you to go and pay him a visit just outta respect," Wizard said, giving Elijah and Big Teflon the keys to one of his old cars to get around in. They saw the projects on their way in, so it wouldn't be a problem for them to find their way there. They just had to bend a couple corners and hit Twenty-Sixth Street where they would see the squad hanging out.

Elijah and Big Teflon gave their daps and appreciation before leaving. "Li'l Nine," Wizard said just as he was about to leave, "all is at your fingertips. Take full advantage of it. Spread your wings as far as you can. The sky's the limit, soldier!"

Elijah nodded and headed out into the cold, *Sky's the limit* forever burned into his brain.

# CHAPTER FIFTEEN

The northeast side of Oklahoma City during the beginning of winter had a cold, crisp chill that could never be felt in South Central LA. It was that biting cold that swept in right before the snow. Like most ghettos in America, liquor stores occupied every other corner and black people moved about unfazed by the weather.

Elijah and Big Teflon stepped from the old Buick Regal to get acquainted with their new environment. Hot breath against the chill caused white smoke to emit from their mouths. The puffy North Carolina Tar Heels jackets, beanies, gloves, and winter work boots they wore did little to shield them from the frost.

If not for the weather, the low-income government projects could easily be a hood in LA. The single-story brick units beginning on northeast Twenty-Fourth Street and Martin Luther King Boulevard and spanned an entire six-block radius. Elijah and Big Teflon felt at home in the urban enclave. They approached the front porch where about fifteen unfamiliar faces stared them down. These were the Oklahoma Nine Os that the Western homies recruited in the late eighties. The Oklahoma Nine Os and a clique off them ('Cousin Hood 'Duce-Seven Neighborhood Crips) shared the projects and surrounding area.

"What's crackin', cuzz? Where the homie Hitt?" Big Teflon asked.

A boy who couldn't have been no more than twelve rose from the porch to extend the two-fingers-and-thumb handshake. "What's up, cuzz? The homie hasn't got over here yet, but he told me to look out for y'all. I'm Li'l Loc."

"I'm Big Teflon." He returned the handshake.

Elijah followed suit. "I'm Li'l 9-Lives. Budlong Aves!"

"That's what's up. The homie Hitt should be here soon. Wanna wait in the homegirl's house till he comes?"

"Nah, we cool. We'll wait out here." Big Teflon studied the rest of the crowd with a dangerous eye.

The cheap screen door swung open and Li'l Cadillac, (or Li'l Cad) stepped onto the porch with a sarcastic smile on his face. Dark skinned with cornrows in his hair, he was short and built like a mini tank. He was "one" on a short list of few from the Western side that all cliques and sides respected. He was fresh out from a seven-year bid in California Youth Authority and Youth Training School for a shooting on the Hoover Crips. While locked up, Li'l Cad earned a reputation as a knockout artist and "rider" for the hood. Unlike most of the Western side Nine Os, Li'l Cad was gang-banged out and not too concerned with hustling. He was the young champion in O.K.C. to serve as the O.G. Western side's muscle.

"Look at what the west wind blew in," he said, dripping with condescension. "The mighty, mighty West Coast boys Li'l 9-Lives and Big Teflon Black! Long time no see. What that original Western Avenue Nine O Gangsta Crip like?"

Elijah and Big Teflon picked up on the sarcasm. Elijah spoke up first. "What's that?" he returned the sarcasm.

"What's what?" Li'l Cad asked, confused.

"I ain't never heard of 'O' and 'Gangsta' going together. O's is Hoodstas, not Gangstas, so I don't recognize nothing about a Nine O Gangsta nigga. We Gangsta killas!" Elijah spat on the ground, then looked away as a gesture that he wasn't worried about Li'l Cad being a threat.

On the contrary, Big Teflon looked Li'l Cad directly in the eye like a game pit bull ready to attack.

"Oh, is that right?" Li'l Cad smiled wickedly. "Should I have said 'Nine O Hoover' instead? Or West Coast? Which one is it now?" He laughed.

Originally when the two sides of the nineties, Western and Budlong, were separate hoods, the Western side were Nine O Gangstas and the West Coaster Budlong side were originally Nine O Hoovers. Now that the Hoovers were one of the nineties main enemies, Li'l Cad took a dig at them for once being Hoovers.

"We from Budlong Ave.," Big Teflon said, "so you can miss us with all the extra shit."

"Oh yeah, I've been hearing a lot about you since I been away. I even heard about y'all hitting the homie Big Cujo's house for a nice li'l lick."

That statement got their full attention. It caught them off guard and Elijah didn't like being caught off guard. He had almost forgotten about their robbery. There was always speculation and rumors about him and the Teflon brothers' involvement, but no one ever came at them about it. They didn't want to risk facing off with Big 9-Lives about fucking with his nephew. Elijah quickly recovered, "You need to get another source of information because you got your shit backward!" he said.

"Oh, y'all didn't think nobody knew? Niggas knew, they were just too pussy to push the issue. One of the homegirls watched y'all from the neighbor's house loading the safe in the trunk. You already know how I get down. I speaks my mind and whoever don't like it, my arms is wide open for beef at all times." Li'l Cad spread his arms wide for emphasis.

Elijah was tired of the back-and-forth verbal sparring. He took off his coat. "Enough of this free-ass talking, I need that."

Big Teflon pushed Elijah aside. "Nah, cuzz, I got it."

Li'l Cad rubbed his palms together in delight. "Yeah, I been wanting some of you, Tef. I heard you can throw them hands. I want to test those rumors out, and I know it was you and your brother who hit the homie Cujo's house. Nine, I got love for you and your uncles even though I don't agree with some of y'all moves. Let this be between me and Teflon."

"Back up, Nine, cuzz just challenged me man-to-man. Respect my call on this one. I want to see what he all about anyways because I ain't convinced he all that." Big Teflon removed his jacket and handed it to Elijah.

"Come on, Mighty Mouse, let's see what you got!" Big Teflon assumed a boxing stance.

Li'l Cad peeled out of his heavy-duty sweatshirt revealing a torso and arms that resembled a He-Man action figure doll. Squaring off, Li'l Cad rushed forward like a bull, his short muscular arms releasing three blows so fast that they all seemed to connect at the same time. The blows stumbled Big Teflon, but he caught his balance before hitting the ground. Re-grouping, Big Teflon bounced lightly on his feet, anticipating the next bull rush. Li'l Cad attacked again, but this time Big Teflon sidestepped and countered with a right cross that knocked Li'l Cad off course. He absorbed the blow and launched another attack immediately. A one-two punch from Li'l Cad landed hard to both sides of Big Teflon's face. Teflon responded simultaneously: straight-right, straight-left, right-hook.

Li'l Cad took the punches like a seasoned boxer that wouldn't be deterred. He crouched low and continued his assault from inside with a flurry of overhands. He knew Big Teflon's reach was much longer than his was, so he had to stay inside up close. While he continued his constant flow of overhand rights and lefts, Teflon worked the short hooks and uppercuts viciously. A solid right hook clipped Li'l Cad's chin and dropped him to one knee. Li'l Cad was up in an instant and back inside Teflon's chest.

The two men fought like Muhammad Ali versus Mike Tyson in their prime. It went on for a full three rounds, with short interludes to catch a quick breath before resuming in the same fashion. The Oklahoma Nine Os were amazed and animated by the spectacle.

"Damn, cuzz! These niggas is lockin' up for real!" one said excitedly.

Elijah couldn't take it anymore. Big Teflon was taking too long to put Li'l Cad down. "Fuck that, cuzz, it's my turn," he said. Before he could join the fight, a voice interrupted the festivities.

"What's the problem here?"

All heads turned to see Hitter walk from the side of the complex. Everything went quiet.

"Li'l Cad, what's all this about? You trippin' on my homies?" He slowly walked toward the group, as everybody stepped off to the side and let him in the circle.

"Nah, homie," Li'l Cad said, breathing heavily. "Me and Tef just had an old issue and we handled it heads-up."

"Li'l Nine, you alright?" Hitter asked.

"Cuzz, I'm straight!" Elijah knew it was time to end the confrontation.

Hitter looked at Big Teflon and Li'l Cad with an unreadable expression on his face. "You two finished puttin' on your little show?" he asked. Both men confirmed it was over. "Embrace as homies then," he ordered.

Reluctantly they shook hands and embraced.

"This li'l cat right here"—he pointed to Elijah— "is my people. I'm responsible for him while he here. If I hear anything else about him having any problems y'all have to answer to me!"

Hitter's two-hundred-fifty-pound frame of stocky muscle made Li'l Cad appear insignificant beside him. His bushy eyebrows and piercing eyes gave him an eerie and threatening look without even trying to appear frightening. His clean-shaven bald head and smooth light brown skin reminded Elijah of an evil-looking albino python he'd once seen in a pet store.

"This is the only warning y'all get!" Hitter shouted, staring at the crowd to make sure they understood. Many averted their eyes under his glare.

With that, Hitter turned and walked away, melting back into the maze of the projects while everyone looked on in silence.

---

For the next few months, Elijah and Big Teflon hustled hard, dumping halves and whole kilo of cocaine into the hands of those throughout the northeast and surrounding counties. It was sweet to get $1,000 an ounce in a single hand-to-hand transaction instead of having to grind all night in LA for the same amount. Wizard was coaching and quarterbacking for them, and encouraging them to become independent. Things were coming together for Elijah. It was time to call Big 9-Lives for round two.

Elijah popped out his cloned cell phone and called his uncle in Atlanta. Big 9-Lives picked up on the third ring.

"What's crackin', Unc?"

"Ain't nothing. Just leaving the gym and 'bout to get something to eat. Hold on one second." Li'l Nine looked at the digital clock on the night stand, 10:15 a.m. He guessed the time in Atlanta to be about noon.

"Alright, I'm back. What's the biz?"

"The basketball game just ended. Tar Heels won in a blowout," Elijah said: *All the coke is sold. We made the money we were expecting.*

"Is that right?"

"Yeah. I'm about to renew my season tickets tomorrow. Gotta support the team. Feel me?" Elijah said: *I'm on my way back to LA tomorrow so I can buy more coke and get back to O.K.C. immediately. Okay?*

Big 9-Lives laughed. "Slow down, young'un. We'll renew our season tickets together and get a discount. I won't be able to get back till next week. Will you be safe there till then?"

"Yeah, I'm straight. I got one of the homegirls from the hood out here, a li'l spooky rat. She's on my team. I'm staying at her house in the boonies most of the time."

"She trustworthy?"

"Yeah. She's solid and do what I tell her. She wants me to fuck her, but I haven't went there . . . not yet anyway. I don't want her thinking I'm just another hoodsta feenin' for her pussy. I'm winging her like you taught me, lacing her up mentally, teaching her how to be a real hoodsta."

Big 9-Lives laughed. "Li'l nigga, you always think these broads want you to fuck on 'em like you Rico Suave or something."

"Don't hate because you starting to lose your touch while I'm catching full stride!" Elijah teased. "Just stay on my hip, ol' man, and I'm gonna carry us to the Land."

"Alright with that 'old man' shit. Ain't nothing old about me. I'm still in my prime. And know you got a long way to go before you catch O.G. Mister 9-Lives with the magnificent gift of persuasion!"

"Now you wanna use big words: magnificent, persuasion. Knock it off!"

"I can't help it if my vocabulary and word play is up to par. Catch up!" Big 9-Lives snickered. "Nigga, let's get back to business. I'll be in route next Saturday, so stand ready."

"I'm getting myself together as we speak. I'll holler at you then."

"Ninety minutes!"

"Nine minutes, no seconds!"

They ended with the original Nine O sign-out. The line went dead.

It was four a.m. on Sunday, the time when South Central Los Angeles slept. The apartment was dimly lit as Big 9-Lives and Elijah sat in the kitchen with the cash machine whirring and beeping in a constant tone as it counted the bills. Big 9-Lives sat in the dinette chair scribbling figures on a piece of scrap paper. His nephew stacked twenties on the tile floor in thousand-dollar stacks. The CD player was on kicking out old-school hip-hop. Empty beer bottles and chips bags filled the counter.

"Two hundred and twenty thousand dollars. All here." Elijah stacked the last bundle atop the rest. "I gave five stacks to the homegirl in Oklahoma."

"Why?"

"To strengthen her loyalty to our structure."

"Good move. I'll eat half the five with you," Big 9-Lives agreed. "I'm goin' to get with Big Cad later to do the same deal as the first, so you need to kick in your twenty-one thousand dollars for your work."

"I'm not doing one-and-half this time," Elijah protested.

Big 9-Lives looked up from flipping through one of the stacks with an expression of consternation. "What do you mean?" he asked deadpanned.

"Unc, I'm going all the way in. The homie Wiz told me the secret to the come up. I'm going to invest everything, the whole sixty-eight stacks. If you loan me the odd two stacks, I can buy five bricks of my own."

"Damn, nephew, that's a real power move. I hadn't even thought about going for more than ten at a time. But now that you've stepped up to the plate, I got no choice but to ride with you. Let me see, you get five and I buy five, we'll get fronted ten . . ."

Big 9-Lives reached for his pencil and pad again and began scribbling figures. "Since I didn't give you a cut out of the work I got fronted on the first trip, I'll throw you the two stacks you need on GP. Now that I see you're serious about gettin' your money, I'll split all profits in the future fifty-fifty. We each take ten bricks to our hustling grounds and grind it out. When it's all said and done, we should come back to the table with a little over a half-a-mil just off two flips! And why stop there We can take that half-a-mil and reinvest it all." Then again, and again, and another one and another one." His voice echoed the thrill he was feeling at the prospect of it all.

"If we can get ten successful trips over the next year without touching the profits to spend on dumb shit like cars, clothes, jewelry, and all the other worthless stuff, we'll be millionaires by this time next year," Elijah estimated.

"Not just millionaires, nephew, but multi-millionaires."

"Oh, and Wiz made me an offer that I forgot to tell you about. He said that he'll take me to two other states where I can push more work, but I would have to enter into a contract with him."

"What kind of contract?"

"Ten percent of all profits from those states, and ten thousand a month for five years even if I decide to stop working those spots."

"Ten percent plus ten thousand a month for five years? That's kind of steep. Shit, that won't even be counting what I'm giving him on the O.K.C. deal."

"Fuck it! We'll still be winning at the end of the day if you think about it. The states will pay for themselves and I don't plan on retiring any time soon, so the five stacks a month from each of us ain't shit."

"Alright if that's how you feel. When you get back down there, tell him we accept the deal."

Elijah cracked a wide smile. "I already did."

# CHAPTER SIXTEEN

**1996**

"Unlock in five minutes, the prison guard announced over the intercom. Li'l Teflon put down the book he was reading, rose from his small metal cot, and scrambled to the crack in his cell door.

"Ju? Don't forget to bring out the chess board!" he yelled down the hall.

"I'm already on it, cuzz!" Ju-Ju hollered back.

All the cell doors cranked and slid open at the same time. The big black guard with an oversized head and thick red lips eyed the inmates as they formed a single-file line. Once he was satisfied with their silent orderly formation, he herded them forward into the dayroom at the front of the unit. A row of plastic orange chairs sat in front of a television mounted to the wall. The rest of the dayroom was a cluster of small circular tables and more plastic chairs for the inmates to play board games or sit and talk.

Most the inmates rushed over to grab the best seats in front of the TV to watch the latest music videos. It was more for the women in the videos than the music itself. Li'l Teflon and Ju-Ju took up a table in the back corner of the room. The Nine Os had so many enemies that strategic positioning was a must.

Li'l Teflon hadn't aged much. Aside from getting a little taller, he was still the thin-as-a-racehorse, shit-talking person he had always been. Ju-Ju, on the other hand, had changed dramatically during his four years of incarceration. The boyhood fat had transformed into solid muscle from all the push-ups, dips, and waterbag lifting. A few inches were added to his height and his hair hung in nine French braids past his shoulders. There was a hardness to him now, a hardness that came when a man had endured the mental tortures of ghetto life.

"Yo skinny ass need to do some push-ups, nigga," Ju-Ju laughed as he unfolded the chessboard and sat across from Li'l Teflon.

Li'l Teflon responded with his usual defense. "Nigga, fuck'a push-up! I already told you, as long as I can throw these hands I'm good."

Li'l Teflon meticulously set up the chess pieces as Ju-Ju filled him in on last night's conversation with his mother. "Li'l Nine was over at Mom's the other night dropping off some bread for me and her. He even spent some quality time with her and ate dinner. That's some 'real nigga' shit in my book. Shit, most of the homies jump ship as soon as a nigga gets locked up. It feels good to know that one of us is out there running shit and making power moves." Ju-Ju was proud that one of his own—his friend Elijah—was the major figure in the whole city. "I can't wait to get out there with the homie." He exhaled deeply.

Li'l Teflon narrowed his eyes and swallowed the lump in his throat. "Humph!" He shook his head and rolled his eyes. "I don't know why you feelin' all special because he dropped a little change off. We in here for his shit. He's supposed to be looking out. From what I'm hearing, him and Bro is playing with major money out there now. We should be getting a little more than what's coming our way." He moved his bishop and yelled, "Check!"

Even though Li'l Teflon pretended to not care, he spent many nights feeling betrayed and abandoned, that his own brother and friend could allow him and Ju-Ju to take the fall.

Ju-Ju moved his king in front of the knight. "Cuzz, us being here is all part of the game. Li'l Nine don't owe us shit. They paid for good lawyers that got us the best deals we could hope for under the circumstances. We haven't wanted for nothing since we been down and my mom is being taken care of. We can't ask for no more than that. He's gone above and beyond his duty."

"I'm not complaining, I'm just saying . . . the shit he do ain't special. Anyways, we have to start thinking about our own moves when we get out of here. The next couple months will fly by in no time and they'll be letting us walk out these doors. I still got fifteen stacks put away. What about you?"

"I fucked off a lot of mines when I was out, but with what I've been getting from Nine, I should have about ten stacks."

"Yeah, I fucked off a lot of mine too. Still, with twenty-five between the two of us, we good. We won't have to get out looking for handouts. We'll get a brick or two and shoot out of town with Bro. That'll give us a chance to scope the scene. Once we make a few trips to flip our bread, we'll go back and lay them country niggas down for all they got." He moved his rook in front of Ju-Ju's king and said, "Check."

Ju-Ju laughed to himself because he knew Li'l Teflon was just talking out the side of his neck. "The homies ain't gonna go for no shit like you talking about. That would fuck they money off if we went out there and robbed all of their customers." He moved his king behind a pawn for protection.

Li'l Teflon wasn't laughing; he was as serious as death. "They won't know . . . we won't let anybody know that we're leaving LA on our final trip. Once we get to Oklahoma, we'll stay out of sight until it's time to handle business. I've thought about it for months. I'm telling you it's gonna be sweet."

Ju-Ju looked at him, concerned. "I don't know, cuzz, that might not be straight." Ju-Ju tapped the table as he contemplated his next move. More concerning was that Li'l Teflon seemed to be serious. While Ju-Ju wanted to make money when they got out, he didn't know how he felt about in crossing Elijah Oklahoma. "It could put the homies in danger down there. Plus, the hood changed since we been gone. It's a chain-of-command since Big 9-Lives moved to Atlanta. Big Wiz and Hitter call most of the shots from up top and Li'l Nine is the general. We couldn't make a move like that without clearing it with one of them first." He moved his bishop in an attack position.

"Fuck all that!" Li'l Teflon shouted, causing some people to look in his direction. His eyes blazed with fury. In a softer tone, he said, "I wasn't out when this new shit started. I'm just as much a general as Nine is, if that's the case. I'm not about to sit back on my heels and take orders. Don't get me wrong, Nine's my nigga, but if they don't want to recognize my status in this hoodsta movement, I'll create my own chain of command. Feel me?" Li'l Teflon abruptly stood up and laughed out loudly, causing more stares.

"Shiddd!" He threw his head back and bellowed. "The Black Bear been in hibernation, but now he's awake and hungry. Nigga, it's time to eat."

With a sinister smile, Li'l Teflon picked up the bishop and carefully placed it on the board two spaces from Ju-Ju's king. "Checkmate," he said calmly.

---

Perched in the nestle of the Hollywood Hills, the eight-bedroom, nine-and-a-half-bathroom mansion was a world away from the warzones of South Central LA. The long wrap-around driveway was packed with expensive cars of different makes and models. At the top of the drive, directly in front of the entrance, an ice-blue Lamborghini Diablo with a vanity plate that read, "Hole-9," sat on full display. Two brand new 1996 Oldsmobile Auroras with twenty-inch Anteras sat behind the Lambo with two huge blue bows lying across the hoods.

2Pac's "Ambitionz as a Rida" jammed throughout the house and property. A big banner posted at the front entrance read, "Welcome Home Li'l Tef and Ju." Plenty of hugs, handshakes, laughter, and loud talk lent the night the proper festive vibe. Sexy women wore their most expensive dresses and heels; even the homegirls who made the trek from the hood sported their best fashion. Champagne bottles popped in a constant flow.

"I'm glad y'all home, li'l bro," Big Teflon said over the loud music.

"Shit, you can't be happier than me. Ju-Ju, come here." Li'l Teflon waved Ju-Ju over to join them.

"What's up, cuzzins?" Ju-Ju took a deep guzzle from his Moet bottle as he walked up.

Li'l Teflon wrapped one arm around Ju-Ju's shoulder. "It's time for a toast among us, road-dogs, for old time's sake."

Before Li'l Teflon could begin to do the honors, Big Teflon stopped him. "We need to wait on Li'l Nine," he suggested. "It won't be long before he come back."

"Man, the homie's Lambo is clean as fuck! Y'all been doin' it since we been gone," Ju-Ju complimented.

"To keep it one hundred, it all seems unreal to me at times how far we've come," Big Teflon said as he surveyed the room. "I mean, Big 9-Lives got the door open for us, but once we got our foot in, Li'l Nine smashed the gas to the max. Everything you see here tonight cuzz is responsible for. What y'all think about the Auroras he got for you?"

"I'm digging it to the fullest!" Ju-Ju exclaimed.

Li'l Teflon didn't comment.

"Nine wouldn't let me put in on the cars—he wanted to do that for y'all himself—but I got some bread I'm going to hit you with."

Li'l Teflon wondered how much bread his brother was talking about laying on them. He took a deep drink from the champagne bottle and looked around the room at all the different faces. "He still getting his work from the Western cats?" he asked in an off-handed manner.

"Hell nah!" Big Teflon twisted his face in disdain. "That stopped a while ago. The homie got a Mexican connect coming straight across the border. I'm telling y'all, this shit is big! Li'l Nine is the general and carrying it well."

Elijah stepped through the front door just at that moment, dressed in a North Carolina Tar Heel sweat suit, powder-blue Air Jordans, and a matching T-shirt. Aside from the $100,000 diamond-encrusted Rolex watch dangling from his left wrist, you would never guess he was a millionaire.

Ju-Ju lost his mind as soon as he saw him. Before Elijah knew it, he was being engulfed in a bear hug. "I love you, nigga!" Ju-Ju screamed in pure joy.

"Damn, cuzz." Elijah laughed. "You gone squeeze the air out of me." It was a nice greeting and he almost forgotten how much he enjoyed Ju-Ju's company. Li'l Teflon, on the other hand, clenched his jaw and tightly smiled.

"I see you've been getting it in, huh?" he said of Ju-Ju's six-three, two-hundred-twenty-five-pound frame "Done got all that baby fat off you. Yeah, I heard about you knocking out enemies up in there. Don't get out thinking you ready for the kid though, because I'm still vicious with these hands." Elijah threw a playful upper cut to Ju-Ju's gut.

"You ain't never gotta worry about that. I'm with you to the end of the earth, my nigga!"

"You already know: Budlong Ave. niggas gonna be standing when all else is gone," Elijah swagged.

"That's right!" Li'l Teflon broke in. "We like cockroaches around this bitch. The Ice Age can come and go, and a million years later when the ice blocks melt, we'll shake it off, lace up our Chucks, and continue mobbing on these lames!" He walked over and embraced Elijah in a strong hug. At the same time, Big Teflon wrapped his arm around them both, and Ju-Ju wasn't going to be left out, so he joined in on the group hug.

When they broke the hug, Elijah waved over a server for four fresh bottles of Cristal. It was now time for the toast. Ju-Ju urged, "Li'l Nine, you do the honors."

Elijah gave it some thought as to what he was going to say. He was genuinely happy to see his homies and had missed them. "This is to the warriors who overcome and shine the brightest. We give thanks for all the trials and tribulations that come our way along with the triumphs. Without hardships, we could never develop the will to be conquerors. Strength created by our blood, sweat, and tears is what makes us the strongest amongst men. Salute!"

"Salute!" All four bottles turned up in unison. After long guzzles, Elijah wiped his mouth and gestured to the room of beautiful women. "Tonight is y'all night. We have plenty of time to catch up with each other to shoot the shit. Tonight, though, grab some of these fine-ass broads and get your party on."

"Say no more." Li'l Teflon looked around at all the possible candidates. "I got to line me up some pussy to eat tonight." He headed for a thick brown bombshell wearing a skintight flimsy dress with no undies and matching heels.

The others laughed as he swooped down on his prey.

"I don't know about eating it," Ju-Ju commented, "but I gotta get a hold of something!" He made his way through the crowd on a conquest of his own, with Big Teflon right on his heels.

Elijah watched them with pride as they made their way to the dance floor. It was good to have the old crew back together again, seeing them enjoying themselves, clowning like back in the days. Partying wasn't really his thing. He needed some alone time.

He grabbed an extra bottle of Cristal and made his way up the wrap-around staircase to the top floor and out onto the terrace. The bright lights of Los Angeles were majestic against the full moon and clear skies. He marveled at LA's energy and nowhere else could match it. It was a forced that flowed through its inhabitants that couldn't be explained, only felt.

He pulled a blunt from his pocket and sparked it, allowing the calmness to overtake him. He felt a sense of accomplishment, yet something still felt missing. A moment when he should be having the time of his life he was instead thinking about the dead: his mother, his uncle, all the dead homies.

He could hear the music playing downstairs, but it, along with the festivities, might as well been in another world because the view and his marijuana-laced thoughts had him lost. Thirty minutes flew by in a flash

*Click, click.*

The meatal-on-metal action of the .380 brought Elijah back to the moment and he froze.

"Don't make a move or make a sound, mutha-fucka!"

Elijah hadn't heard the footsteps come up behind him. He turned around slowly to face his intruder. Even though he had heard the voice, it still surprised him to see a woman standing there. He calmly sized her up. *Petite, cute pistol, definitely wearing a wig and some sort of disguise,* he thought. He looked past the barrel directly into her eyes without fear.

"Take off the watch and run everything in your pockets, bigtimer," she sneered.

He didn't move a muscle. He glared at her with unreadable eyes. Not only was there no fear, there was no anger either, just an eerie stare that seemed to reach down and probe her soul. For a brief moment, she felt hypnotized. The gun trembled slightly in her hands as she tried to regroup.

"I said run your shit. I'm . . . I'm not going to tell you again." She tried sounding more authoritative.

His stare suddenly took on a new dimension, one that invited death. He cocked his head to the left with a curious look that asked, *What're you waiting on to pull the trigger?*

"I'm not the one who hurt you," he said out of nowhere.

The random statement threw her off, and the gun in her hand trembled with more intensity. Her legs began to shake too. She shifted weight to her opposite leg to try to restore stability, only to have that one betray her with the shakes as well.

"What? Shut the . . . shut up and do what I said . . . or you're gonna get it!" she stammered.

"Look, whoever sent you here, tell 'em you wasn't able to do it. Because I promise you one thing: you won't be taking shit of mine by force! You must not know who I am. You would've been better off asking for something from me than trying to take it. I rented this place to party with my homies and I have to return it in the condition that I found it. I don't have time to be cleaning your stupid-ass blood off the walls. Now, take your little gun, that ugly-ass wig, and get the fuck outta here before I decide to kill ya."

Calmly, Elijah turned back to the city view.

The woman was unsure of what to do next. The gun still aimed shakily at his back. She shifted from one foot to another. *Should I run?* she thought. *Fuck that!* "I'm gonna get what I came for . . ."

The words barely escaped her mouth before she was snatched from behind in a deadly chokehold, wrist clamped down on with such pressure that it felt instantly broken. The gun tumbled to the floor. Her windpipe was being crushed and she struggled to breathe.

"Yeah, bitch, you 'bout to get something, but I guarantee you won't like," a man whispered in her ear.

"She wasn't gonna do shit, let her go, Hitter," Elijah said without turning around.

Hitter gave her a hard shove that sent her crashing into the wall and onto the floor. She gasped for air as she massaged her neck.

"Take off that ugly-ass wig and lose the disguise," Elijah ordered. Once she regained her bearings, she slowly removed the wig and peeled the rubber material from her face. Her long black hair fell around her shoulders and her greenish-blue eyes widened with panic.

"Who sent you?" Elijah asked, now facing her. She didn't look like he expected. There was softness and femininity to her, not the hardness she tried to portray earlier.

"Nobody, I came on my—"

"Don't lie to me!"

"I'm not lying. I got an invitation to the party from a promoter guy I know. When I saw where it was going to be, I figured it would be some money here and came to do my work."

Elijah studied her expressionless. '*Work' is what she calls it,* he thought. "Get a fuckin' job if you want work," he snapped.

"Humph. A job like you?"

"First of all, you don't know shit about what my line of work is, and whatever it is it don't consist of going into someone's territory to take what belongs to them, especially not for crumbs like jewelry and pocket change," he scolded her.

Elijah crossed his arms. "Stand up," he ordered.

She slowly rose to her feet with the certainty that he was about to kill her.

Elijah relit the blunt and studied her. She stared back with equal measure of hate, fear, and something else he was trying to put his finger on. Was it . . . familiarity?

He dug into his pocket, making her take an involuntary step backward and closing her eyes in anticipation. When nothing happened, she opened her eyes to see him holding out a wad of one-hundred-dollar bills, five-thousand-dollars' worth. She looked at his hand as if he held a viper. He gestured with his hand for her to take the money. She furrowed her brow in confusion and suspicion.

"Take it!" He shoved it toward her.

Shakily, she reached out and took the money. "Why?" she questioned in a low disbelieving tone.

"I'm giving you the money because I understand that you're just a confused little girl looking for a reason to hate me. We don't know one another, so why should you hate me?" he explained.

She stood there, stunned. *This ain't how it's supposed to go down,* she thought. Not only was he handsome, but there was a genuine sincerity and kindness about him. She saw no motive behind his gesture, only concern. But that couldn't be real, men weren't like this. They always have a hidden agenda. He seemed so different. She suddenly felt an unusual connection to him. *That face, those eyes. . .*

His voice interrupted her thought.

"You just had the misfortune of picking the wrong person to fuck with tonight. So, I made the night a success for both of us. You learned the lesson never to fuck with me again, and you accomplished your mission of getting money, so be happy! Hitt, give her back her gun."

Hitter looked at Elijah as if he'd lost his mind. Was he really going to pay her for trying to rob him, *and* give her back a gun that she might shoot him with in the future? This was ludicrous! "My vote is to wrap the bitch up in saran wrap and throw her in the ocean," he said.

"Yeah, I know, but sometimes the universe tests us to see if we can be merciful, even when we got the power to do otherwise."

"What, you a philosopher or something now, nigga? Kill this bitch and get it over with."

"Can you just trust me on this one?" Elijah asked Hitter. "I know what I'm doing."

Hitter looked at them with consternation on his face. Reluctantly, he removed the clip and dislodged the bullet that was in the chamber, tossing the gun at her feet. "You're very fortunate. Allah spared you this night."

She was perplexed, yet gained the courage to speak without fumbling over her words. "I ain't no little girl, and I'm probably older than you. You never said how tonight is a success for you," she said.

Elijah turned his back on her again. "You may be grown physically," he said, "but emotionally you're still a little girl. Tonight was a success for me because I didn't have to kill your dumb ass. Now get the fuck outta here!"

Tucking the pistol and wad of money in the band under her skirt, she hurried to the door with one last glance at him. He was still looking out over the terrace. *It's time to get the hell out of these hills as quick as possible*, she thought.

Once she was gone, Hitter joined him at the rail. He grabbed the blunt from Elijah's hand without asking and pulled deeply on it as he looked out over the city. Elijah gave him a sidelong glance.

"My vote wasn't really to kill her," Hitter abruptly spoke. "I just wanted her to know she was being spared."

Elijah didn't believe that for a second. Hitter went on with his philosophy, "A person should only kill when it's an issue of self-preservation, disrespect, or upholding the code of honor that we all must live by. Killing solely for money or just because you have the power to do so is to sell your soul."

Elijah watched him out of his peripheral. *He talking about me. Now he trying to be the philosopher,* he thought. *This nigga's crazy, but damn, he's intelligent at the same time. How can a person be so contradictory? What's really going on in his head?*

"Do you think about your brother Big K-Mike a lot?"

"Every day!" Hitter said, looking off into the distance.

"How do you deal with it and still find happiness or peace of mind?"

Hitter sighed as he thought about his older brother being murdered in front of him. He would never forget that day, gunned down by cowards. He turned to look at him. "Life on Earth is an experience to learn lessons that the spirit will take into the next existence. While here, all we can do is enjoy what there is to enjoy and suffer what there is to suffer. That's the reality of the human experience. For whatever reason, peace isn't an option for me in this lifetime, so I learned to be the best warrior possible and not complain or drive myself crazy with sadness. K-Mike taught me that as a kid, and it's the gospel I will live and die by."

He looked out at the city lights below. "I don't spend my time trying to find happiness" he reiterated, "because I know it can never be found. I take every experience for what it's worth. You know, I have brief spurts of joy, not from the money and bitches that y'all seem to be obsessed with."

Elijah wanted to interrupt him but decided not to. Hitter was on a roll and didn't really seem to care if he was listening or not. It was more like he was thinking out loud, something Elijah suspected he did a lot when alone. "I don't care about the street fame," Hitter continued, "nor the money or phony bitches that only come around when the money's good. Don't get me wrong, I respect money, but I give away more than I keep to those who need it more than me. My joy is my daughter, my nieces and nephews—they're too young to know how to be fake. They say and do what's on their mind. I relate to that. I know where I stand with them." He suddenly laughed for no good reason, toking on the blunt that he still hadn't offered back to its rightful owner.

"It's called unconditional love," Elijah said.

"Yeah, yeah," he agreed. "Their love and camaraderie is authentic. You want to know my other joys?"

"Yeah, why not."

"Driving my Porsche up the highway at a hundred miles per hour. It makes me feel alive." Hitter continued in an almost distant tone, "Other than those things, I'm content with ghetto life. Even though I have more than enough money to get away, I won't. I prefer being among the low lives, dodging bullets, sending bullets.

War is the true spice of life! Hell, I know that many people believe I'm psycho, and at times I don't disagree. But the truth is, I don't give a fuck. When the day comes for me to stand before Allah and give an account of my action, I believe Allah will understand."

Elijah gasped to hold back a laugh when Hitter spoke of God, or Allah, as he called him.

Hitter looked at him with questioning eyes. "What the fuck so funny?" he said.

"No disrespect, cuzz. It's just that you and Wiz trip me out. You speak of selling dope and gunning niggas down one minute, then speak of God or Allah the next. Do you really believe in a god?"

Hitter's eyes darkened, his eyebrows squinted together in obvious agitation, his body tensed as if he had been slighted by the question. His feelings poured forth in a controlled rant. "You, like so many others, are brainwashed into believing that God is some man who sits in the sky judging and controlling everyone and everything, and to earn his favor you have to be some perfect mutha-fucka. The same people who spread this doctrine are those who robbed, raped, and killed for centuries. Yet somehow, they're the blessed ones and continue to remain in power while others struggle at the bottom under every curse imaginable. When black men like myself do what's necessary to change their circumstances and that of their tribe, they're labeled evil and ungodly. Fuck that! I won't be fooled. Those in power ain't no better than I am. I acknowledge the god that I am a part of, and reject and fight against the god society tries to force on me. The god of those in power are really the devil in disguise, and I'm their worst nightmare, because I'm a thinker, rebellious, and don't mind dying—as long as it's in combat with my finger on the trigger, I'm a god!" Hitter declared, veins bulging from his neck. "And to the enemy, a frightening evil god. You know the greatest lesson my oldest brother taught me and your mom taught you?" He turned to face him.

"I don't know . . . um, I guess . . . love?" Elijah said in confusion.

"Nah, nigga!" he yelled, pounding his fist against the rail, disgusted by Elijah's perceived ignorance. "They taught us how to die! You see, a person who knows how to die has the most potential and is the most dangerous, because the enemy can no longer use fear as leverage. Embracing death is the greatest accomplishment. It goes against the very nature of the average man."

Elijah nodded in agreement. Even if he didn't agree with what was being said, he sure wasn't going to let him know it.

Suddenly, Hitter looked around suspiciously and lowered his voice. "Be careful of those cats you grew up with," he said. "They not thoroughbreds. Yeah, they'll fight and shoot, but they have no inner substance. They ride out of anger and ignorance that's been instilled in them by their upbringing. They have a purpose, but don't trick yourself into believing that there's true love there. They're not cut from the same cloth. This party, all the material things you give them, don't mean shit. If push comes to shove, they'll betray you because it's been bred into them to be selfish and cut throats."

"I feel you, I—"

"You wanna know how to deal with the emptiness of losing your mom? Let me tell you, there is nothing wrong with thinking about her, but don't let grief consume you. Enjoy what the fuck there is to enjoy, suffer when it's time to suffer, break the backs of those who deserve it, and keep marchin'. That's it and that's all, nigga!"

Thumping the last of the blunt over the balcony, Hitter walked away mumbling under his breath. "Dumb mutha-fuckas" was all Elijah could make out. He watched him as he walked away, trying to figure out the enigma. *Unc was right,* he thought, *that is a dangerous man.*

He turned back to the city view and took a sip from the bottle. "Yeah, Momma, your son'll keep marchin'," he whispered.

# CHAPTER SEVENTEEN

Li'l Teflon took the blunt from Ju-Ju as he bobbed his head to the music. The scenery sped past as they maintained a steady seventy-five up I-40. It was Ju-Ju's turn behind the wheel, so Li'l Teflon took the free time to get his thoughts together and enjoy the view of the Midwest.

"Damn, cuzz, it's taking forever to get there. How much longer?" Ju-Ju complained.

"Not that long." Li'l Teflon continued to stare out the window, tired of Ju-Ju's whining. "Stop crying, nigga. You should enjoy being out here on the open road. Shit, two months ago, our asses was stuck in a cage."

"Yeah, but this shit is still taking too long. We should've took Li'l Nine up on his offer to have this shit moved for us, and we could've been chillin' on a plane right now."

Li'l Teflon didn't bother to respond. He took another toke of the blunt and passed it back to Ju-Ju to shut him up.

*He still don't get it,* Li'l Teflon mused, as he stared at the old Oldsmobile station wagon ahead of them being driven by the homegirls from the 60s. He had recruited them to drive the extra car with two kilos stashed in it. He smiled to himself as he thought of the genius of his plan. The station wagon had a small metal box compartment welded into the top of the gas tank. He'd wrapped the bricks in multiple layers of Saran wrap before coating it with thick, grimy monkey grease. Dropping each brick in a large Ziploc bag, he ran them through the vacuum-sealing machine for extra insurance. This would keep them safe from the drug-sniffing dogs in case they were pulled over and searched. The bricks were packed into the hiding spot in the gas tank and they were on their way. The dashboard fuel gauge had been rewired to disguise the malfunction caused by the abnormal gas tank. State Troopers looked for all those seemingly insignificant flaws that people usually overlooked. But not Li'l Teflon—he was way ahead of the game.

Elijah had given he and Ju-Ju the two kilos free of charge and offered to have it transported for them, but Li'l Teflon had opted to get it there himself. It was best for him and Ju-Ju to come and go as they pleased. He didn't mind the twelve-hour-a-day driving and the stops at night in the roadside motels for a little extra play with the girls.

The drive was smooth until they entered the stretch on I-40 from Albuquerque, New Mexico, to Oklahoma. State Troopers had a roadblock set up to randomly search vehicles. Ju-Ju and Li'l Teflon had been smoking blunts since leaving LA and the interior of the car reeked of marijuana. "Ah, fuck!" they shouted in unison, their hearts dropping when the obese trooper wearing a reflector shade came into view.

"What the fuck we gonna do if they pull us over?" Ju-Ju had rattled off, damn near having a nervous breakdown. "We ain't got the work in here with us, but just the weed smell alone gonna have them mutha-fuckas trippin'."

Traffic came to a crawl as some vehicles were waved through with barely a second glance; others were brought to a complete stop for questioning before being allowed to pass. Those who were unfortunate were directed to the side of the road where more troopers waited to rip their cars apart.

"I gotta take a piss," Ju-Ju had said in what seemed like comic relief.

Ignoring Ju-Ju's stupid outburst, Li'l Teflon said, "I'm gonna let a few cars go in front of me so we ain't directly behind them bitches." He slowed down, allowing a few cars to pass him by. "Shit, two cars with California tags and young blacks in both . . . yeah right! That's a dead giveaway. Them mutha-fuckin' troopers gonna know instantly that something up." They were a few cars back from the front of the line and they waited to see how this would play out.

As the girls pulled up to the trooper's station, they were motioned to stop. Li'l Teflon and Ju-Ju held their breaths. The trooper cautiously approached the driver's window, slightly bent over, leaned in, and looked around the inside of the car.

As the trooper conversed with the girl driving the car, Li'l Teflon started to sweat. *Man, this could be bad,* he thought. "I ain't goin' back to jail," he said nervously.

Just then, the trooper waved the girls through. Li'l Teflon sighed in relief.

As they inched up, the trooper continued to wave them through, and to their surprise, Li'l Teflon and Ju-Ju were waved through without delay. Both exhaled in relief as the car picked up speed again. The rest of the drive was without incident.

⟿

Ten hours later they arrived on the north eastside of Oklahoma City. It was the first time either of them had been out of California and they hit the ground running.

Li'l Teflon swung the station wagon into the driveway of a one-bedroom shack on the verge of collapsing. They had swapped cars with the girls as soon as they'd checked into the Motel 6.

"We 'bout to bubble, cuzz," Ju-Ju said with excitement. "The homies already set up everything for us. All we have to do is reap the benefits."

"Exactly . . ." Li'l Teflon laughed. "I feel it in my bones, this the fuckin' land of opportunity."

They pulled into the garage and parked. Li'l Loc opened the back door for them.

"Everything y'all need's in the kitchen," Li'l Loc called over his shoulder as he went back to playing Nintendo.

"That's what's up, li'l homie, we on it." Li'l Teflon looked around at what they had to work with.

The inside of the house was just as bad as the exterior. Broken-down furniture cluttered the living room, the kitchen was filthy, and mattresses were sprawled on the floor in the bedroom without sheets or blankets.

Neither Li'l Teflon nor Ju-Ju showed any discomfort with the house. They understood that the spot wasn't for looks; it was to sell dope out of, and that was what they were there to do.

Li'l Teflon unwrapped one kilo of cocaine and weighed out nine ounces, took it to the kitchen, and cooked it up.

"Let 'em know the shop's open!" he yelled to Li'l Loc.

"Got you, big homie, 'bout to make some calls now." Li'l Loc ended his game and got to task.

"You bag this shit up and get it off as they come. I'm 'bout to go out and scope the town," Li'l Teflon told Ju-Ju as he put on his jacket.

Ju-Ju eyed him suspiciously. "Alright cuzz, but stick to the script that Li'l Nine laid out for us. We don't wanna fuck up this opportunity."

"Humph," Li'l Teflon grunted sarcastically. "Don't worry about it. Best believe we gonna take full advantage of the opportunity." Then he shouted, "Come on, Li'l Loc, roll with me for a bit." He grabbed the keys, and he and Li'l Loc headed out the back door.

Li'l Teflon shook his head as he started the car. *Ju be acting too damn green sometimes. I ain't no fuckin' dope dealer. Who got the patience to be sitting in a house all day? Not the kid, that's for sure.*

"Show me the town, cuzzo, and all the major players I need to know," Li'l Teflon said as he passed Li'l Loc a fat blunt filled with Cali killer bud. "I know you been fuckin' with the homies who's been coming down here, but stick with me and I'm gonna make you rich in no time. Most of them niggas is for self, I'm for us."

Li'l Loc pulled on the blunt and coughed. "That sounds like a plan to me, big homie."

Li'l Loc took him to a few of the hot spots and introduced him around. They and three Oklahoma homies ended up at Lance's, an after-hours strip club joint.

Li'l Teflon made his way around the club with the Oklahoma homies serving as his makeshift security squad. They introduced him to all the ballers, movers, and shakers that Oklahoma had to offer. He engaged in private conversations with them, offering to sell them cocaine at lower prices than all his competitors. He reasoned that the cocaine didn't cost him anything, so why not get rid of it while meeting the people he needed to meet in the process. It was win-win for him.

By the time he and Li'l Loc made it back to the spot, it was around three in the morning. Ju-Ju had already sold seven of the nine ounces and the spot was still jumping.

Li'l Teflon took a seat on the sofa, kicked his feet up on the coffee table, and laid his head back in exhaustion. "Man, I think we've reached the Promise Land." He chuckled.

Li'l Loc stretched out on the beanbag in the corner and fell asleep.

"Tell me about it," Ju-Ju responded. "If it keep goin' like this, we'll be done with the two birds in no time."

"For sure." Li'l Teflon kicked off his shoes. "I found a couple cats we can sell some real weight to. We won't make as much money off the work, but it'll go quicker and put us in the position we need to be in."

"That's what's up. That'll stop us from having to be here any longer than necessary."

"Yeah, but on this trip, we gonna stay at least a month even though the work'll be gone long before then."

"For what? Once this shit is gone, we need to get back to the Land," Ju-Ju said, reaching for the TV remote to change the channel.

Li'l Teflon looked at him, irritated. "Because, we need to build relationships and trust with who we dealing with here. Look . . . I'm only looking to make about four or five trips before we turn this mutha-fucka upside down. We not tryin' to make no career outta this shit. We strike while the fire's hot, then get ghost."

Ju-Ju didn't respond. He sat back in thought.

Li'l Teflon took his silence as agreement. *I love this city,* he thought. *Where else could we gang bang, get money and not have to worry 'bout gettin' shot at by enemies? I can do anything I want in this town.* A big smile spread across his face. *The city's mine for the taking, and bet your last dollar I'm gonna take it.*

Li'l Teflon reached over to grab his cell phone off the nightstand, being careful not to move his lower body. He leaned back against the headboard and answered it. "What's crackin'?" He used his free hand to press down on the head of the stripper he met the night before.

"Everything's a go," Ju-Ju said with a tinge of anxiety in his voice. "Li'l Loc's bringing the last material you're gonna need over right now."

"Good . . . good." Li'l Teflon smiled at the stripper as she stared up at him with his penis in her mouth. "Once he get there, and you make sure everything we need's there, y'all swing over to my room so I can work my magic."

"That's a bet." Ju-Ju hung up.

Li'l Teflon tossed the phone to the side, rested his hands behind his head, and let her finish sucking him.

After she got through, before she could even wash her face, he jammed a hundred-dollar bill in her hand and ushered her out the door. He slammed the door behind her and cracked the curtains to let some light in. He'd been coming in and out of Oklahoma City for the past four months and the Remington Ramada Inn had become his favorite hideaway.

He turned the heater on to take some of the chill out of the room before getting into the shower. "That bitch had some fucked-up teeth. Got the nerve to buy some fake titties, but bitch should've bought some braces," he chuckled, then burst into laughter, as the hot water beat on his back.

As he covered his toothbrush with Colgate and started brushing his teeth in the shower, his mind running over the last-minute details of his plan. He'd taken care of all the preliminary work with precision. The first step was establishing working relationships, then the next and most important part was getting the eight kilos of cocaine he needed to show the buyers to make his final play a success.

It turned out to be easier than he expected. At the last minute, he realized that he didn't really need the eight kilos because the four that he and Ju-Ju already had was enough to lay the bait. He'd taken the four kilos to the buyer and used a razor blade to cut a rectangular window into each kilo so that he could see and test the powder to ensure the quality was good. Once the buyer was satisfied with the product, Li'l Teflon wrapped a layer of plastic around each kilo to close the window back up. After a little small talk, they made arrangements to make the exchange the following day at a set meeting place. As soon as Li'l Teflon left the meeting, he dropped the four kilos off to another buyer who paid $30,000 per kilo. The $120,000 was packaged and sent off to LA within the hour.

Li'l Teflon toweled off and slipped on his boxers, Levi's, and work boots. Before he could get his shirt on, there was a knock at the door. He peeked out and let Ju-Ju and Li'l Loc in.

Ju-Ju placed bags of McDonald's breakfast on the small table. Li'l Teflon took an Egg McMuffin and orange juice. As he ate, he watched Li'l Loc place a few sheets of dry wall, electrical tape, red tape, and rolls of Saran wrap on the bed.

After a few bites, Li'l Teflon put the sandwich to the side and went to work. He used an industrial razor blade to cut the wood into squares the size of kilos of cocaine. He stacked each square three layers thick. After making each individual square the same size and thickness, he completely wrapped each one with electrical tape. He then used the red tape (the same color tape the buyer saw the cocaine wrapped in the day before) and wrapped multiple layers over the electrical tape.

Ju-Ju and Li'l Loc watched the process in complete silence.

When Li'l Teflon was satisfied with the red-tape finish, he took the razor blade and cut a rectangle peek-window into each one, digging a small portion of the dry-wall out and replacing it with a small amount of cocaine powder. Finally, he wrapped a layer of Saran wrap around each kilo to re-close the window.

"Viola!" Li'l Teflon stood back and marveled at his work. "Exact copies of what I showed him yesterday. You niggas better recognize a real magician at work."

Ju-Ju picked one of the bricks up and turned it over in his hand. "Damn, cuzz, how do you think of this type of shit?" He looked at Li'l Teflon and shook his head.

"It's magic." Li'l Teflon slid on his gray sweat suit and grabbed his goose-down jacket off the chair.

Li'l Loc laughed with excitement. "Cuzz is an evil genius," he said, putting the fake kilos inside a black trash bag.

"Let's make it happen," Li'l Teflon said, checking his .45 Smith and Wesson.

Ju-Ju and Li'l Loc checked their weapons also, and they headed into the frost for the day's adventure.

Li'l Loc waited in the driver's seat as Ju-Ju and Li'l Teflon walked into Rose's Soul Food restaurant on Northeast Twenty-Third Street. Li'l Teflon had the fake kilos in a backpack slung over his shoulder. The restaurant was empty except for an old man wiping tables with a stained rag.

"He's waiting in the back," an overweight youngster said, as he led them through the kitchen to a small office at the very back.

A short black man, with a receding hairline and bulging eyes, stood up from behind the desk. "What's up, folks? I'm Steve." He extended his hand to Li'l Teflon in a familiar handshake.

Li'l Teflon shook his hand and sized him up. "What's up, bro?" He put on a fake smile. "Is everything good?"

"Yeah, everything's gravy . . . go 'head and have a seat." Steve waited for Li'l Teflon to sit before doing the same.

Li'l Teflon took a quick glance at the man standing at Steve's side. *I'm gonna kill you first if this goes bad,* he thought. He slid the backpack across the desk.

Ju-Ju stood near the far wall of the room.

"Eight big ones for you, Steve," Li'l Teflon nodded at the bag.

Steve opened the backpack and placed each kilo on the desk. He turned the last one over in his hand and stared at it intensely. He took out a small knife and sliced the plastic wrap to expose the rectangle window.

Li'l Teflon's hand instinctively dropped to his pistol.

Steve opened the window on the kilo, used the tip of his knife to dig out some of the powder, and placed a small amount on his tongue.

The room was heavy with silence.

Suddenly, a smile creased Steve's face. "That's him!" he exclaimed with satisfaction.

Li'l Teflon breathed a sigh of relief as the tension left the room.

Steve reclosed the window on the brick and placed all the fake kilos back into the backpack. He nodded to his worker, who left the room, and came back with a grocery bag. He emptied the stacks of cash from the grocery bag onto the desk.

"You can count it. It's all there," Steve offered Li'l Teflon.

Li'l Teflon stood and loaded the cash back into the bag. "I trust you, bro." He smiled and extended his hand in for a shake. He grabbed the bag, gave Ju-Ju a head gesture, and they headed to the waiting car. The deal was done.

# CHAPTER EIGHTEEN

At the break of dawn one morning, Elijah, Ju-Ju, and the Teflon brothers all received phone calls from Big 9-Lives to meet in at the family house on Ninety-First Street. Since Big 9-Lives moved to Atlanta and Elijah relocated to a beachfront condo in Malibu, no one officially lived at the family home anymore. It became more of a social meeting spot for their small circle of comrades when they were in town.

Each arrived separately from their prior night's rendezvous. Big 9-Lives, Wizard, Li'l Crip from Underground Crips, P-Nut (Wizard's cousin from Crenshaw Mafia Bloods), and Li'l Nicky Bam from Rollin' 60s showed up. Cars were already lined up in front of the house when Elijah pulled up. He smoked a blunt while he waited in the driveway for the others to arrive. It wasn't long before Ju-Ju hit the block in a black Jaguar, and the Teflon brothers swung up in a gray Suburban. After a brief exchange, they entered the house and found everyone gathered around the huge oak table that took up most of the dining room. Elijah had transformed the house into a ghetto mansion: plush soft white carpet covered the living room, which matched the off-white sofas and the coffee and end tables. The immaculate hardwood floor in the dining room complemented the oak cabinet and twelve-seat table set.

Elijah plopped in one of the chairs and stared around perplexed at those in attendance. "What's this all about?" he directed at Big 9-Lives.

"There's going to be some changes." Big 9-Lives responded, then he pointed at Wizard. "Wiz wants to address the circle. Where's Hitter?"

"He's supposed to already be here, you know how he is. We can get started. I'll fill him in later," Wizard said, standing in preparation of his spiel.

"I made agreements with all of you," he began, "and everybody has benefited more than expected. Now you've brought in more people to make money off what I created, people who're not giving me a cut, and—"

Outside, four eighteen-inch Fosgate woofers beat down the block. At this time of morning, every house on the block was awoken from their sleep. Through the front window, they saw the monster Yukon with its huge tires jump the curb and park on the front lawn. The song "Reality" by the Dogg Pound pounded loudly through the speakers. Big 9-Lives sprinted to the front door immediately.

Big 9-Lives sprinted to the front door. "Turn that shit down! You gonna wake the whole fuckin' block!" he growled, and aggressively gestured with his hand to shut it off.

Hitter shut the ignition off and hopped out with a sarcastic smile. "Calm down, cuzzo, you too uptight," he said as he summoned his dog. "Come on, Hitler." A muscle-bound, all-white pie bull jumped from the backseat and out the driver door.

"Where the fuck you goin' with him?" Big 9-Lives asked.

"Oh him?" Hitter pointed to the dog, "This is Hitler, he come to watch my back. Don't trip. He's house trained. he won't shit in your house."

Before Big 9-Lives could protest, Hitter walked inside the house with Hitler trailing. He led his best friend to the corner of the dining room and gave a command in Swahili, "*Bamoa!*" Hitler squatted and remained as still as a statue. Hitter joined the others at the table and emptied his early morning breakfast contents from his Burger King bag: cheese-egg croissants, hash-brown potato nuggets, and an orange juice. He began eating without acknowledging anyone.

"Back to what I was saying," Wizard picked back up. "The deal we made was specific to each one separately, not your friends and workers. So instead of trying to do the math for everyone working, I'm just putting a blanket tax on everybody."

They all squirmed in their seats. Eyes rolled and teeth smacked in frustration.

"You'll have to decide," Wizard went on as if he didn't detect the negative reactions, "if you'll cover the quota yourself or have each of your partners give a certain amount each. Either way doesn't matter to me as long as I get it."

"How much are we talking? Because for real I feel like ten percent is enough," Li'l Crip said. He was medium built with a shaved head and trimmed goat-tee. "We made an agreement and now you going back on your word."

Wizard shook his head, feigning shock. "My word's my bond at all times. When circumstances change, I gotta change with them. You can't bring people in who weren't part of the original deal and still expect it to be valid. Look, I'm not being greedy, I'm only asking for an additional five percent of all profits."

Some haggling went on around the table while Hitter ate and watched.

"The extra five percent's fair enough," Elijah finally agreed. "Everybody has expanded and is eating good. Why not?" he reasoned.

"I feel like this some sorta extortion goin' down, but it's still enough to go 'round, so I ain't trippin'," Li'l Bam, who was wearing a backward LA Dodgers hat, reluctantly agreed.

"I'm gonna go along with it . . . for now," Li'l Crip agreed, but ill will was written all over his face.

Hitter finished his breakfast, wiped his mouth, and decided it was time to take the floor. "Now that we got that out the way," he paused to burp, "we need to talk about why you three"— he pointed to the Teflon brothers and Ju-Ju— "are here. But before I do that, let me tell all y'all something: Stop driving these high-priced cars, wearing that big country-ass jewelry, and sporting Gucci, Versace, and all that other bullshit over here in the ghetto. We khaki-and-Chucks niggas. We Crips and Bloods. Leave that bootsie shit to them country niggas. All you doing is advertising for the feds. What the hell a 600 Benz doing sittin' in a driveway in South Central?"

No one responded, so he took their silence as agreement and moved on. "I'm not gonna ask y'all if you done the shit or not, because I know you'll lie to my face and that'll really piss me the fuck off. So instead I'm gonna give y'all a solution, an ultimatum."

Hitter turned to Big Teflon. "Teflon, I don't think you was involved, but I'm sure you was aware, at least after the fact and kept quiet to protect your li'l brother. But you two"—he pointed at Ju-Ju and Li'l Teflon— "y'all robbed cuzz down in Oklahoma!"

Ju-Ju and Li'l Teflon tensed up, finally realizing why they had been summoned.

"Don't look surprised. What, you niggas thought you could twist one of our people for over a hundred stacks without us finding out?" Hitter angrily spewed his verbal assault at them.

Big Teflon and Elijah were shocked by the turn of events. "Cuzz, is this true?" he asked in disbelief. *Nah, this ain't true,* he thought. *Hitter gotta be wrong,* he reasoned.

Before Li'l Teflon and Ju-Ju could answer the question, Hitter interrupted, "Don't ask that question, because you'll force them to lie in our face, and if they be so bold to do that, I won't have no choice but to go all the way. Yeah, don't think 'cause I'm fuckin' your sister that I won't twist your head off your shoulders." He directed the last statement directly at the Teflon brothers.

Li'l Teflon shot daggers at him. Even though he didn't much give a shit about his sister Naqael, he still didn't appreciate her being spoken about in that way. It was about respect, but he had to reign in his instincts to react violently. He would talk his way out of this one.

"I'm a man about mines cu—"

"Didn't nobody ask you for a fucking explanation," Hitter cut him off.

The Teflon brothers were taken aback by Hitter's absolute lack of respect. They still held their tongues with the understanding that they were batting out of their league.

Wizard held up his hands. "Calm down, Hitt. Look, y'all go to—"

"Nah, ain't no calming down," Hitter interrupted. "These dudes in major violation. They think 'cause they got a body or two under they belt that they can disregard the chain of command. Li'l Nine, if it wasn't for you, there wouldn't been no talking. I would've been baked both of these black mutha-fuckas—and sidekick too!"

Wizard tried to interrupt to restore some form of order to what was fast heading for chaos. "I know, I know, bro—"

"Nah, fuck that!" Hitter shouted, his eyes bulging. "I stay in my own lane, but you niggas bet not ever forget who's the sledge hammer around this bitch! You bustas go and do a couple years behind the wall, get some muscles, have a few fights, read a few books, now you feel you can call some shots. Let me tell you, y'all better read way more leadership and war strategy books before you think you can fuck with me. I'm war in the flesh! Don't mistake me for my brother. I don't have sympathy for none a you niggas. We're comrades in war, but once you break that code, fuck you! It's that simple."

"So, what do you suggest?" Big 9-Lives asked, trying to bring back some civility to the issue.

Hitter stared at Big 9-Lives in thought. As if reaching a conclusion, he finally spoke. "Since they took ninety-six-thousand dollars, dope, and guns in the robbery, I want all the cash plus twenty-five thousand in violation fees. That's one hundred and twenty thousand dollars and I want it next month. Also, y'all time in O.K.C. is over, officially terminated. Li'l Nine, if you still want to work O.K.C., you'll have to give that part of your operation to the li'l homies. It's time for some of the homies from down there to eat anyway," he concluded bitterly.

Since moving his operation fulltime to Atlanta, Big 9-Lives had tried to stay out of the day-to-day drama of his young homies. He felt that Wizard and Elijah could handle things and keep a grip on Hitter to a certain degree, but the confrontation at hand could turn deadly in a hurry. The Teflon brothers were holding their tongues, but they wouldn't take lightly to what Hitter was saying. Big 9-Lives had to somehow soften the blows Hitter just dealt to their egos.

"Check it out, Hitt. I understand completely where you comin' from, and the li'l homies're in violation for what they did." Big 9-Lives measured his words carefully. "But don't come down so hard on 'em. They're solid homies that made a mistake."

"That wasn't a mistake. That was some snake shit! Solid homies don't snake each other!" Hitter spewed. "I'm not being nearly as hard on 'em as I should. They didn't just disrespect Li'l Nine, but the whole machine."

"You right, cuzz, I'm not disputing that," Big 9-Lives negotiated, "but sometimes we got to correct and educate those who lack discipline and knowledge instead of tearing them down because they don't possess what we have. Look, since the whole machine's been violated, the hundred-twenty stacks should be divided between you, Wiz, and Li'l Nine, and if you feel they need to get put in the circle, then that's the call."

Hitter was shaking his head in disagreement before Big 9-Lives even finished the statement.

"It's ain't gonna happen," Hitter said. "Li'l Nine shoulda controlled those he included in the business. He's definitely not gonna get rewarded for his negligence, and this action, this call, don't have nothing to do with my brother. It's all me! When y'all slip and let shit like this happen, I clean it up, and when I gotta do the cleaning, I get the cleanup fee—period!"

"Shit can't always go your way," Wizard said, frustrated at his brother's stubbornness.

"Today it is," Hitter shot back.

"You know what?" Elijah finally spoke. "Hitt, I don't like the way you goin' about things. It's not what you say, but how you sayin' it. You not the only one who don't give a fuck around here. It's about respect, and I'm gonna get mine. With that being said, you're in the right. I shouldn't have let this happen on my watch, so you can have the money. As for putting them in the circle, that's not for the hood to do. This is my immediate circle, and I'll handle that. Agreed?"

Those who mattered in the room nodded their agreement, all except Hitter. He just stared in silence.

"I guess that's about it." Wizard looked around the room.

"It's a wrap then. We'll get together next month just to stay updated." Big 9-Lives concluded the meeting.

Everyone stood to pack up their phones, pagers, and pistols in preparation to leave. The serious issues were over. The tension that moments earlier was thick in the air had been replaced with small talk and jokes. A slow trek was being made to the front door as the visitors put on their jackets to face the morning frost.

A deafening crack of what sounded like a thick stick breaking in half startled everyone in the room. They all turned in the direction of the sound just as Li'l Teflon was crashing face first into the floor, already unconscious from Hitter's massive right hook to his chin. Big Teflon and Ju-Ju moved on instinct to his defense. Wizard was a split-second behind, grabbing Big Teflon in a mixed martial arts chokehold Big Teflon never saw coming. Before he could react, his lights were already being choked out. He wiggled and clawed at Wizard's arm, but it did no good; Wizard had already leveraged his weight against his back, placing him in an awkward position where he had no balance.

By the time Ju-Ju made it to within a few feet of Hitter, the dog sprung from his crouching position and launched into him. Ju-Ju had a brief second to throw his arm up in a last-ditch effort to protect his face from being mangled. The dog's teeth quickly sank into the soft tissue of his forearm and Ju-Ju let out a howl. The pit bull pulled downward, shaking its head violently back and forth in its death grip, trying to rip Ju-Ju's arm from his body.

"Get this fuckin' dog off me!" he shouted.

With bloodlust in his eyes, Hitter watched his dog at work.

Big 9-Lives snapped. "Nigga, you son-of-a-bitches better stop right fuckin' now in my house or everybody 'bout to die!" he said through gritted teeth, grabbing his .9mm off the table. "Hitter, get this goddamn dog before I kill it!"

Hitter watched for a minute before slowly turning to issue the command. "Chini," he said calmly.

The dog immediately released Ju-Ju and ran to stand beside his master. Big Teflon was nearly unconscious when Wizard let him go.

"Cuzz . . . fuck that! I ain't no bitch. Hitter, nigga you extra'd out." Ju-Ju was close to tears from being so angry. Blood poured from the gashing wound on his arm.

"Shut your bitch ass up," Hitter said in a casual manner. "If any of you niggas ever make a move toward me again like you want problems, you won't live to talk about it."

"Get the fuck out . . . all of you!" Big 9-Lives yelled.

Hitter popped his collar and smiled at Elijah on his way to the door. "Well, Nine, looks like the boys got put in the circle after all," he boasted smugly. "The Hitter's Circle!" He threw his head back and let out a loud, wicked laugh as he walked out to his truck. Hitter sped off the front lawn, jumped the curb, and raced up the block with "Reality" still rumbling through the speakers.

# CHAPTER NINETEEN

Elise and Diabla cruised down La Cienega Boulevard on their way to Fox Hills Mall in Culver City. Diabla wheeled the black-on-black Lexus coupe in and out of traffic like a seasoned getaway-car driver as Elise sat in the passenger seat bobbing her head to Brownstone's "Heard it Through the Grapevine." A silver convertible Mercedes Benz 600SL blew past them in the fast lane. Elise turned down the music and slapped Diabla's leg excitedly.

"That's him . . . that's him right there." Elise squirmed in her seat. "The one I told you about a few months ago from the party."

"Damn, bitch, calm down! Are you sure that's him?"

"Positive!"

"You are out of your mind stupid. Do you know who that is?"

"No, if I knew who he was, it wouldn't have taken me this long to tell you who I was talking about." Elise rolled her eyes.

"That's Li'l 9-Lives from Nine O. I can't believe you tried that and still got your life." Diabla shook her head. "If you would have included me in your plans, I could have warned your crazy ass not to try that. Maybe now you've learned your lesson about trying to do shit on your own."

Elise made a mock sad face and rubbed Diabla's cheek. "Don't be mad I didn't include you," she said.

"Stop playing, bitch," Diabla laughed.

Elise joined in on the laughter, "What's up with this 9-Lives nigga?" she asked, needing to get some more details on this 9-Lives character.

Diabla willingly gave her what little she knew about him. "From what I heard, Li'l 9-Lives is one of the most powerful Crips in LA and is not to be fucked with. He's not only rich, but has an army that will kill for him in a heartbeat. He's even got pull with the Mexican gangs in LA and Compton." The streets talked, and Diabla tried to always stay in the know. "You sure are interested in him," she said suspiciously. "You've been talking about him constantly since that night. You want to give him some pussy or something?"

Elise laughed hard at that. "Fuck no. That mutha-fucka nearly killed me, even though I probably had it coming." She put her little girl face and voice on. "Don't worry, you know I only want you kissin' this pussy, with your jealous ass."

Diabla blushed, peered up at the rearview mirror, and her smile suddenly turned into a look of concern. Elise read her expression and glanced away on instinct.

Diabla hit Elise's thigh and gestured for her to turn back around. "Don't look too obvious, but check out them *vatos* in that little gray bucket a few cars back on the right."

Elise nonchalantly peered through the passenger side mirror and spotted them. Three grimy-looking black dudes with hoodies on. Hoods pulled tight on a sunny California day couldn't have been more obvious that they were up to no good.

Diabla continued to watch the men as she waited for the stop light to turn green. She had noticed them trailing some time ago, about the time Elijah zipped past them.

"The passenger just reached down for something. I think those *vatos* are plotting on Li'l 9-Lives."

"Why do you think it's him?" Elise's hand edged toward her DKNY clutch purse.

"Because that's who they're watching. Every time he changes lanes, they do the same. And they are intentionally staying behind traffic so he can't see them," Diabla said, eyes constantly darting from the traffic ahead to the rearview.

Elise removed the .9mm from her purse and cocked one in the chamber.

"Catch up and pull beside him," she instructed while continuing to watch the men in their rear.

Diabla saw that look in her eyes—the eyes of a she-devil. When those greenish-blue eyes took on that look, Diabla knew not to ask questions and simply did what she was told. She smashed the gas around traffic and caught up to Elijah.

A blunt dangled from his lips as he vibed to the music, and when he saw Elise's face, it surprised him. The light turned green, he smirked, and smashed off.

Diabla smashed behind him as Elise waved frantically for him to slow down and roll down the window.

*I can't believe I'm seeing her again. What she tryin' to do, rob me while we driving?* he thought in amusement. Then he noticed the urgency in her face, so he slowed for them to catch up. Clutching a .357 Desert Eagle in his lap, he rolled down the window halfway.

"What?" he said, as the car continued rolling at a snail's pace.

"Them cats in that gray car following you."

"What, you my guardian angel or something?" he said sarcastically. "I know they following me. I'm waitin' on 'em to play pussy so I can fuck 'em." His eyes darted to the rearview to keep watch on the enemy's position. "Thanks for the heads-up, but mind your business, little girl."

Elijah sped off, cut in front of them, and put on his left turn signal.

"Follow him!" Elise ordered.

Diabla tried to protest. "This none of our business. Plus, he just told us not to get involved."

Elise looked at her with deadly eyes. "Shut up and do what I said."

Diabla, clearly frustrated, put on her left turn signal. The gray bucket did the same a second later.

Once oncoming traffic cleared, Elijah made the turn onto Stocker with the Lexus right behind him. The light changed from yellow to red as the bucket swung onto Stocker almost causing an accident, rapidly picked up speed. By the time they neared the rear of the Lexus, Elise saw that the passenger had donned a blue bandana over his nose and mouth. It was about to go down!

"Get over and let 'em pass on my side," she instructed Diabla.

The bucket darted to the right and passed the Lexus. Up ahead, Elijah took another left onto a side street that led inside the "Jungles," a territory of the B.P.S. Bloods. His pursuers slowed to make the turn as well.

Before they got fully into the turn, Elise raised out of the convertible top and began filling their car with gunfire. The shots were deafening; the car rocked back and forth violently as the slugs penetrated windows and exterior. The driver ducked under the dashboard and smashed the accelerator to the floor. The car shot through the corner diagonally and collided into a big curbside tree. The front window exploded and the car's front end folded in like a crushed soda can. Antifreeze and water sprayed upward in a plume of steam.

Diabla turned behind them so Elise could continue the assault. The .9mm recoiled in her hand, as used shell casings ejected onto the concrete as she emptied the entire nineteen shots.

By the time she was finished, Elijah was running up the sidewalk toward the wreckage, Desert Eagle in hand. Her stunt had thrown a monkey wrench in his own plan. He was intending to surprise them when they made the turn by being on foot, the car parked halfway up the block. Either way, it still worked in his favor. Running to the passenger side of the wrecked car with his gun drawn, he saw no movement. Cautiously, he reached inside and nudged the unconscious passenger's head backward against the rest, using the barrel of the gun to lower the bandana to get a look at his would-be killer's face. "Punk mutha-fucka!" he muttered to himself. It was one of Li'l Crip's homies from U.G.

"You know them?" Elise startled him. He turned to see her peering over his shoulder at her deadly work.

"What the fuck you doin'? Get the fuck outta here!" he yelled, turning back to the carnage.

The passenger's eyes fluttered as he tried to regain consciousness, and a slight moan escaped his mouth. Elijah looked to him, to Elise, then back at him again. Leaning closely he whispered, "Oh, you still alive, huh? When you get to hell, tell Lucifer he owes me one for giving you a ride back home."

He put the Desert Eagle to his head, then paused. Elise was present; he turned to see her watching and he was shocked at her demeanor. There was no fear, no panic evident on her face, only an anticipation of death. He pulled the drawstrings on his hoodie tighter and nodded his head.

"Finish ya dirty work," he said.

"I'm out of bullets," she said casually.

He looked both ways before handing her his gun. She accepted without hesitation. He turned and trotted back to the Benz.

One shot from the small cannon seemed to echo throughout LA. *One point for the bad guy,* Elijah thought. He jumped in the driver's seat and went to drop it in gear when the passenger door flew open and Elise plopped in the seat beside him with the gun still smoking. Her breath raced as she slammed the door shut. Even though he wanted to, there was no time to curse and kick her out. They'd been at the crime scene for far too long already. He dropped it in drive and got ghost.

After making it a few blocks away from the crime scene, his adrenaline began to slow, and he turned to look at her like the crazy bitch she was. "Where did your ride go?"

She stared out the window emotionless, in a sort of daze. "I told her to leave when I got out to make sure you were alright. I didn't want our car to be there too long. Somebody could've gotten the license plate number."

"Shit! Why didn't you just leave instead of getting in my way?" He maneuvered quickly through the Jungles, eyes everywhere at once watching for any signs of police and the Ghetto Bird.

Elise shrugged her shoulders as she stared out the window. "I don't know."

He gave her a double-take. There were no words potent enough to reach the mysterious creature that occupied his passenger seat. With eyes shifting back and forth between her and traffic, he reached over and eased the pistol out her hand. She released it without ever turning to face him. The clouds gathered covering the sun as they rode in silence into the evening.

Li'l Teflon sat slumped in the puffy black leather couch, house shoes kicked up on the coffee table, blunt dangling from his lips as he did battle with his brother in NBA-JAM. Big Teflon worked the controller, cursing at the TV and the animated Michael Jordan from the edge of the couch. The surround sound turned the living room into a real arcade. Ju-Ju had just received a phone call and stepped in the hallway to hear clearly.

Ju-Ju rushed back into the room animated. "The U.G.s and Li'l Crip just tried to hit Li'l Nine over by the Jungles."

Big Teflon immediately dropped the game controller and stood at attention. "Tell me Li'l Nine alright," he said.

"Lady Rawdog said that Li'l Nine's good. The U.G.s caught the bad end of the stick," Ju-Ju explained.

Big Teflon scrambled frantically for his keys. "We gotta get to the hood and catch up with the homie. Niggas gotta pay."

"Hold up, nigga," Li'l Teflon said. "We not 'bout to run out there like chickens with our heads cut off for that dude. You act like you forgot that nigga didn't ride with us when Wiz and Hitter took off and his dog almost tore your fuckin' arm off."

"What the fuck you talking about? Nigga, that's—"

"What I'm talking about is that this shit ain't over!" Li'l Teflon cut Ju-Ju off. "Them niggas gotta pay. We can't handle our business with Hitter and join in Li'l Nine's war at the same time. Nine O ain't got beef with U.G.s; they our allies. What them dudes got goin' on is between them. To keep it 900, I don't give a fuck if they would've got that nigga. He ain't with us no more."

Big Teflon and Ju-Ju couldn't believe what just came from his mouth. It was true that they didn't agree with or like what happened with the Hitter situation, but at times a man had to be big enough to admit his wrongs and accept the consequences of his actions. The bottom line was they were wrong for going to Oklahoma shitting where the homies were eating. In hindsight, it wasn't even necessary, because they were already eating good anyway. To blame Elijah and wish him dead was going too far.

"Li'l Nine is my nigga," Ju-Ju stated, "and I'm ridin' with him. We were in the wrong, accept it! We lucky the homies didn't smoke us behind that shit; we got a pass. Stop looking at Li'l Nine as our childhood runnin' buddy. Cuzz is a boss and can't put us first all the time."

"He ain't my mutha-fuckin' boss!" Li'l Teflon leaned back in the couch and continued the video game.

"You on some bullshit, I'm outta here." Ju-Ju grabbed his strap, cell phone, car keys, and headed out the door.

Big Teflon looked at his brother. Seeing that he had no intentions of moving, he turned and followed Ju-Ju. After they left, Li'l Teflon peeked through the mini blinds. Certain they were gone, he flipped open his cell phone and punched in a number. It was answered on the fourth ring.

"What the fuck happened, cuzz?" Li'l Teflon barked.

"Shit. It got all fucked up. I don't have all the details yet, but from what I gathered so far it's all bad. What about you? What've you heard?"

"The same as you, not much. When I get more info, I'll let you know. What's the progress on Hitter?"

"After how all this went, we gotta hold off on Hitter for now. I'm about to get real low, you feel me? So, won't be no need to hit this number after today."

"Fuck all that. We push forward like we agreed. When shit goes wrong, we just regroup and go at it from a different angle."

"Man, you must didn't hear what I just said. I'm about to get low. I'm outta here! If you wanna press your luck further, be my guest. Good luck, cuzz!" The phone went dead.

"Hello? Li'l Crip? Hello? Fuck!" Li'l Teflon threw the cell phone against the wall in frustration. He would make sure the job was done not matter what it took.

# CHAPTER TWENTY

Elijah pulled the Benz to the front of a six-story condominium complex off Fountain and Whitley Avenue, a nice enclave at the foot of the Hollywood Hills. He dialed a number from his cell and a few seconds later the gate to the underground parking stalls clicked and slowly slid open. The Benz disappeared into the bottom of the complex and parked next to a pearl-white Range Rover. He and Elise got out and entered the elevator. When they exited the sixth floor, a bleached-blonde white girl with the looks of Pamela Anderson and the body of Melyssa Ford waited by an open door. She wore USC sweatpants, house slippers, and an oversized T-shirt that was so tight it seemed like her breasts were trying to escape. Her face lit up with joy when Elijah stepped into view.

"Hey, Daddy." She stood on her tippy-toes to hug him around the neck.

He wrapped his arms around her lower back and lifted her off the ground with a kiss on the neck. "What's up, Snow Bunny?" he said, lowered her back down, and slapped her on the ass.

She giggled in delight. It was the kind of encounter you watched with a smile simply because it is so rare that people genuinely enjoy one another. Noticing Elise, he girl paused with a curious look.

"Oh, my bad." Elijah said nonchalantly. "This is . . . Assata," he pointed to Elise. "Assata, this is Snow Bunny."

She hit his arm playfully, "Don't listen to that 'Snow Bunny' stuff. My name is Lauren," she said, extending her hand to Elise.

Elise looked her up and down with a touch of disdain. "Hey," she said dry as sand before finally shaking Lauren's hand.

Lauren acted as if she didn't detect the rudeness. She turned to Elijah all smiles again. "Why didn't you let me know you were coming so I could've cooked."

"You already know how I am, always spur-of-the-moment," he answered.

"And why haven't you been answering my calls for the past month, fucker?" she asked with a knowing smile.

"Ah, my phone's been messin' up. I didn't get any calls from you. You sure it was me you called?" He smiled to highlight the obvious bullshit he was shooting her way.

Spinning her around, he hugged and kissed her neck again as he guided her into the room. She gave him tender slaps and pinches on the arm. "Your lying ass." She laughed. "You think you can tell me anything. It's alright you're going to call on me one day and I'm going to ignore your ass too."

Elijah smashed his face against hers and bit her earlobe. "Who you tryin' to fool? You can never ignore me. I don't care if you marry one of those corporate clowns you fuck with. You'll always be my bitch!"

"Oh my god!" She broke free from his grasp, laughing. "Don't be saying that in front of guests. You're so rude."

He waved her off. "Don't try to act modest all of a sudden."

He walked to the kitchen and popped open the fridge. Pulling out a family-sized bottle of Ocean Spray Cranberry Juice, he drank straight from the container. "Run me a bath and get me a fresh change a clothes," he told her between gulps. "You do still have some of my clothes, don't you?" he asked.

"Of course, what you think, I'd throw your stuff away for dodging my calls?" she asked sarcastically.

"Girl, ain't nobody dodged your calls. I had to ask because you know you have company sometimes and may need to hide my presence from your little boyfriends."

She rolled her eyes and turned to go carry out his instructions, but not before pausing to give Elise a quick once over.

Elijah copped a squat next to Elise on the plush white sofa and began breaking down some weed on the coffee table.

"Assata, huh?" Elise grunted with an attitude.

He continued with what he was doing. "What was I supposed to say, 'This is the no-name girl'?"

"No, you were supposed to have asked my name before we got here so you would know it when you introduce me to people. It's Elise if you care to know."

"Alright Elise! Your name is Assata to me, so that's what I'll call you. I guess you already know who I am."

"I don't like that name," she protested. "Yeah, I know who you are, *Li'l 9-Lives*."

"If you knew history you would learn who Assata Shakur is and be honored I call you that. Anyways, I don't recall asking you what you like."

Elise sucked her teeth in protest. "I don't care who 'Assata' is. I like my own name thank you.

Elijah ignored her sassy attitude; he needed to know some things. He got straight to the point of asking her a litany of questions: "Who is ol' girl that was driving with you? Where she from? Is she solid? Who name is that Lex in? I need you to tell me everything." There was no time for beating around the bush; he had to know if there were any loose ends that could lead back to her, which would ultimately lead to him.

Elise, on the other hand, felt completely insulted by the interrogation. "What? You think I'm a rat or some kinda weak-ass bitch? You acting like I'd be a liability if shit was to go down." She was furious and she let him know it in no uncertain terms. "You got me fucked up. Not only am I solid, my homegirl Diabla is as solid as they come too. Any concerns you have about the Lexus and Diabla, you can get outta your mind. They're my responsibility and I'll handle it."

Elijah gave no reaction to her ranting and raving; seemingly, his sole focus was getting the information he asked for and breaking down the weed in front of him on the table.

"Don't worry about my end," she said. "I know you think you're God Almighty and the world revolves around you, but it doesn't. This ain't the first work I've put in. I've been busting heads before you jumped off the porch."

*This broad done lost her mind,* he thought. *People don't talk to me like this.*

"Slow your roll," he cautioned, having heard just about enough from her.

But Elise wasn't quite finished. "I ain't slowing nothing," she snapped. "I put myself out there for you. You ought to be thanking me that I didn't let them fools ride up on your slippin' ass and unload a clip in your face. You know what? Go take your little bubble bath that your 'Snow Bunny' is running, let her dress you, and please take me the fuck home!"

Elijah dropped the task of breaking down the weed and gave her a sideward stare. "First off, I don't need to thank you for shit. I didn't ask you to play cowgirl out there. As far as me slipping—never! I'm going to tell you this because I don't never want you thinking you know how I move or that you did me some hell-of-a favor. All of my whips are bulletproofed!"

Elise was even more pissed. She didn't like not having the last word.

Elijah grunted. "Why you think I only rolled my window down halfway when you flagged me down? Catch up, smart ass! Whatever them suckas thought they were gonna do, it sure wasn't going to be emptying a clip in my face – I stay on point!" He went back to rolling his blunt.

"Like you did something," he mumbled to himself. He paused and looked at her with a second thought. "And where you get this bullshit that you've been puttin' in work before I jumped off the porch? You ain't did shit before me. I was born into this street life. I was puttin' in work and seeing death when you was playing with Barbie dolls and counting the new strands of hair on your pussy."

Elise laughed involuntarily. Recovering quickly, she tried to put her mad face back on only to break form again with a second bout of laughter. "What the fuck ever dude," she half snickered. "If you've been puttin' in so much work, why didn't you handle that sucka today instead of having me do it?"

"First, answer why you done it when you didn't have to."

Elise grew serious for a moment. "I don't . . . don't know exactly. I guess I felt I owed you one. You spared my life that night when you had all the right to take it. You showed me kindness I never experienced from a man before."

"Is that right?" He studied her. "Reason I let you finish that dirty work out there is because one, I don't know you like that to blow somebody's brains out in front of you. And two, you owed me one."

She stared, not knowing what to think of him as he lit the blunt. "I guess we're even now. What's next?"

Before he could give her a response, his cell phone vibrated on the table. He picked up to Ju-Ju's voice, upset and animated, "We gotta get with them U.G. bitch-ass mutha-fuckas right now!"

Big Teflon could be heard in the background seconding Ju-Ju's sentiments, "Hell yeah! Them niggas violated!"

Elijah tried to calm them down. "Y'all chill. We gotta wait to hear from Unc and them before making any moves."

Ju-Ju and Big Teflon weren't trying to hear it. "I say we meet up now. Fuck all that waitin' shit," Ju-Ju piped in.

Meanwhile, Elise was busy looking around assessing Lauren's condo as she halfway eavesdropped on his conversation. She rubbed the soft couch in admiration and wondered what type of fabric it was. The artwork was nice too, except for the painting of a woman burning at the stake. *Why in the hell would she buy that?* The furniture and furnishings were all nice, but probably cost a fortune. *She's probably one of his little sugar babies he takes care of. All she gotta do is look pretty and spread her legs when he says so . . .* "Yes, Daddy! No, Daddy!" Elise mimicked with disdain. *Well, at least she has good taste, not as good as mine though.*

"Snow?" Elijah called out.

Elise jumped, jolted from her little mental venture.

Elijah instructed Lauren, "Set up the special line for a conference call with the fellas." He turned to Elise. "You hungry?"

"A little bit."

"Good, make us some sandwiches or something." He leaned back with the remote and began flipping channels on the big screen.

*The audacity of this dude,* she thought. *I need to slap him upside his head. Maybe he'd have some damn sense then.*

"This ain't my house. I can't go in somebody's kitchen and just start cooking."

"When I'm here this is my house. So you not cookin' in just anybody's house, you cookin' in mine." Reluctantly, she got to her feet and went to the kitchen.

Lauren came from the backroom with the phone system with all its' scrambler devices and wiretap detector units attached. After Lauren set up everything, she went to the kitchen to help Elise.

The phone rang. Elijah pushed the intercom button and the speaker crackled to life with all the fellas already there.

"Nephew?" Big 9-Lives spoke with worry in his voice.

"Whaddup, Unc?" Elijah confirmed he was on the line.

"You straight, Li'l Nine?" Wizard was next to confirm his presence.

"Yeah, I'm straight," Elijah reassured, then filled them in on the details of the day including the 'divine intervention of Elise,' as he called it. The U.G.s were the culprits and the main topic of discussion.

"They want it with us like that, huh?" Big 9-Lives speculated.

"I guess so. It's time to make 'em believers," Elijah added.

"*Salaamu alaikum,*" Hitter broke in the call with the slow, deep greeting.

"*Wa alaikum assalaam,*" Wizard returned the greetings, then caught him up on what he'd missed so far. It wasn't necessary to go into all the details of the hit because Lady Rawdog had already given Hitter the run down on that part. She somehow always knew all the hood gossip before anyone else.

"I'm proud of you, soldier." Hitter was excited. "The results were beautiful. I couldn't have handled it better myself."

"To keep it 900, it wasn't my work," said Elijah, "You remember the broad we gave the pass at the party, Hitter?"

"Yeah, yeah, how could I not? I wanted to fuck her and break her neck at the same time. I don't meet women that make me react that way much."

"Yeah, well, she happened to be in the area when it all went down. She performed like a real Budlong Ave."

"Sounds like my kinda girl!" Hitter laughed.

Wizard broke into their little light moment. "Y'all need to quit all that bullshittin' around, because this is some serious shit. I'm gonna have Li'l Wiz come back from Iowa to take care of the retaliations. That way Li'l Nine can lay low until the entire picture becomes clear. Y'all know that Li'l Wiz's specialty is getting his hands dirty in the trenches."

The conference call went silent for a moment. After the pregnant pause, Elijah said what some of the others were thinking. "Don't get me wrong, I appreciate your intentions, Wiz, but I'd rather handle it myself. No disrespect, but Li'l Wiz kinda creep me out and I don't get the creeps easily."

Wizard was a little offended. "Li'l Wiz's as solid as they come, strictly 'bout the business. What the hell you mean the homie give you the creeps? What type of shit is that?"

Elijah took the liberty to explain. "Li'l Wiz take shit too far at times. I took him on a collection mission once. It was supposed to be a simple approach and pressure on the cat who owed. Next thing I knew, he was cutting off fingers and torturing the poor bastard. It's one thing to be a warrior and totally another thing to be a lightweight serial killer. For real, cuzz, it wouldn't surprise me to find out that nigga be eating people like Jeffrey Dahmer or Ted Bundy or some shit."

Everybody on the call burst out laughing except Elijah.

"Y'all niggas think I'm joking. I'm dead serious!" Elijah said.

"I know you serious. It's just the way you said it that's funny." Hitter tried to regain some sense of seriousness, "Look, I don't fuck with Li'l Wiz either. I don't like, or should I say, don't approve of his methods, but you know what? I think y'all overreacting to the situation."

"Fuck you mean?" Big 9-Lives asked.

Hitter explained. "My contacts in the 100s gave me the news that Li'l Crip already skipped town. Going at the U.G.s without Li'l Crip being around defeats the purpose. The U.G.s are the ones who lost homies while Elijah and our squad is still living life. We the winners. My solution is that we should leave it alone for now, act like we don't know the U.G.s was behind the hit. Once Li'l Crip resurfaces, we cut off his balls and mail them to his wife—problem solved."

"Nah!" Elijah immediately disagreed. "We got to let the streets know they can't take shots at us and get away with it. An example must be made!"

"Hell yeah!" Big 9-Lives and Wizard seconded Elijah's opinion.

"Aw, stop beatin' your chest with the King Kong shit," Hitter chided. "You niggas gettin' all emotional and taking a little gun play street politics personal. You act like you ain't never been shot at before. It's just business. Li'l Crip felt if he knocked us down, he'd strengthen himself. It's nothing personal in that. Respect his hustle! Just be patient, his time gonna come. Until then be thankful for your victory and live life. I'll be in town next week. We'll go to the U.G.s' funeral to pay our respects."

As everyone said their good-byes, the line again plunged into an empty silence.

Elijah got up and stretched. He walked to the kitchen to see what Elise had going. The smell of beef and spices made his mouth water. She was just removing the French fries from the hot grease when he entered. She put them on a plate, sprinkled some Lawry's seasoning salt, then dropped some shredded cheddar cheese over the top. Sliced jalapenos, red peppers, and diced bell peppers were then added. She coupled the cheese fries with a jalapeno-laced thick juicy hamburger, then lettuce, pickles and tomatoes were placed on the side of the bun.

"You can add your own mayo or mustard," she said, handing him the plate.

"Thanks, I didn't think you could cook," he joked.

"What would make you think that?" she asked while making her own plate.

Elijah laughed. "Just didn't think women of violence could be cooks too."

"Just because you can't cook," she said, "don't put that jacket on me."

"I don't know what you talkin' 'bout, I'm a beast in the kitchen, on the grill too!"

"Yeah, right." She laughed. "If you can be a killer and cook, why can't I?"

"I'm one of a kind," he boasted. "Multi-talented." He smiled and bit into the burger. He had to pause for a hard swallow. It was good, but spicy as hell. He took a sip of juice and went back in on the burger.

"I know you don't like me, but damn, you didn't have to try and burn my mouth up." he joked.

"What you expect? I'm a Belizean who lived with Mexicans. Of course my food's gonna be spicy."

"Belizean, huh? I knew you had a different look to you." He looked down at his plate as he chewed. "Damn, this is good as hell. You got a nice li'l cookin' hand to you."

Lauren came out and announced, "Your bath is ready."

"Come taste this." He waved her over to try the food. Lauren grabbed the half-eaten burger from his plate and bit into it, handed it to him, then took some fries from Elise's plate. Elise's first instincts were to check her, but she caught herself and let it go.

"You guys are going to have me fat eating like this," Lauren said. "I'll have to jog a few extra miles in the morning to work this off."

"You good, ain't nothing wrong with a couple extra pounds on that ass," Elijah said.

Lauren smiled from ear to ear. "Shut up!" she teased.

"I'm gonna take a bath and get a quick hour of shut-eye. I'm burnt out. It's been a long day. Is it cool if I take you home a li'l later, Assata?"

"Do you," she said, still not appreciating him calling her that.

Taking another handful of cheese fries and stuffing them in his mouth, he headed for the master bedroom. Lauren ate a little more before showing Elise her music selection, giving her the remote, and retiring to the room with Elijah.

⁂

Sitting back in the Jacuzzi bathtub, Elijah tried to calm his thoughts. He closed his eyes to relax, a bit of meditation. It only lasted a brief moment before Lauren interrupted, "Hey, baby. Did you fall asleep in there?"

He opened his eyes to her sensually sliding off her sweatpants. After she tossed them to the side, she lifted off the snug-fitted T-shirt exposing perfectly sculpted breast, tossing it as well. Her blonde hair spilled down her back and around her shoulders as she walked over to grab a washcloth and body scrub. Stepping down into the tub, she sat close, facing him. She squeezed the scrub into her right palm, applied it to his neck and torso, and used the washcloth to scrub the area lightly. She stared into his eyes as she worked her hands lower with the scrub and washcloth. The sight of her naked body already turned him on immensely, and her touch only intensified things. His erection didn't escape her attention; her hand found his dick under the water and stroked it intimately.

She leaned in to kiss him softly on the lips; her wet tongue slipped into his mouth. He sucked and tasted it lightly. She removed the stopper and turned the hot water on full blast to keep it leveled. Beginning her descent, she licked and sucked on his chest, her long hair brushing against his skin. Her kitten-like tongue gave him goose bumps. "Damn, baby," he whispered.

She looked up at him like a sexy white tigress, making sure he saw what she was about to do. She licked his shaft like an ice cream cone.

"I've missed you, Elijah. Did you miss me?" she cooed before licking the tip.

"Yeah, you know Daddy miss this shit."

She melted at the sound of his voice. She let out a moan, closed her eyes, and deep-throated his entire eight inches. His head rolled back in ecstasy as she bobbed up and down with a slow, methodical rhythm, changing angles with each stroke. She seemed to be enjoying it more than him. She moaned from the sensation pleasuring him gave her. Using her hand, she stroked and sucked at the same time, picking up the pace, twisting, pulling . . . the sounds of her hand and saliva mixing turned them both on even more.

"Oh, shit, bitch," he breathed. "Get it . . . get this dick." He grabbed the back of her head and guided her through the motions.

Lauren sucked harder and faster. He watched her with lust-filled admiration as she performed her technique with flawless mastery. As if she felt his eyes on her, she looked up at him without breaking her rhythm, taking him to heaven while she looked into his eyes.

Reaching his breaking point, he grabbed a handful of her hair and pressed down roughly on her head. She moaned. He moaned louder and deeper, his body tensed as he shot long and hard in her mouth. She held still and accepted it like it was juicy nectar.

Body slackened, he opened his eyes to find her watching him with his flesh still in her mouth. She slowly released and kissed it. "Thank you, Daddy," she whispered.

This wasn't over; he was still aroused. Exiting the tub, he lifted her out as if she weighed nothing. She wrapped her legs around him as he carried her dripping wet to the bed and laid her on her back. She threw open her legs. He took notice of her flawlessly pedicured feet. Yeah, it was on!

He climbed on top of her, gently licking her breast with the flat part of his tongue, sliding further down until he was face to face with her soft, pink wet pussy. The walls and lips were dripping with moisture waiting for him. He inserted two fingers inside her and moved the index finger in an upward motion, causing her back to arch and a moan to escape her lips. Both fingers slid in and out in a constant rhythm. She thrusted her body in concert with them.

"Yes, Daddy, yes. You make my pussy feel so good! Yes, Daddy, nobody makes me feel like you do," she chanted.

He slipped his tongue in the top of her slit to play with her clit as he fingered her. "Elijah! Elijah!" She cried out his name over and over. Juices overflowed from her delicious, pink pussy and he lapped up the juices like it was life-giving waters.

Abruptly he pulled back and flipped her on her stomach. She arched her lower back, raising her ass slightly to give him better access. She looked back over her shoulder as she waited. "Come on, Daddy, get it!" she demanded with aggression.

He obliged her. Shivers ran through her body as she buried her face in the pillow and he began his smooth glide backward and forward. "Deeper, Daddy, deeper!" she begged for more, which he gave her with each glide. He always teased her with the dick first to make her beg for it all. She pressed her ass hard against him, trying to force her way from her stomach to her knees. He knew what she wanted but prolonged it a little longer. After a few minutes, he relented and pulled her into the doggy-style position, slapping her ass cheek savagely.

"Oh, shit yeah!" she cried out.

He grabbed her roughly by the hips and plunged into her, using the length of himself to pull nearly all the way out before plunging into her again, slapping her even harder.

"Whose pussy is this?"

"Ooooh, Daddy, it's yours. It'll always be yours!"

"Throw it at me then like its mine, bitch."

She backed into him with all she had. They caught a rhythm and their bodies collided with a constant smacking sound. "Oh my God! You killing this shit . . . yes . . . yes! Punish me . . . punish your bitch, Daddy!" He continued to give her a real Hoodsta Street nigga-fucking. This was what she couldn't get from the square corporate types.

After beating it up doggy style, he turned her on her back again to enter her missionary style. They looked into one another's eyes as he delivered long powerful strokes.

"You like looking in my eyes when you come in me, huh?" she whispered, rolling her hips in rhythm with his strokes.

"You know I do. I love lookin' at ya sexy-ass face when I fill you up with this hard-ass dick." They moaned and talked dirty as they satisfied each other's hunger.

"You 'bout to make me come!" he said.

She picked up the intensity of her grinding against his hardness. "Come on, Daddy, come for your bitch. Shoot it all in this pussy, Daddy."

With three more deep thrusts, his entire body locked up and began to convulse. "Oh shit! Ohhhhhh!"

Worn out, he collapsed on top of her, both breathing heavily. Her hair was pasted to her face and shoulders from sweat. She kissed him lightly on his shoulder blade, wanting to cuddle, but he had no interest in cuddling. He rolled off her and they both fell into a deep sleep.

Irritated by what she felt was fake theatrics coming from Lauren in the next room, Elise combed through the music selection and chose Sade's greatest hits to drown out the excessive moaning and screaming. She put on the oversized headphones and dozed off to "Sweetest Taboo."

# CHAPTER TWENTY-ONE

"Let me get a box of Phillies and some Swisher Sweets," Elijah said to the Arab cashier as he ate from an open bag of Skittles. The 7-11 mini mart was empty except for the two of them. Elijah pulled out a wad of bills and placed a twenty on the counter for the items. The cashier made no move to take the money, standing stark still looking Elijah in the eye with a diabolical smile.

"What the fuck up with you?" Elijah asked, confused. The cashier continued to smile and stare. Words began to resonate in Elijah's ears from the cashier even though his mouth remained closed.

"You tell me, my servant," the words traveled.

"Servant? Who you callin' servant, bitch?" Elijah reached for his waistband but the pistol wasn't there. Suddenly, the Arab's eyes turned a burning bright red. Elijah stepped back cautiously.

"Give me what you owe!" came the voice, deep and ominous. Without moving his legs or leaning forward, the Arab's hands stretched across the counter and snatched him in a death grip, and the counter that once separated them disappeared, bringing the two face to face.

The man's face began to melt yet the eyes continued to blaze fiercely. Elijah struggled to break free as the face transformed into features, part-man, part-goat, horns on top of its head. It laughed demonically as Elijah made his futile attempt at getting loose. He felt like an infant in the grasp of the beast.

"Give me what you owe!" it roared again.

A terrified scream emerged from Elijah's core. The grip abruptly released.

Elijah wasted no time sprinting for the door. He glanced back to see the beast dissolve into three smaller demons that immediately started chasing him. He ran with all his might yet his feet seemed to not move fast enough. He suddenly remembered that he could fly in this world. Taking to the air, he traveled instantaneously to a different time and place.

The scenery changed from city to a breathtaking green countryside. He landed in an open field surrounded by the most beautiful flowers and butterflies imaginable. He walked over a hill and came upon a crystal-clear lake with exotic fish swimming freely at the bottom with the plant life. He sat next to the lake feeling a peace that he'd never experienced before.

Out of nowhere, his pit bull that died years ago, ran up beside him. She looked renewed, vigorous, far from the sick dog he had watched wither away. "Hey, Ne-Ne!" He rubbed her head and ears as she jumped into his arms.

"Hello my child," a voice came from his rear. He turned around startled. His mom stood before him dressed in all white, so pure, so lovely. A light seemed to emanate from her presence.

"Momma?" She nodded and smiled. He ran to embrace her with tears running down his cheeks. "Momma, where've you been? I've missed you so much!" She looks just like he remembered, but even more radiant. Her skin glowed and her eyes glistened with joy. There was an aura of peace and strength that permeated through her body to his.

"I know, baby." She rubbed his back. "I've missed you, too, but don't worry yourself when you don't see me, I'm always close. I told you I'd always be with you."

"Don't leave no more, Momma," he cried. "If you leave again I want to come with you."

"You can't come right now. You still have duties to fulfill."

"I don't want the duties. I want to be with you. I'm tired Momma, so tired." He held on to her with all his strength not wanting to ever let her go again.

Hands placed on his shoulders, she strongly pushed him back to stare into his eyes. With a stern tone she admonished him, "Never speak like that again. There is no time to be tired. Weaklings give in to tiredness. God's warriors press on, never neglecting their duties."

Elijah, shocked by her outburst, questioned, "What are my duties? Why is God putting me through so much pain? I'm tired, confused, and lost. I need rest."

"'Why'; is a coward's question," she scolded. "Endure what you must and let God lead your path. You don't have to be perfect but you must work towards perfecting the mind and spirit. You have the power, but the power is a gift and a curse—perfect the gift, son . . ."

"Fatima, we have to go." Elijah turned to the unexpected voice of his uncle Cannon.

"Unc? Damn, what's up, cuzz?" Elijah stammered. —

Cannon smiled. "You look good, Elijah." He paused, hearing something in the distance. "Continue your march, soldier, and never forget that we love you." Cannon looked toward the sky as a shadow began to spread. "Me and your mother have to go. Take care of yourself. There is much evil ahead."

*Whooo . . . whooo . . .*

With his eyes, Elijah followed the sound to a huge Redwood tree that stretched far into the sky. On one of the branches sat a freakishly large owl watching him with the eyes of an evil man. It sent shivers down his spine. When he turned back to his mom and uncle, they were gone. Looking toward the woods, he caught a glimpse of them accompanied by a short light-skinned woman just as they were entering the brush. The unknown woman turned to stare at him; she had the same greenish-blue eyes as Elise. After a long pause, she turned and disappeared along with the others.

"There he is!" came a shout.

Elijah looked to see an army of men with weapons charging out of the hills toward him.

"Get him!" one of them howled.

"Come on, cuzz, this way." Elijah felt a tug on his arm; it was Li'l Teflon. He ran through the brush; on instinct, Elijah ran behind him. He could hear the men's footsteps and calls behind them; they were gaining ground. They were certainly going to be caught.

Elijah wished he had his pistol . . . wish granted—a pistol appeared in his right hand. He stopped to let off a few shots. He had to slow his pursuers down. But when he squeezed the trigger nothing happened. He began running again, at the same time trying to unjam the gun. Finally, a bullet succeeded in sliding into the chamber. He turned and squeezed again—nothing!

"This way, cuzz." Li'l Teflon detoured down a well-hidden pathway. As soon as Elijah reached the path, the scenery shifted to a desert in the middle of nowhere.

"Just a little further," said Li'l Teflon. "right over that hill."

They hurried toward a little sand hill. Just as they made it to the top, a gigantic bull with fiery red eyes and smoke coming from his nostrils was waiting for them. The bull had facial features like that of a man and horns long and sharp. It locked eyes with Elijah and charged.

Li'l Teflon laughed and disappeared into thin air, leaving Elijah to do battle with the beast. His fear quickly turned to anger and rage. He raised the pistol and charged the bull head on. Within a few feet he squeezed the trigger. Nothing! The gun was useless. He needed another weapon, which was granted. Instantly, the hatchet he and his three friends had stolen from their first robbery appeared in his opposite hand. He launched into the air and swung with all his might. "Ugh!" he grunted.

The blade of the hatchet embedded into the forehead of the creature. It absorbed the blow and countered with a wild plunge, ripping a hole in the flesh of Elijah's thigh. The bull then made a full turn, scraped the sand with its hooves, and charged again.

With the hatchet still stuck in the bull's head, Elijah was weaponless. He knew that death was certain and braced himself for the blow. "Come on, mutha-fucka!" he yelled as he beat on his chest.

"Elijah?"

Elijah looked up to see Elise standing on a plateau fifty yards away. She threw something his way that reached his hands instantly—the .357 Desert Eagle she'd used to kill earlier. Immediately, he jacked one in the chamber. The bull was inches away. It dipped its head and aimed its horns directly for his heart.

*Bang, bang, bang.*

Three slugs ripped through the bull's head as momentum still carried it forward.

"No!" Elise screamed, her echo carrying across the empty desert as the horns slammed into his chest.

"Elijah bolted straight up, grabbing for the hole in his chest. His head was pounding and sweat soaked the sheets beneath him. He looked around. Lauren was still sound asleep. He slowly laid his head back on the pillow.

In the living room, Elise was jolted from her sleep as well. Sweat dampened her hair, her heart beating rapidly as tears rolled from her eyes. "It was only a dream," she whispered. "Only a dream." She laid back into the softness of the couch, staring at the ceiling. Sade's "Your Love is King" played as she drifted back into a dreamless sleep.

Elijah woke up a couple hours later to Lauren giving him head. A nice consolation prize for the nightmares he had earlier. As always, her gorgeous face and supreme head game sent him over the top before he knew it. They hit the shower together. He had to cleanse himself of not just the sex but of all the day's events.

Feeling fresh, he slipped on the brand new Girbaud jeans, socks, and Rockport shoes Lauren had laid out for him. Lauren lingered in the bathroom getting her hair and makeup together. He walked back in as she stood naked in the mirror. Hugging her from behind, he kissed her neck. She tilted her head to give him access to another. They locked eyes in the mirror as he gave her a quizzical gaze. *How can creatures so beautiful be so wicked?* he thought. They enjoyed the sight of one another for a while before he broke the spell. Kissing her cheek, he loosened his embrace.

"Don't take too long," he told her. "We need to get to the restaurant at least forty minutes before closing time. Oh yeah, get Assata an outfit and shoes to wear. Y'all 'bout the same size, —your titties and ass is just a li'l bigger."

"I told you to stop talking about me being fat."

He wasn't about to stroke her ego. She knew that she was only fat in all the right places; she just wanted him to tell her that. "Hurry up and get your ass ready to go!" He walked out laughing.

Elijah went to the kitchen for a drink of water then to the living room where he stood over Elise for a minute, watching her sleep. *This one is a little more complicated than Lauren,* he thought. He bent down and gently lifted one side of the headphones. *Sade, huh? Good choice.* He leaned in and whispered in her ear, "Wicked . . . wake up, wicked."

Elise rolled toward him, barely opening her eyes. It took a few seconds for her to bring his face into focus. She yawned and stretched. "Who the hell is wicked?" Her voice was groggy.

Elijah stood upright and laughed. "You! Now get up, we goin' out to eat before I take you home. Snow got some clothes for you. You need to rush your shower 'cause we don't have a lot of time."

"Make your mind up, is it Wicked or Assata? And I don't wanna wear her clothes."

"Stop tryin' to wrestle with me on everything. You got gunshot residue all over those clothes, your hands, not to mention who might've seen you in those. That shit goin' in the trash." He slipped his tank top over his head and went back to the kitchen.

Lauren came out wearing black-laced panties and matching bra. She handed Elise a white Gucci blouse and charcoal gray Donna Karan slacks. "I have really tiny feet, so I'm not sure if these will fit," Lauren warned, holding some Gucci mules in front of her. "My makeup is in the bedroom, so feel free to use whatever you want. Towels and scrub are already laid out for you in the bathroom."

"I don't wear makeup," Elise said with a barely disguised attitude, "but I could use a brush."

Lauren smirked at her childishness. "Come on." She looked Elise up and down, amused. "You can choose whatever you want to use." She led her to the room.

Elise couldn't help feeling a tinge of envy seeing Lauren's fat ass cheeks swallow up the thong. She reluctantly followed behind her.

It was an hour before the girls were dressed and ready to go, which was considered fast. Elijah threw on his Girbaud sweatshirt over the tank top, grabbed his phone, keys, pistol, and headed out. When they got in the parking garage, he put a car cover over the Benz, then climbed into the back seat of Lauren's Range Rover. "Don't forget to call Ahmed in the morning so you can holla at him about trading in the Benz for something else," he reminded Lauren as they prepared to leave.

As Lauren backed out the parking space, he tapped on the headrest. "I hope you got something in your CD changer I can listen to. I know how you get with your music sometimes," he said jokingly.

"Leave my music alone!" she smiled. "I got something for you." She pressed a button and the sound system sprung to life.

"That's what I'm talkin' 'bout, white girl!" he yelled, and began his Hoodsta dance to Notorious B.I.G. and Bone Thugs-N-Harmony.

Lauren laughed as she watched him through the rearview mirror. Elise turned to get a glimpse and laughed too. She tried to turn her head back toward the front so he wouldn't see her laughing.

It took about twenty minutes to reach Elijah's favorite restaurant, Crustaceans, a Euro-Asian cuisine in Beverly Hills. This was Elise's first trip to the five-star spot, and she was blown away by the layout. The front door sat between two floor-to-ceiling glass picture windows with a display inside that featured a beautiful waterfall. Inside, the entire floor was made of a scuff-resistant Plexiglas, a fish tank built into the floor of the restaurant that gave a view of the coy pond beneath with colorful goldfish swimming lazily. It was spectacular. The furniture was also unique. Each table and chair set different from the next.

The place was buzzing with chatter. Soft jazz played faintly in the bar area. Elderly Armenian and white men sat at the bar smoking cigars and talking multimillion-dollar deals. Arrogance oozed from their conversations and laughter while their trophy wives posed in diamonds and couture designs.

Elijah loved this environment. Though he was well aware that most of these people could boast having more legal money than him, he still felt richer than them all. He couldn't sing or dance, wasn't a professional athlete, wasn't particularly educated by society's standards, and he damn sure wasn't born into money, yet here he was, a black ghetto kid who statistics had counted out long ago. These were the times he felt proud of who he was—*a successful, rebellious nigga.*

They enjoyed the bar while they waited on a table. Lauren ordered wine for herself and Elise, and Elijah clipped a cigar and smoked with the Big Dogs. Many had their eyes on Lauren and

Elise, which Elijah appreciated. He wasn't no hater; he smiled as some of the men tried to flirt with them.

The host finally called their name and seated them at a table. The aroma of seafood and garlic permeated throughout the dining area. Elijah did the ordering: beef spring rolls with mint leaves and crab cakes were the appetizer; a feast of garlic roasted Dungeness crab, butterflied garlic prawns in heavy pepper, and garlic noodles sautéed in a rich butter sauce for the entree. Between the three of them, they ran through a bottle of Cristal and a bottle of Moet White Star, which Elijah preferred over the more expensive champagne; it tasted better and didn't leave a nasty hangover after a hard night out. Needless to say, they were feeling bubbly.

Elijah joked and talked shit the entire night. For the moment, they forgot all about life's problems and enjoyed one another's company. Even Elise, who didn't enjoy much of anything was having a good time.

They left the restaurant with a nice buzz and in good spirits. Elise gave Lauren directions to her apartment in Westwood, an upscale area in west LA.

Everything was quiet when they arrived. Lauren needed to use the restroom, the alcohol was running through her, so Elise invited them up. Elijah went just to check out the spot. He was diggin' the newly built complex.

Elijah was impressed when he entered Elise's place. A soft peach-colored French provincial couch wrapped around the living room, matching throw rugs and floor pillows were strategically placed, artificial logs burned in the fireplace giving off a comforting warmth and soothing sound, a big screen covered an entire section of wall, the dinette set was modern oriental-style made of heavy Plexiglas. Elijah took a mental note; he'd have to get one of the all-glass sets for one of his spots. *Very classy,* he thought. He was tired of those ugly overstuffed leather couches and African statues and art that every black person with a little bit of money had in their houses. This place had style and class.

Diabla came out with a worried look when she heard them come in. A thousand-pound weight seemed to lift off her when she saw Elise. She hugged her without acknowledging the company. "I've been worried like shit about you! You left your phone in the car so I couldn't . . . why didn't you call to let me know you were alright?"

"I didn't want to use any phones," Elise said emotionless, "then I fell asleep for a little bit. I was tired from all the activity." She cut her eyes at Elijah.

Diabla narrowed her eyes with Elise's dry explanation and her look said it.

Elise gestured to Lauren and Elijah, "You already know him. This is his . . . this is Lauren," Elise hesitated. "This is my people, Diabla," she introduced.

Lauren shook her hand. "Diabla, so you're the lady devil, huh?" she said with a smile.

"In the flesh!" Diabla said proudly.

"The bathroom's this way." Elise led Lauren down the hall.

Elijah and Diabla were left to stare at each in an awkward silence. Neither broke eye contact until Elise walked back in to break up their standoff. "You want something to drink?" she asked.

"Nah, I'm good." He still stared at Diabla.

Elise sensed the tension in the room. "I gotta give your girl back her clothes," she said, attempting to ease some of the tension.

"Don't worry about it. She don't sweat the small stuff." He looked at Diabla. "Do you mind if I holla at her in private for a minute?"

Diabla gave no response to his demand disguised as a request. She looked at Elise, who nodded her head. With another prolonged stare-down, she walked to the bedroom.

"Before you start I want to tell you something important," Elise said before he had a chance to speak. "It may sound crazy, but I'm going to say it anyways. I had a dream—"

"And?" he interrupted.

"Let me finish. I won't go into details, but in the dream I saw that somebody close to you tried to have you killed."

"What? You a dream interpreter, a psychic or something?" he said, not trying to hide his sarcasm.

"No, but since I was a kid, I've had dreams that sometimes come true . . . or I can understand their meaning. I don't know how I know, I just do."

Elijah studied her closely. He wasn't going to tell her about his own dream. Was this a freak coincidence or some sign? Either way he couldn't deny that this was some deep shit. "I'll keep that in mind." He remained cool, ignoring the shivers running down his spine. "Truthfully speaking, I was already feeling that somebody close was trying to pull a grimy move. That brings me to what I wanted to holla at you about."

"Speak ya mind."

"This what I'm thinking. Until I get to the bottom of things, I'm gonna keep a li'l distance between me and my guys. I'll take care of business with them when it's necessary, but I won't give any of them the upper hand. That brings me to my proposal: I want you on my team. Before you answer, I wanna be clear, you'll have to give up the robberies and theft game. Second, you'll have to gain control over your hate. Not get rid of it, control it, and only unleash it when necessary. I don't need undisciplined soldiers on my team. Last and most important, you'll follow my lead in all matters. You'll get paid well and will have my support and honor for as long as you remain solid. So?" He watched her closely.

Elise dropped her eyes to the floor as she thought, running through the implications of his offer. She had never trusted a man before and wasn't sure she could now, but something within was compelling her to believe him. Even though she didn't fully understand the new emotions she was feeling, she decided to take a chance. She finally looked up and locked eyes with him nodding the affirmation. "I'm with you," she said hesitantly, "but you gotta promise to have my back in the same way I'm going to have yours—to the death."

"That goes without saying. You take two steps for me, I take nine for you."

They exchanged numbers. Hers he locked into his memory without writing it down, but his he wrote down for her. "Make sure you memorize it ASAP and get rid of the paper." Suddenly, he walked up on her, so close that she thought he was going to try to kiss her. She looked up at him confused. "Diabla's your responsibility," he hissed. "Get it through her head that I ain't tryin' to take her bitch. I have access to more pussy than I can keep up with. Assure her that yours ain't my concern. You're my comrade, my sister, a soldier—that's it, that's all! She better put that jealousy shit up or she'll get her feelings hurt. Feel me?"

Elise averted her eyes, embarrassed that somehow he knew that she and Diabla were intimately involved. "Don't worry, I got it," she nearly whispered.

Elijah affectionately grabbed her chin and forced her to look at him, making her feel like a child standing before her father. "Ain't nothin' to be embarrassed about," he told her. "You my nigga now. You can keep it real with me about any and everything 'cause I'm gonna do the same with you. We clear?" She nodded her head.

He heard Lauren and Diabla's voices in the hallway. "Stop runnin' your damn mouth and come on, girl!" he yelled.

"Okay, I'm coming." Lauren laughed. She and Diabla walked out together talking about one of the paintings in the hallway.

Elijah tapped Elise on the chin. "Have a good night, little girl." He winked.

To Elise's surprise, Lauren hugged her and kissed her cheek. Elise had no choice but to reciprocate the gesture. She tripped off Lauren's real and outgoing personality.

Lauren waved to Diabla, "Nice meeting you, Lady Devil."

"You too, *mami*, be safe," Diabla responded.

"Ninety minutes." Elijah smiled at the women, then walked out with Lauren a step behind.

Elijah and Elise . . . the beginning of a true unholy alliance founded on pain, sustained by bullets and death. This one was for the history books.

# CHAPTER TWENTY-TWO

Crips from all over LA, along with family and friends of the deceased, filled the big pink church on 111th and Broadway to capacity to pay respect to the U.G.'s fallen comrades.

The entire Rollin' 100s cars were out flying their flags to the fullest. All six sets that comprised the Rollin' 100s were there representing. Blue bandanas, Loc's, Chucks, khaki suits, and R-I-P shirts were everywhere in the chapel. Everyone sat silent as the overweight preacher, in his too-tight suit and dried-out perm, screamed his fire-and-brimstone sermon. He dabbed the sweat from his brows as he noticed, with some concern, a new crowd of men gathered at the front entrance. They began making their way up the aisle toward the casket, grabbing everyone's attention as heads turned to see what was going on. The black sweatshirts with large white "90" on the backs couldn't be missed, as the buzzing whispers grew louder.

The Nine Os were in the building, around fifty of them. Abruptly stopping their march at the end of the aisle, an individual not dressed like the rest walked forward to the casket. He wore a tight K-Mart Sunday suit, some Buster Brown shoes that looked much too big, and large bifocals. He looked completely out of place with this crowd. He approached the casket and gently raised the white lace that unnecessarily served as a covering for the deceased. Leaning in, he kissed Li'l Dirt on the cheek and placed a powder-blue bandana inside the casket. He turned and walked for the exit with the small army in tow.

Outside the church, more Nine Os posted up in the parking lot. Elijah sat on the hood of the bulletproofed Hummer, Elise by his side, vigilant, serving as his constant shadow.

Hitter drove up in a classic 1955 Chevy with three of his soldiers. They hopped out, Cripped-down with mob-style derby fedoras, like a scene straight out of an old mobster movie. The suicide doors on the Chevy remained opened as the three didn't stray far from the car. Hitter walked up and eyed Elise before speaking to Elijah. "What's the business?" They shook hands.

"You late, homie," Elijah said, eyeing the church's front door.

"I usually don't do funerals—not even family—so me not showing up at all would've been on time for me. All these fake muthafuckas here pretending they care when most of them couldn't give a give a fuck. They ass just wanna be nosy and get in these people's business." Hitter really didn't like being there. For his own peace of mind, he would rather remember people as they were when alive. At the point of death, it was none of his business; it was a matter between the individual and his creator.

They kicked around a little small talk. The fifty-man squad finally exited the church. Hitter caught sight and had to do a double-take. "What the fuck? Why is he here?" he muttered to himself, then looked to Elijah believing that he was responsible for this. "Cuzz, if you was bringing this nigga you shoulda let me know, I coulda kept my ass at home."

"This wasn't my doing," Elijah responded, "I didn't know he was coming till I drove up and saw them walking into the church."

"What's up, cuzz?" Li'l Wizard walked up and addressed them.

"Alright, what's crackin', homie?" Elijah shook his hand.

Hitter didn't respond. He looked Li'l Wizard up and down with a critical eye, shook his head, and averted his gaze back to the church. The cheap suit and bifocals only added to the belief by some that Li'l Wizard carried a serial killer's aura—Hitter was convinced they were right.

"What's up, Hitt?" Li'l Wizard addressed him with a smile. He seemed to enjoy getting under Hitter's skin. Hitter gave him a delayed chin-up and looked back at the church.

Li'l Wizard chuckled. Elijah had witnessed the two interact with one another on numerous occasions, yet never failed to find humor in their tension-filled relationship. Big Wiz was the only reason the two tolerated each other. Li'l Wizard thought his actions toward Hitter was a joke, but Hitter didn't find it funny at all, and on many occasions considered ending Li'l Wizard's career.

Elijah tried to lighten the atmosphere by striking up a frivolous conversation with Li'l Wiz, but he really didn't want to rap. Looking into the distance, Li'l Wiz jumped to a topic that had nothing to do with what Elijah's was talking about. "I got things on my mind, things y'all will know soon. I'm tired of all the hidden agendas. I promised Big Wiz that I'd look into matters and that's what I'm gonna do," he said with unwarranted venom.

Elijah wasn't feeling his state of mind. *I need to get this psycho away from here,* he thought.

"You know, Li'l Nine, I don't like the way you niggas get on this secret, politically correct bullshit . . . you-kill-me, I-kill-you in secret." Li'l Wizard mocked. "Why does everything gotta be a goddamn secret? Fuck a secret! I'm sending a message: you fuck with the Nine Os and we bring it to you loud and at your front door!"

"I hear you, but we've already discussed it. We gonna do things a li'l different this time," Elijah tried to reason.

Li'l Wizard's face was blank. "What that gotta do with me?"

That statement officially pissed off Hitter. "Cuzz, I wash my hands of this shit. This dude is gonna make me do something to him. Li'l Nine, you be careful, homie, I'm outta here." He eyed Li'l Wizard with the look of death. "Respect the family; they not part of this gang shit. Whatever you gonna do, do it away from here. Let's bounce, cuzz." He and his three-man entourage jumped in the bomb and swerved out of the parking lot.

The Rollin' 100s filed out of the church and gathered in a cluster, eyes on the Nine Os. After a couple minutes of posturing between the two sides, Li'l Wack from U.G. walked from the crowd to approach Elijah. Elise and a few others cut off his path. "Let me holla at you, Li'l Nine," he said from a respectful distance.

Elijah hopped from the hood and broke through the human wall formed around him. "Y'all chill for a minute and let me hear what he gotta say," he told Elise and the others. The homeboys backed off but not Elise. Not moving an inch, she stood maintaining her position at Elijah's side, turning her gaze back to Li'l Wack. Elijah knew it would be a winless argument with her, not worth the time it would take tongue wrestling with her being as stubborn as she was. He turned to Li'l Wack and nodded. "Go ahead, speak your peace."

"I'm aware of the rumors about who tried to hit you and ended up dead," Li'l Wack said, his eyes scanning their faces. "No actual facts been presented to us, so we in the blind. The U.G.s got love for Nine Os, and I can't see my homies making a move like that," he assured Elijah.

Li'l Wack shifted his eyes back and forth, almost in a nervous manner. Elijah picked up on it. In a shaky voice, Li'l Wack said, "Cuzz, did you kill the homies?"

"I ain't killed nobody. I'm just here to pay my respects," Elijah said. "You might want to ask Li'l Crip—he seems to have all the answers nowadays. Is he here?"

"Li'l Crip nowhere to be found," Li'l Wack confirmed.

"If the beef 's between y'all two, that's where it should stay. It shouldn't turn into a Nine O underground beef," he suggested.

Li'l Wizard grew defiant. "Since you claim this Li'l Crip's beef, then this how it'll go. Y'all turn him over to us for questioning by tonight. If not, all bets are off!" He looked to Elijah. "Come on, cuzz, this conversation's over."

Elijah didn't want to show any disunity among the ranks, so he turned and yelled to his machine, "Ninety-Crips, roll it up!" They all retreated to their rides and peeled away from the church.

The Rollin'100s had an after-funeral party at a two-story house in the One-Eleven Neighborhood Crips. It was strictly a Crip affair; no elderly family members were allowed. Loud music could be heard from blocks away.

The Nine Os parked a couple blocks over and walked the rest of the way to the party just in case a quick getaway became necessary. Elijah and Li'l Wizard led the pack as they appeared out of the darkness like ghosts. The 100s saw them coming and formed up. Bear from Eleven-Tray Block stepped up as the official spokesman for the 100s.

"We don't know the full situation between you and the U.G.s, but we know it's tension," Bear said to Elijah. "So check it out: this an Eleven-Tray Block party, and tonight it's all 100 love! So if you came to kick it off with the U.G.s, I suggest you do it somewhere else, because tonight is a Rollin'100s night and we ain't gonna lose!"

Elijah stared at Bear, unmoved by the implied threat. "You the spokesman for the U.G.s or something? They can't speak for themselves?"

Kickaboo from U.G.s heard Elijah's remark and took offense. "Don't nobody speak for U.G.s! We don't back down or bow down to nothin', nigga!"

Elijah smirked as the rest of the U.G.s gathered beside Kickaboo in the standoff.

Kickaboo knew they had the numbers on their side. He continued the tough talk. "You told the homie Li'l Wack that we better give Li'l Crip up by tonight. Well, we don't know where he is and even if we did, we wouldn't hand him over to you. So, do what you feel you have to do—"

Ju-Ju blindsided him with a wild haymaker. Li'l Wizard took the next U.G. in line with a flurry of blows.

The gang rumble was on.

For all the talk of 100-love, the rest weren't quick to come to the U.G.s' aid. They watched for the first couple minutes while the U.G.s got pummeled. Finally gaining some courage, a few jumped in. Even outnumbered, the Nine Os force was too much. The U.G.s and the few stragglers who had tried to assist had to retreat to the mob that didn't join the melee.

"Nine Os, pull back," Elijah ordered.

The 100s regrouped and began approaching the back-pedaling 90s as one unit. Out of nowhere, a youngster from Eleven-Tray Block fired his pistol in the air and all hell broke loose.

Li'l Wizard unleashed his .44 Bulldog directly into the 100s crowd, followed by the rest of the Nine Os. They rained bullets on them from every direction. Wherever possible, the 100s fired back, and for a full two minutes it was Vietnam on a residential street in South Central.

The Hummer swung on the block, skidded to a halt and the door flew open. Elise stepped out with a fully automatic MAC-11 and emptied the clip as Elijah and Li'l Wizard jumped in the truck. The rest of the Nine Os fled on foot to their cars as Elise jumped back in the driver's seat and reversed it off the block tires screeching.

Result: one dead, five down with gunshot wounds. All Nine Os escaped unscathed. Nine Os won.

On the drive back to the hood, Li'l Wizard was hyped. "That's what the fuck I'm talkin' 'bout!" he yelled. "That's how you do it, face to face—beat they ass, then serve 'em all in the same night! Nine! Nine!" He beat on the back of Elijah's seat. "What Puff Daddy say? 'Take that, take that, take that!'" He laughed wildly.

Elijah took it all in silence. No rejoicing, no remorse either, just an acceptance of the experience as a necessary event in his life.

# CHAPTER TWENTY-THREE

Lauren rolled over from her sleep to Elijah's phone vibrating on the nightstand. She answered it, "Hello."

"Let me talk to Nine," a male voice said.

"Call back later. He's sleeping right now," she tried to tell him, but whoever he was wouldn't hear none of it.

"I need to talk to him *now*." She relented and shook Elijah awake, handing him the phone.

"Hello?" he mumbled half-asleep.

"Ay, cuzz, this Fat Jack from U.G. We need to rap."

Elijah perked up. "I'm listening." This had to be some interesting news for Fat Jack to be calling him.

"Look, cuzz, that was foul what went down at that party. None of ours fell, just one of the big homies from one of the other 100s went down. They declared war on y'all."

"Yeah, so?"

"I'm speaking for the U.G. and U.G. only: we wanna squash this beef before it go any further. I got some info that'll bring things to light for you. It's a peace offering. But if I give it to you, I want your word that you'll call off the war."

Elijah leaned back against the headboard. "How can I give you my word when I don't know if the info is going to be true or even worth knowing?"

"Li'l Nine, you know me, cuzz. We've always been straight up with each other. I wouldn't even play with you with some bogus shit. I'm a man before anything, and my word is my bond."

"I'll tell you what, if what you tell me proves worthy and warrants peace, then you have my word that I'll work toward peace. But that don't extend to Li'l Crip."

"Fuck Li'l Crip! He's the reason all this is where it's at. Then he dips outta state and leave homies to die over his bullshit! I heard he's in Texas. As soon as I get an exact location, you'll have it. Trip, though, he wasn't the only one involved. Your homeboy Li'l Teflon plotted with him to make that happen. Hitter was next on they list, but as you already know things didn't go as planned."

Elijah fell silent. This couldn't be true, not after all he'd done for Li'l Telfon's family. True they've have their differences, but to plot to take his life, that was a whole other level. "Why should I believe some shit like that about my homeboy?" he said, yet feeling in his gut that it was true.

"Because it's true. They felt if they could get you and Hitter out the way without nobody knowing, the balance of power would shift toward them. Look, I didn't expect you to go on my word alone, so I got something that'll let you see the truth. Listen . . ."

Fat Jack clicked over to access his voicemail, then clicked back on the line so Elijah could hear:

> *Ay, Fat Jack, this Li'l Tef. I need you to get back at me ASAP.I need to catch up with Li'l Crip like yesterday, ya feel me? He ain't been answering his phone. Man, it's real important that I holla at him 'bout that situation. Get back at me!*

Anger coursed through Elijah's veins as he listened to Li'l Teflon sell him out.

Fat Jack sighed. "Everybody and they momma know that you and Li'l Crip is beefing," he said. "Why in the hell would Li'l Teflon be tryin' to catch up with him at a time like this? To keep it all the way 100, Li'l Crip had told me about all this before he skipped town, but it was none of my business so I kept quiet. But now, it's a situation where homies' lives at stake that have nothing to do with y'all business. I have to do what I can do to prevent that."

Elijah had to respect Fat Jack's straightforwardness. He could have easily lied or stayed quiet that Li'l Crip had personally given him details of the plot. For that Elijah gave his word. "On the hood, I'll do whatever's in my power to stop the beef between our hoods from escalating. As a matter of fact, I'm gonna slide you some paper for your assistance and future cooperation. Don't nobody else need to know about this conversation or our agreement. That's strictly between us."

"You got my word," Fat Jack told him. "And I'm gonna be keepin' my eyes open for when Li'l Crip raises his head."

"Alright, that's a bet. You stay safe."

"You do the same."

Elijah sat in stunned silence for over thirty minutes, trying to wrap his head around the news. *It's time to make some serious moves and changes,* he thought. *It's time for Plan B to go into motion.*

He needed to see Elise. For some reason, he found calm and security in her presence. He called out to Lauren, "Get Assata on the line and let her know we gotta make an emergency trip outta town."

He crawled out of bed and to the bathroom. For the first thirty minutes, he didn't even bother lathering up; he allowed the hot water to run over him as his mind raced in overdrive. *How did it come to this? After all we'd been through together.* He wondered if Ju-Ju and

Big Teflon were also involved? For the first time since his mother's death, he felt a tightness in his throat, as if his eyes would fill with tears. But he restrained himself and clenched his hands into fist. It was a few moments before he realized that the water had turned cold. *One thing's for sure: when I figure this shit out, those mutha-fuckas gonna feel my wrath!*

Earlier, Big Teflon had received a call from his brother who sounded distraught. He rushed over to the apartment as soon as he got off the phone. When he walked through the door, Li'l Teflon was sitting slouched in the Lazy-Z-Boy drinking a bottle of Hennessy. The lights were off throughout the apartment, and the only light was the sun's rays creeping through the blinds.

Li'l Teflon lit a blunt to try to calm his nerves. "I . . . I need to talk to you about some . . . something serious. I know you ain't gonna like it, but I can't leave you in the dark." He pulled hard on the blunt, following it with a deep gulp of the Hennessey. "Just to be safe, we need to go lay low for a while, get outta town until things blow over."

"What the fuck you talkin' about? You losin' me." Big Teflon was baffled by his brother's erratic behavior and talk.

"There's talk in the city that I plotted with Li'l Crip on the move against Li'l Nine."

Big Teflon gasped. "Talk in the city? I haven't heard no . . ." The realization of what his brother was really trying to say hit him at that moment. "Aw, nah, cuzz . . ." He shook his head. "Tell me you didn't do that. Tell me you didn't try to kill the homie." Big Teflon was instantly close to tears.

Li'l Teflon's silence told the truth of his involvement. He couldn't look his brother in the eyes. Big Teflon felt so many emotions: hurt and anger at his brother, but he still wanted to protect him in spite of the betrayal.

"Why would you pull a stupid-ass move like that? We eating more than we could've ever dreamed of all because of Li'l Nine. He made shit better for our family. Hell, he paid for Naqael's college tuition. What more did you want?"

"We all played a part in this success," Li'l Teflon snapped. "I went to jail for that nigga, and how does he show his appreciation? He let them niggas take off on us and sat back and watched, that's how. Right or wrong, he was supposed to ride with us. Why you don't see that? Look, Bro, we don't need them."

Li'l Teflon stood and grabbed his brother by the shoulders to plead his case. Truth be told, he felt scared and alone. "It can be just us, like the old times. We can lay low, then come back and put our own machine together. I got a team of young Tiny-Toons that follow my lead. Just ride with me. I ain't never let you down before, have I?" Li'l Teflon spoke with the conviction of a delusional lunatic.

Big Teflon stared in disbelief. He had the urge to slap the shit out of him. "You really starting to buy your own bullshit." He slowly shook his head. "You know what? You just being who you always been: a greedy, jealous, selfish mutha-fucka." He knocked Li'l Teflon's hands away from his shoulders. "But this time you on your own. You won't drag me down with you. My advice to you: find a rock and crawl under it! All this talk of starting your own machine with the Tiny-Toons, nothing gonna come of it but you and them ending up dead. This ain't a game, Bro. We ain't kids, no more. Look, you my brother and I'll always love you, but I gotta turn my back on you on this one."

Heartbroken and conflicted, Big Teflon left the apartment without looking back. For the first time in their lives, he showed his back to his brother in a time of turmoil. The world was changing.

Li'l Teflon knew the gig was up. Grabbing his bags that had been packed earlier, stuffed with money, guns, clothing, and jewelry, he put them in the trunk of his BMW. Before the sun set on

Los Angeles, he was on the I-15 heading for his hideaway in Las Vegas where he had a Laotian stripper waiting. A tear slid down his face as he sped the interstate. *This ain't over,* he thought. *Nah, they'll hear from me again . . .*

# CHAPTER TWENTY-FOUR

Elijah moved around Lauren's place making last-minute preparations and phone calls while she packed his clothes for the upcoming trip. He had to go to Mexico before heading to Atlanta then Nashville. It was time to rearrange the way he did business, time to downsize and maximize.

Elise paced the living room while talking on the phone, making all the necessary travel arrangements. Elijah was trying to do so much at once that he interrupted her every five minutes with a different question, making her more irritated every time she heard her name. "You need to stop acting like I'm a kid who needs to be constantly reminded about things," she told him for what seemed like the thousandth time.

"I'm not treating you like a kid," he said for the umpteenth time. "I'm just making sure everything's in order. Where in the hell are your clothes, your luggage?"

"I didn't bring none." Elise sulked. "You had me rushing over here like it was some real emergency. I didn't have time to pack anything. Besides, you need to buy me some extra clothes anyways."

"We going on a business trip. There ain't no time for no damn shopping."

"Well, they have malls where we going, and if you buying, I can save my money like you keep telling me." She smiled mischievously, putting her ear back to the phone.

He didn't bother responding; he gave her a stop-being-a-smart-ass look and went back to tying up loose ends. "Lauren, I need you to take care of a few things while I'm gone. Take Tiny Droop's grandmother two grand for her late mortgage, give Lady Rawdog a grand, and get with the director of Jesse Owen's Park to give her a donation for the Pop Warner football team's new uniforms."

"Alright, I'll get it done tomorrow when I leave the office," Lauren assured him.

Elijah grabbed his keys and belongings, looked around the room a second time to make sure he wasn't forgetting anything. Satisfied, he pecked Lauren on the lips on his way to the door. "Douche that li'l pussy while I'm gone," he snickered, "and don't let your boyfriends put too many miles on it."

"Kiss my ass, you jerk!" Lauren laughed.

"That'll have to wait until I get back."

"Oh, you get on my nerves." She looked at Elise. "Assata, take care of him. You know he can't be trusted to take care of himself."

"Don't worry." Elise winked and smiled. "I'll keep him in line."

He hurried out the door before they decided to gang up on him again, which seemed to be happening a lot lately.

Elise and Elijah were on I-5 South floating the BMW 850i like a cruise ship through the ocean. The sky was clear, energy pulsating, making for a beautiful sunny southern California day. Elise worked the CD changer in accordance to their unwritten rule that whoever drove controlled the music. R&B-soul was always her choice. Today, at least for the moment, it was Soul II Soul's "Keep On Movin'." It set a soothing vibe for them to ride and think.

All morning Elijah had been in deep thought on how he was going to execute Plan B to perfection. During their ride to San Diego, he played scenarios over and over in his head. He finally turned down the music to lay out his plans to Elise.

"You are going to be my queen on the chessboard." He turned to look at her. She nodded as an invitation for him to tell her more. I need to be sure you're fully onboard. The first step is the meeting in Tijuana with Guzman, my Mexican drug connect. I want you to sit through the meeting with me to pick up on their conversation whenever they switch to speaking Spanish so you can tell me whatever they say after we leave." It made him uncomfortable to have people talk about him in his face and he couldn't understand. That would change now with Elise present, and they wouldn't expect a black girl to speak Spanish, so that was a leg up.

"If everything goes as expected, we'll go into the next phase of the plan in which you'll be the focal point. Until I figure out exactly who in the hood is for me and who is against me, I only want you and Lauren to have access to me. Wizard'll play a part, but I won't be dealing directly with him. He paused to gather his thoughts and to give Elise a moment to absorb what he just told her.

"It'll work like this," he continued. "You'll be the go-between with the Mexicans, my out-of-state workers, and Wizard. There'll be one person in each state where I do business that you'll be in communication with. You'll use untraceable phones that'll change monthly to instruct Guzman's people where and how much to deliver to each state. Once the work is safely at its destination, you'll then let the designated person know where to pick it up, how much money is expected back, and when the money should be ready for shipment back to LA. You're not going to meet anyone in person. You'll just be directing traffic, quarterbacking from the phone only."

Elise listened intently as if she was recording every single detail of every word he relayed to her. To his surprise, she didn't interrupt him at any time. He continued laying out the plan. "When the money lands back in LA, Wizard'll pick it up and meet with you to give you our cut. From there you convert the money into big bills and postal money orders and get it to Snow once a month. At that point, you're finished and Snow will handle the rest.

"To jumpstart the new operation, I'll put up the initial money, then get it back after the first flip. The profits from that first trip will be used from then on. From that point forward, all profits that come back after Wiz take his cut will be split fifty percent for me, thirty percent for you, and twenty percent for Snow. Once we get back from this trip, you and me only gonna meet once a month for updates. No more talking on a daily basis. I plan on this new program running for a year, two at most. Then I walk away from all this shit. I'll leave the door open for you to keep going on your own if that's what you wanna do. Can you handle what I need from you?" He concluded, putting the ball in her court.

Elise's expression answered that the question was unnecessary. "I already told you when I agreed to be down with you that I got your back to the death. Whatever you need me to do, I'll do it as you say. Don't ever second guess that."

Elijah leaned over to the driver seat and kissed her roughly on the cheek, like a brother would his little sister. The car swerved slightly before she quickly straightened it out. "Boy, you gonna make me crash with your crazy ass." She laughed.

Elijah settled back in the seat to enjoy the scenery of Oceanside, California. Total's "Can't You See" banged through the speakers like an earthquake. They rode the rest of the way without conversation.

---

They checked in to the Beachfront Marriott in San Diego. The meeting wasn't scheduled to take place until the following morning.

They hit the nearby mall to do some shopping before returning to order room service.

After dinner, they decided to take a walk on the beach. For a while they walked in silence. She watched him whenever he wasn't looking. There were so many questions she wanted to ask. Finally, she worked up the nerve and asked, "Can I know some personal things about you?"

Elijah paused to gaze at the waves rolling in. "Shoot," he said.

"Why do you always talk about your uncle but never your mother or father?"

"My uncle raised me," he spoke casually. "I don't know my father, and my mom . . . killed herself when I was a kid. I don't have anybody else." He reached down, picked up a pebble, and pitched it into the ocean.

"Is that why you're always sad . . . because of your mother?"

Elijah looked at her quizzically. *What make her think I'm sad?*

She spoke as if she read his mind. "I see it in your eyes. I can feel it. You smile and laugh a lot, but I know your pain."

"Here we go with the psychic stuff again. If you really wanna know, I don't know if I would call myself sad, but there's a lot in life I'm not happy about. I feel like I've been cursed my whole life. One bad thing after another. I try to do good but still get fucked-up results. Even with all the money, there's still no happiness, just more death, more poison. I feel like I sold my soul for this shit." He took a deep breath and turned to face her. "I don't like having to kill, but it seems like that is my fate, my duty, no matter how hard I try and change it. So I have to play the cards I was dealt." He looked back out to the ocean and turned the topic to her. "What's your story? Who hurt you and made you so full of hate and anger?"

At first she was hesitant—she'd never shared her entire life story with anyone, not even Diabla. She wasn't sure how to talk about some of the things that had happened to her. Then somehow she overcame her fear and began talking, and when she did it poured out like Niagara Falls. It had all been bottled up for so long that it seemed to explode from her. She shared everything with him: her mom, her aunt and uncle, the rape, the murder—everything. She searched his face for any signs of change. Would he look down on her now? Would he not trust her?

Elijah's expression never changed except for a hint of sympathy in his eyes. "I understand you. We're one and the same." But he did have a question that had been nagging at him. "What drew you to me, made you give your loyalty and dedication to my cause?" he asked softly.

Elise paused. "I don't know how to answer that without you thinking I'm crazy." she said sheepishly.

"Try me."

"Well . . . no, I'm not gonna say."

"Girl, come on with the bullshit and speak your mind."

"Okay . . ." She studied the sand on her feet. "Well, I had a dream about you before we ever met." She looked up at him waiting for another sly psychic comment. When one didn't come and she saw his serious expression, she continued. "It wasn't until we were alone on that balcony and I looked in your eyes that it all came back to me. I wanted to turn and run but my feet wouldn't let me. Then that first night at Snow's, I dreamed about you, and my mother was in the dream too. She told me that you were sent to take care of me and in return it's my duty to take care of you. I know it sounds crazy, but it's the truth."

Elijah brushed aside the strands of hair blowing across her face. "I don't think you're crazy. I believe you. I've had experiences of my own that are mysteries I don't tell anyone about."

"So, are we gonna take care of each other?" she asked quietly.

"It's already written in stone, li'l girl."

Without warning she leaned in and kissed him on the lips, but he pulled back with a confused look. "What was that all about?" he asked.

"What's wrong, only Snow can kiss you? What? I'm not pretty enough or white enough? We've spent nights together in the same room, you've been in the bathroom while I showered, and you never give me a second look. What, I'm not woman enough, or is it that Snow is the only one who can get your real love?"

Elijah didn't appreciate her speaking on Lauren in that way. He wanted to flip on her but calmed himself. "First of all, Snow is my soldier, not my girl. There's more to our relationship than you'll probably ever understand. She's loyal to a fault. She worships me. If I do have any love to give, she gets her share because she has earned it. Me and Snow are comrades in the struggle before anything else."

Elise sucked her teeth, averting her eyes as he checked her on the race issue. "She isn't the average suburban white girl. She has bumps and bruises, fought the same curse as us. Color is irrelevant when it comes to her. Snow is folks and you need to understand that." His voice softened. "Look, I look at you as a little sister. I don't wanna be lusting and fiending over you because you don't need that. Above all, while you are confused in your feelings for Diabla, I intend to respect that, got it?"

A tear formed at the corner of her eye. She tried to look away. "I just want you to love me like you love her." The tears began to fall. "I want you to make me feel the same way you make her. Why can't I have that?"

Elijah was taken back by her sudden show of vulnerability. He knew he had to really think about what she was saying and feeling at that moment. "Listen, I don't want you to confuse your emotions, your loyalty to me, with lust. You dealing with a lot inside and I want to be the one to help you work through that and get some clarity about yourself, not tear you down and confuse you even more. I tell you what: if once you get your vision clear, you have my word that if you still want us to share ourselves in that way, I won't deny you. But not right now." He wiped her tears away with his thumb and kissed her gently on the lips. Grabbing her by the hand, they walked back to the hotel. Preparations had to be made for the meeting in the morning.

Crossing the border from San Diego into Tijuana was like stepping into a different world. Dirty children ran to the car windows trying to sell tourists everything from knockoff clothes to piggy banks. No longer a sleazy border town, half Old West and half whorehouses, but rather a shiny metropolis with a million or more inhabitants. Corporate logos were everywhere. Still, a Mexican presidential candidate had been assassinated here, and a chief of police had been ambushed and gunned down. The wealth of drugs was entwined with all of it. Anyone with any street sense could easily detect this was a dangerous place.

Elijah half listened to the Spanish chatter while looking out at Tijuana. The blinding dayglow colors of the taxis, the main boulevard, Calle Revolucion, with miles of businesses, all aimed at Americans on a day visit. The beggar women with their babies, the cantinas, strip joints, and whores were abundant.

Then the scenery changed. The streets became dirt or rutted macadam, the few vehicles tended toward pickup trucks and old Fords and Chevys. The driver turned up a long dirt road that ended on a spacious ranch with chickens running about freely. The Bronco came to a stop. Elijah and Elise got out and surveyed their surroundings. They felt and looked out of place. The driver who had been sent to pick them up from San Diego led them toward the modest dwelling at the center of the ranch. Mexicans in tight jeans, cowboy boots, and hats eyed them suspiciously. The man Elijah was there to see stepped out on the porch with a welcoming smile. In contrast to his security, he dressed like an American businessman: sports coat, slacks, and a buttoned-down shirt with no tie. He had the looks of Antonio Banderas.

"Welcome, my friend!" Guzman said with overly dramatic cheer.

"Thank you for having me." Elijah gave him a firm handshake.

Guzman led them inside the modest dwelling where he served chilled lemonade. The inside of the house was nothing extravagant, but cozy compared to the surrounding property. The air conditioner blew cool breeze throughout the house. The simple terracotta tiled floor and festively painted walls gave the place a Spanish Mediterranean look. The furniture and other decorative pieces reflected Mexican culture and the *telenovela* playing on the fifteen-inch TV, propped on a glass stand, completed the home's simplistic charm.

"*Nueve en vivo.*" Guzman smiled. "I've always been curious, why do they call you Nine Lives?"

Elijah gave an arrogant chuckle. "I'm called that because I come from a jungle that was designed to kill me long ago, but instead I became a lion, the king of the cat family, and you know what they say, cats have nine lives." He smiled.

"I like that, yeah, I like it!" Guzman feigned excitement. "I, too, am a lion, but I must be careful because there are many more lions around who are just as hungry as me. They've been trying to eat me for the past nineteen years, so I should be called Nineteen Lives." He laughed as if it was the funniest joke in the world.

The next instant Guzman became serious and businesslike. He leaned in his chair, folded his arms, and spoke firmly in heavily accented English. "My pressing concern is what is so urgent that you request a face-to-face meeting. It is no secret that I prefer our prior arrangement of seeing one another as less as possible."

In his own no-nonsense businesslike demeanor, Elijah responded without missing a beat. "I needed to speak directly to you because it is time for major changes and I want a full and clear understanding that we are on the same page in order for things to run smoothly."

Elijah presented in detail the changes to Guzman with the control of a CEO at a board meeting, changes pertain to method of delivery, the amount of cocaine and the prices. "Instead of you delivering the product to San Diego as usual, I want the deliveries to be made to the States where they will be distributed: Oklahoma, Iowa, Tennessee, Arkansas, and Georgia. For you having to use your resources to transport the work, I will up the amount I buy. Instead of fifty to one hundred kilos as needed, I will commit to two hundred a month for a one-year period. I want the kilos at the price of $9,000 a piece, half to be paid up front, the other half upon delivery. The upfront money will be given to the usual contact in San Diego. The additional $900,000 you will have your drivers pick up in LA." Elijah paused to let Guzman process the information. Guzman remained silent, staring and nodding attentively.

Elijah then proceeded. "Once the year contract is up, we can either renegotiate a new deal or simply walk away depending on our circumstances at that time. Also, this will be the last time I cross the border on drug business." It was too risky for him. If something went wrong on Guzman's end, he couldn't have them knowing his face.

"This is a very interesting proposal." Guzman rubbed his chin in thought. "Do you mind if I take a few minutes to discuss this with my cousin Eduardo?"

"I'm your guest. Take as long as you need."

Guzman gestured to the greasy Mexican to his left and they walked to the kitchen.

Elijah could still hear their voices as they went back and forth in rapid Spanish. Elise tilted her head without being too obvious, recording everything in her memory.

*"Eduardo, Quiero arreglar este asunto . . . los pros y los contras?"*

*"¡No, me importa un comino precios en alza!"* Eduardo said.

*"Te lo vendo barato todo es lo mismo."* Guzman lowered his voice.

*"¡No, me gustó en absoluto! . . . es lo que quiera la gente."*

*"Yo hago lo que tengo de ser es tiempo para todo."*

*"Haz lo que tengas que hace todo eso es ente."*

*"Ya hice mi mente!"* Guzman snapped and walked out of the kitchen.

Elise shifted her attention back to Elijah when they walked back in.

Guzman strolled and sat down facing Elijah as Eduardo stood by with a look of frustration. "Nine Lives, I like your offer, but I would like to suggest a few changes of my own."

"What part of it don't you like?" Elijah engaged him in negotiations.

"It is not that I do not 'like'," Guzman flashed his million-dollar smile, "it is just parts that I would like to adjust, to benefit us both. If you only commit to one year, I will have to charge ten thousand per kilo. But, if you agree to two years I will give them for nine thousand like you ask. To get this deal, you will have to take an extra fifty kilos on consignment with each shipment for a price of ten thousand a piece on the ones fronted."

Elijah had already anticipated this counter offer when he made the initial pitch. He smiled inside for being able to predict his opponent's next move. "I don't like consignment." He paused. "It makes me feel . . . indebted. I don't like being indebted to no man, but I can understand you wanting to maximize the opportunity—that's business."

After some more word sparring, Elijah agreed to the two-year contract at $9,500 on each kilo that was fronted and with a grace period if necessary of two months to pay.

"You are a very smart man," said Guzman. "I like dealing with smart lions because they outlast the lions that rely solely on brute strength. I accept your offer, but I have one condition. I want your word that you will avoid war for the next two years. Murder brings heat. I am making a big investment into you, and I need you safe and free to get my returns."

"That's difficult to do, the jungle is unpredictable."

"I know, I know, but you must be wise now. I am not asking you to accept disrespect; I am asking you to postpone your vengeance until the right time. If something comes up that is too dangerous to ignore, I have men who specialize in making problems go away. As long as we are making millions together you are part of my extended family. All you have to do is get word to my people and things will be handled. You are to stay in the shadows and be untouchable."

Elijah was hesitant, but finally gave in and agreed to the condition. "I will do as you ask and keep a problem free low profile. The first $900,000 payment will be in San Diego by week's end." The agreement was settled.

Guzman smiled, then stood to shake his hand.

Elijah flashed his usual charismatic smile. "*Gracias*," he said. "I better get back across the border before I miss my engagements."

"No. Thank you, *mi amigo*! Be safe in the jungle."

Elijah walked out with Elise trailing. Right before she made it out the door Guzman stopped her and extended his hand.

"*Me gusta mujeres inteligentes. ¿Dónde aprendió a hablar español?*" he said with a knowing smile. (I like smart women. Where did you learn to speak Spanish?)

Elise returned the smile, politely disengaging his handshake. "Thank you for having me as your guest," she spoke in English, then walked to the awaiting truck. The smile never left Guzman's face as he watched them drive away.

Elijah relaxed in his seat and smiled inside. *Phase 1 complete. Machine in motion once again*, he thought.

# CHAPTER TWENTY-FIVE

**1999**

Li'l Teflon's blood pumped wildly as he and the crew made their way to the destination. Today was the day he'd been working toward for months. All the hard work of surveillance, obtaining the necessary tools, and doing homework was about to pay off big time. He couldn't help thinking of the phone call he had with his brother days earlier. Big Teflon had been so dry, so cold toward him. It had been two years since the move on Elijah, and despite Elijah never getting at Ju-Ju or his brother concerning his involvement, Big Teflon still refused to accept him back in his life.

Big Teflon was no fool; Elijah had pulled back from them. He'd only seen him twice in nearly two years, and at those times Elijah never showed any animosity, but neither did he fully embrace him. He acted the same way with Ju-Ju. His excuse for not seeing them much was that he was in and out of town a lot on business. Big Teflon knew better; he'd known him all his life and knew when something was wrong. Another telltale sign was he never once asked the whereabouts of Li'l Teflon.

*Bro is just being a paranoid, scared little bitch!* Li'l Teflon thought. *Fuck 'em all! I ain't sweating Li'l Nine, Hitter, or none of 'em.* He was in Vegas living lovely. He had the li'l homies down there, they were hitting licks, and he had a down-loyal bitch on his team, and after today it was going to get even sweeter. And when it did, he was going to smash back on the set and be just as strong as Elijah and the rest. He'd heard it said that a man shouldn't go to war until he had his money right. Well, he was about to have his right, and he was definitely going to want war!

Both vehicles pulled into an alley at the back of Las Vegas Boulevard. The van following Li'l Teflon came to a stop and three males, dressed in black fatigues and boots, hopped out with ski masks, burners, and large bags strapped to their backs. Li'l Teflon's female driver, a Laotian stripper named Murder-Min," put the car in park and left it running. Li'l Teflon got out with the same attire as his three crime partners. He activated the radio scanner for police communications, put the earpiece deep in his ear, then double-checked his stopwatch and nodded to the others. "Let's get it!" he said.

They all jogged through the passageway between two buildings that led from the back alley out next to a large parking lot that served a mini mall and bank. They turned up the speed a notch and sprinted for the door of Bank of America.

Li'l Teflon leaped on top of the counter and waved his gun methodically at the patrons and bank workers. "Everybody down!" he screamed. The patrons and workers hit the floor, some covering their heads with arms and hands as if that could shield from any potential danger.

The other three masked men leaped over the counter while he began his little speech. "We're here for the bank's money not yours," he said calmly, "so lay your asses still, stay calm, and we'll be outta here in no time . . . and you can get back to your lives. Look at it on the bright side: you'll have a nice story to tell your grandkids one day."

One of the robbers dashed straight for the vault when he cleared the counter, while the other two emptied the cashier's drawers. They packed their specialized bags with neat stacks of large bills only.

"Thirty seconds!" Li'l Teflon warned.

The three sped up their packing to a frantic pace.

"Fifteen seconds!" He kept the .9mm roving on those lying face down. "Times up, fellas!"

The robber who had entered the vault lugged out two bags; he pitched one to Li'l Teflon who strapped it across his back. The other two zipped their duffle bags, leaped back over the counter, and ran out the front door.

"Thank you for your time and cooperation, people. Enjoy the rest of your day," Li'l Teflon announced before leaping down to follow the others.

A few feet out the door, dye packs exploded in two of the bags. Purple and red dye in the form of smoke spread over the bags and clothes. They'd anticipated the possibility of this happening ahead of time, so it wasn't a surprise. They continued their run to the stolen van. Once inside the van, they dropped the bags of money into large ice coolers filled with water. This was used to kill any electronic tracking devices hidden inside the stacks of money.

Ten blocks away from the bank the van was ditched and the coolers were placed in an SUV that Li'l Teflon and Murder-Min switched over to. He lay down in the backseat while she drove. The other three got into a nondescript Chrysler Concord and drove in the opposite direction from the SUV.

Li'l Teflon made it back to his secret hideout, a white two-bedroom, single-story house in a quiet residential neighborhood. He entered through the back entrance, walked to the living room, and immediately began sifting through the money for tracking devices. He then took each bag to the bathroom where he placed the money in a bathtub filled with fingernail polish remover, where it would soak there for the rest of the day, then he'd drain the tub, rewash it one more time, and voila! Dye stains gone. Once the cleaning cycle was complete, some of it would still have a faint reddish tint, but it would be spendable.

The other crime partners weren't privy to the cleaning and counting process. They waited at another location for their cut of money to be delivered. The final count for Li'l Teflon was $397,000. By the time the money reached the others it'll have dwindled to $105,000. The additional $292,000 was hidden in Li'l Teflon's wall safe.

Li'l Teflon drove over to the small house outside of downtown that had been rented for the young homies when they arrived from LA. Pulling all the way to the back of the driveway, he entered through the back door. He walked in smiling from ear to ear and slammed the duffle bag with the $105,000 on the table. "This how it's done, li'l homies!" he boasted. "I told y'all that Vegas wasn't ready for us. We gonna teach niggas how to eat for real." He unzipped the bag and threw each one a $25,000 bundle. Not knowing too much about money, they felt as if he'd just given them a million dollars. Never in their wildest dreams would any of them had imagined coming up on this much money so quickly. They smiled at one another in disbelief as they fondled and tossed the money from hand to hand, feeling its weight. Li'l Teflon took a $25,000 bundle for himself as if it was his only share of the money.

"We can use the extra five Gs to snatch up some assault rifles and pistols at the gun show if it's cool with y'all?" he asked as if their vote really counted. All the youngsters quickly agreed to the purchase.

"Once we strap up like the mutha-fuckin' mob, we going back to the hood to run shit. It's time to celebrate young bucks!" Li'l Teflon exclaimed. What y'all know about this Tony Montana?" He produced a sandwich bag from his pocket containing two ounces of powder cocaine and placed it on the table. He used a playing card to separate it into long lines. Using a small straw, he sniffed two deep lines through each nostril, stood up straight and threw his head backward to ensure he inhaled it all. The young homies then each took their turn getting introduced to the White-Girl.

"That's right, you li'l niggas just got your cherries popped! We 'bout to take this shit all the way to the top my way." Li'l Teflon grinned.

---

Brenda prepared breakfast while getting dressed for work at the same time. She scampered around in her nurse's uniform still wearing house slippers. When Ju-Ju was a kid this was her everyday routine, but now that he had moved out, her days were usually a little less hectic, but at least once a week he'd stumble in drunk to spend the night. Even though she would fuss, she really looked forward to his visits. That still didn't change the fact that she wasn't going to be his servant and bring him breakfast in bed.

"Julius, Julius, get your ass up and come to the table to eat. I'm not going to tell you again!" Her voice echoed throughout the house.

Ju-Ju rolled over, grumbled, and smashed a pillow over his head. "Damn, I'm trying to sleep. I'll eat later!" he yelled back, half asleep.

She hollered even louder. "Boy, don't let me have to come in there and snatch you out that bed!" She didn't see him enough anyway, so he was definitely going to at least eat breakfast with her before she left for work.

"Ugh!" He threw the covers back in irritation. *I shoulda took my ass home last night,* he thought.

"Ugh, my ass!" she mocked, letting him know she'd heard his smart outburst.

Ju-Ju rolled out of bed and drunk-walked to the bathroom to piss and wash his face. He then joined his mother at the kitchen table for a spread of turkey bacon, cheese eggs, flaky biscuits, grits, and orange juice. He slapped a pad of butter on a biscuit, overloaded it with eggs, and crammed it into his mouth like a savage.

"You act like you haven't eaten in years and ain't got no home training," she scolded him as she always did.

Ju-Ju smiled big around a mouth full of food. Taking a hard swallow, he told her to stop fussing. *She such a trip,* he thought. *First she force me to come eat with her, now she complaining about how I eat . . . women!* To get on her nerves, he filled another biscuit to the max with turkey bacon and eggs and forced it all down while staring at her. He couldn't hold his composure for long; they both burst out laughing, food flying from his mouth.

When they settled down, he complimented her on the new furniture and decorations, "This real cool how you got it looking in here. I still don't understand why you won't let me move you to a better neighborhood."

Brenda was set in her ways. "I don't need a new house. This is my home and this where I'm gonna stay," she snapped at him. "Julius, you need to stop doing what you're doing," she suddenly pleaded.

"Aw, here we go again. Momma, don't start this morning."

That was all it took to send her on one. "I'm your mother; it's my job to keep telling you until you understand. It's time for you to change and do something positive with your money, because if you don't, it won't last long. Drug money is the devil's money. He gives it to you as a trick to gain your soul. Once he have you, he takes it all back, and you lucky if you walk away with your life. Y'all youngsters nowadays don't understand that. Y'all believe you the first ones to get ahold of that tainted money. Not knowing you just following a cycle that's been done many times before. The story always end the same—the devil use you up, and when he's through, he comes for it all and then some!"

Ju-Ju hated her redundant philosophies on his lifestyle. *She need to be done with this topic already, I don't need a sermon this morning,* he thought.

Sensing his irritation, she switched topics, but not before reiterating, "All I can do is warn you, the rest is your responsibility." She wanted to make sure she got her point across regardless of how he took it.

"Why hasn't my other son, Elijah, been by to see me in so long? Have you and him fell out over something?" she pried, tilting her head so she could look more into his eyes, trying to detect any form of deception.

"No, Momma. Stop trying to read between the lines on everything. Me and Nine don't have any problems. We good, and we'll always be good."

"His name is Elijah. And it's not like him to go so long without checking on me. I hope he's alright. I hope you Negros haven't done nothin' to that boy." She looked at him with accusatory eyes.

Ju-Ju stuffed his mouth with more food. "Ain't nobody done nothing to him," he grumbled. "I told you he's good. I think he's just laying low after those suckas tried to hit him a while back."

Brenda thought of how heartbroken she would have been if they had succeeded in hurting Elijah. It was good he was staying away for a while. Most of the people he came to help out and visit in the neighborhood didn't like him anyway. They just wanted a handout, at least that was her opinion. Envious jealous black people hated to see him doing good. She had heard all the talk and hater's venom going around the hood from the same people who smiled in his face and had their hands out when he came around. They didn't realize how good of a heart he had. He did his share of dirt, but that was only because of the circumstances he found himself in. The dirt really wasn't him. She knew and loved the real Elijah.

"He's a beautiful person inside," she voiced her thoughts without realizing it. "He has a heart of gold. The devil's just trying to steal him like he's doing with all of you. He wants him more though, because of his good heart."

"Damn, you talk about him like you love him more than me," Ju-Ju whined.

This tickled her. "Don't be jealous," she slid in and smiled.

"Ain't nobody jealous, just don't let me find out you got a crush on my homeboy," he half joked. "Make me put you over my knees."

Brenda found that statement even funnier. "Hell, you ain't got that big. I brought you into this world, and I can take you out of it. Talking about putting me over your knees." She shook her head and laughed, knowing she didn't mean a word of it.

"Julius, I want to tell you something, and I want you to take it to heart." She became serious again. "I want you to promise me that no matter what goes on in them streets, you'll never go against Elijah. He's a real friend. He took care of me and you while you was locked up, and he was a real son and provider when I needed it most. Never forget that, because friends like that don't come around but once in a lifetime, so you need to cherish it. You need to be careful of them black brothers. After all these years, something about them Teflons I still don't like."

"That's a promise. Nine is my guy, so it really goes without saying."

"I know, but it's more to it than him just being your 'guy. He gave me a promise when you both were kids, and he stuck to it. You're a man now, so it's a must that we return that love and loyalty back to him."

"What promise did he make you when we were kids?" Ju-Ju asked with suspicion, lowering his fork.

"That's between me and him," she snapped. "Just do what I asked. Now, can I count on you to do that?"

He looked at her for a minute, then nodded, "Always!"

Brenda took another bite of bacon and rose from her chair to kiss his forehead before grabbing the rest of her things to head out to work.

Ju-Ju sat in a daze, moving the food around on his plate with the fork lazily. *What's Mom really trying to tell me,* he thought. *Why Li'l Nine and Li'l Tef grown so far apart from us?* His thoughts drifted on as he tried to piece together a difficult puzzle.

# CHAPTER TWENTY-SIX

Elise's eyes roamed the crowded club as she stood in the corner against the wall. Strobe lights slashed across the dance floor in red, purple, yellow, and blue. House music, not familiar to her ears, blasted from the speakers and seemed to energize the mostly white partygoers. Some popped ecstasy pills freely on the dance floor, while others swung glow sticks and danced offbeat into a sweating frenzy. Most them, male and female, wore makeup on their faces and dark clothes that represented their Gothic lifestyle. The atmosphere made Elise a little uncomfortable. Never in a million years had she thought this would be the place Lauren would choose for their celebration night.

The name of the club was the Coven, a block-shaped building located on the fringe of Hollywood. When Elise first entered, she thought she was at a cult meeting or among devil worshippers, until Elijah explained to her the difference between Goths, witches, and devil worshippers.

"I never would've thought an attorney could be a devil worshiper too," she laughed.

“Well, you wouldn’t have expected her to be fuckin’ with a hoodsta like me either,” Elijah said sarcastically. “That’s why it’s not good to judge a book by its cover. And she’s not a devil worshiper. She practices, or should I say, has knowledge of her own form of witchcraft and metaphysics.”

Elise’s face said that she had a healthy dose of the creeps. She now understood why Lauren’s mani-pedis were always done in black, and why her makeup and clothes were dark. She hoped the bitch hadn’t put a spell on her.

Elijah laughed. “Don’t get scared now, Ms. Tough Ass.”

Lauren walked up before Elise could respond to his smart remark. She was carrying a tray with two bottles of champagne, a bottle of tequila, and three shot glasses. She sat the tray down and hugged Elise excitedly. “Hey, girl. You look cute tonight.”

“Thank you, you look cute too. Those boots are kicking ass.” Elise looked her up and down. Lauren’s boots, black knee-high Gucci, really were a hit. They set off her tight black miniskirt that barely went past her hips. The matching see-through black blouse and black lace bra were accompanied by a thin black cape that flowed behind her. The dark eyeshadow, lipstick, and manicured black nails, gave her the look of an exotic beautiful vampire.

“We ain’t ’bout to have no damn fashion talk show.” Elijah cut their girl-power moment short. “Let’s toast and get drunk so I can go home and get some sleep.”

Both women chided him for trying to rush. The past two years had gone too well for them to downplay what the night represented.

Elise had worked flawlessly with Guzman, Wizard, and the out-of-state workers. Lauren executed the finances with the precision of a Wall Street accountant. She was well versed in burying illegal funds into small businesses and real estate for Elijah and herself without detection. Being a lawyer gave her a lot of flexibility because she generated enough legal funds to cover for a lot of the investments. A little tinkering with the accounting books and adding a couple of zeros and commas to the incoming funds of the small businesses, and they were sitting nice. Whatever money she couldn't wash they stashed away in a water-fire weather-proof ground safe that was custom built at one of their properties in San Bernardino County.

Elise always took her cut of the money and used it separately, although she took pointers from Lauren on how she should hide and invest it. Lauren gave her twenty percent to Elijah every time. In her world, what was hers was his first. Together they had amassed a stash just over fifteen million dollars, from the two-year run alone, that didn't include what money they had before the new deal with Guzman. Elise was also now a millionaire; she'd come a long way since Elijah came into her life.

Lauren filled their shot glasses with tequila. "We're starting off with the strong stuff first," she announced. Elise looked at the liquor with some apprehension; she wasn't much of a drinker. *What the hell,* she thought, *may as well give it a go. After all, tonight is about celebration.*

Lauren gave the first toast. "This is to you, Daddy." She smiled at Elijah, "Everything we've been able to accomplish is due to you. You came into my life and rescued me not only from the vultures but from myself as well. I'll always be loyal to you. You are my savior, my god. Salute!"

"Salute!" Elijah and Elise echoed, raised their glasses, then downed their shots.

Elise made a face that cracked the other two up. "Shit," she exclaimed, "it tastes like rubbing alcohol." She looked at the empty glass in her hand and whipped her head side to side as if she could shake the taste out of her mouth.

Lauren leaned in and kissed Elijah, then pulled Elise by the arm and gestured for her to kiss him too. "It's your turn."

Elise was surprised by the request, but Lauren's look assured her that she wouldn't get jealous. "I know you love him too," Lauren admitted.

Elise looked to Elijah, who was enjoying the exchange between the two, and the look on Elise's face. He knew Elise had been caught off guard and was confused as hell. He smiled at her being speechless. Not often did he have a chance to see her little smart ass at a loss for words. She surprised him though. She leaned in and kissed his lips in a shy manner.

Elijah laughed and bear-hugged them both, smothering them with kisses to the face like they were his daughters. Both enjoyed his affection.

"This is powerful. Three mutha-fuckas born of pain, rising from nothin' to be on top. I want you both to know I appreciate you and you owe me no more debt." He wanted to make sure they understood that their jobs were completed. "Take your money and live well. I still got unfinished business in the streets, so we gotta walk our separate ways now. But you'll always have my respect, honor, and support. How could you not? We jumped the moon together—three orphans."

After Elijah voiced his sentiments, Elise caught an immediate attitude. "I ain't trying to hear shit about goin' separate ways. I promised to ride with you to the death and ain't a fuckin' thing changed. Wherever you go, whatever you do, I plan on being right there with you."

Lauren didn't even waste her time responding. He was stuck with her to the end, and he knew it.

Elijah suddenly became sullen. He shook his head as if it pained him to say the words he was about to share. He'd never voiced these feelings to anyone.

"I won't live long," he began slowly. "I've known that somewhere inside of me since I was a kid. It may not be tonight, it may not be next year, but at some point soon my story will end in tragedy. I wasn't put on earth to live long . . . it's part of my legend."

In Elijah's mind, the last pieces to the puzzle was to first kill his enemies. Next, he needed to have a son to leave his riches and wisdom to and to carry on the family name. If Elise and Lauren ever wanted to find peace and happiness, they needed to invest their emotions into someone else.

He gulped another shot of tequila and slammed the glass on the bar. "I'm cursed," he said with a burst of rage. "To love me is to love death. My final trail leads to hell. I'm cool with it though. I've accomplished a lot in my short life, and if the price of those accomplishments and struggle is an early death, then so be it! But I want better for you two. You've both overcome your demons. Don't make the mistake of re-awakening that curse by making the wrong decisions."

Elise smacked her teeth and stared at him. "Yeah, I hear all that and I respect what you're saying, but it still remains the same with me," she said with a dismissive wave of her hand. "If you go to hell, we go together. And when we get there we'd take that muthafucka over too."

"We're supposed to be celebrating success, not talking about curses and demons," Lauren said sadly. She grabbed her purse, dug out a long blue jewelry box, and handed it to Elijah. "A token of my appreciation."

Elijah opened the box and slowly removed the eighteen-karat gold heavy link necklace laced with sharply cut baguette diamonds. Before he could respond, Elise gave him another gift, a smaller square box that appeared to be from the same company. He smiled and popped it open. It held a solid gold face of the Sphinx, with diamonds covering each side of the head wear. The eyes and mouth were inlaid with diamonds in the form of a five-pointed star enclosed in a circle—the pentacle, or ancient symbol of magic. The Sphinx had been custom made to fit the chain Lauren had given him.

"I came up with the concept and Elise helped me design everything. Do you like it?" Lauren asked excitedly.

"Like it? That's not even the word. This is sick! You know what the crazy part is? My uncle just sent me a book a few weeks ago on the Egyptian mysteries. The Sphinx is a symbol of the perfect blend of divine man and his animal nature." He admired it further as he thought of what he'd learned from the book. He would keep this gift for life.

Lauren already had much knowledge of the Egyptian mysteries and metaphysics, so the revelation about how the gift related to the book his uncle had just sent him intrigued her. "This event is called 'affinity,' man attracting to himself, persons, and circumstances that are compatible to his level of consciousness. I believe the universe has given you this gift to confirm that you have the same potential greatness of the ancient pharaohs," she explained.

Elijah was feeling some kind of way about the both of them. He was coming to the realization that they really loved him. Not because of the money or his status as Li'l 9-Lives, but because of him, the man—Elijah. "I lost my mom when I was eight," he said. "And since that time, I haven't said to a woman what I'm about to say to y'all, so don't take this lightly. I love you both, in my own special way."

Both were shocked to hear those words come from his mouth. His actions had always showed that he had love for them, but he had never come out and expressed it. He expected Lauren to show the most emotions when he said it, but to his surprise, Elise teared up first. She hugged him tight and buried her face in his chest. He embraced her and kissed the top of her head. Lauren joined in the hug with tears in her eyes as well.

"We love you too." Lauren said for both of them.

"It's time for more drinks and fun now," he said to lighten the emotions.

The remainder of their time in the club was spent drinking, smoking, dancing, and talking shit. Lauren danced them both into exhaustion. Elise couldn't believe that she had more rhythm and dance skills than most Black girls. Lauren worked her ass and hips like a stripper.

In between all the partying, Elise made clear to Elijah her intentions of continuing her working relationship with Guzman and the operation they had going. Even though Elijah reiterated that he was officially retired, she insisted that she still give him ten percent of all profits. Of course he gave her his blessings.

They left the club at two in the morning feeling on top of the world. Each drove separate cars and were equally tipsy. Evidently, driving under the influence didn't apply to them. They made a quick stop at Larry Parker's restaurant in Beverly Hills to grab a bite to eat. Elijah's plan was to eat some greasy food, drink a Pulp Fiction strawberry shake, and get to his condo for some much-needed rest.

"Why don't we all go back to my place for the night since it's closest?" Lauren offered.

"Nah," he declined. "This my week to kick it at my beach spot."

"Well, then, we'll go with you. We haven't earned that yet?" Lauren asked slyly.

Elijah never took anyone to his condo, not even his uncle, and Lauren knew that. When Elijah spent time with women, he took them to hotels or to their place. The condo was where he got his peace of mind.

"Now you know that's my own private hideaway." He was forced to explain to Lauren again for the hundredth time. But just as in the past, she was insistent on seeing his condo.

"Well, tonight that's gonna change," Elise chimed in, "even if we have to follow you, I'm going."

"Me too!" Lauren added.

Elijah shook his head. "What am I gonna do with you two? Y'all are like spoiled daughters. Alright, just this one night, but don't ask me again," he relented.

Elise concealed a smile, enjoying the fact that she made him give her way . . . again.

# CHAPTER TWENTY-SEVEN

The Santa Monica Freeway west ended and let them off onto Pacific Coast Highway where they continued into Malibu. About fifteen minutes later, they came to a stop at a condominium complex that was dug into the face of a rocked cliff. The electric gates to the parking garage opened to allow them entrance.

The elevator let them off on the top floor directly into Elijah's living room. It connected to the dining room as one space, like a loft. The furniture was minimal, modern Asian décor. A thin glass and metal dinette set was on an uncarpeted section of the room. Marble tile blended nicely with the set in its color and design, and plush white carpet ran throughout the rest of the penthouse. The only other furniture in the entry room was a thin leather cushioned futon with bamboo framing and an entertainment center complete with a movie screen TV and state-of-the-art stereo system. The bay windows gave a view of the ocean from anywhere inside the penthouse, two lounge chairs, and a small table on the balcony.

What caught the girls' eyes was the beautifully painted mural that covered an entire side of the wall beginning with a big portrait of his mother Fatima, and progressing into a collage of smaller pictures: Cannon, Malcolm X, 2Pac, Harriet Tubman, Napoléon Bonaparte, Hannibal the Conqueror, George and Jonathan Jackson, Assata Shakur, Big K-Mike, Che Guevara, Fidel Castro, Winnie Mandela, Ho Chi Min, Big Mikeron, Mao Tse Tung, Tiny Smokey, and to the girls' surprise, the drawing ended with a picture of the both of them together that they'd taken at a fight in Las Vegas.

"That's us," Lauren stated the obvious.

Elise's eyes never left Fatima's face. She knew this was his mom without having to be told. "She was so beautiful," she muttered. Elijah walked to the kitchen so he wouldn't have to talk about his mom.

"I'm going to see the rest of your secret lair," Lauren called behind him. "I need to see what's so secret and special." She made her way through the hallway.

Elijah hurried from the kitchen to catch up with her. *She needed to slow her little ass down, running all through my spot,* he thought. He caught her just as she entered the first bedroom. Grabbing her arm playfully, he warned her, "Chill with all the nosiness. You might learn something you don't want to know."

Lauren wasn't trying to hear it. She needed to know what he had going on in this place where he could stay away for months at a time without being lonely. "Maybe I can learn some ideas on how to make my place to your liking so you can stay there with me . . . forever," she said, hinting at them moving in together.

He laughed. "We not about to go into this topic again." *She know she need to cut out the nonsense,* he thought.

For Lauren, it was the exact time to broach the topic again. "I want you to be with me more now, some sort of commitment. Don't worry," she said, placing her hands on her hips, "you can still have your other little girlfriend in there, but only her."

"Oh, you givin' me permission now?" Elijah joked.

"Elijah, I've never sweated you about all the women you've had in the past because I felt it wasn't my place at the time. Now I feel that Assata and I have earned our place in your life. What do you need other women for? I don't understand."

"Slow down, Ma." Elijah smirked. "We don't need to fix something that ain't broken. Our relationship works because we don't put stipulations and impossible expectations on each other."

Lauren sucked her teeth in defiance. "Yeah, well life has changed. I'm not saying it hasn't been great between us, I have no complaints, but it's time for the next step. I want stipulations and expectations not just for me but for you too. I want you to tell me I can't be with other men. You never told me you loved me before tonight, and that's what I've been looking for. I want to be your love, or should I say, *one* of your loves."

"Why do you keep bringing up Assata? She ain't my girlfriend. She's family. Diabla is her love."

Lauren stepped closer and lowered her voice. "A blind person can see that Assata's in love with you. Diabla's just a friend, a crutch that she leans on emotionally." Lauren understood that all the bad things that happened to Assata as a child had killed her trust in men. Until Elijah came along, Diabla was all she had. Women were emotional, so that was what she was doing—acting out of emotions.

"She loves you," Lauren whispered, "and she'll run through fire for you. You love her, too, but you're trying to keep everything in perspective and not think with your dick because you're a good man. That's what I love about you. It's okay to let go sometimes though. It's safe to love us the way we love you."

"You guys hiding from me?" Elise stepped into the doorway. She had been lost in looking at Fatima's picture so intensely that she hadn't realized the two had left her standing there alone.

Lauren immediately switched topics. "Mr. Man here was just showing me around, being my tour guide." She nudged him to continue the tour.

Elijah took her cue and began moving, though he smiled to himself. It always amazed him how quick on her feet she was.

"It's not much to see," he told them as he led the way. "This is obviously my personal gym." He led them into a room was filled with top-of-the-line fitness equipment: treadmill, rowing machine, free weights, etc. "Y'all will get more acquainted with this room in the morning," he promised.

Lauren welcomed the challenge. "You know I'm always down for a good workout." She exercised five days a week faithfully and believed she was in better shape than him. Elise kept quiet on that topic; she wasn't lifting shit but some food or a pistol.

Elijah moved them down the hall to the next room. It had no furniture, only a miniature man-made waterfall with water crashing onto artificial rocks that took up one corner of the room. A large oriental rug sat in the middle floor and assorted candles placed strategically around the room gave off a soothing orange glow. Wrapped around the room between the ceiling and upper wall were words and characters painted in Hebrew, Arabic, Sanskrit, Chinese, and ended in the English phrase: "Man knows thyself."

Elise was confused. "What in the hell is this room all about?"

"This is my meditation room," he responded.

"I love it." Lauren squealed with a little too much enthusiasm. She knew what it was from the get-go and had already envisioned it as being her new "Room of Ceremonies."

They had seen enough of his meditation room; he couldn't have them disturbing the energy. He lazily walked them to the master bedroom where his tour guide duties would end. The room impressed with a California king-sized bed that sat three feet off the floor. The black-silver comforter and pillows matched the artwork and blinds. Two metal and glass nightstands sat on each side of the bed, and a sixty-inch screen TV was mounted into the entertainment center with a home computer and stereo.

Through a widely spaced open doorway, the sleeping area transitioned into the master bathroom with the floor, sink, and shower all in black Italian marble. The glass-encased shower was in its own corner separated from the deep sunken bathtub. The aroma of sandalwood overcame the senses as soon as they entered.

"Wow!" Lauren exclaimed. "I could really get comfortable here." She winked at him with a mischievous smile. "Who helped with the decoration? And don't say nobody because even though you have style, a woman's hand is all over this. Not only that, somebody's definitely been here to do the cleaning."

Elijah looked at her as if he was insulted. "The decorating is all me down to the last detail. And for your information, I clean every morning when I'm here. Y'all got it twisted if you think I don't have skills in interior designing. I got 'natural style.' I didn't need the help of professionals or women," he bragged.

He entered the walk-in closet to grab some socks, a pair of boxers, a muscle shirt, a pair of sweatpants, and his house slippers. "Well, that's the end of the tour," he said as he came back out. "I'm gonna take a shower. I never intended on having company, so I apologize for not having a guest room. This'll have to do for the both of you. I got floor duty." He began walking for the door before he paused and gave them a devious smirk. "You girls play nice," he said, walking out.

"You would like that, wouldn't you, asshole?" Lauren grinned. Elise laughed to herself as she watched him go.

Elijah went to the guest bathroom where he showered then put on his comfortable house wear. He grabbed his weed box and blunts, then went out on the balcony for some fresh air and solitude.

Lauren had a nice soak in the tub while Elise showered. Elise finished well before her and found one of Elijah's T-shirts to put on with her boy shorts, then went to the kitchen for something to drink when she saw him out on the balcony. She poured herself a glass of water and went to join him. Without asking, she squeezed in next to him on the narrow lounge chair.

"A penny for your thoughts," she said, looking up at the sky.

He blew out a cloud of smoke. "I was thinking about what I always think about: life." He gazed up at the stars.

She laid her head on his shoulder. "Have you figured it out yet . . . life?"

"Life can never be figured out. Only analyzed to try to gain some perspective. What about you? What do you want out of life?"

She thought for a minute. "I . . . don't know. I guess happiness."

"That's a good answer. Most people want material shit when happiness is really what they should be aiming for. A lot of us want happiness, too, but achieving it is the problem. I've pretty much given up on happiness; I'd be content with a bit of peace within."

Elise took the blunt from his hand. "How do you get peace within?" She pulled from the blunt and coughed.

"I'll tell you when I figure it out. For right now I just learn to enjoy the good moments with no intentions of holding on to them forever."

"Just live in the moment then, huh?"

"I guess you can call it that." He paused to contemplate. "Like right now, just sitting here with you watching the night sky . . . that's peace." He paused again, then went completely off topic. "You got some pretty feet." He stared down at her tiny feet with soft pink polish.

She raised her head to look at him. "Nigga, don't tell me you got a foot fetish." She laughed at the thought of it.

He laughed, too, because she was somewhat right: he did have some sort of attraction to women with nice feet, but it wasn't a damn foot fetish. "Cut it out. Ain't nothing wrong with me taking notice when a woman have nice feet."

"Sounds like a foot fetish to me," she clowned, snuggling back up against him.

"See, I can't even give you a compliment. Don't worry about it, I lied, your feet are funny looking."

She ribbed him with her elbow. "You better not call my feet funny looking." She raised them up. "You know you like 'em." She laughed.

"They probably stink."

"Fuck you. Yours probably stink! My feet are always fresh."

He suddenly raised up to grab one and she instinctively tucked them under her, screaming for him to stop through her laughter. He maneuvered over her and pried it from under her as she struggled.

"Leave me alone," she pleaded while still laughing.

He overpowered her, raising her foot to his nose for a whiff. "Ugh, they do stink!"

"Fuck you!" She still couldn't stop laughing.

"Scoot your ass over and give me my spot back." He tried to push her legs over.

She had taken over the entire recliner during their struggle. "Nope, it's mine now," she said like a stubborn child.

He disregarded her protest and still went to reclaim his spot. She planted both feet on his chest to block the way, and the move caused her T-shirt to hike up above her waist, giving him a clear view of her boy shorts. She watched as his eyes got stuck on her crotch area and made no move to obstruct his view. It was as if he was momentarily under a spell.

Slowly, he looked up at her and knew immediately that she had caught him in one of his moments. Still, her feet rested on his chest as a long pregnant pause ensued, the two looked into each other's eyes. Finally, he gently took one of her feet and kissed the sole of it, then did the same with the other. She gave no resistance; her eyes invited him to move forward.

"Elijah?" came Lauren's voice from the hallway, interrupting the moment.

"We're out here on the balcony." He slowly lowered Elise's feet back to the chair, pausing to look in her eyes one more time before turning his attention to Lauren's approach.

Lauren wore one of his T-shirts as well, but she'd chose a smaller one than Elise and it barely went past her hips. Any slight movement on her part gave a nice shot of her lace thong. "You having a meeting without me?" She toweled off her hair. "Damn, I really enjoyed my bath. I see why this is your hideaway. Everything is so peaceful. I love this view. You should've shared this place with me way before now."

Elise diverted her eyes as she spoke, her panties wet and feeling aroused.

Elijah kissed Lauren's cheek. "I'm glad it's up to your standards," he told her as he made his way back inside. "Bring my weed box in when y'all finish. I'm goin' to get some sleep," he called over his shoulder. The weed, alcohol, and partying had finally caught up to him.

He went to the linen closet and grabbed a sheet, blanket, and pillow, then swung back through the living room for one of the cushions before heading for the meditation room where he would sleep for the night. The girls were still on the balcony chilling when he walked to the room. Making a pallet on the floor, he lay down to clear his head. The calming glow of the candles and sound of the waterfall relaxed him. He was asleep before he knew it.

During the late night and early morning hours, he felt the blanket pull back and a soft warm body nestled up against him. Turning over he saw Elise's face in the predawn light. He rubbed his eyes and squinted. Was he dreaming or just plain trippin'? She looked deep into his eyes and pulled him closer to let him know it wasn't a dream. He was now fully awake, and fully erect.

"You sure this what you want?" he whispered. She pulled his shoulder toward her as she lay on her back in answer to his question.

Elijah mounted her and prepared to go inside her when she suddenly tensed up. "You alright? Did I do something wrong?"

"No, don't stop," she purred. "I . . . just . . . this is my first time being with a man *willingly*. I don't know exactly what I should be doing."

"Just relax." Elijah brushed his hand across her lips. "I got you." He kissed her softly on the lips and slowly moved downward. The kisses went from her neck to her collarbone, then to her breasts. Her breathing sped up as he took them into his mouth one at a time, teasing, sucking, and kissing. She gripped the back of his head not knowing what else to do with her hands. Trailing kisses down her stomach, he finally reached her moist slit, licking her juices sliding his tongue inside her. Elise grinded against his face, pressing on the back of his head aggressively.

"Oh shit, Elijah . . . yes," she moaned. Hearing her call his name in ecstasy put him into overdrive. It was time to rev things up a notch. He slid two fingers inside her hot wetness as he continued to work his tongue magic. Her moans and hip thrust intensified.

"Oh . . . you're gonna make me come in your face, baby. Oh, I'm about to come!" Her legs trembled uncontrollably, as her back bent like a contortionist. She screamed wildly, and her body convulsed in a massive orgasm.

Being fully experienced in pleasing a woman, he knew the first part of the task was complete. He climbed on top of an already exhausted Elise and entered her. Her tight walls felt like a mink-lined glove on his rock-hard dick. The long, slow strokes caused her to claw at his back. He continued his rhythm; the deeper he went, the further her nails dug into his back.

"Oh, God! Elijah! Give it to me! Fuck me!" she groaned.

His concentration was focused solely on touching every pleasure spot inside of her as he picked up the pace. At first she lay there without moving her hips, but before long her fighter's spirit emerged and she threw it back at him fiercely. Beads of sweat formed on her chest and forehead, sparking the savage in him. He worked her without mercy. Her nails were embedded so deep in his back that blood began to seep from the wounds. The pain from her nails only excited him more. He felt like a gorilla ravishing a fragile, beautiful creature with pleasure and pain. Elise was making enough noise to wake the entire complex, so to quiet her a little he began sucking on her lips. She responded by sticking her tongue as far as it would go into his mouth. Both were in a frenzy as he slammed deeper and deeper. Elijah considered flipping her doggy style, but her face was too enticing to turn away from. Her walls felt like a piece of heaven, and instead of loosening up with the moisture, it seemed to grow tighter. He felt like his dick had swollen an extra three inches inside of her. Losing control, he started a tremble dance of his own. His ass cheeks compressed as he buried every inch of himself in her soft, wet pussy.

"Oh shit . . ." he panted. "Oh . . . oh shit . . . ohhhh!" He came inside of her, harder than he had with anyone before. He rolled on to his back to catch his breath.

"Go get a wet towel," he gasped.

In response, she slung one of her legs across his and snuggled up against him. She didn't want their closeness to end. She never thought being with a man would feel so amazing. The tenderness and care Elijah showed her, covered the open wound left in her would by her uncle. "No," she whispered. I want us to lay here in what we created."

He was about to say something when she let out a sudden giggle. "What's so funny?" he said, looking at the top of her head.

"You. I finally figured out what I have to do to get you to call me Elise." She laughed, caressing his chest.

"Girl, knock it off. Didn't nobody call out your name. You must've been hearing things," he said with a smile.

"Yeah, I was hearing things alright. 'Oh Elise'! 'Oh Elise'!" she mocked. "Don't worry, I won't tell anybody." She cracked up even harder.

He rubbed his hand through her hair and kissed her forehead. "Kiss my ass . . . Elise," he chuckled. She fell asleep in his arms. Listening to each other's heartbeat, they both soon drifted off into deep sleep.

---

Elijah woke up and lay motionless as he listened to the waterfall. The smell of frying turkey sausage and turkey bacon hit nostrils and made his mouth water. It took him a few seconds to remember the events of last night and how he came to be sleeping on the floor in his meditation room.

He stood and stretched. With a swift jerk of his hand against his chin, he cracked the kinks out of his neck, then headed to the shower. He smiled at the thought of why he was butt-naked. In the bathroom, he relieved himself, brushed his teeth, and then soaked under the hot shower water for a good while. Finished, he slipped on his boxers, sweatpants and slippers, then went to the kitchen where Lauren and Elise were working their magic.

"You finally up, huh?", Lauren said. "I thought you were going to sleep the rest of the day away."

"I just needed a li'l extra rest," he dryly commented, getting a glass from the cupboard.

"Yeah, I bet you did with all that activity you two had going on in the middle of the night."

Elijah pretended not to hear her. He preoccupied himself with pouring the cranberry juice. Elise played dumb as well, keeping her eyes in the pot of potatoes she stirred unnecessarily. The embarrassed smirk on her face revealed that she had heard Lauren loud and clear.

"Um . . . hum . . . my ass," Lauren continued with her slight saltiness. "I almost came and interrupted your little *meeting*, but she sounded like she was enjoying herself too much, so I decided since it was her first time with you, I'd let it be her night." She took the glass from his hand, drinking the last of the juice as she stared with accusatory eyes. "From here on out," she said once the juice was gone, "you at least better invite me to your bed and let me decide whether I want to sleep alone or not."

Elise felt uncomfortable even though she knew Lauren wasn't trippin'. For whatever reason, Elise still viewed her as his girlfriend, regardless of them both saying otherwise.

"What you talking about?" Elijah continued his playing-dumb game. "I did invite you to my bed, how you think I ended up on the floor?"

Lauren wasn't in the mood for his bullshit. She was serious and it was time for all of them to come to an understanding. She rolled her eyes at him and looked at Elise. "And you, Miss Elise . . . yeah, that's right, *Elise*, don't be trying to look all innocent. We may as well get this all out on the table here and now."

Elise finally turned to face her, allowing Lauren to give it to her like the straight shooter she was. "I know how much you love him," Lauren started in on her, "and you know I love him just as much. I'm a real bitch, which you should already know, so you and I are not gonna play the jealousy game . . . at least not with each other. We're not gonna make him have to sneak between us like we're high school kids or some lame ass couple. I'm gonna accept you, and you're gonna accept me. We'll love him and each other at the same time. Do we have an understanding?" Lauren stood, hands on hips.

Elise didn't take orders from anyone but Elijah. She respected Lauren, never feared her, but at that moment the respect level elevated to the utmost. It was completely clear to her that this white girl was a full-blooded thoroughbred. All Elise could do was nod her agreement.

With that part out of the way, Lauren turned her attention back to him. It was time for the ultimatum. "You gotta uphold your part in this new arrangement if we're willing to. It's gonna be me and Elise. No more bitches. This is our circle . . . just us three."

Elijah watched in amusement. "I told you before, just because you got a fat ass don't mean you have real weight to throw around."

"Stop playing, I'm serious," Lauren said sternly.

He bit into his turkey sausage and studied Lauren for a minute. "You know what?" he said, coming to a decision. "I respect you for coming at me and Elise like a real one. Y'all are more solid than most of these niggas who call themselves 'real soldiers'. So, you have my word, I'll keep it solid with just you two . . . except for the strippers and call girls on my trips to Vegas." They all laughed. "Nah, I'm just playin'. You got my word."

"Then, that's that!" Lauren began to pile food on his plate. "Now, let's get you fed. You owe me for neglecting me last night. You better eat your Wheaties."

# CHAPTER TWENTY-EIGHT

Elise and Lauren cleaned the kitchen in silence. Elise had a question that had been on her mind for some time. She inquired to Elijah about it in the past but could never get an answer out of him. He would always tell her to ask Lauren herself. That was just how he was, feeling that telling her details of Lauren's past without her being present was somehow betraying her trust. She suspected that he hadn't told Lauren of her own past either for the same reason.

She never felt comfortable enough in the past to ask Lauren, but now that they had shared so much of themselves with each other, she felt the time was right.

"I want to ask you a personal question," she began. "I mean . . . I don't know if it should be considered personal if we're family."

"Stop beating around the bush and just ask what you want to ask." Lauren set aside the rag she was using to wipe the centerpiece.

"Why are you so loyal to Elijah?"

Lauren knew this question would come eventually, had even considered in advance how she would answer it, *if* 'IF' she decided to at all.

She weighed Elise with her eyes for a moment. Heaving a sigh, she stared out the window into the distance allowing herself to remember, to go back and relive those dark moments in her past. Her sophomore year at the University of Southern California was the turning point in her life, but it all started long before then.

She had been born to meth-head parents in Val Verde, California. At nine years old, her father, in a delusional methamphetamine-induced rage, strangled her mother to death in their tiny shack. He received a life sentence in prison for the crime and Lauren was taken in by her maternal grandmother who was already on her last leg. By the time Lauren reached the age of eleven, her grandmother died of a sudden heart attack, leaving her an orphan.

Most families looking to adopt weren't usually in the market for pre-teens and teenagers, but were more likely than not searching for infants or toddlers. Older kids getting adopted was a somewhat crap shoot, with the odds leaning toward "not going to happen."

Lauren was a victim of those odds. She spent her teenage years in foster homes where she learned to fight and survive. Through her hard and lonely times, education became her only refuge. She devoured books on many different subjects in her time alone and excelled in the classroom. In her senior year of high school, her aptitude for learning landed her on the Dean's list, and ultimately earned her a full academic scholarship to USC. Though book smart and drop dead gorgeous by any standard, she was inexperienced and extremely insecure.

In her freshman year at the university, she worked part-time at a local campus pizza joint. One evening while working the cash register a young Puerto Rican guy came in. He was pretty to the point of almost appearing feminine. His black Polo sweat suit and matching sneakers complimented his jet-black curly hair. The diamonds around his neck and wrist and those in his ear seemed to make him glow. The well-trimmed mustache and manicured fingernails topped off his pretty-boy swag. She was speechless when he asked, "Beautiful, what's your name?" after placing his order.

It took him asking a second time before she clumsily stammered out, "La-Lauren."

His compliments on her beauty and seasoned smooth talk had her blushing red. She self-consciously fidgeted with her hair, avoiding direct eye contact. She had never been in an official relationship before, being that she was too ashamed and insecure in herself and all the things she felt she lacked. When Monolinthe, ("Mono" for short) left the restaurant that evening, he had a pizza in one hand and her mind in the other.

At the beginning of their relationship, he wined and dined her and bought her nice things. Gradually he became more possessive, convincing her to quit her job on the promise that he would take care of her. He later had her move out of the dorm and into his apartment.

By her sophomore year he wanted her in his presence at all times, at least when he was home. She began missing classes and her grades dropped. When she voiced her concerns about missing school, he presented her with a choice: she could either be his woman or she could continue in that "bullshit of a school," but she couldn't do both.

Desperately not wanting to lose the only person in the world who loved her, she gave up school. Now that she was totally dependent on him, his behavior grew more and more abusive by the day. First it was verbally, then it became physical. He had a way of speaking that made her feel minor and insignificant. The chokes and slaps he doled out only reinforced those feelings. She couldn't understand what it was she did wrong. *Why can't I get it right,* she told herself, *I need to do better.* She loved him unconditionally.

It wasn't long before Mono introduced her to powder cocaine. The first line she snorted was to appease him, but once she got a taste of the white euphoria, she loved it. It took away all her mental and physical pains. She could be free, alive, and for the first time in her life feel sexually attractive.

She never wanted to come down from the high, wanting more and more. He always had it but began refusing her access. As time wore on, he'd make her beg before giving her a little taste. Then the time came when he broke the news. "My paper getting low. Bitch, you spending up all my shit. You can't just be around here doing nothin' with your lazy ass. If you want to keep snorting blow, living good and keep me, you gotta pitch in and move something. Do your mother-fuckin' part."

He then moved in for the kill. "I got a homie who would love to kick it with you and he willing to break a nigga off for making it happen." She couldn't believe her ears, that he was willing to trade her body for some drugs. The expression on his face let her know that he was dead serious.

"Have you lost your fucking mind?" she had protested.

His demeanor was calm and cool. "Get out," was all he told her.

"I have nowhere to go," she cried hysterically. He simply stared at her emotionless, her tears not meaning a thing to him.

Faced with the dilemma, she felt there was no choice but to relent and do what he said. As it so happened, the one friend led to another the next day, then another the day after that, and so on and so forth until finally it was four to five men a day. She never saw any of the money. When she complained, he would give her more cocaine and told her to shut up. Eventually, her will to resist was broken and she became a defeated slave to him and the cocaine.

One day out of the blue, he came home with a new outfit and shoes for her. "I'm gonna take you to get your hair and nails done," he told her. At first, she thought her old love was back, but the optimistic air was soon let out of her balloon.

"I have a meeting with some important mutha-fuckas whose team I'm trying be down with and I need you to help me make a good impression. You know, like my dime-piece bitch." He explained like he was on some real pimp shit. "All you have to do is look good and do what the fuck you're told."

Elijah walked into Boulevard Café on Martin Luther King Boulevard like he owned the place. The quaint soul-food restaurant had the vibe of a down South hole-in-the-wall dining room. The aroma of fried chicken and home-style potatoes hung thick in the air. The host and waitresses were all middle-aged heavy-set black women who would scold or flirt in a heartbeat, depending on the circumstances. When they saw him come in, a few of the waitresses stopped what they were doing to embrace him. He treated them like aunts, even though a few seemed like they wanted to be more like incestuous aunts.

He was finally able to get away from their flirting and affection and made his way over to the table where Mono stood waiting. Though Mono stood a full three inches taller, he appeared unimposing in the presence of Elijah.

Lauren always had the impression of Mono being smooth and in control, but from the moment Elijah shook his hand and gave eye contact, Mono grew erratic and nervous in his movements. For the first time, she witnessed the chink in his armor. She wondered, *Who's this man? He doesn't look over twenty. He's making Mono behave like a little schoolgirl?*

The meeting began with Mono trying his best to convince Elijah of how good an asset he could be to the organization, and how much of a loyal soldier he was. Elijah's expression was unreadable. Every so often he would stare at Lauren with intimidating eyes.

About twenty minutes in, Mono was still rambling about the drug spots he could operate and how much money his "hoes" could bring in. In the middle of Mono's sentence, Elijah turned to her and asked, "What's your name?"

The question caught her off guard, and Mono, too, for that matter. For a split second, Mono's face betrayed the perceived disrespect but he recovered quickly and let out a fake chuckle.

"What's funny?" Elijah asked without a hint of humor.

"My bad . . . I didn't mean no disrespect, man," Mono stumbled over his words.

Focusing back on Lauren, he asked again, "What's your name?"

Drawing his full attention, her hand started to tremble. She self-consciously ran it through her hair. "My name is Lauren," she told him timidly.

Elijah then asked Mono, "Where did you get her from?" Without waiting for an answer, he added, "Why in hell would you bring her to a business meeting?"

"I . . . uh . . . I cracked her at a pizza joint in the USC Village," he boasted with nervous laughter. "She was going to school at USC. Now she's my best earner. I brought her because I thought you might want to test the merchandise I had to offer." He smiled.

Elijah was offended but his face never showed it. "Lauren, are you still in school?" he asked, ignoring Mono.

Before she could respond, Mono answered for her, "I made the bitch quit so she could hustle for me full time."

"I didn't ask you anything," Elijah calmly stated.

Mono shut his mouth unless he was asked a question directly. Elijah then asked Lauren a string of questions: What had she majored in? What was her GPA? What was her SAT scores leaving high school?

At first it felt like an interrogation, but after a few questions it became refreshing to talk about something she was familiar with. She was new to dealing with black people from the streets, and the previous ones she'd met through Mono, their conversations didn't go past sex, music, clothes, and violence. She was surprised by his interest and knowledge in academics. For a while, she'd forgotten that she was a prostitute and cokehead.

After the meeting, Elijah stood and assured Mono, "I'll give your proposition some thought and get back to you." He paused and scrutinized Mono briefly.

"One thing I need to ask before leaving: Why would you take a girl out of college to sell her body?" He turned and walked for the door before Mono could give an answer.

Before exiting, he stopped at the host working the front entrance and whispered in her ear. She nodded her understanding and scribbled something on a piece of paper.

As Lauren and Mono gathered their belongings to leave, the host came over to them. "The tab has already been taken care of," she announced with a big smile. "You're always welcome here, because a friend of Li'l Nine's is a friend of mine," she told Mono, and gave him a friendly hug good-bye.

She then embraced Lauren and whispered, "I'm putting something in your pocket. Read it when you're alone."

"Let's go," Mono barked at Lauren as he headed for the exit. She simply lowered her head and picked up the pace, quickly following his footsteps out of the restaurant.

The weeks and months following the meeting had Mono more violent and unpredictable than ever. He blamed Lauren for Elijah not calling him to join the team. He took to beating her on a regular basis. One of her eyes had become permanently blackened it seemed. Looking in the mirror one day, she lightly touched her eye and winced from the pain. Her lips were swollen and specked with dried, crusted blood. She barely recognized herself. *How did I get to this place in my life?* she thought. Tears ran down her face as she broke down on her knees and sobbed.

She needed somewhere to turn, someone to save her. She got up and went to her hiding place where she hid the piece of paper she had gotten months earlier. She'd been through this routine on three different occasions, but always backed out at the last minute. Finally gaining enough courage, she dialed the seven digits into the cell phone.

"Hello?" the male voice answered, but before she could speak, her sobbing overtook her.

A week later, Mono got the call he had been waiting on. Elijah would be at his apartment within the hour to discuss the terms of their new business arrangement.

Mono nearly tripped over himself when he heard the doorbell ring. Opening the door to admit Elijah and Big Teflon, he was all smiles and giddy with nervous energy in his greetings. Elijah took a seat on the sofa while Big Teflon continued to stand, eyes surveying the apartment.

"Hey, come get them something to drink," he called for Lauren to serve his guest.

She stepped out from the back room, head down, looking frailer than the last time Elijah had seen her. "What would you like?" she asked nervously.

"Nothing for my guy, water for me," Elijah answered.

She brought the water and handed it to him. "Have a seat." Elijah patted the spot next to him. "Come on . . . right here."

She hesitantly sat, looking over to Mono as she did so.

"So, Mono . . ." Elijah took a sip of his water and rested his hand on Lauren's knee. "I come to tell you that I don't believe this thing with me and you gonna work out."

Mono looked around confused. "What? I thought . . . I thought everything was good."

"Nah, Mono, it isn't." Elijah sat the glass on the coffee table and relaxed back. "You see, you just too damn pretty. Shit, you more pretty than most of my bitches and you look like you can give better head too. I can't work with a mutha-fucka prettier than my bitches."

Mono frowned in anger. He had a healthy fear of Elijah, but a man could only take so much. "Get the fuck out of—"

Big Teflon's blow landed so hard that Lauren jumped at the sound. Mono crumpled to the floor and rolled around holding his nose, moaning in pain.

"You don't look so tough now, pretty boy," Elijah said. "It's not so easy when it comes from a man, huh? You like beating women, Mono? Makes you feel like a man?"

Lauren watched as Mono rolled on the ground crying. A suppressed hatred bubbled up to the surface. She saw him for what he really was . . . a coward bitch.

"Go get the money and jewelry," Elijah told her.

She stood, gave Mono a double-take, then collected everything he had of any value and brought it back to Elijah. At that point, Mono had been propped up on the couch being held at gunpoint, blood pouring from his broken nose soaking the front of his shirt like red paint.

Mono glared at Lauren with pure hatred. "You traitor bitch. I've taken care of you and this is how you thank me? I'm gonna kill you, bitch!"

"This is what you call taking care of me?" she screamed. "Look at me . . . look what you did. You destroyed me, you piece of shit." She slapped his face as hard as her weak hands allowed. He accepted the slap with a mask of venom.

Elijah placed his hand on her shoulder from behind. "Today you have an option," he told her. "I offer you your honor, your dignity, and your power back." He spoke close to her ear.

He nodded to Big Teflon, who stepped forward and placed the silencer equipped .22 Luger in her hand. She looked at the gun, then to Mono. Slowly, she raised it to his face. Her hands trembled, and time stood still in the room.

"It's up to you," Elijah whispered. "I only gave you the option, and now you decide whether he lives or dies. There is no judgment on whatever you choose."

Five shots spat from the gun in rapid succession, .22 slugs burning through his face like hot butter. The metal-on-metal action from the gun's firing mechanism was all that could be heard, explosion suppressed entirely. Tiny specks of blood sprayed into Lauren's face as Mono's head whipped backward, then pitched forward in a dead-man's dive.

Elijah and Big Teflon looked on emotionless. To Lauren's own surprise, her nervousness disappeared, she felt . . . powerful! There was no sympathy for Mono; he'd gotten what he deserved, and she was in some odd way proud of herself.

---

Lauren spent the next six months on a ranch in the Mojave Desert outside of California City. The first three months was hell for her. Elijah made her go cold turkey to kick the coke habit. He locked her in a small room when she went through withdrawal symptoms, only opening the door to give her fruit, water, and juice. No matter how much she pleaded for him to stop the torture it fell on deaf ears.

After the three-month cleanse, she began to feel normal again. He then took her into town to see a private doctor where she had a series of tests ran and given a general physical. Luckily, she was given a clean bill of health.

The next three months she was forced to exercise with him every morning and maintain an all-natural diet. The rest of her free time was spent reading from his personal library of books on metaphysics and history.

Once he felt that she was ready to be on her own, he told her, "My job is done. I got in touch with your old guidance counselor at USC and we were able to work together and get you accepted back in school. Your scholarship couldn't be reinstated so I'm gonna cover that myself."

Lauren was speechless. "Why?" was all she could ask. He never gave an answer.

Never once during the six months did he ever try to make an advance toward her. She got the impression that he didn't have any interest in her sexually. Upon their return to LA, he gave her a Nissan Maxima, ten thousand dollars, and wished her luck.

He never called or visited her in school. She made it her business to call him at least once every two weeks to ask for advice or to see if he needed her to do anything. Occasionally, he'd have her run a few errands, but most times he would talk to her for a while then let her go on about her life. To her, he was her best friend and the family she never had.

After numerous attempts of trying to seduce him, in her senior year she finally got her wish. After a night of drinking and partying with him she ended up in his suite at the Hotel Nikko in Beverly Hills. He made love to her in a way that she had never experienced. The college boys she dated here and there were cool, but Elijah was her world.

He wouldn't commit to a formal relationship, instead encouraging her to experience life and graduate so she could go on to law school and become *his* lawyer. Accomplishing this was what would be important, not trying to be his girlfriend. He drilled into her head to be completely independent and never have to look to no one but herself.

She had to respect and accept his honesty and the role he wanted her to play in his life. She promised herself that she would play that role well, and that was how she would repay him for all that he had done for her.

Elise was close to tears when Lauren finished her story. Her love and respect for Lauren and Elijah grew even more, if that was at all possible.

"Thank you for sharing that with me." She hugged Lauren.

"Thank you for asking." She kissed Elise softly on the neck.

# CHAPTER TWENTY-NINE

Big Teflon sat on the hood of his '64 Chevy as Ju-Ju drove into Jesse Owens Park. Since Elijah and Li'l Teflon had been off doing their own thing, it gave Ju-Ju and Big Teflon the opportunity to grow closer. Together they shared the responsibility of keeping the next generation of Nine Os in line when the others were out of town. Since they couldn't hustle in none of Wizard and Hitter's states any longer, they had opened up dope spots on both sides of the hood and grinded locally.

Big Teflon appeared gloomy as Ju-Ju jumped out of his Suburban. One of the little homies had been killed the night before by the Hoovers. The youngster was hanging out on Western without a gun when some members of the Hoovers drove up and pumped him full of lead. Teflon had warned them over and over to be careful, but like most teenagers that thought they knew it all. It wasn't until slugs ripped through him that he realized Super Nigga only existed in the movies.

"What's crackin' with the retaliation?" Ju-Ju asked.

"It's already in motion," Big Teflon said, sparking the morning blunt. "I gave about ten of the Tiny-Toons straps and G-rides. As we speak they should be hittin' the Nine-Deuces, Seven-Foes and Eight-Tray Snoovas."

Ju-Ju felt they shouldn't have wasted time on the Nine-Deuces because they were a non-factor, but he kept his opinion to himself, already knowing how Big Teflon felt. To him a Snoova was a Snoova and should all get a taste of the 90 Crip wrath.

"I wonder if Li'l Tef and Nine gonna come back for the funeral," Ju-Ju speculated as he accepted the blunt.

"Ain't no tellin', cuzz," Big Teflon looked conflicted. "It's a lot going on with them that we don't know about."

"A lot like what?"

"Just a lot of bullshit. Hood politics, you know how they get down."

Ju-Ju exhaled a cloud of smoke, watching the traffic flow up and down Western. "Yeah, well they need to figure it out, we suppose' to be one unit. It seems to me like money and power is separating us."

Big Teflon didn't want to talk about his brother or Elijah. That topic was too sensitive, too raw. He redirected the conversation. "It is what it is" he said. "How's your mom doing?"

Ju-Ju turned somber. "I don't know, cuzz. She try to put on a brave face for me, but that chemotherapy and radiation is destroying her. She's lost her hair and so much weight that I don't know how she's still standing. It's killin' me to see her like that. Makes me want to kill up the whole world."

Big Teflon was sad for him, but it wasn't much he could do or say to help the situation. "I know, cuzz" he tried to give Ju-Ju some assurance, "but you got to keep your head. Be strong for her. Everything gonna be alright, Just a small bump in the road."

"I hope so, cuzz. I hope so."

Elise slid Diabla a black duffle bag across the table as they sat facing each other. Diabla had been Elise's friend and companion when she had no one else, and they would always be friends. Diabla, for her part, eyed Elise suspiciously. Something about this entire visit felt awkward for her, like Elise was trying to tell her something but not coming right out and saying it. A peek inside the bag revealed ten individually wrapped bundles of money, a hundred thousand dollars.

Elise was struggling with the awkward encounter as well and knew she had to be careful with her words. The last thing she wanted to do was damage their friendship with her new decision. She had given her the money to make sure Diabla would be well taken care of in her absence.

"I was going to tell you sooner," Elise hesitated, "but things hadn't been finalized yet. I just bought a house in Malibu. I'm moving out."

Diabla stopped fiddling with the money and leaned back in her chair. She already knew this day would come, she just didn't know when. "Was this your decision or that *vato* Nine-Lives?"

"It was mine. It's just time for us to have our own space, do some soul searching. I want to take my life in a different direction."

Diabla leaned forward, stacking the bundles on the table as she gathered her thoughts. "Are you fuckin' him?" she asked without looking at Elise.

"Do you really want to know?"

"Yeah, I do." She sat back again, crossing her arms. "As much as we've been through, you at least owe me the truth."

Diabla was right, Elise knew it, so she laid it on her. "Elijah's my man now and I have to honor that. Me and you started as friends and somehow it became something else. It's time to put things back in perspective. I honor you as a friend and I'm not ashamed nor have any regrets about what we shared. I love you and always will, but something in my soul tells me that loving Elijah is my rightful place in life, and that's what I have to follow."

Diabla studied her. "So you really love him?"

"To the fullest." Elise answered without hesitation.

A knowing smirk creased Diabla's face. A part of her was upset, but not to the point where she was going to hate on Elise. She had already known for a while that Elise was in love with him, so she guessed she had already prepared herself for this moment. At the end of the day, if they loved each other, and he could give her more happiness, then Elise had to give it a chance. She deserved that.

"I'm happy to see you happy, *mami*"," Diabla said. "I'd be a hater if I tried to stop you from what you feel inside. But you tell that *vato* he better take care of you, because if he doesn't, it's a badass Mexican bitch in the cut waitin' to take his place."

Elise smiled. They stood up and hugged each other good-bye. It felt good to close another chapter in her life, only to start a new, promising, hopeful one.

# CHAPTER THIRTY

A heavyset dark-skinned woman in her late forties dressed in a nurse's uniform opened the door to Brenda's house. Her presence alone made Elijah feel like a stranger to the house. Over the years, Brenda's place had always felt like a second home to him, but today the house was much too quiet and a depressing energy hung thick in the air. The smell of industrial-strength disinfection products and something he couldn't quite put his finger on gave him the feeling of being in a hospital or morgue. The hospice nurse allowed him in, gave a dry greeting, then scurried back to the kitchen to continue whatever she was doing before he came.

Elijah made his way to Brenda's room with a sense of anxiety and apprehension. He paused at the door before inching it open to peek inside. The scene before him sent a tingle up his spine. The room had been transformed into a miniature I.C.U. ward. The queen-sized bed that was normally there was replaced by a traditional adjustable county hospital bed. A machine that dispensed heavy pain medication sat next to it, and monitoring components and other medical devices and tubes were positioned strategically around the bed.

Elijah's instincts told him to get out of there as quickly as possible, but something inside him compelled him forward. When he had gotten the call from Lady Rawdog that Brenda was at home sick on hospice, he had no idea this was what she meant. The philosophy behind hospice was to allow the terminally ill patient to die at home among family and friends with some form of dignity. If this was the aim, he surely missed the logic. He made a silent plea to never go through this form of death; he'd prefer a swift, hot bullet to the head while he was still young and strong.

Brenda lay staring at the ceiling, all motherly plumpness reduced to skin and bone. A white skullcap covered her head to hide her baldness, a result of the radiation. Even in this horrible condition, her face managed to have a peaceful resonance about it.

She turned to smile at him. "Elijah?" she practically whispered. "Hey, baby. I thought you'd forgotten about the old gal."

Elijah kissed her forehead. "Now you know that could never happen. How could I forget my favorite girl?" He tried his best to act normal and disguise the hurt he was feeling for her. "Nobody told me what was going on with you until yesterday, I woulda been here sooner if I knew. Why didn't you call or have somebody call me before now?"

"Aw, chile, I didn't want to worry you with my stuff. You have enough going on in your life. I can handle this end." She strained a soft laugh.

He sat on the bed next to her and kissed her bone-thin hand. "I don't know what I can do, but if there's anything you need all you have to do is say the word," he offered with the utmost sincerity.

Brenda smiled up at him. After all that he had done for her, he was still trying to help. She adjusted her position to be able to see his face better. The movement took a big effort on her part. "I'm just happy you came to see me. Elijah . . . this is the end of my road. It'll probably be the last time we'll be able to talk. I'm dying, baby, but I'm ok with it." She paused when she saw the cloud come over his face. "Aw now, now, baby, don't get sad on me."

Elijah hadn't shed tears in years; he'd come to believe himself above sentimental emotions at this point in his life. He'd endured so much hardship and grief that he felt himself immune to it all. But Brenda's words, in that moment, broke something inside of him. The floodgates opened, and everything he had kept bottled up over the years came pouring out. The grief from his mother, uncle, and friends' deaths, his anger at the forces in life that caused so much tribulation in his world, the men that his hands had killed due to circumstances and forces he couldn't seem to gain control over, the taint on his soul . . . All these feelings of the past and present merged to spill from his eyes.

Brenda rubbed his head as only a real mother could. "Go ahead and let it out," she consoled him. "It's okay, baby, crying cleanses the soul."

It took quite a while to regain some form of composure before he excused himself to go to the bathroom and wash his face. He came back holding a damp towel and sat next to her. "I'm sorry for breaking down in front of you like this. I'm supposed to be giving you strength not the other way around." He felt embarrassed.

Sensing that, Brenda took his hand in hers. "It doesn't make you any less of a man to accept support from others or to show feelings," she said. "We all need that in life at some point or another. That is part of God's mercy for us, to give us people to lean on when we need it."

Elijah grunted in disdain. "With no disrespect toward you, God is the last thing I want to hear about right now."

"What do you mean?" Brenda asked, incredulous.

Elijah vented his rage toward God even though he knew that he probably shouldn't, giving her condition, but anger overrode his logic. "God don't care about us. Look at what he constantly put us through. You a good person, tried your best in life, and look at your reward—an unspeakable death. Where's the goodness? Where's the mercy? Where's the love?"

Brenda shook her head. "I don't have all the answers to your questions," she said sadly. "Some questions in life never get answered. One thing is certain, you need to start focusing on and counting your blessings and stop dwelling on the negativity. If you don't, your blessings will pass you by without you truly enjoying them. No, I don't want to die this way, but if it's God's will then I have to accept it. I didn't complain when God blessed me with all the wonderful things and gave me all the good experiences. Why should I question him and complain now? If I can accept my fate and keep on believing, you who is much stronger than me should definitely have no problem being a strong soldier for God through all the struggles."

She paused to adjust her position and put together what she needed to say. It had been on her heart for a long time to have this conversation with him. Being that this would probably be her last chance to do so, she knew she had to be clear and thorough with her message.

"It's all a test to see who is going to remain faithful to God and who is going to fold." She reached up and caressed his cheek. "Many are called but few are chosen, baby. You are a chosen one. All you have to do is look around you to see how blessed you are. You're not dead, in prison, or strung out on drugs. Elijah, you defied the odds, you took the hell that life dealt you and still triumphed. For this you should be thankful and proud, because Lord knows I'm proud of you."

Elijah's eyes glossed over as he listened intently, contemplating all that she was saying.

"When a strong, young black man does what he has to do to ensure the survival and progress of his family, even if it's by illegal means, society says we're supposed to look down on and criticize them. But I won't do it. You're a hero. So, don't never let anyone make you feel bad about what you had to do to survive. And remember that God knows your heart, and the goodness that's in there is what makes him continue to love you."

Her strength began to fade, but she willed herself to give him what she believed was the most important part of her message. "Now that you are successful, Elijah, change your line of work. Don't keep doing things that'll allow these people to come and take all you worked for and cage or kill you like they do all our great men. Get out of the game now—you've already won."

A light tap on the door gave Brenda a moment to rest her eyes for a brief second. The nurse peeked her head in. "Your lady friend wants to know if it's alright to come in now."

Elijah wiped his face with the towel and gestured for the nurse to let Elise in.

One look at him and Elise knew he was taking the situation extremely hard. She walked over, draped her arms around his neck, and kissed his cheek.

Brenda's eyes fluttered opened to get a good look at Elise. Her brief rest had given her just a little more energy. "And who's this beautiful child?" She smiled.

"I'm Elise," she introduced herself and walked over to hug Brenda.

*This is new,* Brenda thought curiously. Elijah had never brought a woman to her house before. "Elijah, did you bring her to meet me 'cause I'm sick or because she's special?" Brenda asked, amused.

"It better be because I'm special," Elise sassed, smiling. "Go ahead, answer her question." She waited for his response look.

Elijah stared at the floor and shook his head. "Women!"

Brenda got a kick out of this. Elijah had finally met his match. *This is a strong one. This is a good thing, he needs someone to look after him when he fails to lookout for himself.*

"Don't be laughing at me, woman," he told Brenda playfully.

"Yeah, my baby done fell in love," she teased, then turned serious. "Elise, I want you to do me a favor." She spoke as if he was no longer in the room. "Make sure you take care of my son here after I'm gone."

"Stop talking that 'gone' stuff. Sounds too much like giving up," Elijah interrupted. It earned him a dismissive wave of the hand from Brenda.

Suddenly, the windows and walls began a subtle rumbling that gradually grew into a mild earthquake inside the house. DMX barked through the speakers.

"Here comes that boy with all that damn loud music disturbing my neighbors," Brenda complained. Somehow, she knew his music from the countless others who drove up and down the street daily. "Elijah, go tell him to cut that damn music down and give me and Elise here a few minutes to have a little girl talk."

Elijah stood and smiled, mumbling under his breath, "She ain't too sick. She still have the energy to fuss and gossip." He walked to the living room and peeked through the window.

Ju-Ju was pulling his truck into the driveway. He was alone, but activities were still shaky in the hood for Elijah. He took the .9mm from his waistband and released the safety before tucking it back in place and walking out on the porch.

Ju-Ju hadn't expected anyone but the nurse to be there when he arrived. Elijah and Elise had purposely driven a low-key Plymouth so that attention would not be drawn to them. Ju-Ju's face lit up with joy when he saw him. Not shutting off the truck or music, he jumped out and ran to hug Elijah.

"My nigga." Ju-Ju exclaimed. "Where the hell you been, cuzz?"

Elijah watched him closely, with a major lack of enthusiasm. "Just under the radar, homie," he said.

Ju-Ju knew that look well. He threw up his hands in exasperation. "Nine, man, you need to come off the bullshit." He looked Elijah directly in the eyes. "Cuzz, you need to stop leaving me in the dark. If I done something wrong then let me know, put the shit on the table like men do. Niggas is letting money come between us. I'm still the same, ain't nothin' changed with me."

Elijah continued to study him in a dry, serious fashion. "What the fuck you trying to insinuate, that I switched up on niggas? Ain't nothing funny style about the beast Li'l 9-Lives nigga."

"Look, homie" Ju-Ju tried to reason. "I ain't trying to say nothing as an insult to you. I'm referring to us all as a whole. Just so you know, whatever I got to say or however I feel you welcome to know it. I don't do no corner cuttin'; I just want us to get whatever the problem is out in front of us. We better than all this secretive hood politic shit. Like I said, if I did something wrong hit me in my mutha-fuckin' mouth. I'd rather that than having you trying to read my thoughts when we see each other."

Elijah didn't respond to the question; he just looked at him as if he was actually considering socking him in the mouth. The bass line from the truck reminded him of what he was sent out to do in the first place. "Go turn that shit down before I do decide to punch you in the mouth. Your mom don't wanna hear all that."

Ju-Ju was so caught up with seeing him that he'd forgotten the truck was still running. He ran back to turn it off. Before he reached inside for the keys he looked over his shoulder and said teasingly, "I'm ready for your Indian-lookin' ass to try and hit me in the mouth. We ain't kids no more. I can slang these thangs like Iron Mike Tyson."

"Boxing ain't a weightlifting competition." Elijah eyed him from the porch. "You'll need way more than what you got to fuck with the kid." No smile followed that statement.

*Nigga think 'cause he got a little muscle on him now, he's ready for me,* thought Elijah. "I'll still tip his ass up." Elijah pulled a blunt from his pocket and lit it, watching Ju-Ju as he made his way back to the porch. It was time for a real conversation to take place.

"How you handling your mom's situation?" Elijah opened the conversation.

Both knew it was an unnecessary question. "Shit, what other way could I be taking it? It's fuckin' me up, plain and simple. You only get one momma." Elijah already knew that, and how it felt to lose that one.

"For the most part, I try not to think about it when I'm out in the streets, but when I come here that's a different story. Reality's a mutha-fucka."

Elijah couldn't give him much advice on how to deal with Brenda's impending death, because he wasn't sure how he dealt with losing his mom. They said time healed all wounds, but Elijah wasn't too sure that was a complete truth. Time helped to cover the wound, but his still hadn't healed.

"All I can say is keep living. Keep surviving, embrace the pain," he advised Ju-Ju. "It makes no sense to try and run from it. I don't know what kind of assistance I can be, but if you need something on her behalf let me know. I woulda been through here sooner if I knew, but Lady Rawdog just caught up with me a few days ago and put a bug in my ear."

"I appreciate the offer but there ain't much to be done. The medical expenses are covered, now it's just a matter of waiting for the end," he added. "Yeah, I'm the one who told the homegirl to call you because I can't seem to catch you these days, and mom was constantly asking about you."

"You know how it is. I've just been staying low, scoping things from a distance. It's a lot of funny-style shit going on in the hood."

"Nine, cuzz, come clean with me. What's really going on? What's on your mind?" Ju-Ju pleaded with him.

Elijah pulled on his blunt, staring off into the distance at the kids playing tackle football in the front yard down the street. "Wouldn't it be beautiful to have their carefree innocence?" He pointed lazily at the kids. "I feel like I never had that. Like I've been dealing with grown man problems all my life."

Ju-Ju looked at the kids but didn't respond. He knew Elijah was just thinking out loud, not wanting an answer at all.

"Ju, are we friends, brothers, or comrades?"

The question caught Ju-Ju by surprise. He'd never thought about their relationship in specific terms. "I guess we all three."

"Would you kill me for money, or power, or position?" Elijah asked straight up.

"Fuck no, nigga! Where you goin' with these off-the-wall ass questions?" he responded, feeling uneasy by what Elijah was asking him.

"Would you kill me for crossing the game, like snitching, or trying to kill somebody in our circle for money or jealousy?"

"I'm not feelin' all these fucked-up questions you asking me. I deal in reality, not hypothetical bullshit," Ju-Ju said agitated.

"I ask for a reason." Elijah turned to look at Ju-Ju. "I got love for you and I love your mom, but if I ever find out that you betrayed me or betrayed what we stand for, I wouldn't hesitate to end you, and I expect for you to hold me to thc same standards."

Ju-Ju was openly offended. *This where our relationship at now,* he thought, *where we contemplating what offense would make us kill one another*? Ju-Ju had too many problems in his life at the moment to be dealing with the shit Elijah was dishing out.

"Cuzz you can miss me with what you talkin' 'bout." He tensed up. "My mom's on her deathbed, and you gettin' at me with this irrelevant shit? Let me tell you something, nigga, I tried to be the one to keep us all together, but I see now y'all don't want unity. So fuck it, I don't give a fuck either."

Elijah pulled on the blunt, watching as Ju-Ju continued his rant.

"I don't care about dying or killing either. Hell, I don't have shit to lose no way. From now on, you niggas do your own thing and I'll do mine, and if it comes down to us having to go at each other, so be it. But know, just this one time I'll forgive you for talking to me like a fool on my mother's porch. If you ever do it again, be ready to go all the way. I probably can't win in the long run, but before I let you disrespect me at my momma's house, I'll take my chances."

Elijah watched him calmly. "Nigga, slow down with all that yappin'. You need to drop ya mutha-fuckin' tone a few notches," he warned. He knew Ju-Ju was going through a lot at the moment, but emotion got people into wrecks.

"The time is coming where you'll have to choose sides," he told Ju-Ju, "between me . . . and Li'l Tef."

Ju-Ju was confused. *What the hell's this dude talking about choosing sides?*

"What I'm about to tell you has to stay between us. Should it ever get out that you mentioned it to anybody, I'd consider it betrayal." Elijah needed to see Ju-Ju's reaction to the revelation. It was time to put it all out there and know who was friend or foe. He wanted to believe Ju-Ju's profession of loyalty but too much had happened. He waited for Ju-Ju to nod his agreement. Once Ju-Ju did so, he revealed the plot behind the attempted hit against him, and Li'l Teflon's involvement.

"Nah, cuzz." Ju-Ju shook his head in disbelief. "I can't, I won't believe that. I know cuzz is cutthroat, but I can't see him going that far. If you felt that way, why did you take nearly two years to speak on it?"

"I have my reasons. The bottom line is what I'm telling you is fact not speculation. Open your eyes. Think about it. Why would he disappear from the hood for all this time?"

Elijah filled him in on the details of how and why the move went down, and the fact that the source of information came from one of Li'l Crip's own homies.

Ju-Ju could only drop his head at the news. "This shit's too much. I don't even know what to say or think. But it all make sense now."

"Think long and hard," Elijah said, "because before long, you 'will' have to choose." With that, Elijah turned and walked back in the house.

The next hour or so was spent laughing and talking with Brenda. The nurse finally came to break it up, telling them that it was time for her to administer the pain medication, which would put her to sleep. Both Elijah and Elise hugged and kissed Brenda good–bye. Her weak smile and eyes told Elijah that this would be the last time that he'd ever see her alive.

"I love you, Elijah." Brenda managed to say with the little strength she had.

"I love you too, Mom." He turned to leave before anyone could see the tears in his eyes.

Ju-Ju caught up to him on the porch. Even though they had spent the last hour being cordial as a good showing for Brenda, there was still an awkward energy between the two. Ju-Ju was still trying to process what he had been told and how he was to act on it.

"I don't know what the future holds for us, homie," Ju-Ju said, "but what I do know is I never want me and you to be enemies. My mom loves you like a son and I gave her my word that I'd never go against you. I intend to honor that."

Elijah examined him the way he'd done since they were kids. Without words, he embraced Ju-Ju in a hug that he returned. Disengaging, he turned and walked to the car where Elise waited in the driver's seat.

"Nine?" Ju-Ju called out just as he was grabbing the door handle.

Elijah half-turned to see what he wanted.

Ju-Ju smiled a big smile, "Ninety minutes, cuzzin."

Elijah smirked. "Nine minutes, no seconds!" He jumped in the passenger seat.

Elise stared at him with concern as he leaned his seat back and put his feet on the dashboard. "Me and Snow have a surprise for you, baby," she said, trying to cheer him up.

"I don't know if I'm in the mood for surprises right now," he said, still staring at Ju-Ju on the porch.

"Trust me, you'll like this one." She looked him over closely. "Are you alright?" she asked, caressing his head.

"Yeah, I'm straight."

"Can I have a kiss then?" she asked in her sweetest voice.

He turned to look curiously at her. *What is she up to?* he pondered before leaning over to kiss her sexy lips.

Satisfied, she cranked up the volume on En Vogue's "Hold On" and smashed off toward the sunset.

# CHAPTER THIRTY-ONE

"Nah, cuzz, no bullshit," Li'l Teflon said, dying with laughter. "This li'l bitch couldn't have been no more than four feet tall. I'm talkin' a pair of high-heel shoes away from being a midget. She had some mutha-fuckin' missiles for titties. She leaned back when she walked 'cause they were weighing her down. She walk in the spot like this . . ." He demonstrated in a penguin-like walk.

Like always, Li'l Teflon had taken the initiative of being the entertainment of the night for his crew. The living room was his stage and the squad of youngsters hung on his every word. The weed they'd smoked made his story twice as funny. From the good cheer in the room, this could have easily been a social evening among friends. The three-bedroom house in Inglewood, California, was nice and tidy. Minus the array of guns and ammunition lying loosely about, the house was normal enough. The neighborhood was considered upper middle-class, though predominantly African American, the well-to-do professional-type stuff.

As the rest of the country discovered, poverty was not always a prerequisite for gang influence. Inglewood (or at least this part of it) was the territory of the Inglewood Family Bloods. In short, initially they were a group of kids from good homes who despite their good upbringings decided they preferred to live the lives of outlaws.

Li'l Teflon chose this location for his new headquarters with all this in mind. Being in a Blood hood lessened the possibility of some of the Nine Os rival from another clique stumbling upon his hide out by happenstance, which happened a lot when homies tried to set up shop in their own neighborhoods. It was only a matter of time before the rest of the homeboys knew where you were, no matter how hard you tried to keep it a secret. Li'l Teflon reasoned that as long as he and the crew used the backdoor at the end of the driveway to come and go, and never hung out front flying their colors, the Bloods would never know they were there. Another plus was the Bloods would unknowingly be supplying an extra layer of protection from his real enemies. A Crip couldn't just show up in a Blood hood snooping around or asking questions without putting themselves in danger. This was the ideal location to launch his coming-out party. He was back and soon the streets would know it.

He continued with his outrageous story that had the youngsters laughing tears.

"I'm thinking to myself," he clowned, "this broad gotta have back problems. That's too much weight to be carrying around on that short-ass body. You know me though, midget or no midget, I'm 'bout to get in where I fit in."

He mellowed his tone and said as if he was reliving the moment. "We sip on some Cognac. I really just wanna take her clothes off 'cause I'm dying to see these big-ass titties. So, you know, I try to ease into it. I'm like, 'Baby, why don't you take all that off for Daddy'. She try and play the shy role, talking about, 'Let's just kick it and talk for a while first'. I guess her breath mint had worn off cause her breath flew across the room smelling like pure dog shit, but I still couldn't just let her walk out. It wasn't even about fucking her at that point. I had to see how those titties fit on that little body. I definitely wasn't gonna let a little bad breath get in the way."

"Pass the blunt, cuzz," one of the li'l homies urged the other while he kept his eyes pinned to Li'l Teflon as if he had to not only listen but also watch his movements to get the full story.

"So I'm trying to speed up the process while she's acting like we're on a real romantic date, like there could possibly be a future between us. I'm getting irritated . . . she got to know this ain't no get-married-have-kids type thing. I'm not 'bout to have no mini midgets with you, bitch. At the same time, I still have to fake like I'm interested in her conversation.

"Finally, I can't take no more. We gotta get down to business. I say, 'Come on, baby, let's get in the Jacuzzi.' I'm thinking, I got her now. She at least got to strip down to her panties and bra. She tells me to dim the lights. Damn. I had to think fast. I go to the Jacuzzi area and turn down the lights and get butt-naked. She comes over and starts to get undressed. I wait until she bends down to pull off her panties and I inch toward the turn knob for the lights. Soon as she straightened back up—surprise, bitch. I turned that muthafucka up as bright as it would go. I thought they were gonna be hanging to the floor like some African saggers. She smiled like she knew what I was try'na do all along. Naked and proud she let me get a full view. She had the most pretty, firm titties I've ever seen in my life. I was hypnotized. My dick stood up like, 'We the people'!"

One of the youngsters laughed so hard that soda sprayed from his mouth and leaked from his nose. The scene made the others laugh even harder.

"Damn, nigga, let me finish my story. Gonna make me lose my train of thought." Li'l Teflon paused for a second before continuing. "Anyway, I didn't even feel my feet moving—all I know is I'm up on her rubbing them. I said, 'Damn, bitch, are they implants or something? She's like, 'Nah, Daddy, these are all natural, baby.'

I picked her up and propped her on the sink, kissing and sucking on them titties like they were my most prized possessions. She leaned back against the mirror with her heels on the edge of the sink. All of a sudden, she grabbed the back of my head like a savage and pulled me face first into her pussy. I went along with it, eating that pussy like a starving dog."

He was interrupted by a burst of laugher and comments. "Ugh, cuzz, you ate that bitch's pussy? You didn't even know her," blurted Baby Devil.

"Aw, li'l nigga, you still in ya momma's bathroom jacking off. How you gonna say what's nasty?" Li'l Teflon waved him off. What the hell did this wet-behind-the-ears kid know? "For ya information, in my book, I did know her. I knew her long enough to buy her food and drinks, so I knew her long enough to suck her pussy!"

He picked back up where he left off. "So I'm sucking the pussy and she's pressing the back of my head and grinding my face, smothering me—literally. I had to force my head back every so often just to catch a breath. As soon as I'd get a little air she'd slam my face back into her. Finally, I'm like, 'Damn, hold up, you gotta let me catch my breath.' Do you know this broad turned into the Exorcist? She said, 'Shut the fuck up and eat this pussy,' in a deep voice. Scared the shit out of me. I did what I was told quick. So, after a while she tells me to take her to the bed. She was so demanding that I forgot she was a midget. She hopped off the sink like it was a two-story building. I follow her to the bed and she tells me to lay on my back. When I do, she climbs over me and sits on my face, bucking like she's riding a bull. After getting her li'l rocks off she goes down and starts giving me head like a true pro. I'm ready to nut in forty seconds flat but she stops and tell me to wait. Once she knew I had calmed down she got back into it, licking my balls. She's going lower and lower, I'm thinking what the hell is she doing? Next thing I know she starts licking my ass . . ."

The room erupted.

"Aw, nah, cuzz, say it ain't so." Baby Devil choked out through his laughter.

Li'l Teflon couldn't stop himself from laughing with the rest of the room. "Hold up, cuzz." He tried to calm them down so he could finish, but even he couldn't control his laughter.

"This cat is nasty!" one youngster shouted.

"Dude is crazy," said another. The youngsters couldn't control their hysteria. Eventually, he was able to gain some measure of control over himself and the others that allowed him to continue.

"I ain't never had no bitch do no shit like that," he said with exaggerated hand gestures. "I said, 'Hold up, bitch. What you doin'?' But really I ain't making no real effort to stop her, so she keep doing her thing. My mind was telling me to stop her but my body was overruling me. Before I knew it, she got my legs in the air like I'm the bitch. I felt so vulnerable."

The youngsters were laughing hysterically.

"Afterwards, I'm laying there feeling violated. She done bossed me around during the sex session, and on top of that she done tickled my whistle. I didn't know if I should slap her or thank her. I didn't even feel like a hard nigga no more. I done got raped by a mutha-fuckin' troll. I had to redeem myself somehow. I got up to get dressed. I said, 'Get your ass up, you got to go.' She had the nerve to ask me what was wrong. I said, 'I don't know, but bitch you got to go.' As she's grabbing her clothes, them big-ass titties were swinging. Seeing that I started to have second thoughts. I'm getting hard again just seeing her naked. I change my tone, I said, 'Hold up, baby, I'm over reacting, I apologize, I'm just going through some things.' Ten minutes later, I had a smile on my face and my legs back in the air. Booty licks on the line!" he yelled, and they burst into laughter again.

Murder-Min walked in on their joke session. She had been out on a scouting mission for the crew. She was pretty in the typical young Asian girl fashion: nice face but not much of a body. She had a faded scar that ran from her temple down to her chin, an old wound she'd gotten from a John in Laos who had sliced her with a machete. Though faded, it was still visible. It gave her exotic beauty, an edge of evil that seemed to turn men on. For Li'l Teflon she was the ultimate asset: pretty, petite, street smart, ruthless, and loyal. Her deceptive appearance was what he liked most. She could drive or walk past police without so much as a second glance from them. She could also lure a sucker into harm's way without him once suspecting himself to be in danger. To most men, women of her description were non-threatening. It took an experienced eye to look past her exterior and see what was really behind those flat, empty black eyes.

Li'l Teflon realized she was watching and knew it was time to end the funnies and get serious. Composing himself, he joined her at the dining room table and began rummaging through the shopping bag she brought with her. Only items of importance were the Houston Astros baseball caps. A simple block-lettered "H" with an orange star in its backdrop, the official hood hat of the West Side Hoovers. Six orange bandanas put the finishing touch on the crew's outfits of the evening.

Murder-Min's scouting report: fifteen or more Hoovers hanging out in the back of Manchester Park near the Denver Ave entrance/exit.

"Alright, fellas, it's time to shine." He handed each of his soldiers one of the baseball caps.

Two of the youngsters, Droopy and Bam, had never put in any work on Los Angeles soil. They had been recruited in Vegas to help with Li'l Teflon's criminal activities there. Now they found themselves in the land on a mission of a lifetime, and they were anxious to prove their mettle.

"Look, this is our statement move," Li'l Teflon said, "to let niggas know we're back and playing for keeps. The suckas who supposed to be running the hood let the li'l homeboy get his brains blew out by the Snoovas and sent some rookies to do some bullshit drive-bys as payback. We're gonna show them how it's really supposed to be. Afterwards we'll let the seeds be planted that it came from our clique in a way that won't give the police any solid links. It will be an open secret."

"What we waiting on?" Baby Devil said excitedly. "Let's rain on these bustas." He put his cap on backward. Droopy, Bam, and the others, Skip and Tiny Looney, all grabbed their guns and hats with youthful enthusiasm.

For Li'l Teflon, there was one more thing they needed to do before the mission. He placed two thick lines of cocaine on the table and put his face in it, Scarface-style. His soldiers each followed suit. Feeling like war gods, they left the house and got into the black van with tinted windows that had been purchased solely for this occasion.

The sun hung low, a fluorescent orange bulb, as they made their way through the city streets. Moving across Van Ness, they proceeded purposefully into the heart of South Central with murder in mind.

The Hoovers stood bunched together in the back of Manchester Park smoking sherm. The park spanned a two-block radius (north-south) from Eighty-Eighth to Ninetieth Street in the middle of a residential area. Hoover Street gave open access to the park for the entire two blocks. This spot had been the territory of the Hoover Crips since the seventies, when East Side-West Side Crips began breaking up into individual sub-sets. There were many Hoover sets, each distinguished by its street number. They all came together to touch base at Manchester Park.

The six were at a distance, and being that the sun was on its way down, it was difficult to make out the faces clearly. "Y'all stay cool,"

Li'l Teflon said. The approaching group walked carefree, nothing visible in their hands, as the Hoovers watched them closely. As they drew closer, it was easier to make out the orange bandana slung over one of their shoulders. Orange was the Hoover's color, just as powder blue was the color of the 90 Crips. At the same time, the big "H" on the front of the ball caps also became visible.

"Hoooooovaaaaa!" Li'l Teflon and his group bellowed as if using a bullhorn.

The Hoovers returned the call: "Hoooooovaaaaa!"

As Li'l Teflon's group approached, he said, "What's up, Groove?" and extended the Hoover handshake.

The handshake was reciprocated by the Hoovers. The rest of Li'l Teflon's group gave and received greetings as well.

But something felt out of place . . . forced, they all felt it. An eerie silence fell over them. The Hoovers began eyeing the visitors with suspicion.

"So, what bring y'all from the Fifties?" one of the Hoover's asked with a hint of apprehension.

"The Fifties?" Li'l Teflon looked with feigned confusion. "What you mean bring us from the Fifties?"

"Ain't y'all from the Deuce?"

"Nah, cuzz, we from Ninetieth Street." Li'l Teflon said it with such calm that it took the Hoovers a few seconds for his words to register, likely the result of the sherm they smoked. Finally realizing the implications of his words, their eyes went wide with fear. Li'l Teflon allowed an evil smile to spread across his face.

A young Hoover turned and bolted without warning. His sudden movement caused a chain reaction and the Hoovers scattered. Baby Devil reacted just as fast, pulling the .40 Glock from his waistline and squeezing the trigger, catching one of them just as he turned to make his getaway. The velocity from the bullet knocked him forward off his feet at a freakish rate of speed, his face crashed into the grass as if he'd high dived into a swimming pool. The back of his head was a mess, leaving no question as to his status. On cue, the rest of the Nine Os drew their pistols and began firing.

An explosion of what sounded like an elephant gun blasted from Li'l Teflon's blind side. A wave of hot air and flying debris rushed past them, making him duck for cover. Out of his peripheral vision he saw Droopy go down. Another blast sent more buck shots in their direction, though this time he saw exactly where the flash came from. The chain-link fence overran by green shrubbery had a barely noticeable hole cut in it.

Just then, one of the Hoovers wielding the shotgun had blown one of his enemies off his feet and now he was hell-bent on killing the rest. The recoil from the shotgun and the effects of the sherm had him feeling like the most powerful man on Earth. His adrenaline-spiked intoxicated mind encouraged him to abandon his strategic position and emerge from the shrubbery letting the shotgun rip with fury. He couldn't be touched. "Get some, muthafuckas!" he yelled in madness.

Li'l Teflon couldn't let this madman get any closer or they would be doomed. Raising up on one knee, he squeezed off eight shots. The Hoover made no attempt at retreat or taking cover as the bullets whizzed by him. He continued to work the riot pump.

Baby Devil, without even raising his head to look, let off his last three shots in the Hoover's direction. By pure luck, one of the slugs hit its mark, knocking the shotgun from his hands, leaving him writhing on the ground in agony.

Li'l Teflon wasn't going to waste the opportunity. He was on his feet in an instant, in an all-out sprint. "Let's go, cuzz!" he called out as he ran.

"The homie down!" Baby Devil alerted the others. "We can't just leave him, cuzz!"

Li'l Teflon never heard those words or at least acted as if he didn't. He was doing his best impression of Jesse Owens and getting the hell out of there.

Bam answered Baby Devil's call for assistance. They lifted their fallen comrade, placing one of his arms on each of their shoulders as they carried him. He'd taken a host of buckshot to the side abdomen but was still alive. His weak legs could only help so much, but it was better than dead weight.

Luckily, they didn't have to travel too far. The others had made it to the van and picked them up before Droopy became too heavy. It went without saying that they couldn't take him to the hospital for treatment. All gunshot wounds had to be reported to the police upon entry to an emergency room. Li'l Teflon checked the wounds and determined that while the buckshot would hurt like hell, they were not life threatening.

They made it back to the hideout in Inglewood where Droopy was given lines of cocaine to hold him over until they could arrange some sort of medical attention. They ended up settling for one of Li'l Teflon's cousins who worked as a nurse at Martin Luther King Hospital. She came and removed as much of the lead as possible without inflicting further damage. She then cleaned the wound, patched him up real nice, set up an IV drip to fight off infection, and left them with the instructions to get him some real medical attention as soon as they could. After handing over her personal stash of Percocet to be given to Droopy on an as needed basis, she collected her $5,000 and hauled ass out of there.

Even though the mission had been a near disaster, Li'l Teflon had accomplished his objective. He made the phone call to Lady Rawdog, telling her to spread the word that the Hoovers had just took some losses at Manchester Park and the homies needed to be on the lookout for retaliation. He knew that she would spread the word among the homeboys as to where she'd gotten the information and they would naturally assume that he was somehow responsible even though they had no real evidence.

As expected, the word spread like wildfire among the Nine Os. Li'l Teflon Black was back.

# CHAPTER THIRTY-TWO

Big Teflon mumbled under his breath as he cleared the table of drug paraphernalia stemming from his mother's week-long binge. Cleaning the shabby low-income apartment at least once a week became a routine that he upheld religiously.

After Virginia's first stint in rehab, he'd moved her to a nicer place on the other side of town, but it didn't do any good. She did well for the first few months, but then ended up finding her way right back to the hood. After a few more tries, Big Teflon was forced to realize and accept the fact that no matter how bad he wanted her to change his effort would always be in vain if she didn't want change for herself. This was her place in life, and all he could do was try his best at making sure she didn't end up completely homeless.

The apartment was a pitiful sight: roaches of all sizes ran about freely, furniture was in the poorest of condition, and the brown-imitation velvet couch was heavily stained and reeked of piss. Like the couch, the carpet was filthy and worn beyond repair. Replacing it was the only option, which he had done three times over the past year, yet somehow she and her junkie friends seemed to return it to the same condition within a month's time. Same thing with the furniture: he had purchased more expensive items hoping that the better quality would last longer, only to find that it had been sold for crack and replaced with the same old furniture he'd set out on the curb for the garbage man.

His thoughts ran as they always did when he saw his mother in this downtrodden condition. *Why do I even put myself through this shit with her*? he questioned. *Why did I have to be born to somebody like her? How can I get her to be normal? I need to walk away from this house, this neighborhood, and never look back. What would I do?* His mind roamed while his hands cleaned.

"Come on, baby, give me a hundred dollars," Virginia pleaded, disturbing his train of thought.

He continued cleaning as if he didn't hear her.

"You know you hear me!" she persisted.

"You know I'm not about to put no money in your hands, so why you keep asking?" he said without bothering to look her way. "Tell me what you need and I'll get it for you."

"You ain't my daddy! I don't need you to go and get me nothing. I need a hundred dollars to take care of some personal business. I'm grown! I ain't gotta tell you everything I do."

The stench from her breath reached him from three feet away. To stop from gagging, he walked away from her and entered the kitchen. "If you grown and don't want me in your business then don't ask me for nothing. Grown folks handle their own affairs," he said looking through the cabinet for more cleaning supplies.

She was on his heels from the living room to the kitchen, knowing that eventually he would relent and give her what she wanted. She wouldn't even try this with her younger son. That stingy bastard, she could beg and plead with him until her head popped and he still wouldn't give her shit. But Akili, he would break. Regardless of his tough talk, he was still her sweetheart.

"Nigga, don't get smart with me. All the money you got and you can't give your own momma a hundred dollars?" When he gave no response, she began with her fake crying act. "I. . . I don't know why . . . you treat your mother so bad. I know I wasn't perfect and all but . . . but I did my best."

He had been through this routine a thousand times, if not more. It used to work when he was younger, but now it was just hot air. He continued spraying and scrubbing, her fake tears and pleading a distant background noise that held no relevance. He let his thoughts drift to his son, Akili Junior, and the future.

Suddenly, she wrapped her bony arms around his neck in an attempt at false affection that jolted him out of his reverie. "Come on, baby," she pleaded like a child, "I promise it's not to buy drugs." Her mortifying breath, yellow teeth, and filthy body made him cringe. He used his elbow to shrug her off, irritated by her obvious bullshit.

"Miss me with the drama. I already told you once—no!"

"Well, you can get the fuck out of my house then," she snapped, tears and affection magically nonexistent. "You black mutha-fucka."

He had heard the phrase "black mutha-fucka and "black jungle bunny" so much growing up that he still carried a complex about the color of his skin. Hearing her say those words again was like reopening an old wound. He was furious.

*How can she talk to me like this,* he thought with rage growing, *after I go out my way constantly to help her funky ass?* Abruptly, he threw a plate against the wall, and she jumped in fear at his sudden outburst. Shards of porcelain erupted throughout the kitchen.

"You ungrateful, evil-ass lady. No matter what I do for you it is never enough," he screamed. "I'm done with you. Take care of your damn self!" He stormed out.

"I'm done with you too, mutha-fucka," she called out behind him. "I don't need you no damn way. Ya ass ain't gonna do nothin' but end up dead or in jail. What you gonna do then, you black bastard?" She followed him out the door, screaming at the top of her lungs for the world to hear. "Yeah, Mister Big Man, get in your fancy car! You better enjoy it while you can."

Closing the door muted her out, but he could still see her mouthing obscenities and performing for the neighbors to see. He started the car and sped out onto the road. She continued her rant even as the car sped up the block. He felt so disappointed and mad that tears welled up in his eyes, but he refused to let them fall. To divert his attention elsewhere, he grabbed his cell phone and called his voicemail. First message was from his baby sister, Naqael, who was away at college. She was crying about Hitter not returning her calls and having a kid by another woman. "What the fuck she want me to do?" He shook his head. He had told her to leave that nigga alone long time ago but she wanted to be hard headed, so now she could deal with it.

He received an incoming call just as he was about to check the next message. It was Lady Rawdog.

"Hey, baby." Lady Rawdog said in her aunty voice.

"Hey, what's the business?"

"I just wanted to give you a heads-up. The Snoovas got served real tough and the finger points back to the hood, so be careful. Yo li'l brother told me to let you know."

Big Teflon clenched his jaw and remained silent. *What the fuck that fool thinking?* Over the last few years, they had grown apart. The last time he saw him was two years ago, when he refused to be part of his schemes . . .

"My li'l brother?" he finally said.

"Yeah, you didn't know? He's back in town."

Another pregnant pause. *That son of a—*

"Hello, you there?"

"Yeah, yeah, I'm here. I was just trying to get over to make this turn," he lied. "Alright, good lookin' out on the heads-up. I'll swing by there later on."

"That's what's up. Holla at your bro too. He can give you more details."

"For sure, for sure." he said, mind already racing.

"Ninety minutes!"

"Nine minutes, no seconds!"

He pulled over on a side street and jammed the car in park. *What the fuck this nigga doing showing back up?* he thought. His brain was scrambling a thousand thoughts a minute. Beyond frustrated, he pounded his hands against the steering wheel. "Son of a bitch," he ranted. "My own family's worse than my enemies in the streets."

His phone rang again. He was hesitant to even answer. With a huff, he picked up. "Hello?" he said somberly.

"Where the fuck are you? I told yo' mutha-fuckin' ass that our son had to go to the doctor and I need money to pay for it," Keisha barked through the phone.

Keisha had been such a sweet girl when he first met her. She had a full-time job, attended night school at Southwest Junior College, and was trying to do something with her life, or so he thought. It seemed like overnight she turned into a monster. She had told him she was on the pill, then the next thing he knew she broke the news that she was pregnant. She agreed to have an abortion because they were "just sex partners," she told him, "with no love for each other or plans for the future. She had also told him that she wanted her life to be on a better foundation when she had kids. After coming to a mutual understanding, he forked over the money for the abortion. Lo and behold, five months later she was walking around with a huge belly. When he questioned her about not having the abortion, she went into some rehearsed drama about how abortions messed women's bodies up, that it was morally wrong . . .

Trying to be a man about it, he accepted his responsibility and committed to doing his part in raising his son even though he knew she had trapped him on purpose. From that point forward, it was all downhill. Keisha had quit her job, dropped out of school, and made it her life's work to nag, lie, disrupt, and make his life miserable. No matter what he gave her or did for her, it was never enough. Once she realized that he had no plans of being her man, she vowed he would never be with any other woman in peace. Damn that he provided for his son, which was irrelevant if he wasn't going to be her man and cash cow. She'd go through periods of not wanting him to spend time with or see his son if she wasn't allowed to tag along. The kid became a tool, something to barter with to get to him. Every now and then she'd be cooperative, only to get him into thinking there was a chance they could at least have a civil relationship for his son's sake. Within a week or so she would revert to the bitch-from-hell: showing up at his hangouts to make a scene, being belligerent with any females who happened to be around, neck swinging, hand waving, screaming, cursing like a sailor, etc. Putting it on extra thick was her whole M.O.

Her voice alone, barking like a Chihuahua, caused his head to hurt. Today wasn't the day for this shit. Big Teflon took the phone from his ear and looked at it disgusted. Even from this distance, he could hear her voice loud and clear, grating on his nerves.

"Use the thousand dollars I gave you two weeks ago to pay for the visit," he said dryly.

"I told you I had to use that money to get the car fixed. So you need to get—"

"I don't *need* to do shit, bitch," he said through gritted teeth. "What you need to do is get a fucking job and a fucking life! Until then, sell the car I gave you to pay for it, bitch!"

"Fuck you, mutha—"

Big Teflon hung up the phone and tossed it on the passenger seat. He relaxed against the headrest, sinking deeper into the soft leather seats. "Never no rest," he whispered.

# CHAPTER THIRTY-THREE

Elijah looked to Elise, puzzled that she missed the exit leading to his condo. She flashed him a look that said, "I know where the hell I'm going." He smiled faintly and stared back out the window.

Pacific Coast Highway, unlike the LA freeways, flowed at a nice pace. The sky was an odd mixture of purple, orange, yellow, and blue. The sun disappeared into the ocean in picture-perfect beauty. Seagulls squawked in flight, couples and children walked or rode bikes and roller blades on the bike path next to the ocean, while others jogged listening to their headphones. It all appeared so . . . peaceful. Elijah shook his head in contempt. *All an illusion,* he thought.

Up to that point, the ride from Brenda's house was without communication. They rode to the music, both in their own thoughts. He hadn't earlier given much notice to the heavy traffic on the 110 Harbor Freeway and the Santa Monica 10. Life was beginning to wear him down. Seeing Brenda in that condition was a reminder of how fragile life truly was. All the hustling, all the war, all the stress . . . was it really worth it at the end of the day? Everything that was gained on Earth would become dust and a distant memory anyway. *Could I be as brave as Brenda in the face of certain death? Am I sure that I would be going to a better place after death like she is?* he wondered.

In theory, he had been courting death since he was a young boy, but not knowing the when and how of it made it more of a distant probability that he had long ago accepted. But what Brenda was facing was much different. It was a whole different ballgame when death was a definite finality at your front door, with time to live with that knowledge and ponder it. Would and could he be so brave about death under those circumstances?

Ten minutes past the turnoff to the condo, Elise made a right turn on Malibu Parkway. A few minutes more and they were making the ascent into the hilly mountains until they reached a driveway fronted by two eight-foot-high cast-iron gates with a large coat-of-arms connecting between them. The shield was adorned with two hatchets crossing at all four corners, with three old English letters, E-E-L, interlocked together in a clever design. Through the gate, about half a city block away, he got a view of the fifteen-thousand-square-foot majestic mansion looming at the top of the hill, a Spanish colonial-style estate with Mediterranean accents. The plush green lawns and different variation of trees and flowers were immaculately manicured. The well-placed lighting fixtures lit up the estate as though the sun was at its zenith.

The gates parted to allow them access. He still hadn't asked any questions, just sat back and gazed in fascination at the beautiful work of art this place presented. Elise drove slowly up the long winding driveway until they reached the top. There, a stone sculpture stood over the coy pond with a waterfall flowing at its back. Elijah recognized it as a stone version of the picture in his condo of Hannibal the Conqueror," a general of the victorious Carthaginian hordes.

"Damn," he said in amazement. "Whose house is this?"

"You'll see, come on." Elise exited the car.

As he got out, Lauren stepped out of the large oak wood double doors with a smile. Even in a modest knee-length Dolce and Gabbana skirt, white ruffled blouse, and Prada heels, she still bore the sex appeal of a half-naked Vegas stripper.

"Welcome home, Daddy." She dipped a mock curtsy.

"What you mean? This your house?" he asked, leaning in for a peck on the lips.

"This is *our* house," Lauren emphasized.

Elijah looked around in disbelief. "You gotta be shitting me!"

"I told you that we had a surprise," Elise interjected. "Come on, let us give you a tour." She grabbed his hand in excitement.

Entering the house, the hardwood floor was a polished high quality walnut. The design points were impeccable: a mixture of elegance and intuitive design. On the wall of the living room hung a six-foot hand-painted portrait replicated from a picture the three of them had taken together at a black-tie affair. Elijah had worn a traditional black-and-white Armani tuxedo with Bertoni loafers. Both Elise and Lauren had worn identical red Versace dresses, tailored to hug every curve on their bodies, with matching Manolo stilettos. It was one of their best and brightest moments together, and the painting captured it perfectly. The furniture was patterned after the condo, a blend of sophistication and grandeur with a medieval touch. The pearl-white baby grand piano was Elise's own personal addition. The house split into three levels connected by a wrap-around staircase.

"I'm impressed with the interior designing," he said proudly. "I see y'all bit the kid's style."

Elise rolled her eyes. "Boy, take some of the air out your big head. We just wanted to make you feel comfortable so you could be pried out of that damn condo. So, we decided to make this a bigger better version." She winked. "That's the same reason why we picked this location. Now let us show you your private space."

Lauren giggled at his expression. "Yeah, that's right, you have your own private space. We won't bother you there unless invited." With her suggestive look, he didn't need her to elaborate to know what she meant.

He was led up to his personal domain on the top floor. It consisted of three bedrooms and two baths in addition to the master bedroom and bath. The latter was deliberately designed to be a carbon copy of his room at the condo: the bed, the artwork, the entertainment center, the marble floors in the bathroom, even the sandalwood scent. It was all the exact same, only bigger.

The additional three bedrooms were converted to his gym, meditation room, and media room, respectively. The girls even had pictures taken of the collage in his condo that was given to an artist who duplicated the work inside of the new meditation room. The writings that wrapped around the upper wall were included.

One extra drawing was there that wasn't in the original. A single figure covered half the back wall. It was a life-like image of him dressed in the uniform of a medieval warrior, holding a hatchet in one hand and the head of an opponent in the other.

Elijah studied the picture closely. "Who came up with this?" he asked.

"That was Elise's idea," Lauren volunteered.

"Where . . . why did you think to do this?" he directed at Elise.

"I don't know." She shrugged, "It just came to me."

"Bullshit! What does it mean?"

Elise's eyes widened in surprise. "God! Why do you think there is always something more to what I say and do?"

"Because there always is!"

She hesitated, embarrassed. But she knew he wasn't going to let it go until she gave him an explanation. She let out a deep breath in frustration. "Okay, the truth is . . . this is how I saw you in my dream before we ever met. I never forgot it, so I described it to the artist and he brought my vision to life in this painting."

Elijah studied it as though the figure would speak some unknown mystery. Elise watched Elijah, wondering what he was thinking.

"This is . . . profound," he stated with sincere admiration. "The most profound aspect of this entire house!"

Elise smiled, relieved that he approved. "Sorry we didn't put the mural in the living room," she said to deflect his compliment. "We thought it would be better to put it in here."

"Nah, it's cool, it's better up here." He nodded.

"Let's go downstairs, I have a gift for you." Lauren led him by the hand to the second level where their rooms were.

Lauren's room was the complete opposite from her last place when it came to style. This one resembled the bedroom of a spoiled teenaged girl instead of a sophisticated, complex woman. Everything from the carpet, to the paint, the drapes, and the bedspread were a bright pink with fringes of white. The bed and shelves were littered with a variety of stuffed animals of all shapes and sizes. Elijah didn't even comment when he stepped in; he just gave a slight chuckle. She knew him well enough to know what that meant.

"Shut up, don't start with me," she quipped before he had the chance to say something smart.

He feigned ignorance. "What? I haven't even said anything."

"You don't have to. I already know how your little slick mind works," she said, entering the walk-in closet.

Elijah laughed.

"Ha-ha, asshole," Lauren mocked as she emerged from the closet carrying a crate. "Here." She handed it to him.

He took the small crate, turning it around to get a look inside. To his delight, it contained an all-black baby pit bull with a blue ribbon bow around its neck.

"You like him? His name is Cannon." Lauren smiled in anticipation.

Elijah sat the crate down and opened the front slide. The puppy shot out instantly in a frenzy. He grabbed him by the scruff of his neck, shook him, then alternated to the skin on his hind legs. The puppy growled and snapped with his baby teeth as Elijah laughed and continued the rough play. The pup seemed to be enjoying it just as much as he was. Once he stopped roughhousing the pup, it jumped in his lap with his tail wagging furiously. He rubbed and hugged him like a little boy.

Elise and Lauren watched him with pure joy. Lauren kneeled next to him and the puppy wasted no time jumping on her lap, allowing her to scratch his ears and belly.

"Now you have a responsibility," Lauren said. "He's not to leave here. This is his home. So you have no choice but to be here because he's going to be waiting on you."

"I'm not getting rid of my condo if that's what you're insinuating."

"Why not?" Elise pouted. "Keeping it would be a waste of money. This is your home now."

"You know how I am." He put the puppy back into the create. "The condo is a part of me. I'm not comfortable just leaving it."

"Well, we won't make the decision right now," Lauren said. "We'll talk about it again in seven months or so?" She looked to Elise and they both smiled.

"Aw, here we go with this secret-smile shit. I'm goin' out back before the drama gets started." He headed for the stairs with their laughter behind him.

"Wait, baby . . . come here," Lauren teased as they burst into more laughter.

*These girls are crazy,* he thought as he rounded the staircase. Once downstairs he went through the arched French doors to the patio. Padded lounge chairs lined the concrete in a neat row. Two iron-accented glass patio tables with matching chairs sat at a short distance, and a concrete and stainless steel barbeque was built into an isolated structure eight feet wide. The interior of the house was seamlessly integrated with its exterior. The lawn faded into a green linoleum towel that in turn made a flawless transition into the infinity pool, giving the illusion that the water disappeared into thin air.

The surrounding view put the condo to shame by a long shot. He could see the ocean in one direction, Century City, the traffic on the freeways, and downtown LA in another. *This is truly magnificent,* he thought.

Removing a Cuban cigar from his jacket pocket, he clipped the end, moistened it, and lit it up, inhaling the smoke. The distinctive sweet taste felt like a piece of heaven as it stimulated his senses. The pool looked inviting. On impulse he removed his clothes down to his boxers and stepped down into the water until he was shoulder deep, keeping his smoking hand free.

"So, we're not invited to your little private party?" Lauren interrupted as she and Elise exited the house.

"You said this is our house, so why would you need an invitation?"

"Say no more. I'm going to get some champagne for us." She turned and walked toward the kitchen.

Elise stood watching him for a minute.

"Come get in," he ordered more than asked.

"I don't have a bathing suit."

"Your panties and bra will do."

She looked at his expression and knew he wasn't kidding. She shook her head and began to strip down to her underclothes. She entered the pool gingerly, complaining about the temperature. Once in, she glided over to him and wrapped her arms around his neck. They didn't need words to dialogue with one another. He kissed her forehead. For her part, she was content to rest her head on his shoulder and enjoy his presence.

Lauren came back with a bottle of Moet and two glasses. Without any reservation, she sat down the items, kicked off her shoes, and stripped down completely nude. Picking the bottle and glasses back up, she stepped down into the pool. She took his cigar and handed him the bottle to open. While he popped the cork, she took a couple of pulls from the cigar like a true cigar connoisseur. He filled the two glasses for them and drank from the bottle he held for himself.

"Are you ready for your surprise?" Elise said.

"Hell, I thought I already got the surprise of a lifetime with this house. How can you top all this?" He waved at the surroundings.

"The real surprise is . . . Elise is pregnant. You're going to be a daddy!" Lauren exclaimed. She had been holding this secret with Elise for nearly two months and was dying to let it out.

"Are you serious?" He looked to Elise, trying to read her expression for a practical joke. "How long have you known?" he asked.

"I guess a little over two months."

"So, we keeping secrets now? I'm the only one who didn't know. Is that how we doing it now?"

"Boy, be quiet," Lauren came to Elise's defense, "we just wanted it to be special when we told you."

"Are you mad that I'm pregnant?" Elise asked with uncertainty in her voice.

"Mad?" he asked, incredulous. "Hell nah, I'm not mad. If not by one of you, then who else would I want my seeds to come through?" He grabbed her with his free arm and kissed her aimlessly on the eye. With the bottle still in hand, he wrapped the other around Lauren. "You're next." He told her before kissing her too. She nearly burned him with the cigar.

"I'm going to get your cigar wet." Lauren laughed.

"To hell with that cigar." He took it from her and tossed it in the water, letting it float away on the surface.

All their faces were inches apart, their bodies pressed against one another as he held them both. Although he knew he could have had them both at the same time, he had never initiated it in the past because he believed it would foster jealousy and alter their relationship. But having them both so close, so intimate . . .

his desire triumphed all rationale. The girls seemed to read his thoughts or expression. Lauren leaned forward and kissed him passionately, then pulled back to allow Elise to do the same. Elise kissed him long and deep. When she stopped, she looked to Lauren with passion in her eyes, then back to him in a questioning manner. He nodded in consent.

Lauren took the cue and ran her fingers through the back of Elise's hair, pulling her gently forward. She licked her lips softly. Elise's mouth parted, allowing Lauren's tongue to enter. Eyes closed, Elise returned the affection, her hand finding Lauren's lovely breast. Her soft touch made Lauren moan.

Elijah had never witnessed a sight so beautiful and erotic. Immediately, his dick grew hard as penitentiary steel. Lauren felt it rubbing against her and reached down to massage it while still locked in a kiss with Elise. Elise raised one of Lauren's breasts from the water and moved down to lick the nipple, making her back arch in ecstasy. Elijah let go and moved to the opposite wall to get a better view.

Lauren watched him with raw lust and desire, "Is this what you want, Daddy?" she moaned.

"This one isn't about me, this is something you both been wanting. Since y'all gave me so much today, I give you the gift of each other." He leaned back and propped both elbows on the wall.

Elise paused in her stimulation of Lauren's breast and pulled her close. In her most obedient tone, she turned seductively to Elijah and asked, "Is Lauren mine tonight?"

Elijah nodded. She immediately slid her hand between Lauren's naked thighs and began fingering her expertly. Lauren wrapped her legs loosely around Elise's waist allowing her to navigate her weightless body to the edge of the pool. Against the wall, Lauren used the leverage the water gave to raise and spread her legs, using her elbows for stability. Elise touched and probed every spot inside her, making her tremble with pleasure.

Elijah watched the show as he drank from the Moet bottle. It was Lauren's turn to be the aggressor. She went under water to slide Elise's panties off. Coming back up, she half-turned to look at him over her shoulder and threw the panties in his direction. His smirk let her know that he was enjoying the show. She slowly dipped under water again and licked Elise's clit. Her head fell backward as Lauren's tongue made magic. It took every ounce of his self-control to stop from joining in.

Coming back to the sucked, Lauren sucked Elise's breast and fingered her with the same expertise she had received moments earlier. Elise's pussy felt wetter than the water somehow. Lauren kissed her lips tenderly. "You ready to take this to the bed?" she whispered.

Elise nodded, and they both made their way out of the pool, naked and dripping wet.

*This is shit you only see in the movies,* Elijah thought as the girls walked hand-in-hand toward the house. Once they reached the patio door, Lauren turned with an inviting look.

"What are you waiting on?" she called.

"Shit. I thought I wasn't welcome."

"Well, it's been offered, the rest is up to you." She led Elise inside.

"Wait . . . hold up." He dropped the bottle in haste, letting it float with the cigar and champagne glasses. He nearly broke his neck trying to catch up.

By the time he made it in the house, they were no longer in sight. But knowing them the way he did, he figured they were taking the party to his room. His assumption was correct; he heard them soon as he reached the top of the stairs.

Stepping into the doorway, Lauren was lying on her back, legs spread wide with Elise between her legs licking and sucking her wet flesh. Elise hadn't even realized he was present, but Lauren looked him directly in the eye as soon as he appeared. She licked her lips seductively as Elise pleasured her. Without consciously being aware of what he was doing, he began massaging himself. Something about him watching but not touching turned Lauren on immensely. She had the desire to tease him further. While continuing to stare at him, she talked to Elise.

"You like how this pussy taste?"

"Um-hum," Elise moaned.

"How good does it taste?"

Elise paused to look up at her. "Really good . . . like ice cream."

Lauren let out a sexy giggle. "I'm glad you like it." She caressed Elise's hair. "You're making me feel *sooo* good. I love the way your tongue feels in my pussy."

Lauren's encouragement fueled Elise to work even harder at pleasing her. The scene had Elijah fully jacking off.

"Let me eat some with you," Lauren cooed. Elise came up to let her suck the juices from her lips.

Lauren slowly reversed positions and made her way down to get a taste of Elise. Only then did Elise notice Elijah standing in the doorway stroking himself. But she didn't have the self-control to watch him as Lauren did. Lauren's tongue and fingers were making her feel too good. She closed her eyes in the thrill of such pleasure. A woman knew exactly what to do to make another woman feel good. It wasn't long before Elise began convulsing as her hot come soaked Lauren's lips. Making her way back up Elise's aroused body, Lauren left a trail of soft kisses.

Elijah moaned involuntarily. He couldn't resist any longer, and it was time to make his way over. Before he could get in the bed, Lauren was already pulling and sucking on his dick. He lay on his back to let her dominate. Elise got on her knees beside her. Lauren drew back but kept her hand on his shaft, stroking him as Elise took her turn sucking. Lauren gave her a few minutes then nudged Elise so she could have another turn at him. Lauren had more experience in the head department, a fact not lost on Elise, which was why she took mental notes of all Lauren's techniques. When it was her turn again, she tried her best to duplicate every move. They alternated pleasing him with Lauren controlling the pace.

On Elise's final go at it, she moved Lauren's hand aside and took full control. Sucking him long, deep and fast, she caught a perfect rhythm with her head and hand motion.

"Oh shit!" Elijah was reaching his peak. "Damn, Elise." His body tensed, his breathing increased. She didn't break rhythm, just continued to make love to his dick with her tongue, lips, and hands.

Lauren was all too familiar with those sounds and movements. She went to move Elise aside again, but Elise resisted this time and kept sucking.

"Ohhh shit!" he said louder.

"Give it to me," Lauren told Elise.

"Un-un," Elise breathed, continuing her work.

"Ahhhh!" Elijah moaned as he started to explode.

Lauren was certain that he was coming. *This is my part,* she told herself, *Fuck this.* With a more forceful shove, she nudged Elise off and deep-throated him, taking all that he had left. She licked it gently after he was finished, knowing that he would be tender. She'd mastered how not to touch it too rough at that point, giving just enough contact to arouse him again without having to wait the usual refractory period. Elise took notes.

Once she got him fully erect again, she pulled back. "I want to watch you fuck her." Lauren encouraged Elijah. That was all she had to say. He commenced to satisfying Elise, working her through multiple positions at different speeds and angles while Lauren watched and masturbated. Elise competed with his aggression with intense hip grinding and dirty talk of her own.

"Alright, I'm getting jealous now. It's my turn." Lauren pulled him over to her. He took her missionary for only a few minutes before wanting her in their favorite position. He flipped her doggy-style and served her without pity.

Elise lay on her back in front of Lauren to give her a full view of the pink walls as she masturbated. Between thrusts, Lauren randomly tasted Elise's sweetness. This was too much for Elijah's senses and he was about to blow again. He tried to avert the orgasm by pausing his motion, but it didn't work. Giving in, he gave her five more deep thrusts before erupting inside her. Lauren bounced her fat ass against him unmercifully, making sure he shot every last drop into her.

Exhausted, he pulled out. Lauren's motor was still running. She climbed directly into Elise with her tongue again. He was done for the moment. He needed to rest his eyes, just shut them for a quick second.

Sleep overtook him.

---

The next morning, Elijah was abruptly woken up by Elise shoving a phone in his face. "It's Wiz, he says it's important," she said.

Elijah reluctantly grabbed the phone and looked at the clock—8:15. He squinted against the bright sun beaming through the window.

"Shit," he mumbled. "What's so damn important he gotta call me this early in the morning?"

"Get up, nigga," Wiz shouted a little too loudly. "We'll have plenty of time to sleep when we check into Inglewood Cemetery."

"I ain't goin' to no mutha-fuckin' Inglewood Cemetery. They can burn me up and sprinkle my ashes in the hood when I go."

"Yeah, yeah. I didn't call you to hear about your after-death plans. Turn on Channel 9 news."

Elijah told Elise to turn on the TV. They watched in intense silence as an attractive Hispanic reported from the scene.

"We are reporting live from Manchester Park in South Central Los Angeles where one man is confirmed dead and another has been transported to the hospital with life-threatening injuries suffered from gunshot wounds. This shooting occurred last night. Sources say the shooting stems from a long-running feud between rival gangs that escalated a week ago when a member from one of the gangs was murdered not far from here, *near* Jesse Owens Park."

The reporter adjusted her earpiece and flung her hair back. "It is suspected that the victims in this present incident were members of the Hoover Crips, or Criminals as they now call themselves, and the assailants were members of the Nine Os Crips. We are receiving information as we make this broadcast. We will continue to bring you coverage throughout the morning as it comes in . . ."

Elijah put the phone back up to his ear. "What was so important about that? The homies laid something down, that's nothing new or special. How long has this shit been on?"

"They've been running it over and over since I woke up at about six," Wizard said. "I had already got a call from my bro last night telling me about the situation. I was supposed to let you know last night, but it got late and I fell asleep. What the hell are you doin' still laid up?"

"I had a long night." He looked at Elise who cracked a smile. "You still haven't told me why you had to call me this early in the morning to tell me about some every-day gang shit."

"Stop complaining about it being early, save that for somebody who really gives a fuck. It's not what happen that's important, it's who's behind it. Our little black friend is back and he's supposed to be the crowd mover."

Elijah knew exactly whom Wiz was speaking of: Li'l Teflon.

"Oh yeah?" Elijah said slowly. "That's a hell of a way to announce his presence. But it doesn't surprise me, he's always had a flair for the dramatic."

"We're meeting at *Jummah,* twelve o'clock," Wizard said.

"The Islamic center?"

"Nah, Jefferson."

"I'm there."

After he hung up. Elijah quickly got up and made his way to the bathroom. Elise came in while he was showering and sat on the sink.

"Is everything okay?" she asked.

"Yeah . . . nothing I can't handle," he responded, soaping up.

"Do we have some business to handle?"

"No. Not we. Look, now that you're pregnant, carrying my seed, your criminal career is over. Your role is different now so you may as well get at Guzman to let him know that you're done. If you want to give the role to Diabla, then I'll leave you that choice, but you, personally, that's over. It's just like Snow—once she put in her work and proved herself, things changed. She's my legal side, touching nothing but money, and that's only after it's safely in hand. It's time for you to do the same. Your job now is to be the teacher and mother of this household. You got it?"

Elise nodded in a way that wasn't complete agreement or obedience, but not defiant either.

Elijah had no time to get a more definitive answer; there were more pressing matters to wrestle with. He got dressed and went downstairs to the kitchen where Lauren had a light healthy breakfast prepared.

"I need one of you to take me to pick up the Diablo from the condo," he said, biting into a piece of wheat toast.

"It's already in the garage," Lauren responded. "I had all your cars . . . well, at least your favorite ones, moved here yesterday after you left the condo."

He shook his head at their craftiness. Standing from the table, he grabbed his jacket from the chair and cell phone from the table.

"The keys are on the rack leading to the garage." Lauren gestured in the direction of the backdoor.

"Alright, I got business to handle." He kissed them both. "Love y'all."

"Love you too." They spoke in unison. "Be careful, and come back home," Elise added, clearly worried about him.

He paused to stare at her for a moment with one of those smiles that could mean everything or nothing at all. He turned and walked out without comment.

Firing up the Diablo, he felt the roar of the engine when he hit the gas pedal. He knew things had been going too good for him. Hell had to come on the heels of a night in heaven—his life story. "No rest for the wicked," he mumbled. Turning up the volume on Scarface and Tupac's, "Smile," he braced himself to face the concrete jungle another day.

# CHAPTER THIRTY-FOUR

Inside the small tidy mosque on Jefferson and Fourth Avenue, men and women of all different ages and stations in life sat shoeless on a bright red carpet with Middle Eastern designs, engaged by the sermon being delivered. Aside from the Imam's voice, the mosque was so quiet that time seemed to stand still. The men and women were separated by a thick partition while *Jummah* was in session; they did not exist to one another. The Imam was of short stature. His tight white *kufi* made his head appear abnormally large, and his smooth dark skin and physical vitality gave him a much more youthful appearance than his sixty-seven years would indicate. In a somber tone, he began the reading of the Quran:

> "*Bismillah –ir-rahman-ir-raheem.* "Verily thou cannot make the dead to hear, nor can thou make the deaf to hear the call when they show their backs and turn away. Nor can thou lead back the blind from their straying. Only those wilts thou make to hear, who believe in our signs and submit their wills to Islam. On the Day of Judgment, no excuse

> of theirs will avail the transgressors, nor will they be invited then to seek grace by repentance. Thus does Allah seal up the hearts of those who understand not so patiently persevere: for verily the promise of Allah is true, nor let those shake thy firmness who have themselves no certainty of faith."

The Imam continued in a louder voice. "Is then the man who believes no better than the man who is rebellious and wicked? Not equal are they! For those who believe and do righteous good deeds are gardens as hospitable homes for their good deeds. As to those who are rebellious and wicked, their abode will be the fire. Every time they wish to get away therefrom, they will be forced thereto, and it will be said to them: taste ye the penalty of the fire, that which you rejected as false. And indeed, we will make them taste the penalty of this life prior to the supreme penalty in order that they may repent. Surely Allah speaks the truth." He concluded his reading, then followed up with elaborating on the verses he'd read.

He held the audience's attention with a style of speech that was clear and effective. His eyes roved from one end of the room to the other, lingering from time to time on individuals to ensure his connection separately and as a group. They soon landed on one individual who sat at the back of the room; their eyes locked and both seemed to find some sense of familiarity. The Imam's attention was held there and he directed the remainder of his *khutba* to this individual exclusively.

*I hate coming to these places,* Elijah thought. *Why does Wiz always want to meet in one of these damn places? There are plenty of other places where we could talk without wiretaps. Hell, we can't talk while this preacher is up there running his mouth.* Every time he came to one of these places, he felt like the preacher was talking directly to him, and it always made him uncomfortable. Last thing he needed to hear was about heaven and hell. *Why's this dude looking at me?* Was someone behind him . . .

Elijah checked over his shoulder, but he wasn't surprised not to see anyone there. Turning back to the front, the Imam was still staring directly at him. Now he knew he wasn't tripping; the guy was really talking to him.

The Imam looked around the room and suddenly switched topics from his original sermon. *"Subhana Allah!"* he said. "I want to ask you brothers and sisters to excuse me. I want to go off course briefly to touch on another area Allah has given me inspiration to speak on, a topic that I feel someone desperately needs to hear."

No one spoke, but many in the congregation nodded their heads encouraging the Imam to speak what was in his heart. In a very thoughtful and careful manner, he proceeded forward with his message:

> "Allah says in the Quran that he who supports and promotes a righteous cause will receive the fruits of that cause, and he who supports and promotes an evil or unrighteous cause will receive the fruits therefrom. O ye who believe, die only as Muslims!"

He looked at Elijah again and smiled. "Many of you young warriors are using your talents and gifts for the wrong cause. It is Allah who gives you strength, who gives you intelligence, gives you courage, and gives you substance so that you may be thankful and glorify him, and to use those gifts to further the righteous cause.

"You do not realize you are being ungrateful and rebellious toward Allah. It is not that you are evil, that you don't realize or understand your rebelliousness, it is because the *dunya* has dulled your senses, clouded your consciousness, causing you to become spiritually blind.

"The heart is still good, the intentions are good, but anger and ignorance is contaminating your heart with a deadly disease that is in turn affecting your actions. It is solely up to you to curtail this disease before it becomes incurable. Do not allow events and circumstances from your past to choke and deprive you of your blessings and happiness in the present."

"All of Allah's righteous people have had enormous hardships. You're not the only one who has suffered. This is how Allah tests and refines us. In the Bible, it is called being put through the furnace of affliction. All our experiences of pain, all our experiences of tragedy, give us lessons that we must accept and grow from. This is how we reach the greatness that Allah had ordained for us. We must pass our test and not become disgruntled toward Allah for allowing us to experience those hardships. It should have the opposite effect. Allow your appreciation to grow even more for Allah for giving you the strength, fortitude, and resilience to overcome those obstacles and tragedies.

"You have come through unbroken, but you are already victorious! Allah calls you to strive in his cause. You are needed in the Muslim *Ummah.* You have a duty to Allah, to the Muslims who are not as strong as you, to the elders, women, and orphans who look to the Muslim champions to ease their burdens. Most importantly, you owe it to yourself. Loosen the bonds that the *Shaytan* is using in his attempt to enslave you.

"Allah is extending his grace and mercy to you in this moment, do not delay. Run to Allah as if in a race!"

With these words, he broke eye contact with Elijah and shuffled his notes around on the podium.

His words resonated to the core of Elijah's spirit. He gave a quick glance over his shoulder to see if his three companions were aware of what just happened between him and the Iman. Big Wizard and Hitter's heads were bowed in thought. Little Wizard's mind seemed to be in the distance. He stared straight ahead with tears in his eyes.

*I wonder what the hell he's thinking about,* Elijah thought before directing his attention back to the front of the room.

*"Qad kama tis salaat,"* the Imam announced.

Elijah didn't know exactly what those words meant, but he knew from prior experience that when the preacher said them, everyone gathered together for a group prayer. Like always, he stood with everyone else. The Imam prayed in a rhythmic tone in Arabic. Elijah peeked out of the corner of his eye to see what Hitter was doing so that he could follow his movements to keep up with the congregation. He hated the part where he had to prostrate his head to the floor—it felt unmanly—but out of respect he did it anyway.

Usually, he went through these motions mechanically, but this day felt different. While in prostration, he voiced his own prayer. "God forgive me for my faults," he asked simply. He didn't know why he was doing this, he wasn't even sure God existed, yet he felt the need to voice these prayers.

With the prayer completed, the four of them sat closely together. Aside from the few stragglers lingering to make extra supplications or make-up prayers, the mosque had emptied out. Still, they lowered their voices to a nearly inaudible pitch wanting to keep the meeting short and sweet.

Wizard leaned in. "This is the situation," he spoke in hushed tones, "we've put in much work getting money and knocking suckas down, and it's time to back all the way up. I got word that the feds and murder detectives along with 77-Crash Unit have formed a special task force specifically for us. Too many murders have been going unsolved on their watch and they are being pressured to do something about it. With this new shit all over the news they're really gonna try to turn up the heat. It's time for us to fall back and enjoy our money . . . and grow fat. The situation with the little Black dude, we can't leave that unresolved. We take care of him, then we disappear for a while. We can regroup in a year or so and start the next phase after things die down."

Elijah listened closely. He let the different scenarios play over in his mind.

"I'll take care of Li'l Teflon," Li'l Wizard volunteered, eyes glazed over as if already envisioning the pain he would inflict.

"Nah, cuzz." Elijah spoke up. "I would feel more comfortable taking care of that myself. I grew up with him. Letting somebody else hit him seems too much like betrayal. Even though he betrayed me, I gotta still stay true to myself and this game."

Hitter broke his silence. "Traitors get no honor, so fuck him. You don't have no exclusive rights on killing him. Whoever gets to him first gets the prize. To keep it real, I don't think it's the time to be doing anymore killing. It's too hot with the pigs, but I'm not planning on doing no running. This is my life! My run will end when I'm in the grave or in a concrete box. I love this shit. I don't know what I would do without the streets. Leave Li'l Teflon to me; y'all go ahead and lay low for a while."

"Man, you sound like a damn fool," Big Wizard scolded his brother. "If you don't know when to step back when the time calls for it, then you may as well go and give yourself to the feds or kill yourself. It's time to get ourselves in a better position. The hoods from state to state are crawling with the feds, all with our names in their mouths. After we move on Li'l Teflon, if we stick around, it's just gonna be an unnecessary war that will only draw more heat. If word gets out that we crushed him, then we'll have to crush his brother. Then the homies that favor them will want revenge, meaning we gotta hit them too . . ."

"Fuck it, let's kill 'em all," Li'l Wizard interrupted.

Hitter shook his head in frustration. "Why are you even here?" He looked at Li'l Wizard like he was the biggest idiot on the planet. Li'l Wiz sat expressionless, oblivious to what he said that pissed Hitter off.

"Look . . . it doesn't have anything to do with me having some exclusive rights to the hit, as you say. I grew up with him, and I'm the one who brought him in so he is my responsibility. And on top of that, I don't want it to happen right now. Like Li'l Wiz said, it's too much heat right now. It would be just our luck to fuck off everything on a mutha-fucka who's not worth the bullet it's going to take to shoot his dumb ass with. Even dead, he still serves the purpose of destroying all that we built."

Hitter glared at Elijah suspiciously. "So, what are you saying? We're just supposed to let him get away with what he did?"

Elijah didn't like the way Hitter presented the last question and the frustration was obvious on his face. "It's not always about 'us' giving our enemies a pass or not. Karma is always gonna dish out what a mutha-fucka has coming. Let's not look at it as giving him a pass—this is about us giving ourselves a pass. A real chance at success, the kind of success that comes with peace of mind. If somewhere in the future the opportunity presents itself, we can take the issue up then."

"Ah, here we go with this shit," Li'l Wizard blurted. "I think y'all let that Imam get too far in your heads. With no disrespect, that sermon was heartfelt, but I don't buy into the spookism and karma and all the other mystical shit." His agitation caused his voice to rise a few decimals, earning a serious look and a gesture of the hand for him to lower his voice from Hitter.

"My bad," he said, lowering his voice. "As I was saying, the decisions I make won't be based on some mysterious force that another man speaks on as if he has some secret knowledge that no one else has. If God wanted us to be good boys, and wanted us to do good he should have created a good world. I tried to love God, but for some reason he doesn't fuck with my kind so I'm not going to kiss his ass."

"Man, I don't want to hear all this emotional garbage this dude got goin on in his head. I'm 'bout to go." Hitter rose to leave.

"Calm down." Big Wizard gestured to his younger brother. "We didn't come here to bicker with each other or get divided in our aims. Li'l Nine, we respected your wishes for the past couple years on dealing with Li'l Teflon because we understood that you gave Guzman your word on holding off on going to war until the money contract was up. You don't have that to lean on anymore, but I'm not going to press you about taking care of it because I agree with you that now may not be the time. As you know, timing is not going to be perfect for every move. Sometimes things gotta be done even if we disagree. So, if you two feel that Li'l Teflon must be dealt with, I won't tell you otherwise, but I do suggest that we hold off for a few months. Let's go to the young homie's funeral to pay our respects and after a while we'll take care of it."

Hitter and Li'l Wizard nodded their agreement, but Elijah only stared. For some reason, he was still preoccupied with the Imam's sermon. He couldn't seem to get the man's face out of his mind.

Big Wizard rose from the carpet, signaling that the meeting was over. On the way out, they stopped at the *Zakat* window. Hitter and Wizard both gave large sums of money to the brown-skinned man doing the collections. Seeing the large amount they dropped, he stared in disbelief. "*As salaamu alaikum,* brothers," he said in gratitude. "*Wa alaikum as salaam,*" they intoned, walking for the exit.

As they filed out, Hitter and Wizard received greetings, hugs, and handshakes from many of the elders who obviously knew them since childhood by the way they inquired about their parents.

A dark-skinned middle-age woman dressed in full *hijab* had a table set up out front of the mosque selling red snapper dinners. Hitter bought four dinners and four slices of her pineapple coconut cake. When he put two $100 bills in her hand she looked confused, but she caught on by the smile on his face that he was engaging in an act of charity. She smiled and placed her hand over her heart with a slight bow of the head in appreciation.

Elijah held his Styrofoam container with the intentions of eating the food later, while the rest of them tore into their food right there on the streets. Their conversation turned to much lighter matters as they laughed and talked among themselves. Hitter and Wizard were interrupted by or joined in other conversations with people Elijah and Li'l Wizard didn't know. Elijah wondered to himself how the two could appear so perfectly in their element in so many diverse settings: from the housing projects to a college campus, they never seemed to be out of place. They had the ability to blend in wherever they go. *Maybe it's part of their survival instincts developed over the years,* he thought. Unconsciously he took a piece of the fried red snapper from the container and popped it in his mouth. One bite was all it took; he was finishing off the entire plate before he knew it.

"Oh yeah," Li'l Wizard said as he put the last piece of cake in his mouth. "I meant to tell y'all, I came up on two hundred pounds of weed today on a fluke. Nothin' special, just some regular stress. I'm trying to get rid of it for a li'l bit of nothin'. The price the dude was trying to charge me was three-fifty a pound. but I'll take two hundred for each and I'm good."

"I don't need it," Hitter said with attitude. Li'l Wizard wasn't talking to him anyway; he knew Hitter was the last person that would buy anything from him.

"That's a come-up." Big Wiz looked to Elijah. "You wanna go half with me?"

Elijah nodded. "I'm with it. We can get together later and check it out."

"What do we need to wait until later for? I got it in the car." Li'l Wizard said.

Big Wizard looked at him in disbelief. "You mean to tell me you came to *Jummah* with two hundred pounds in the car and left it parked on the streets?"

"Yeah. I was in the midst of getting it when you called me to meet you here."

"Man, you could've dropped it off before you came . . . never mind, it's too late for all that. Let's just check it out so we can get it the hell away from here." Big Wizard walked for the car followed by the rest.

Li'l Wizard walked in front of him once they got near the cars. "It's right here in the trunk." He fumbled for the keys before inserting the right one and twisting the lock.

Elijah and Big Wizard were discussing who would be the best Laker in his prime—Shaq or Kareem—when Li'l Wiz popped the trunk. "Check it out, cuzz." He motioned them over.

They all leaned in to get a better look at the product. Instead of the newer model cars the rest drove, Li'l Wizard preferred old buckets that looked like shit on the outside but had the secret sauce under the hood. He equipped them with brand new engines with headers, cams, and Edelbrock carburetors. The pieces of shits could fly like NASCAR racer, and with them being all metal he had no problem with getting into a high-speed chase, because he knew if he crashed his chances of survival were great. The person he may happen to hit—not so much.

The other benefit of driving a 1970 battle-axe mobile was the huge trunk. He wrestled one of the large bundles forward. Using a pocketknife, he cut open the plastic and broke off a chunk of weed for their examination.

Elijah looked it over and took a sniff. "Yeah, it looks decent for some bullshit bammer." He passed it to Big Wizard.

Li'l Wiz pulled another bundle forward. "Here's the rest," he said. Just as the block edged forward, a portion of the trunk that had been shielded by the weed became exposed, revealing a man's bound feet.

"Oh shit! What the fuck!" Elijah and Big Wizard almost jumped out of their skin. Both took a few steps back, eyes still glued to the inside of the trunk.

As soon as he saw the man's feet, Hitter, without question or comment, turned on his heels and walked as swiftly as possible without breaking into an actual run to his car. While the other two stood stuck in the moment, Hitter was firing up his Range Rover getting the hell out of Dodge.

The bound feet began struggling against the ropes as they looked on.

"What the fuck, cuzz. Who is that?" Big Wizard asked from a distance.

"Aw, that ain't nobody. Just some El Salvadorian cat who was selling me the weed." He waved his hand in a no-big-deal sort of way. "Y'all wanna buy the weed?" he asked with childlike innocence, as if nothing was out of place with the scene.

Big Wizard shook his head at his little homeboy's madness. There were no words that could add to or take away from what he just witnessed. Though a couple minutes late in figuring it out, it was time to follow his brother's lead. With a paranoid glance up and down Fourth Avenue, he high-stepped it to his car.

"Where you goin', cuzz?" Li'l Wizard asked, arms raised in confusion.

When Big Wizard jumped in his car, Li'l Wizard shook his head. "Damn, you niggas act like you ain't never seen a nigga tied up before," he mumbled, then turned to see Elijah still standing there. He reacted as if it was his first time seeing him that day. Pushing his bifocals up the bridge of his nose, he squinted at Elijah. "You wanna buy some weed?" he asked with a blank stare.

Elijah looked him directly in the eyes, incredulous, then not being able to hold it any longer, burst into uncontrollable laughter.

# CHAPTER THIRTY-FIVE

The large pink structure sat like an oasis of peace in the middle of the concrete jungle. The plush green lawns rolled with elaborate headstones for as far as the eyes could see. Well-placed shrubbery and palm trees swayed with the breeze as the sun shone bright against a slightly overcast sky. A quiet, calm energy prevailed over the cemetery as if it was guarded by invisible forces that protected it from the everyday hustle and bustle that went on right outside the gates.

Li'l Teflon drove through the front entrance at Inglewood Park Cemetery where cars were jammed in a line leading up to the chapel. He had been to so many funerals over the years that he'd become calloused to what they really represented—death. For him, and many others in attendance, a homeboy's funeral was nothing more than a "hood function," a social event to network, dress up, and represent. Mourning was reserved for the family members and tightest comrades of the deceased. Death and destruction was so common in the fabric of South Central that most were numb to its effects.

Without any emotion, Li'l Teflon observed the throng of attendees loitering outside the chapel. His powder-blue '64 Chevy lowrider moved up the roadway at a snail's pace. Murder-Min followed in a low-key Pontiac Grand Prix with a Tech-9 at the ready. The four youngsters brought up the rear in identical powder-blue '77 Cutlass Supremes. Li'l Teflon had recommended the youngsters get the Cutlass as a reminder of the days he and his brother used to kick up dust out of the same vehicles. The only additions were that the youngsters Cut Dogs were equipped with hydraulics and thirteen-inch Daytons, which gave the cars a bowlegged appearance in the front so the pressure could be absorbed when the hydraulics were activated in the "leap show."

Baby Devil, who was the third car in line behind Murder-Min, broke their single-file formation to squeeze past the other two and move up to the front with his powder-blue bandana tied to the car's antenna at half-mast. He was the unofficial second-in-command in their small group, but on this day he felt bigger than Li'l Teflon. He had a confirmed kill on the enemy and was the one who carried the homie to safety when Li'l Teflon left him for dead. He was Baby Devil, the *real beast* of the squad.

Disregarding the spaces reserved for parking, Baby Devil slammed to a stop in the middle of the roadway in front of the funeral-goers, forcing his caravan to stop as well. He hopped out wearing cut-off blue Dickies that were creased razor-sharp, long white socks, blue Chucks, blue-gray Charlie Brown shirt, Locs, and a gray derby sitting on top of his freshly twisted French braids, which gave him the look and feel of the Tiny-Loc of the Century.

"The gorillas are here," he announced, arms opened wide.

The younger generation of Tiny-Toons hadn't seen Baby Devil in a while; they all surrounded and embraced him. One of their own was shining and it gave them all a sense of pride.

*This ain't part of the script,* Li'l Teflon thought as he watched them from his driver seat. They were supposed to park in a strategic position away from the crowd. "This stupid little fuck," he mumbled. The roadway was too narrow for him to get around Baby Devil's car, so he was forced to park and get out. All the others except Murder-Min followed suit; she stayed put as the watchdog.

The homeboys and homegirls who grew up with Li'l Teflon embraced him just as the youngsters had Baby Devil. The open secret about the park episode was out there, and them showing up looking good and riding clean only added to the hero's welcome. Outside of Elijah and his crew, the rest of the homies didn't know about the in-house friction going on with the two cliques.

In the parking lot on the side of the chapel, Big Teflon and Ju-Ju stood smoking a blunt as they watched the show Li'l Teflon and Baby Devil were putting on. Teflon's son, Little Akili, clung to him as he drank from his bottle of milk.

Further up the hill in an area near Florence Avenue cameras clicked away like a stenographer's typewriter. The task force made up of the FBI, South Bureau homicide detectives, and Seventy-Seventh CRASH officers were in the cut documenting and photographing everyone in attendance. John Berrigan, the lead agent, a forty-six-year-old Irishman, was the classic example of a workaholic. He was a third generation Irish-American born in Boston, Massachusetts. He joined the FBI after graduating with a master's degree in criminology from Princeton and quickly excelled at the FBI Academy both physically and academically.

Berrigan made a name for himself as a young agent prosecuting Russian and Irish mafia figures on the East Coast in the 1980s, going undercover and infiltrating some of those circles. A stickler for details, geared toward perfection in all he did, the cases he worked on would consume him to the point where nothing else mattered. This made him almost unbearable in his personal life but endearing to the top brass in Washington, DC, who considered him one of the Bureau's sharpshooters against organized crime. Now, a middle-aged agent, whose once-young six-five, two-hundred-forty-pound ex-college basketball athletic body was turning into a bulge of yeast from a bit too many beers, on his third marriage. He was hot on the trail of new prey.

News of the Nine Os criminal activities had reached all the way to the Department of Justice in DC. The drug trafficking and multiple multi-state murders had gone beyond the limit and could not be allowed to continue. Agent Berrigan was given the task and resources to bring down the entire gang by any means necessary, and best believe he was taking the "any means" part literal. It was his first experience dealing with black men involvement in organized crime, and it apparently irked him more than the Irish and Russian cases he'd worked on in the past. From the initial meeting when the case opened a year earlier, the first time he saw the charted picture board with the faces of all the members involved in the investigation, he felt a deep hatred them. He missed much of the meeting's dialogue due to his intense fixation with the photo labeled "Elijah 'Little Nine-Lives' Hassahn." Over the year following that meeting, he somehow convinced himself that it was his cosmic duty to take down and destroy Elijah, even if the others got away. Thoughts of Elijah and the case consumed him day and night. It was no longer just about dedication to his job; he'd moved into the realm of personal obsession.

Somber faces filled the inside of the chapel. The sounds of shuffling as people filled the pews, mourners' light sniffles along with the underlying silence, gave the atmosphere an eerie vibe.

Tiny Torpedo was the man-of-honor on this occasion. He lay at the front of the chapel in a black-and-white suit, encased in a sky-blue casket adorned with heavy-metal trimmings. Floral arrangements covered the bottom half of the casket and surrounding platform. Before being gunned down by the Hoovers, he was a bright, handsome youth full of bravado and life. On this day, he laid as a simple child at rest. The dull texture of his skin and hard-to-touch exterior was the true indication that the fifteen-year-old boy would never awake from his sleep.

The theme of the preacher's sermon: "The tragic waste of life to senseless violence," and "Tiny Torpedo's home going to paradise." The tone and content of the sermon caused his mother and immediate family to cry out in agony.

Li'l Teflon looked on stone-faced. The sermon was nothing but static to him. *This mutha-fucka need to hurry up with all this irrelevant bullshit,* he thought. He had seen his brother Big Teflon and Ju-Ju come in a little after he'd taken his seat, but neither of them had acknowledged him when they made eye contact. *Fuck 'em,* he thought, *I don't need their acknowledgement. Ungrateful sons of bitches! I made them who they are.*

Just then, a group of four entered the chapel from a side door dressed in tailor-made Italian suits, dark shades, and derbies. They took seats in the front alongside the family members of the deceased.

"There they go, cuzz." Li'l Teflon nudged Baby Devil. "Let the homies know."

Baby Devil passed the word down the line in hushed tones. The other youngsters grew visibly nervous. Clashing with Big Wizard and Elijah in conversation when they were amongst themselves was one thing, but carrying it out was something altogether different. Now that their adversaries were in the same building, the idea didn't seem too flattering. Big Wizard and Hitter were hood legends and hadn't gotten to that level by being pushovers.

The preacher concluded his sermon, a few brief statements by family and friends followed, then a beautiful rendition of Walter Hawkins's "Goin' Up Yonder" was sung by an attractive young woman. Her powerful vocals had even the hardest among them moved in a soul-stirring moment.

The service ended with a viewing of the body. A single-file line began at the back of the chapel. As it moved forward, the pews emptied out to keep the procession going.

This gave Elijah and their squad the opportunity to see everyone in attendance. Elijah made eye contact with Li'l Teflon just as he turned from viewing the body. Li'l Teflon gave them a look of defiance before exiting the chapel with his crew.

Li'l Wizard chuckled quietly before abruptly getting up to leave, exiting the same door in which they entered. The remaining three looked at one another in confusion, knowing it wasn't a good thing to let Li'l Wizard run loose. They immediately stood up and hurried to catch up with him.

The side door led to a private parking area used for employees. It was on the opposite side of the building where everyone congregated, consoled and talked to each other. Elijah, Big Wizard, and Hitter stepped out to the smoggy gray skies overhead, with Li'l Wizard nowhere in sight. The three had arrived together in a bulletproof Hummer. Li'l Wiz had already been waiting at the prearranged meeting spot. They had never bothered to ask him how he'd gotten there or where he parked, a detail they now regretted.

Big Wizard looked around thinking of the next move. "I don't know where this cat went." He strained to focus his vision. "Y'all go ahead and drive around to the front. I'll walk through the cut and blend in to see if I see him without drawing too much attention.

Hitter nodded and he and Elijah headed to the truck. Big Wizard took his .9mm from his shoulder holster, jacked a bullet in the chamber, re-holstered it, and walked to the edge of the building. They quickly made the decision that Hitter and Elijah would drive around to the front while Big Wizard walked to blend in with the rest of the crowd so he could look for Li'l Wizard without drawing too much attention.

The Hummer swung onto the roadway with Hitter at the wheel. Li'l Teflon and crew lowriders still had the road blocked. Hitter pulled up to the last car and edged up to the bumper, slowly accelerating. The Cutlass slid forward into the car in front of it, which in turn slid into the next. None of it caused any real damage, just a mild display of bumper cars.

"Hold up, cuzz." Baby Devil was the first to respond. Running to the Hummer, he banged on the hood with his fist. "What the fuck is you niggas problem?" he growled.

Hitter was out the driver's seat in an instant with Elijah not far behind. "You li'l bitch! You put your hands on my truck?" Hitter approached in attack mode.

Baby Devil took a precautionary step backward as Li'l Teflon and the others approached the confrontation. "Hold up, this is the li'l homie, cuzz." Li'l Teflon took the stance of an aggressive peacemaker.

"I wouldn't give a fuck who he is." Hitter shifted his focus to Li'l Teflon. "And who the fuck you supposed to be, his protector, nigga?"

"Since you put it that way, I'm whoever the fuck you want me to be."

Hitter mocked a fake surprise. "Oh, I see you've grown some balls since I knocked your ass out. Either that or you lost your fuckin' mind, but I can help you find it real quick." Hitter began removing his suit coat.

Li'l Teflon snatched his hat off and threw it on the trunk of the nearest car. "Let's get to it then, nigga!" he shouted.

This was about to be the clash of the Titans. All the youngsters except Baby Devil backed up a few feet, hesitant about being in the fray once it started. Baby Devil stood side by side with Li'l Teflon, ready for whatever.

"Have y'all lost your fuckin' minds?" The voice gave everyone cause for pause. It was Big Peso, a solid homie allied to all sides of the 90s, yet not committed to any clique or side. He was a homie with that unique ability of being able to lead and sway others by love and less by fear. Hated by the enemies, but loved and respected by his own tribe. His role was that of the unbiased arbitrator for the hood. His word carried weight with every generation because they all knew that his word on an issue would always come from a good place. Brown-skinned, solidly built, with shifty eyes burning with anger and disappointment, he stepped in-between the two parties.

"This is the young homie's funeral and y'all come with this bullshit? Hitter, cuzz, you too sharp to be out here like this. You my nigga, but you know better. Let's keep it all the way solid, my guy. Whatever y'all need to deal with, do it somewhere else. We have to respect his folks." He spoke in an even tone.

Ju-Ju and Big Teflon stood next to Big Peso to show their solidarity of purpose.

Hitter glared at them all aggressively. Big Wizard showed up just in time to prevent Hitter from jumping the gun. He already knew Hitter didn't take orders and ultimatums well, regardless of who or where they came from.

"Everybody fall back." Big Wizard stepped in. "The homie Peso is right. It's not the time for this. Go ahead and back the truck up, Hitt."

Hitter hesitated, head swiveling back and forth as he seemed to be contemplating what he should do. Finally, for reasons of his own, he jumped in the Hummer and backed it off the Cutlass' bumper.

The little boy standing next to Big Teflon caught Elijah's attention. He was a carbon copy of his father. Little Akili smiled at him, forcing Elijah to smile back.

"Everything good?" Peso asked both sides.

They all stared each other down with animosity until Wizard finally spoke. "Yeah, we good. It's all gravy." He glared at Li'l Teflon.

Li'l Teflon grabbed his hat, and he and his crew faded back into the crowd without comment.

Elijah, Ju-Ju, and Big Teflon were the last ones standing there. Elijah looked to the boy. "I didn't know you had a son."

"Yeah, he's a year old," Big Teflon said proudly.

"Make sure you raise him different from us. We grew up too fast, seen too much, and now we've become the things we seen."

There was a pregnant pause as all of them thought about what Elijah had just said. Ju-Ju finally tried to alter the mood a bit. "What's up, homie? What's the word?" He smiled.

"Aw, you know, trying to do all I can before it's my turn to check into a place like this for good." Elijah indicated the cemetery.

"Check it out, Li'l Nine, I know it's a lot going on that I have no control over," Big Teflon attempted to be sincere, "but I'm my own man and I have nothing but the utmost love and respect for you. I have always been loyal to you and Big 9-Lives, you know that, so don't judge me with anybody else. This is me and you."

"Who said anything about judging you? I'm just here to pay my respects to the li'l homie."

"Knock off the bullshit," Big Teflon said. "We've been doing this too long to not know each other's ways. You can analyze and politic all you want, but I'm trying to get at you on some real shit. I just want you to know before I leave that you are still my bro. I've been riding with you from day one, and it will always be love on my part. I want you to really know that because I don't know when we'll see each other again. I'm moving to San Diego to do something better for me and my son. Shit, ain't the same around here no more."

"Tell me 'bout it. That's good to hear though, and I wish you well on your new start," Elijah said insincerely. He ended his well wishes with a handshake and a hug.

Agent Berrigan leaned against the large scraggly oak tree, sun-worn face bloodshot, blue eyes pressed against the binoculars watching the exchange. "Aw, isn't that sweet?" he said more to himself than anyone else. "Looks like our C.I. was a little off about Little 9-Lives and the Teflon boys being at odds. Seems like they kissed and made up."

The double doors to the chapel opened and six pallbearers in blue khaki suits, Chuck Taylors, and dark glasses exited carrying the casket. The family members followed in somber silence. The casket was loaded into the hearse as the attendees retreated to their cars to follow it on the slow trek up the hill to the burial site.

Up on the hill a few Bible passages were read, then the preacher somberly pronounced, "Ashes to ashes, dust to dust, as he tossed a handful of dirt and flowers onto the casket as it was lowered into the ground. The mother and sisters wailed in anguish at the realization that this was the final scene of their loved one's physical presence.

Murder-Min observed the burial from the car parked not far away. On the drive over from the chapel, she had separated from the rest, just enough to maintain a safe distance. Though it deviated from her original instructions a bit, Li'l Teflon decided not to make a big deal of it. In hindsight, he felt he should have thought of it himself.

With the ceremony officially over, everyone headed for their rides to make the drive over to Tiny Torpedo's family house for food and socializing. Li'l Teflon had no interest in the after-funeral festivities; he wanted to make his presence felt and he'd accomplished that. Now it was time to strike out for the hideout not far away and get some head from Murder-Min.

Li'l Teflon and his entourage exited the cemetery on Manchester, and Murder-Min brought up the rear as they headed southbound. At Arbor Vitae, they made a left going east toward Crenshaw. She used this stretch of space to accelerate past the others and squeeze in behind Li'l Teflon. The stop light at the entrance to Darby Park turned yellow causing her to slow in anticipation of having to stop. Li'l Teflon instead sped up, running through the light. At the last minute, Murder-Min pressed hard on the gas to make it through just as it turned red, while the others were forced to stop.

Li'l Teflon saw through his rearview that the red light had caught the others. "Why the hell didn't they just run the light?" he mumbled. He figured he'd just slow up a bit and they would catch him at the next light on Crenshaw. Murder-Min continued to be on pace with him.

Stopping at the light on Crenshaw, he bobbed his head to the old-school Eazy-E blaring from the speakers. Murder-Min pulled alongside him, gesturing that he lowers his window. *What does this bitch want now?* he thought. Lowering the music, he rolled down the window. "What's up . . . ?"

Before he could finish the question, Li'l Wizard popped up in her passenger seat like jack-in-the-box with an evil grin behind a Glock-40.

Li'l Teflon's eyes grew the size of golf balls, and fear swept sickeningly from his testicles into his stomach. "How . . ."

Darkness.

# CHAPTER THIRTY-SIX

When the confrontation had taken place between Baby Devil and Hitter at the cemetery, everyone including the task force had their focus on the altercation. No one noticed Li'l Wizard move from the crowd into Murder-Min's passenger seat, including her. She, too, was distracted by the commotion to notice his presence until it was too late. Before she could react, he had the Glock-40 pressed against her side and was removing the Tech-9 from her hand. "Bitch, if you make a sound or even think about tryin' to do something, I'll blow ya mutha-fuckin' intestines through ya back. Try me!" he warned. From the look on his face, she was more than convinced that he was eager to carry out the threat.

"Now, drive up on the grass and go around the cars blocking the way," he directed her. It all happened so fast that by the time the confrontation was over he was in full control of her and the situation. Crouching next to her on the floor, gun at the ready, she had no choice but to do what she was told and relay to him how and where the caravan was moving.

Soon Li'l Wizard found himself face to face with the object of his desire. The pistol roared death, and the slug penetrated the left side of Li'l Teflon's face, sending blood, flesh, and teeth splattering throughout the car's interior. The '64 Chevy slowly veered right coming to rest on the curb.

Li'l Wizard slammed on the break from the passenger position and snatched the keys from the ignition. "You betta not move from this seat, bitch," he growled before exiting the car with the Glock-40 in one hand and her Tech-9 in the other. He moved swiftly to the driver's side of Li'l Teflon's car.

The entourage was now fast approaching. Baby Devil reached for his .45 Colt when he saw Li'l Wizard. Before he could make it to the scene, Li'l Wizard reached inside the immobile Chevy with the Glock and pumped three more rounds into Li'l Teflon's body.

Baby Devil knew there was no time to stop and get out, nor would it have been beneficial to hang his gun out the window to let off, so he did the next best thing: he squeezed rounds directly through his own front windshield as he approached the death scene.

Li'l Wizard dive toward the front of the Chevy for cover. The Cutlass came to a stop about fifteen feet away from his position. Tucking the Glock into his waistline, he came up firing the Tech-9: the first six shots into Baby Devil's already-busted windshield, the next fifteen were aimed at the other three. No return fire came back. The youngsters were all ducking for cover.

Li'l Wizard, in the midst of changing positions, turned just in the nick of time to see Murder-Min aiming a .25 caliber at him. The gun had been in her boot the entire time; she just never had a chance to go for it until he got out the car.

On instinct Li'l Wizard dived left the instant two bullets burst from her gun. He felt the sensation from one of the bullets run through his arm. Hitting the ground, he immediately tucked and rolled. She let off three more shots that all missed him and hit the

Chevy. As he came out of his roll, he sprung to his feet spraying a barrage of bullets in her direction. One shot hit her in the shoulder and another in the thigh, knocking her against the car. She screamed a high-pitched shrill.

Li'l Wizard let out a demonic laugh as he ran around to the passenger side of Li'l Teflon's Chevy. By now the youngsters were returning fire. He ducked low as their bullets flew overhead and dragged Li'l Teflon out of the passenger door onto the pavement face-first. He crawled over to the driver's seat, and without raising his head, he squeezed off seven shots out the back window to buy a few seconds. When Baby Devil and the others ducked the shots, it gave him enough time to reverse the Chevy off the cur, then drop it into drive.

As he burned rubber wildly onto Crenshaw, more bullets whizzed past his head. He laughed hysterically in the wind. His arm throbbed with a dull ache as blood soaked his suit coat and pants, but none of it fazed him in the least. He was in the zone. He had won.

Within twenty-four hours of the hit on Li'l Teflon, the Nine Os neighborhood was crawling with the Alphabet Boys: FBI, ATF, DEA, and cops of every description. Drug houses were raided and the homes of well-known gang members were being kicked-in and shook down regardless of who was inside, the elderly and kids included.

The tides had turned on the Nine Os. They were being hauled in and dragged off to LA County Jail by the dozen. Over twenty members were arrested on charges from loitering to suspicion of murder.

The word had spread quicker than syphilis in a whorehouse: Li'l Teflon was dead, and all-out war was to follow. A strange thing happened. Instead of gunshots, the hood fell silent. Law enforcement couldn't understand how all the major players, the real street figures and head busters, could simply walk away after such a major blow. The way they saw it, guys of Li'l Teflon's pedigree didn't get hit without others dying. There was supposed to be retaliation.

The Nine Os disappearing act pissed Agent Berrigan off to the highest degree. In his book, black street hoodlums weren't supposed to be this smart. Back to his chain-smoking, he swore with intense anger and rage, "I will not, cannot give up. I don't care if it takes me until my last breath: Elijah and his crew will fall. Somehow, some way!"

# CHAPTER THIRTY-SEVEN

Elise gave birth to an eight-pound, seven-ounce beautiful baby boy that Elijah named Amaru. He was born with the caramel-brown skin complexion of his father and the greenish-blue eyes of his mother. For the first time in his adult life, Elijah felt a sense of real purpose. Playing with his son, changing his diapers, feeding him, rocking him to sleep, gave him the greatest joy he'd ever felt.

By the time Elise delivered their son, Lauren was beginning her pregnancy. For Elijah, life was good: he'd made it out of the drug game, he had a beautiful healthy son and another on the way, he had two of the most beautiful and loyal women a man could ask for, and his name was still good in the streets.

Rumors ran amuck as to Li'l Teflon. He was said to be dead, cremated by his family without funeral services due to speculation that his homeboys had killed him and his family didn't want them being able to come and gloat over his dead body. Another rumor had the Inglewood Bloods killing him. There was another rumor that he was alive and recovering in a private location out of state.

As for Elijah, he accepted Li'l Wizard's confirmation that Li'l Teflon was standing in line awaiting his name to be called for his place in the dark kingdom.

Hitter and Wizard went underground at the same time as he did. Elijah simply stayed in at the mansion with the girls and the baby. Hitter relocated to Warner Robbins, Georgia, where he had a similar situation set up with his two children's mothers. He was home schooling his children and heavily involved with the Islamic community there. Being near Big 9-Lives, who still lived in Atlanta, they were able to get together for socializing and a few legal business ventures.

Big Wizard and Li'l Wizard were holed up in Denmark, South Carolina, at Big Wizard's hundred-acre ranch out in the boondocks. Their nearest neighbor was five miles away from the edge of the property, which meant ten miles or more away from the actual dwelling. The ranch was well stocked with quarter horses, dogs, a fishing pond and pigeon coups filled with show birds.

They were two city boys living out their favorite outlaw cowboy movies. There were no live-in women, but a constant stream of strippers from Georgia and North Carolina was more than adequate entertainment for them. But more than the women, they enjoyed the military-style war games they conducted at least four times a week that consisted of a break-of-dawn five-mile run, calisthenics, shooting practice on the self-made gun range, and paint paint-gun battles through the surrounding brush. They included some of the women from time to time if they were athletic and adventurous enough. They were having the time of their lives just living and strategizing for the next phase of life.

Big Wizard, Hitter, and Elijah communicated with each other through clone cell phones at least once a month. Except for these phone calls, each pretty much did their own thing in worlds a million miles away from the hood.

In the year that passed, they kept an ear to the streets through various trusted sources. All reports were that things had gone quiet since their timely retreat. All the heat and harassment from the task force that had been in full force immediately following the hit on Li'l Teflon had simmered down. The hood was back to business as usual.

Big Wizard felt it was time for the four to meet and discuss the future. Though none of them had voiced it, they all missed the hood terribly. Only a native of LA would understand when it was said that there was no place on Earth like South Central. Despite the tragedy, poverty, and grief that South Central breeds, there was still an undeniable energetic pull on its' natives when away.

The monthly conference call between Big Wizard, Hitter, and Elijah was short and sweet:

"We meet next Friday in the Land at our usual spot."

"That's a bet," Hitter and Elijah affirmed.

"Ninety minutes!"

"Nine minutes, no seconds!"

# CHAPTER THIRTY-EIGHT

**2001**

Standing on top of one of the many boulders mounted into the cliff, Elijah looked out over the Pacific Ocean. From his perch he tasted the salt on his lips, felt the mist on his face, and heard the comforting sound of the surf crash against the rocks below in a symphony of natural poetry in motion. The full moon provided a fitting backdrop for a cruise heading out to sea. Inhaling lightly from the Cuban cigar, it mingled with the salt for a unique taste. He savored the rich sensation. *Heaven*, he thought.

Meditation and contemplation had brought him to the belief that heaven and hell wasn't a destination to be reached after death, but was rather a condition or state of mind right here on Earth. For the past year he had lived in heaven, then came the conference call with the fellas earlier that day that left him feeling uneasy. Something about Big Wizard's tone, the seriousness of it sounded too agenda-driven. Intuition warned him that his present heaven could spiral into hell in no time if he wasn't careful.

Aaliyah's "One in a Million" played faintly in the background of his thoughts. The scenery was so serene that he had become hypnotized by the beauty and forgotten that the music was still playing in the Diablo. Aaliyah's melody broke through his reverie, and for some reason brought Elise to mind. The thought of her made him smile. Yet, his spirit was uneasy, fluctuating between euphoria and anxiety. Intuitively, he knew that his life was at a crucial tipping point and he need divine answers to the mystery of his purpose and destiny.

Taking a final toke from the cigar, he thumped it over the cliff into the ocean and turned his head skyward to blow out a poof of smoke. "God, if you do exist . . ." he said, as he looked up at the stars, "I know that I've become a product of the things I have seen, but that doesn't mean I am unappreciative. I appreciate the blessings I have experienced on this earth. Things have been good for me lately, but I understand that nothing good lasts forever. Sometimes I feel like I've sold my soul for money and power when all along all I was searching for was peace."

He took a deep breath. "Now I know that peace comes from within and is not something that can be bought with money. It was hard to figure out when constantly dealing with envy, hate, jealousy, tragedy, and wicked niggas. But I won't make excuses. I take full responsibility for my actions. You gave me the power to manifest my reality and this is what I created for myself. So now I know that I have to work for any other change that I desire. It says in the Holy Quran that you won't change the condition of a person until they change what is in their hearts. I really want to make that change, but if it's too late, then I'm ready to go when it's my time. Until then, I have to play my part as circumstances dictate. I guess it's up to you to decide if I'm your soldier or Satan's angel. I guess I'll learn which it is at some point, or when the game of life is over. One thing for sure that you and the world can say about Elijah—I'm a survivor. Come what may!"

With a big smile towards the sky, he wiped the tears from his eyes. "Can't stop, won't stop," he affirmed to his invisible allies, ghosts, and demons, then turned to go. Hopping in the Diablo, he smashed off the dirt gravel onto Pacific Coast Highway leaving dust in his wake.

# EPILOGUE

For a moment, he thought he was dreaming because the lights in the room were extremely bright. He was lying on a thick narrow hospital bed. He looked around bewildered. The ceiling was polished an opaque white. Beside him, a machine beeped in a continuous rhythm, a slow, rhythmic beeping sound. Tubes and wires seemed to run through every hole on his body. A crucifix on the wall overhead came into focus. *What the . . .?* he thought aghast.

"Hey, big guy."

He turned to see a man sitting there in a sports coat smiling at him behind tobacco-stained teeth. "You've been out for quite some time. Was afraid we lost you for a minute there."

He attempted to speak, but pain from the effort shot up the side of his face like an explosion, causing him to moan weakly.

"Oh, no need in trying to speak. You have a tube so far down your throat that you'd be talking shit, literally. Not to mention the metal in your mouth from the surgery." The strange man shook his head.

"You know, someone must have really been praying for you, because you are a fucking miracle. When I got the call that your vitals were picking up and you were expected to come out of the coma soon, I rushed down here. I thought it couldn't be true, that someone was pulling my chain bigtime. That bullet that went through your face did some real damage; it only missed your brain by mere inches. Still, the three shots to your body should have been more than enough to end your career. Yet here you are, still with us. I guess you really are Teflon." The man laughed at his own lame attempt at a joke.

Li'l Teflon focused on him through the medicated fog as a tear slid down his left cheek.

"I know, I know." The man patted his leg with feigned compassion. "Li'l 9-Lives, Wizard, and Hitter are pieces of shit for doing this to you. I don't know if that tear is out of pain or out of anger, but you have my word. With me on your team, you best believe that you won't be the only one shedding tears."

The man leaned forward, placing his elbows on the hospital bed. "Don't worry, Li'l Teflon . . . can I call you that?" he said amusedly. "You are I are going to be great friends. You can call me Agent Berrigan, by the way."

Li'l Teflon looked back at the ceiling, exhausted. With an effort, he tried to collect himself. *Who the fuck is this white man?* he thought. *Where the hell am I? He* remembered Li'l Wizard being in the car with Murder-Min. *How the fuck did that happen?* Then it dawned on him: *I think Baby Devil was there. We were coming from a funeral. I could hear their voices . . . and that laugh, the laugh of the devil . . . Li'l Wiz shot me. Them niggas caught me slipping.* He remembered the pain, and trying to speak but not being able to move his mouth. He remembered the darkness that filled his vison, how he was screaming in his mind but no sound came out. The barrel of a gun and Li'l Wiz's face before the pain and darkness.

*I swear on my word, on all that I stand for, once I'm back on my feet, there ain't no more rules, no boundaries. Everybody gonna suffer. Muthafuckas gotta pay. They all gonna die!*

Li'l Teflon's weakness overcame him and he fell into dreamless sleep.

To Be Continued . . .

# ACKNOWLEDGEMENT

We give thanks to the struggle, and all those who righteously endure its blows. For without it, we would not become who we are. Without hardship, we would never develop the will to be conquerors.

CAN'T STOP! WON'T STOP!

# AUTHOR'S BIO

Toni T-Shakir, owner and CEO of Shakir Publishing, is a Jamaican native who grew up in the Bay Area of Northern California, subsequently relocating to Los Angeles. She is an avid reader who acquired a love for writing during her lengthy federal prison sentence for conspiracy in a nationally publicized case. Her debut novel, *Land Of No Pity,* is her attempt to take all the negatives, turn them into positives, and triumph over all that was meant to destroy her.

Shakir Publishing is the conception of Toni's dream of bringing awareness to the stories of urban life throughout the world, being a voice for those who are often unheard.

CPSIA information can be obtained
at www.ICGtesting.com
Printed in the USA
LVOW03s1148080517
533702LV00005B/1164/P

9 780998 609201